They were humans. The aliens wanted to use their world for war games. They were to leave or die. Some left. Some died. Some didn't.

THIS IS THEIR STORY.

Fire on the Border

by Kevin O'Donnell, Jr.

A ROC BOOK

ROC
Published by the Penguin Group
Penguin Books USA Inc., 375 Hudson Street, New York, New York 10014, U.S.A.
Penguin Books Ltd, 27 Wrights Lane, London W8 5TZ, England
Penguin Books Australia Ltd, Ringwood, Victoria, Australia
Penguin Books Canada, Ltd, 2801 John Street, Markham, Ontario, Canada L3R 1B4
Penguin Books (N.Z.) Ltd, 182—190 Wairau Road, Auckland 10, New Zealand

Penguin Books Ltd, Registered Offices: Harmondsworth, Middlesex, England

First published by ROC, an imprint of New American Library, a division of
Penguin Books USA Inc.

First Printing, September, 1990
10 9 8 7 6 5 4 3 2 1

 ROC IS A TRADEMARK OF PENGUIN BOOKS, USA INC.

Printed in the United States of America

To Mary L. O'Donnell, grandmother extraordinaire, for all the warmth and all the fun, I dedicate this book with gratitude and love.

Acknowledgments

I began this book in 1985. During the somewhat torturous process of writing it, I asked a number of people for assistance, information, and critical evaluation. For all they said—and for all they didn't say—I'd like to thank Craig F. Cook, Jim Falbo, Marina Fitch, Janet Gluckman, Amy Hansen, Robert P. Howd, Ginger LaJeunnesse, Mark J. McGarry, Sasha Miller, Howard Morhaim, Neil P. O'Donnell, J.B. Post, Donald Robertson, John Staley, Christopher Schelling, John Silbersack, Lisa Swallow, and above all, Kim Tchang.

Chapter 1

The holophone chimed while Kajiwara Hiroshi was doing his push-ups.

He reacted with a grunt that mingled gratitude and annoyance. Exercise bored him; any interruption of the daily workout came as a relief. Yet Kajiwara Hiroshi, over commander of Octant Sagittarius, had a duty to set an example for his forces, and he could not ignore even the least of his responsibilities without a flush of intense, private shame. He would finish his push-ups, then. For the fortieth time that morning, he forced his tired muscles to lift him, then to lower him back almost to the deck. "Gravity to Earth normal."

The plants in the vegetable wall to his left rustled and straightened as the artificial gravity field slackened. Kajiwara's triceps, still pitted against a 1.5-G pull, popped him to full extension. He smiled wistfully. A man of 167 years rarely felt so strong. Panting, he got to his knees and wiped sweat off his forehead. "Retract the stationary bicycle and the weight machine."

The machines in the center of the 4-by-5-meter over-command module dropped out of sight. With a soft hiss, deck panels slid over the open shafts.

Kajiwara rose to his full 220 centimeters and stepped off the exercise mat. "Retract the mat."

A take-up roller behind the rear bulkhead whined; the mat disappeared through a slot just above the deck.

Yes. Now the place began to look less like a gymnasium, and more like the office and living quarters of an octant over commander. "Holo on. Accept call."

A hologram of Admiral Franklin Munez, Kajiwara's executive officer, shimmered alive in the far right corner, between the dinette set and the door to the bathroom. Munez's collar hung open; the blood had drained out of his normally ruddy cheeks. His eyes darted from side to side as he searched the holo generated at his end. "Sir, are you there?"

In all the years of their acquaintanceship, Kajiwara had never seen his aide so distraught. He moved to the near-right corner, into range of the holocameras aimed at his desk. He walked like an old panther—tired and timeworn, but still poised, still dangerous. Draping a towel around his damp neck, he raised his eyebrows in wordless question.

"Mayday from New Napa, sir. The Wayholder have attacked."

During his first command, news of a rebellion had stunned Kajiwara like a blow to the head. *Preposterous*, he had thought, and for long minutes he had simply refused to believe that a small colony would challenge the entire Association. When astonishment had faded, his heart had begun pounding. Hot adrenaline had sizzled through his veins. Finally, exhilarated by the prospect of fulfilling his purpose, he had leaped into action.

The next 113 years, twenty-one commands, and five uprisings had taught him to accept the inevitability, and the unpredictability, of war. It happened, as earthquakes and solar storms did, and only rarely at the time and place forecast by the experts. Yet the true warrior must face even the most unexpected outbreaks with aplomb, for the warrior inhabits the reality of the instant, where perfect balance is the sole defense against cataclysm.

Kajiwara closed his eyes and tasted the great sadness welling up in him. Anger spiced that sorrow—the anger of knowing that in order to save, he must destroy.

Save he would, though, no matter what the cost, for he was samurai, and the executives of the Terran Association had entrusted him with the defense of Octant Sagittarius.

"So." Weariness whistled through his soul like an autumn wind. He lowered his 130 kilograms into the desk chair. "Finally." The emptiness of a galactic rift separated humankind from the only alien civilization it had ever met, but Kajiwara Hiroshi had studied too much history to expect the species to coexist peacefully. Expanding societies collide in showers of sparks, and cascading sparks eventually ignite fires. It did surprise him that the Wayholder Empire had struck first—and at New Napa, of all places. What could they want *there*? "How long ago?"

"Twenty-nine minutes, sir. The 79th is up. The *Morocco*."

A good fleetship, the *Morocco*. "Have our modules moved and attached immediately. Notify Admiral Wiegand that I hereby assume tactical control of the *Morocco*'s operations groups." A familiar itch, like a mental hunger, awakened within his brain. Faced with a problem, his subconscious was demanding data in cold, precise, and calculable formats. He could not ignore it, for it would plague him until he fed it what it wanted. Annoying, but not, he knew, unusual. Under stress, most officers of the Astro Corps seemed to lose a little humanity, seemed almost to emulate the operating procedures of the computers implanted in their skulls. "A moment, please."

"Yes, sir."

Fingertip to the subcutaneous switch just below his left ear, Kajiwara Hiroshi closed his eyes. The smell of his own perspiration filled his nostrils. "Subject, fleets of Octant Sagittarius; query, list status of all fleets sorted by degree of readiness."

After the briefest of pauses, numbers and names scrolled up inside his brain, as though projected directly onto his retinas:

FLEET	LOCATION	STATUS	READINESS	NOTES
79th	Cheyenne/OSHQ	Red	ready	
76th	Nihu-Almocksy	Red	ready	on peace-keeping mission
78th	Cheyenne/OSHQ	Yellow	6 hours	
77th	Cheyenne/OSHQ	Green	12 hours	
71st	Titan	off-duty	48 hours	on R&R
75th	Hsing P'ing	off-duty	72 hours	new Premier's inauguration
72nd	Cheyenne/OSHQ	unready	96 hours	recruit training
73rd	Fila	MedEvac	11 days	asteroid strike survivors
70th	Cheyenne Astro-yard	disabled	21 days	overhaul
74th	unknown	unknown	unknown	on maneuvers

The itch subsided. Kajiwara sighed. Octant Sagittarius Headquarters in the Cheyenne System served as home port to over thirty thousand Astro Corps vessels. He commanded all of them, as well as their attached army and air force contingents. Soon he might need all of them.

Munez said, "We are under way, sir. Docking with *Morocco* in five minutes. Full functional attachment in five more."

"Thank you, Frank." Again he touched the switch behind his ear. "Subject, 79th Fleet, operations groups; query, list all with status of full readiness. Audio."

This time the implant directly manipulated Kajiwara's auditory nerve. #Operations Group One; the *Kathmandu*. Operations Group Two, the *Lima*.#

He released the pressure plate. "Frank, send Ops Group One to look things over. Its commander has discretionary power to engage the invaders."

"Sir." Through his own implant, Munez relayed the orders to Admiral Wiegand's command module.

Kajiwara rubbed his brush-cut hair, thick as a youth's, white as Fuji's crown, ''Raise ops groups Three through Ten to full red alert. Call up the 77th and 78th, as well.''

''Sir.'' Pressing his neck, the admiral subvocalized some more.

Kajiwara folded his hands and waited till his aide looked directly out of the holo at him. ''Details, please. How many ships did the Wayholder Empire commit to attack, and what kind were they?''

''One skirmish control craft and sixteen fighters, sir.''

Kajiwara triggered the implant. ''Subject, New Napa; query, list functioning defenses against space attack.''

#None.#

He winced. Though he had expected nothing different, he had hoped for at least one satellite laser system. Kajiwara had crushed rebellions on half a dozen colony worlds. Those with harmless skies fell most quickly. ''Subject, Operations Group One, commander; query, list full name.''

#Mikhailaivitch, Commander Yuri Petrov.#

Removing his hand, he pondered the name. The computer could project a desktop holo for him more quickly, but images generated by personnel files lacked emotional resonance. Mikhailaivitch . . . ah. High cheekbones. Gleaming brown eyes. So. He nodded, satisfied. Yuri Petrov Mikhailaivitch. A smoldering Slav. Born on Mars, if he remembered correctly. Dark, intense, wiry. Exuded competence. But perhaps a bit . . . reckless? A trifle . . . eager? ''Launch the *Lima*, Frank.''

''Sir.'' He relayed the instructions, paused a moment, then blinked. ''*Kathmandu* is off the framework and estimates threshold speed in eighteen minutes. *Lima* glitched its launch; three-minute delay in takeoff.''

Kajiwara swallowed an angry comment about fully ready ops groups that hung fire on the rack. Time enough for that later, after the skirmish tapered off. Admiral Pamela Wiegand would have some explaining to do. ''*Lima* is to guard *Kathmandu* against surprise attack from the rear.''

''Sir.'' Munez muttered briefly, listened, then spoke.

"A message from New Napa. A Wayholder shuttle has landed at the shuttleport and is unloading combat infantry who are storming the control tower."

Kajiwara pursed his lips as he thought. Mikhailaivitch carried three thousand rangers aboard the *Kathmandu*. They would deal with the ground forces. Would standard infantry tactics suffice? He did not know. At least rangers had a reputation for ingenuity. . . . But no human had ever fought the Wayholder Empire. Kajiwara Hiroshi wondered how the aliens would respond to his counterattack.

"Frank, disperse ops groups Eleven through Thirty in optimum surveillance pattern around the Cheyenne; they must be ready to bounce back to the *Morocco* on a moment's notice. Inform High Commander Santiago of the situation. Request him to have Over Commander Bjorgeson bring all Octant Auriga forces to full alert. We might need reinforcements."

Munez looked surprised. "Do you think that will be necessary, sir? The fleetship has thirty carriers, each with thirty fighters, giving us—"

"I can multiply, too." He stopped himself. Munez was only succumbing to the same need to quantify that overcame all of them in moments of uncertainty. "I apologize for the discourtesy, Frank."

"It's all right, sir."

Kajiwara touched his neck. "Subject, Wayholder Empire; query, list best intelligence estimate of total Wayholder forces in sector nearest to New Napa."

TYPE	QUANTITY	TAAC EQUIVALENT COMMAND LEVEL
Sector control craft	1	Over commander
War zone control craft	16	Fleet admirals
Battle control craft	256	Commanders
Skirmish control craft	4,096	Captains
Fighter craft	65,536	Lieutenants
TOTAL	69,905	

Kajiwara lifted his finger. The table faded from his mind's eye. He took a deep breath. "Yes," he said, "reinforcements might be necessary."

"As you wish, sir." Munez stared at something off-camera and began to subvocalize the messages into his implant.

The *Morocco* receded to the north as the *Kathmandu* sped down the acceleration lane toward the pop-out point. Commander Yuri P. Mikhailaivitch took short, sharp breaths and kept glancing from the relative velocity indicators to the fighter craft status lights and back again. His mouth dried quickly; his tongue felt stiff; the command module cramped him like an undersized spacesuit.

He noticed then that he was panting like a dog. He sat. He forced his respiration to slow, to deepen, but that did not break his mounting tension. The *Kathmandu* was accelerating into her first combat mission since he had taken command. He ached to prove himself worthy.

For a moment, the intensity of his desire embarrassed him. While people were dying on New Napa, he was focusing on his career. People were dying, and . . .

He swallowed hard. He did not want to admit, even to himself, that he might be flying toward his own death. He had to ignore the gooseflesh, the hollow queasiness in his gut. He had to keep thinking of it as a game, an exercise, a clean metallic encounter in which he put this piece here and that piece there and nothing had a name or a face or a family. He had to see it as a contest, or else he—

No. A contest. With a commendation—perhaps even an admiralship—for anyone who came out of it covered with glory.

Opportunities for glory happened about as often as shirt-sleeve weather on Mars. Fifty-two years old, thirty-three of them spent on active duty in the Terran Association Astro Corps, Mikhailaivitch had flown against an enemy exactly once, fifteen years ago, at Rubio.

He supposed he could have had less experience. His own father had spent forty years in TAAC—eight in command of a carrier—and God knew how many on full readiness in the carrier's musty command module, waiting for a call to action that never came.

Waiting was dull. Mikhailaivitch had done too much of it.

Worse, the statistical analyses proved that carrier commanders who never saw combat never saw promotion, either. And that would not do at all.

Fortunately, memories of that spot of action at Rubio had suggested some very interesting tactics which he thought would catch the Wayholder entirely off guard.

Seven minutes to threshold speed. For all that she looked like a kilometer-long winerack, the Catman was already doing 52,000 kilometers a second, and adding another 4,000 every minute. By the time the Catman hit the eighty kilokay per second her gravpipes needed to create the singularity that would bore an infinitely short tunnel between herself and the New Napa system, she would have covered 48,000,000 kilometers.

Mikhailaivitch leaned into the microphone. Starscapes filled the screens; readouts, the consoles. "Lieutenant Jenkins, have a situation update capsule ready to drop and bounce one minute after arrival in the New Napa. Drop subsequent SitUps every sixty seconds."

"Yes, sir," came the disembodied voice of the communications engineer.

"Also, give me an audio-video feed of any colonial broadcasts about the invasion. I don't want everything you give Intelligence. Just local transmissions. I want to know what's going on down there."

"Yes, sir."

Mikhailaivitch checked the gravpipe lights. All green. Good-oh. Not that he could do anything if one went red besides scream for his chief engineer. The physics of even a simple gravity generator baffled Mikhailaivitch; those of the pipe made his head hurt.

Catman had fifty pipes. When he deployed them, each telescoped out of its housing into an iridescent tube a meter wide and a kilometer long. The hardware rode at the far end of the tube, in an aluminum sphere about the size of a basketball. According to the techies, that hardware took every gravity wave reaching the ship from every gram of mass in the universe, and bent it so it seemed to originate right at the end of the tube. Once the coherent gravity beam thus generated had accelerated the ship to threshold speed—eighty thousand kilometers or eighty kilokay per second—the pipe could create a finely calibrated, short-lived singularity through which the Catman could travel instantaneously to any spot in the galaxy.

Flying is falling into a black hole, he thought, *a black hole that keeps us at arm's length by receding at the same speed we're approaching.* Sometimes it scared him. Sometimes he admitted it.

At least he knew how to *use* it.

He drew a mug of tea from the dispenser. The software download light flashed emerald. He set the mug on the console. "Wing leaders." Wiping his palms on the couch, he waited for Captains Hardesty, Cheung, and M'tano to respond. "I show download complete; acknowledge."

One by one they told him their onboards had received his instructions.

"Good. At last word, one Wayholder skirmish control craft was in geosynch over New Napa City, the capital. All of its fighters are off the rack, taking out commsats and landsats. One of the skirk's shuttles is ferrying infantry to the port. No word on the other shuttles. Our main worry is the skirk. We'll bounce in eight megakay above the plane of the ecliptic, and I hope to God we're pointing in the right direction."

They laughed at that. They always did. But then Hardesty coughed, his standard prelude to an objection. "Sir, isn't that too close? Even at max deceleration we'll pass New Napa at um . . . seventy-three kilokay a second."

"You're not going to decelerate."

"We have to!"

Mikhailaivitch frowned. Hardesty had no imagination. "The object, Captain Hardesty, is to surprise hell out of them, clean as many as possible on the first pass."

"But—"

"They'll have over a minute to get ready for us. Tell me, Captain—what could your pilots do with that much warning of an attack?"

Hardesty hesitated, then gave an almost-sigh of acquiescence. "Yes, sir."

"I'd rather come in closer, but we need time for targeting and course correction." He sipped his tea and made a face. He had forgotten to add the lemon.

A grunt of comprehension came over the speakers. Larry Cheung, by the sound of it.

"All right," said Mikhailaivitch. "The onboards will toss all fighters off the rack right after bounce. Able Wing, you're aimed at the skirk, and the onboards have your tactics. Bravo Wing, the software will pair you off and space your pairs twenty-five hundred kay apart. You'll be scouring the sunward face of the planet. Corsair Wing, same software but the nightside."

Hardesty said, "And once we've flashed past?"

"The software will bounce you—"

Three gasps interrupted him.

"No!" said M'tano. "The regs call for a five-minute cooldown after a bounce."

"Dammit," said Mikhailaivitch, "they wrote those regs to keep maintenance costs down, not to win a war!"

Cheung said, "Yes. Okay. But if the pipes blow—"

"They won't. Look, I'm no physicist, but I can plug numbers into an equation and have the onboards crunch it for me. You cool your pipes to smooth out grav distortions. After five minutes, you've got one warped pipe in every hundred thousand. But we're dealing with an inverse square, here. After cooling for a hundred seconds, only nine pipes in a hundred thousand will blow. I have fifty pipes. Each fighter has two. Good odds.''

Hardesty coughed. ''Wag-End'll have your balls for bearings, Yuri.''

''Yeah. Maybe. She's not running this operation, though. Kajiwara Hiroshi is, and I don't think he'll mind at all.''

''But why not do it by the book?'' Exasperation sharpened M'tano's tone.

'' 'Cause the book only has two ways to do it, Soji. Bounce to the standard pop-in point forty-eight mega-kay up, brake at max along the decel lane, and take twenty minutes to reach New Napa. That gives the Way-holder seventeen minutes and twenty seconds to pre-pare. Or come in close, flash by, and go into a braking loop. I did that at Rubio, and let me tell you, it takes over an hour to get back with a reasonable velocity. Uh-uh.''

Cheung said, ''Okay. So we do it your way. Where do we bounce to the second time?''

''That's when we go to the standard pop-in point. We'll get back with enough velocity to take up orbit. Wing leaders, complete you missions as you see fit. Break orbit to pursue at your discretion. The Catman will drop rang-ers, then go to the aid of Able Wing, which will disap-point me greatly if it needs help. Watch the pipes; we're shielded but New Napa's not. The last thing they need right now is gravity updrafts. All right?''

The three responded.

''Sixty seconds.'' He took a deep breath. ''Do good, now.''

Strapped into the control couch of the sleek, thirty-meter-long Zulu-class fighter, Lieutenant Mei-liang ''Darcy'' Lee checked every light on the board one last time. The hatch in the carrier's rack gaped open; the sling mechanism held full tension to hurl *Kathmandu 18* into the dark of space.

She wondered what she would face. Not space—after nineteen years in a pilot's uniform she knew all about that—but war. A broken leg had kept her out of the invasion of Rubio, the only planet to rebel since she had left the Academy. Service with the occupation forces had entailed little more than routine flying. For the first time in her life she would meet a pilot trying to kill her. How would she react?

She was scared, and not ashamed to admit it. Sane pilots accepted fear, even welcomed a taste of it, because, properly controlled, it could sharpen reflexes and hone concentration

Today she had to be a stiletto. If it took a giant gulp of fear to transform her, so be it.

She braced for the bounce, due to happen—

NOW!

The Catman dropped into the artificial singularity created by its gravpipes. The stars in her forward screens winked out. Her stomach lurched; the breath caught in her throat.

The singularity warped space and time to juxtapose two points forty light-years apart.

For an instant the screen blazed white, then blackened. New stars appeared. They had arrived.

Immediately the sling catapulted the Zulu away from the Catman at a hundred Gs. The generator in front of her flicked on at the same instant, preventing the massive instantaneous force from crushing her. Gravpipes popped out fore and aft.

The count-down clock overlaid on the forward viewscreen flashed **1 minute 40 seconds,** then flicked to **1:39.**

The carrier fell behind. In front, a point of blue light shone steady in a field of steely stars. New Napa. It looked like her home planet, Hsing P'ing, fifty light-years west. "Magnify."

Hardesty's voice crackled through her implants: "Able Wing, you'll ride through contact—everything's in software for the next twenty-one minutes and forty seconds. Sit back and enjoy the view."

Oh, sure.

Under magnification, the blue light ahead displayed a visible disk.

The onboards steered her Zulu into a line with the rest of the wing. Meshing mass detector readings with radar images with microwaved ID beacons, they slipped Catman 18 a few kay to starboard, switched on the forward gravpipe, and sped the fighter to widen the gap between Catman 19, directly behind, and herself. Dead ahead, the glass brains of Billy Wong's 17 did the same, but with a slightly greater acceleration, and so on to Hardesty in Catman 10.

New Napa looked like a blue marble. No, a blue balloon, and a giant was inflating it as she hurtled toward it. A giant with a fly-swatter. She stiffened. For a moment her mind veered away from what awaited her, and turned to afterward. Maybe she and Billy could get down on the surface. Do some hiking. The settlers had tamed barely half the planet; the trailblazing would be good. Throw in exotic *lepidopterons* and a keg of local brew. Sure. The makings of a perfect vacation. But first—

The onboards said, #Target located.#

Lee checked. Yes, the target lock-on light glowed green.

1:20.

Weapons lights glittered. The onboards had selected pinwheels and time-fused torpedoes. Good choices, she thought. A skirk resembled the skeleton of a pancake ten kilometers in diameter and one kilometer thick, with its ''bones'' arranged in an intricate pattern that reminded her of lace. To use antimatter guns on that, at this point, would be a waste.

#Weapons systems activated.#

A faint hum came through her implants, as if the onboards were chuckling.

The portside screens showed two stubby torpedoes leaping away on minuscule tails of chemical flame.

A hatch opened; a spotlight flicked on. The ejection mechanism pitched out a package.

1:00.

The spotlight tracked the packet for visual confirmation of deployment, which came at once as eight small,

shaped charges burst. Each threw a fifty-meter length
of iron chain away from the center.

As the pinwheel unfurled, she thought, *They should
call it a spiderweb—that's what it really looks like.*

0:50.

Since the pinwheel's inertial velocity matched Catman 18's, it traveled by her side, but the gap between
them widened rapidly. Even as the webbing opened to
its full, deadly diameter it dwindled to a glittery point
in the spotlight's piercing cone.

"Deployment confirmed," she said. "Spotlight off."

A skirmish control craft looked about as much like a
carrier of the Unified Security Forces as a hockey puck
does a toothpick, but the Wayholder architects had obviously come to some of the same conclusions as their
Terran counterparts. Both vessels were composed of
small life-support modules and large individual hangars
strung on an open framework of struts and tubing. When
attacking, you had to time-fuse your torpedoes, because
a cylinder one meter in diameter had a high chance of
passing through all the holes and not touching a thing.

0:40.

Even a torpedo that burst exactly where desired would
probably not do significant damage. On a ship like that,
nothing was close to anything.

But a chain-link spiderweb a hundred meters in diameter had to hit something. From long-range holograms of skirks taken thirty-five years earlier, Terran
Association engineers had determined that no passage
through the interior of the ships failed to narrow to at
least fifty meters in diameter. As long as the pinwheels
did not miss the skirk completely, they would slash
through like grapeshot.

0:30.

The implants relayed Hardesty's voice: "We're coming up on it. Expect to bounce right after flyby. Switch
to manual and go into a braking loop if it doesn't happen."

Not much chance of that. Sometimes she wondered
why TAAC bothered to put a human on the control

couch. They had reduced the entire process to silicon decisions and turned the pilot into extra mass. Worse, it hampered the ship's effectiveness—the ship could take more G-force than the gravity generators could compensate for. You red-lined on braking force halfway to actual max. At 75 percent of actual max, you wound up smeared along the bulkheads, a gruesome jelly.

0:20.

But she knew why. She controlled this sleek, slick slaying machine. She weighed the intangibles, then made the value judgments that no piece of gallium arsenide could begin to cope with.

0:15.

Then it hit her: *Jesus Buddha, a bounce!* Too soon, much too soon! Sweat prickled her armpits. Did Hardesty know what he was doing?

The Wayholder craft resolved into a discrete image on her forward screens. She leaned forward slightly, eyes narrowed, watching for pinpoints of light. Even at high magnification, she could barely make out Billy's ship. Would the damn torpedoes never go off?

0:10.

A match flared. But straight ahead, not to port. It burned Billy in 17, not the Wayholder.

In the harsh nuclear light, her cameras recorded 17's instant dissolution into a cloud of shrapnel, a cloud that began to expand outward from its center while the center still sped ahead at eighty thousand kilometers a second.

She would have to pass through that cloud. Through the dust of a dead lover.

She bit her lip, then snapped her helmet down as a safety precaution. The face plate readout pulsed: SUIT INTEGRITY INTACT.

0:05.

Darcy Lee tongued the radio control. "Wing Leader, 17's been hit." Well in front of the Wayholder, a torpedo burst like a micronova.

Hardesty said, "Bad?" More tiny stars flashed and

faded on the path to the skeletal giant that filled half
her screen.

She blinked very rapidly as she said, "Totaled," She
would have to grieve for Billy later.

0:00.

#Bouncing.#

Her Zulu tumbled into its gravpipe's singularity. The
forward screens strobed. Her gut knotted.

The singularity popped a timeless tunnel through normal space.

She and her ship came out the far end.

#Braking commenced.#

Forty-eight million kilometers ahead hung the blue
light of New Napa.

It occurred to her that now she did not need to worry
about the ashes of Catman 17. . . .

Some of the tension went out of her. Only some, for
Billy was gone, forever, never to laugh with again. She
had also picked up many, many millirems of radiation,
which meant eventual purging—or sterility. She wanted
children. Not just yet, of course, but she had to keep
the option open. Though they would never be Billy's.
"Give me a slow-motion replay of the attack on the
Wayholder."

The screen flickered. Here and there the framework
of the enemy carrier reflected sunlight till the whole
sparkled like a giant Christmas ornament. Hundreds of
thousands of kilometers before it, torpedoes burst two
at a time. Each fiery blast spat millions of pieces of
microshrapnel in an expanding cone centered on its line
of travel.

Taffy-pulling realtime into a form she could perceive,
the onboards reached into the infrared to find the hot
grains of metal. She held her breath as the convex base
of each cone spread outward.

The first spanned a bare hundred meters when it
reached the Wayholder vessel. The computer retarded
the replay by another factor of ten, but Darcy Lee
blinked and missed the shrapnel's traversal of the skirk.

The other torpedoes blossomed, some widely separated, some overlapping. They rolled in on the Way-holder like a gritty desert wind. Then they were gone.

"Damn. Did anything happen?"

The onboards did not answer.

She cursed again. You could tell the computer to do anything, but if you wanted it to answer you, you had to use the formula. "Subject, torpedo attack on Way-holder; query, results."

#Unknown.#

She sighed. "Compare and contrast pre- and post-attack holographic blueprints and radio emissions; estimate the attack's effectiveness. Subject, analysis of pre- and post-attack holograms; query, list the differences."

#One thousand seven hundred thirty-one instances of broken frameworking. Twelve missing life-support modules. Seventy-three life-support modules apparently ruptured.#

"Subject, Wayholder vessel; query, total of pre-attack life-support systems."

#Four thousand nine hundred thirteen.#

And they had hit eighty-five, all told? Well, in less than twenty minutes they would be back on the scene, traveling slowly enough for the radio-seeking torps and the antimatter weapons to work. Of course, they would also be traveling slowly enough for the Wayholder defenses to work better, too. . . .

Lieutenant Darcy Lee shivered once, and waited.

Chapter 2

Through the overcommand module's thick hull vibrated faint dings and thumps—the familiar sounds of lock-on to the framework of a fleetship. Kajiwara Hiroshi reminded himself to commend the support crews of the *Morocco* for their quickness, then ignored the noise.

He sat at his desk, hands folded, all the muscles of his face and body deliberately relaxed. His absent gaze drifted to the bulkhead by his right shoulder, to the silver and white phosphorescence of the star coral in the shallow vacuum case.

The case meant as much to him as did the tiny creatures he had tended for the last fifty-six years. Thirty centimeters wide by fifty high by five deep, of dark unglazed porcelain faced with clear quartz, the case bore on its back the incised inscription "To Great-grandfather on his 111th birthday, with love from his great-grandson, Michael O'Reilly."

A remarkable concession to convention, that inscription, for Michael made a fetish of informality—the Irish in him must have rebelled against the etiquette of his Japanese ancestors. Otherwise a fine boy, though.

Sudden moisture blurred Kajiwara's vision. Michael and all Michael's family—his children, grandchildren, and, already, great-grandchildren—lived on Longfall, another colony world in Octant Sagittarius. Were the Wayholder attacking the Association itself, and not merely New Napa, Longfall and her O'Reillys would know war soon.

Kajiwara Hiroshi could not abide that thought.

He sighed heavily. The secret to elegant tactical success lies in coaxing an opponent to defeat itself. Frighten it into retreat, beguile it into misdeploying its forces, lure it into ambush . . . but to do any of those demanded a knowledge of the foe that Kajiwara Hiroshi did not have.

"To know and to act are one and the same." Wang Yang Ming's equation had long guided true samurai, yet must it necessarily have the converse, "Not to know is not to act"?

If Kajiwara could infer even one reason for the attack, he could better organize both a defense and a counter-offensive. But what was the aliens' objective? What did they hope to gain? The invasion made no sense!

Ah, but the Wayholder had never made sense, at least not to the Terrans who had been trying to comprehend them for thirty-five years.

On 8 February 2313, in the expansion cycle during which the Association had colonized most of Octant Sagittarius, the survey ship *Cheng Ho* bounced farther than any previous human explorer—to a star system beyond the rift between galactic arms. During its initial, threshold-speed passage through the system, it detected a vessel the size of a large asteroid, cloaked in fighter-craft and approaching at nearly eighty kilokay per second. Captain Voloshka, an intelligent woman, immediately bounced to Octant HQ in the Cheyenne.

The aliens followed—creating their own singularity, yet arriving at the same destination—thereby proving a technology that Terran engineers could not understand, much less imitate.

The visitors made no hostile moves. They pulled back to the comet belt, slipped into orbit, and waited for Raul Santiago, then over commander of Octant Sagittarius, to attempt communications—to which they made instant, unintelligible reply.

The linguists on each side wheeled out their super-computers. A year's intensive labor earned each near-mastery of the other's language. True communication with a different species became feasible for the first time in Terran history. Whereupon the extraterrestrials sent a diplomatic communiqúe to the Terran Association. Its complete text read:

"We are the Wayholder. We are your defense. In the midst of the dark lie our borders. Respect them, as we shall respect yours. Goodbye."

Over Commander Santiago requested a clarification. He received silence. The Wayholder had gone.

In the thirty-four years since, no Wayholder ship had entered Association space. Inquisitive and adventurous Terrans had ventured into the Wayholder Empire—but had not returned to tell about it.

And now the Wayholder were attacking New Napa. Why?

Self-defense? No. According to the computers, New Napa only had two ships capable of an interstellar bounce. Besides, settlers of a young colony attacked their immediate environment, not their distant neighbors. If Kajiwara knew the colonial mind—and, with descendants on at least three new worlds, he thought he did—those optimistic farmers with their houses full of children had never provoked this. They might look to the Wayholder Empire for commerce, but never for combat.

Why, then?

Retaliation for an Association infringement? No. The ops groups of Octant Sagittarius did patrol the stars along the rift, but they sailed with locked flight recorders that the fleetship computers drained dry after every mission. Had one of them encroached on Wayholder territory by even a meter, Kajiwara would have heard of it.

Expansion? No. Or at least highly implausible. The aliens needed gravity two and a half times Earth normal, and an atmosphere richer in nitrogen oxides than New Napa's. They could never survive suitless there. And the New Napa system offered no other planets suitable for their use.

Why? Why?

The clamor of lock-on had ended. Ready lights had

come to life on his desk. He had not noticed. Eyes blank, lips compressed, he turned the question over and over, but could not answer it to his satisfaction.

He could only watch the star coral cast their silver glow, and wonder if Michael O'Reilly would survive.

Admiral Munez broke into his reverie. "Message from Ops Group One, sir. They have arrived and are about to engage the Wayholder in battle."

"Already?" To take the offensive so quickly, Mikhailaivitch must have bounced his ops group nearly to the end of the deceleration lane. Kajiwara presumed the young hothead was attempting to minimize the time the enemy had to prepare for his attack. "The boy probably chose not to decelerate, either. He is a fool."

"Perhaps." Munez's tone meant that he disagreed, but would not contradict his superior while the over-command module's recorders were running.

Kajiwara raised an eyebrow. "Oh?"

"The SitUp contains an explanation of his tactics."

"Then I withdraw my criticism, and shall reserve judgment till I have looked at his statement. And—"

"It also contains a fragment of a video, sir. Apparently broadcast from the space port and picked up by the *Kathmandu*. I've queued it to your desk."

Kajiwara touched a button. A silver swirl in the corner of his desk resolved into a grainy black-and-white image.

A middle-aged man in a business blouse ran across a parking lot, his arms pumping, his mouth open in a soundless but obvious howl. Behind him, a pressure-suited alien raised a boxy object that terminated in a long, slender protrusion. A light glowed on the end of the object facing the Wayholder. The pointed end swung, tracking the human. A light flashed. A brilliant beam sliced the man's head from his shoulders.

The video went black.

Kajiwara unclenched his jaws. "So." *They murder fleeing civilians.* Revulsion's acid burned the back of his throat. He closed his eyes and breathed deeply. *So. For all their technology, they are savages.* Silently he swore to destroy them. He opened his eyes. "And the *Lima*?"

"One minute from threshold speed, sir."

Braking at the maximum allowable rate, the *Kathmandu* and its fighters slipped into the formation Yuri Mikhailaivitch had designed for his second strike. He would give his legs to know the formation the aliens were assuming, 33 million kilometers down the decel lane.

Voices whispered in his ear constantly; he replied through his throat mike even as his hands and eyes prepared for the attack.

"Barnard, Commander. Rangers are ready to take back the spaceport. How do we go?"

"Dropcaps." Some COs would shuttle their rangers down, but not Yuri Mikhailaivitch. Shuttles made better targets than landing capsules. Until his computers had defined the accuracy of Wayholder antiaircraft, he would not take the risk.

"All of us?"

"Yes, Captain. You'll go off the rack from a megakay out." Packed securely and individually into capsules barely larger than they were, the three thousand rangers would loop around the planet, strike air in a shower of fire, and thunder-roll down to the spaceport. They would hate the ride, but the turbulence would get their juices flowing, put them in the mood to fight.

"Roger, Commander. Out."

Mikhailaivitch glanced at the video frame frozen in the corner of his main screen. A white line linked the alien's weapon to the civilian's neck. The man's head was just starting to roll off his shoulders. *Poor bastard. We'll get them for you, though. Trust me.*

He bit a thumbnail. His battle command board registered too damned many enemy fighters still functional. And the alien mothership checked in at 93.78 percent effective. What the hell had happened to Able Wing?

"Intelligence, Mikhailaivitch. Report."

"Forget OBI, sir. The Order of Battle Intelligence computers are picking up all sorts of transmissions, but they're gibberish. We've got no idea what normal Way-holder levels and modes should look like.''

"Roger, Intelligence. Out." In the *next* engagement, TAAC's OBI computers would have a baseline referent, but he doubted Howland Island would credit him for it.

He addressed his onboard computers: "When we get there, match velocities with the Wayholder skirmish control craft. Provide one-hundred-kilometer vertical separation and zero lateral separation, with *Kathmandu* in the higher orbit. On arrival in stable orbit, divert fifty percent of gravity generator capacity to antimatter ammunition production. Subject, skirk; query, count intact life-support modules in direct line of sight to *Kathmandu*'s destination.''

The carrier wave hummed on the edge of audibility. #Three hundred twelve.#

"Arm 312 shrapnel torpedoes; target individually at skirk life-support modules in direct line of sight to *Kathmandu*'s destination—'' he took a breath, mentally replayed his command to make certain that he and the computer were using the same variables, and then continued—"on a one-module, one-torpedo basis; launch at earliest feasible moment.''

A soft tone chimed. Impatiently, he swiveled his chair around and said, "Holo on. Accept call.''

On the right corner of his desk, his onboards generated a holocube labeled EXTERNAL COMM. Inside that transparent box, a face took shape, a long face, with thin lips, and prominent cheekbones that cradled pale blue eyes. The thin lips moved. The eyes did not. "Hans Bremenschmidt, Commanding Officer, Operations Group Two USFCS *Lima,* reporting with all hands. Present separation from New Napa, 48 million kilometers. Braking at max.''

Mikhailaivitch twitched his nose in irritation. He had wanted to have the situation wrapped up before Bremenschmidt arrived.

"Hello, Hans.'' He turned back to his board. Unlike his colleague, he could not stare stone-faced into a camera bank while radio waves crawled from Catman to Big

Green and back again. He had neither the temperament nor the time.

"Damage Control, Mikhailaivitch, report."

"All techs mobilized, sir. Won't be long. We figure another few minutes."

"Roger, Damage Control. Out."

He had lost five ships. Granted, the enemy had paid for them, and his chosen tactics would still work, but it would not look good on his record. Not good at all. What aspect of his next pass could he optimize?

Ninety-two seconds after his voice first sounded in Mikhailaivitch's module, Bremenschmidt said, "Yuri. All fighters still on the rack. Where do you want us?"

He looked over his shoulder at Bremenschmidt's blond head. "Ah—when you reach the planet, Hans, englobe it at 500 kilokay. Cut off any escapees. Shrink the radius gradually until you reach geosynch. Hold there for further instructions. Oh, and Hans? I expect we'll have mopped them all up, but do feel free to take potshots at any that wander into your neighborhood."

Ignoring completely the comm cube and Bremenschmidt's patient face, Mikhailaivitch turned his attention back to the control lights. He would have eighty, eighty-five seconds before he had to listen to Big Green's captain again. A good commander could—no, make that *should*—win an entire war in eighty-five seconds.

Twenty-four megakay yet to go. A little over fourteen minutes. He cued his onboards. "Subject, dropcaps; query, status."

#All activated. None sealed. None ready for drop.#

He touched a button. "Barnard, Mikhailaivitch. Why the hell aren't the rangers ready to go?"

"Final equipment check, sir. We're almost ready to seal."

"Get it done, Barnard. Out."

His Zulus held formation nicely. At least his pilots did their jobs.

Bremenschmidt's dry voice cut into his frettings. "Don't feel obliged to do it all yourself, Yuri."

"It's no problem, Hans. I don't expect we'll have any trouble."

He truly did not. The Wayholder skirmish control craft presented the main obstacle, but his first wave of torpedoes would cripple it. His second wave would put its lights out forever.

Eighteen megakay. Twelve minutes, more or less.

"Communications, Mikhailaivitch. Are you dropping SitUps on schedule?"

"Yes, sir," said Jenkins.

"Commander, Damage Control. All repairs complete. All techs and repairmechs have returned to combat stations."

"Thank you, Damage Control. Out."

"Commander, Intelligence. The main radio station in New Napa City has gone off the air. We don't know if the Wayholder stormed it or cut power to its transmitting antenna or what."

"Roger, Intelligence. The instant we hit orbit, launch surveillance satellites to detail the disposition of enemy forces. Beam a scrambled feed down to the surface for Captain Barnard and the rangers."

"Roger, Commander. Out."

The *Kathmandu* shuddered as torpedoes spurted from its tubes.

Mikhailaivitch smiled. He would leave *nothing* for Bremenschmidt, nothing at all. Yuri Petrov Mikhailaivitch would win the Battle of New Napa, and Howland Island would *have* to promote him.

One million kilometers to go. "Rangers off the rack!"

"Roger, Commander," said Barnard.

#Dropcaps away,# said the onboards.

Something seized the *Kathmandu* then. That something shook the ship so viciously that for a moment Mikhailaivitch thought they must have plunged into New Napa's atmosphere. He checked his screens.

New stars crowded them as 312 torpedoes burst far, too far, from the Wayholder.

And fighter status lights on his battle command board began to wink from green to red.

* * *

Feeling very much alone, trying hard to avoid looking at the video frame that Commander Mikhailaivitch had programmed to appear in the corner of her main screen, Lieutenant Darcy Lee arrowed toward the skirk. Captain Hardesty was dead, blown to small pieces not ninety seconds earlier. No one else in the chain of command had spoken up. She wondered if anyone was left to speak up—in the air or on the ground.

She could not tear her gaze away from the giant vessel displayed on screen. The alien defenses had to be manipulating gravity in a way that Terran researchers had never suspected possible. She did not even bother to switch over to antimatter production. She might as well throw wet firecrackers at a brick wall.

But how had Able Wing's first volley penetrated those defenses?

For that matter, how had Able Wing survived its flash-by?

She reenacted the attack in her mind. The wing had passed at threshold speed plus the catapult's increment. Except for the slight adjustments immediately after ejection, the wing had neither accelerated nor decelerated. They had not used their gravpipes. The Wayholder had gotten only two of them.

They had struck with pinwheels driven by inertia, and time-fused shrapnel torpedoes powered by chemical rockets. Both traveled at eighty-one kilokay per second plus.

Conjecture: The enemy defenses could interfere with gravpipes, but not with stuff traveling inertially near threshold speed.

Cold sweat bathed her as she realized she had slowed almost to orbital velocity. One thought, and one thought alone, staved off panic. Her best weapon moved at nearly four times threshold speed. She needed facts, though. She needed facts, data, knowledge, numbers— quick hard cold things that did not bleed or cry out or crumple headless to the ground.

"Display probable location of major gravity generators aboard Wayholder skirmish control craft."

The image on the screen dissolved. A blueprint of the giant enemy vessel formed in its place. Four large enclosures within the skeletal pancake pulsed bright, then dim.

"Maximum—" her voice shook; she steadied it—"acceleration." Immense G-forces reached to smash her flat, but the compensators erased them before they touched her.

"Random corkscrew trajectory to intersect mathematical center point of Wayholder mothership. Target lasers for nearest major gravity generator and maintain focus throughout trajectory."

She was taking a terrible chance. On her own authority, yet. But what choice did she have? If she did not do *something,* soon, her ashes would join Billy Wong's in their long slow fall around New Napa's sun.

"Expect impact with Wayholder gravity shield. On impact, cancel all acceleration. On impact, divert full energy production to lasers. On impact, fire lasers at preselected target."

And if she was wrong? She would die.

"Display skirk."

Reality replaced outline. And swiftly grew as she plummeted toward it.

Turning her head, she inspected the starboard screen. She turned away immediately. The Wayholder defenses had torn the Catman strut from strut; it sailed on, a twinkling metal cloud. Hundreds of crewmembers. Scores of friends. Gone.

Abruptly, Catman 18 shuddered. The gravpipe lights blanked—the onboard computer had shut the system down. Rubies sparkled on her board as the lasers fired.

Tight beams lanced out, flared as they punched through the layer of dust and debris compressed by the enemy shields, and demolished the nearest gravity generator.

"Broadcast, scramble, all ships: Attention." Swiftly

she described the experimental assault method, and fell silent, awaiting a reply.

None came.

No matter. The Wayholder Empire had attacked a Terran Association colony. Most of the extended Lee clan lived on a similar colony world not far away. It seemed to her that if she expected her fellow TAAC officers to protect her family, she had damn well better protect theirs. Even at the cost of her life.

"Break off. Loop back. Repeat previous maneuver."

Just as the computer began to carry out her instructions, her aft screen blinked with a new image. She gasped.

And she wondered how much it would hurt when she died.

Chapter 3

Silver light glowed in the far right corner of the over-command module, then faded into a hologram of Admiral Franklin Munez. "Over Commander."

"Yes, Frank?"

"*Kathmandu* has dropped its rangers' capsules and is to engage the skirk at close range. It reports the destruction of ten Wayholder fighters, sir. That leaves six surviving fighters and the skirk against—" he frowned into the camera—"against twenty-five Zulus and the *Kathmandu.*"

"He trades one of ours for two of theirs." Kajiwara inhaled sharply, in anger and anguish alike. Had he sent the wrong man? The intolerable loss-kill ratio suggested that he had—at Rubio, he had sacked a commander with a far better ratio. But then, in the Rubio conflict, TAAC had flown against raw recruits, not seasoned veterans. Kajiwara drew another lungful of the module's cool, dry air. He shook his head. He could not judge Mikhailaivitch by performance benchmarks set against untrained rebels. "What of the *Lima*?"

"Decelerating into an englobement position."

57-7, he thought. Till the battle ended, a part of his mind would track each side's active forces, adding reinforcements and subtracting casualties without conscious prompting. The fleet computers did the same with greater speed and accuracy, but Kajiwara Hiroshi felt the ebb and flow of fortune more vividly, more intimately, when he kept score on his own. That the running tally also insulated him from the suffering it summarized would bother him later, but not now, not when he needed to think in terms of forces and vectors—and victory.

If only he could see the fight in its entirety, in real-time! Though the rise and fall of numbers offered insight, triumph rode more on deployment than on strength.

He wished it were worth summoning the battle command holo now. The module's computers would project an image of the New Napa system and place all warcraft at the coordinates reported in the latest SitUps—but the data could be as much as twenty minutes old, and that time lag would make the exercise worthless. He would have to wait.

"Over Commander, the rangers are popping their capsules and beginning to engage the Wayholder invaders. *Kathmandu* reports the destruction of fourteen Wayholder craft, the loss of seven of its own, and superficial damage to itself."

55-3. He gave a soft hiss of frustration. The firefight would die down soon, and he had deduced nothing of value. What would the—

"*Lima*—" Munez's voice cracked; he coughed to clear his throat—"*Lima* reports the arrival of two additional Wayholder skirmish control craft, each with a complement of sixteen fighters."

55-37. Kajiwara flattened his palms on the smooth desktop. "Dispatch Three and Four."

"Sir." Munez whispered to his implant.

The extra ops groups would give TAAC a decided advantage. That almost comforted Kajiwara. Unfortunately, the ships he had just sent would arrive long after the *Lima* clashed with the new Wayholder.

Munez said, "Three and Four are off the rack and accelerating."

"Are ops groups Eleven through Thirty maintaining surveillance?"

"Yes, sir."

"Have they reported any unusual sightings at all?"

"No, sir." The Admiral paused. Sudden sweat sheened his dark forehead. "*Lima* reports the total destruction of *Kathmandu*. No count on how many of its fighters survived. The trajectory of the second enemy force will put it in geosynch orbit around New Napa.''

31 + ? to 37. ''How did the Wayholder destroy the *Kathmandu*?''

''No word on that, sir.''

Kajiwara bowed his head. Never had he lost a carrier. The occasional fighter, yes, though few rebels had had both the equipment and the training to outwit a TAAC flyer. The grief that shot through him caught him by surprise.

So many next of kin to notify. . . .

And he still did not know why the war had started.

He controlled his breathing, then slowed his pulse. He looked into the glossy, soulless eyes of the cameras, conscious that they recorded his every word and every act for later review by Raul Santiago, TAAC high commander, and by Han Tachun, first commander of the Unified Security Forces. ''Pull in Eleven through Thirty. Each group is to leave behind one survey/reconnaissance vessel in maximum-surveillance, minimum-noise mode, with orders to avoid all contact with the Wayholder, and to retreat to Octant Auriga upon sighting any incoming Wayholder.''

''Sir.''

''Inform me when all ops groups are on the rack.'' Kajiwara licked his lips, and tasted salt.

''Sir.'' Munez mumbled to the system. Then listened hard. He wobbled. *''Lima* reports a third wave. Four skirks, sixty-four fighters, with a trajectory that will trap *Lima* between itself and the ships in geosynch. Four Wayholder killed.''

31 + ? to 101. With only sixty-two more on the way. ''Launch Five through Ten in support. Warn them the Wayholder have some way of destroying a carrier. Tell them to find out what it is.''

''Sir.'' Munez spoke softly, then cocked an ear. He nodded. ''Off the rack.''

* * *

"Eleven through Thirty on the rack, sir. Lockdown nearly complete."

Kajiwara nodded. "Situation?"

"Five to Ten are about to bounce. We are receiving SitUps from Three and Four, which entered the New Napa at the standard pop-in point. They are decelerating, and will attempt to peel the third enemy wave off *Lima*'s back. That wave has fully englobed *Lima* and its fighters. *Lima* reports radio contact with three survivors from the *Kathmandu,* who are fighting up the gravity well. A survivor suggests that the Wayholder use gravity fields both to defend against slow-moving projectiles, and to tear our pipes apart. She recommends that we shut down our pipes and disable the enemy gravity generator with lasers before firing torpedoes."

"Pass it on," said Kajiwara.

"Sir. Thirty-one Wayholder remain effective within *Lima*'s globe. The rangers have captured the spaceport. They report heavy casualties—the enemy does not surrender." The muscles of his jaw tightened visibly. It took him a moment to continue. "They also report that the Wayholder were engaged in systematic slaughter of civilians when they landed."

"Slaughter?" Nausea rippled through Kajiwara, rising to leave a sourness at the back of his mouth. These enemies had no honor. Were they not killing Terrans, to destroy them would be to disgrace himself.

96-99. 186 en route. And slaughter on the ground. "You are relaying all this to TAAC High Command?"

"Of course, sir." Wounded pride filled Munez's voice.

He inclined his head slightly. "I apologize for that, Frank. It is unusual, though, for Howland Island to remain silent for so long."

"Perhaps they have nothing to say, sir."

Kajiwara thought, but did not say, *They have no precedent to quote.* Raul Santiago gave his over commanders free rein, but Han Tachun went by the book. Officially, USF HQ encouraged originality. In reality, it punished unsuccessful innovation while excusing fail-

ure based on precedent. But what precedent defined the
best response to extraterrestrial invasion? The situation
demanded creativity. So Han and his staff must have
decided to let Kajiwara Hiroshi innovate—and bear the
consequences.

"Admiral Munez—"

The admiral's eyes widened at the unfamiliar term of
address.

"I hereby appoint you acting over commander of Octant Sagittarius. Have your module detached from the
Morocco and returned to base."

"Sir—"

He held up a hand. "The *Morocco* is going to New
Napa. We might well need reinforcements. Be prepared
to send whatever is available. Also be prepared to defend the Cheyenne System—or to evacuate it. Inform
TAAC High Command and USF HQ of all developments as they occur."

With disappointment and resignation on his face,
Munez saluted. An instant later, his image faded out of
the corner.

"Ah, Frank," said Kajiwara Hiroshi to the empty
shadows, "would I order you to stay behind if I did not
truly need you in the Cheyenne?" He tapped the nail
of his index finger on the desktop. A new image formed
in the holo area, an image of a gray-haired woman with
flinty eyes and a square jaw: Admiral Pamela Wiegand,
commanding officer of the *Morocco*. She looked up,
apparently noticed the new holo on her bridge, and
flicked her right temple with the tip of her right index
finger. "Over Commander."

"Admiral."

"Are we going in?"

He admired her directness. "Yes."

Grim pleasure sparkled in her blue eyes. "Will you
patch directly to my tactical officers?"

"I will speak only to you, Admiral. Have all status
reports and Situation Update synopses routed to my
computer."

"Yes, sir."

"As soon as Admiral Munez's module is clear, bring the *Morocco* to threshold speed and hold. Be ready to bounce for New Napa. All ops groups to stay at full alert until further notice."

The admiral nodded and turned to her officers.

Kajiwara's implant crackled like autumn leaves. #Five through Ten have bounced.# It fell silent, then a moment later said, #SitUp, *Lima.* Third Wayholder wave has opened fire. OG Two strength at twenty, including *Lima.* OG One strength at two. Enemy losses total fifty-two vessels.#

208-67.

Kajiwara detected a pattern. If it held, Wayholder reinforcements would show up some twenty minutes after ops groups Three and Four had entered the New Napa. More would pop in about that long after Five through Ten arrived. If the pattern held . . .

He squinted at the silver glow of the star coral. If the pattern held, the fourth wave would contain 136 ships. Given the current loss-kill ratio, TAAC would win handily—unless that fifth wave appeared. He sighed. The Wayholder would reinforce. His every instinct said so.

#SitUp, *Nairobi.* Five through Ten in New Napa system. Assuming penta-flake with full mandala around each carrier, five hundred kay separation. SitUp, *Lima.* Two more enemy down.#

208-65.

Wiegand said, "Over Commander, estimated time to threshold, 17 minutes 30 seconds. We have just moved out of SitUp reception range."

"And still nothing from Howland Island?"

"That's correct, sir."

"So." Message capsules from USF HQ would not reach the *Morocco* until it took up a predictable trajectory, and gave Howland Island its location, heading, and speed.

Kajiwara Hiroshi was on his own. He preferred it that way. He might make mistakes, but he could recover more easily from his own than from someone else's.

Yet moving the *Morocco* had also cut him off from his own forces. For roughly seventeen minutes he would receive no news from the front. That worried him. One foolish mistake, or one marvelous hunch, could change the course of this battle in seconds. He wondered how many of his fighters would survive to meet him.

For seventeen minutes he could do nothing to help his warriors except maintain harmony with a dissonant universe.

Aware of the eyebrows that would shoot up when the USF HQ staff reviewed the recordings of activity within the module, he took from the desk drawer a sheet of rice paper, a calligraphy brush, and ink the shade of midnight.

Brush in hand, he gazed at the paper and breathed softly, evenly. He did not try to block events or emotions from his mind. Rather, he let everything flow in, like surf in a tidal pool, splashing and surging till each swell canceled another and equilibrium reigned.

Now. While he and the ship and the great galaxy beyond trembled together like a single plucked string—

The brush skated down the paper, leaving tracks of glistening black kanji:

Spasms shake the land;
Calm warriors ride surprise.
Clouds sleep undisturbed.

Ah, so desu. He cleaned the brush, replaced the ink. He set the haiku in the center of his desk and folded his hands.

Wiegand said, "Five seconds to threshold speed."

"Bounce to New Napa. Standard pop-in point."

Kajiwara Hiroshi held his breath. He had developed the reflex as a cadet at the Academy, and suspected he would not rid himself of it before he died. It made him feel foolish, though. The jump across 450 light-years made almost no sign within the overcommand module. Gravity wavered for a millisecond. Indicator lights flickered on his desk. And that was that. Very prosaic. Not at all worth holding one's breath for. He let it out.

They materialized at the "north" end of the deceleration lane, 48 million kilometers away from New Napa. Wiegand said, "Decelerating at maximum."

Display panels gleamed, flashed, and finally strobed as radio messages five and six minutes old poured in. He disregarded them. The computer and Wiegand would swiftly tell him everything he needed to know.

He had to reset his mental computer, though. He touched his neck. "Subject, space vehicles in New Napa system; query, total surviving TAAC versus total surviving Wayholder."

Even the stealthiest of warships sweats electromagnetic radiation constantly, even at rest. Its heat pumps infrared; its comm devices spit microwaves; its armaments leak X-rays. You can dampen and cloak and insulate all you want, but you cannot make a ship of the line invisible.

All you can do is make it dangerous.

Sensors on the *Morocco*'s framework opened up to a flood of EM radiation. Awash in it, they analyzed, identified, and triangulated.

The computer whispered to Kajiwara: #191 surviving TAAC vessels; forty-eight surviving Wayholder vessels. Caution: farthest point sources 160-plus light-seconds distant.#

191-48. And subject to change as light from the farthest skirmishes reached the *Morocco*. He pressed his finger against his neck. "Wayholder reinforcements will arrive. When they do, tell me how many have come."

It did not even wait. #One hundred thirty-six.#

191-184.

"Admiral Wiegand." He stroked the silk of his tunic as he thought. "Send groups Eleven through Twenty-six at the latest arrivals, with two groups joining forces to take out one Wayholder mothership. Groups Twenty-seven through Twenty-nine are to med-evac ranger casualties from New Napa. Thirty is to shield the other three until they lift off again."

"Sir!" Her holographic image swiveled to relay the orders.

671-184.

They had finally come close enough for him to see the battlefield for himself. He told his computer, "Generate battle command holo."

The programs ran swift and smooth. All furniture save the desk retracted into the walls and floor. A smooth panel slid down in front of the vegetable wall, to keep him from breaking the plants while he paced the room. The lights dimmed. A hologram of the system filled the small module.

The software painted astronomical bodies green and placed the emerald ball representing New Napa's sun in the middle of the bulkhead to Kajiwara's right. The planets on *Morocco*'s side of the sun winked into position. A glitter of asteroids streaked the over commander's face.

It made him feel like God.

Friend and foe stacked up over New Napa in alternate layers. At forty kilokay orbited one skirk and twelve Wayholder fighters. Just above them darted the *Lima* and two Zulus—all that survived of OGs One and Two. A thousand kilometers over the *Lima,* three skirks and a haze of fighters dodged fire dropping from the remnants of Three and Four.

A five-armed snowflake ten thousand kilometers in diameter fell toward New Napa's north pole. Groups Five through Ten would strike within minutes.

Eighteen minutes behind them came the *Morocco* and its warships.

Yet from the "south" swarmed the latest Wayholder reinforcements. Eight skirks flew in single file a thousand kilometers apart; their fighters formed two rings around each mothership, four in the inner ring and twelve in the outer. The spear-shaped formation would reach New Napa seconds after the *Morocco.*

"Inform me verbally of each loss as it occurs."

#Cumulative: TAAC losses equal seven; enemy losses equal fifteen.#

664-169.

Good odds, but he had nothing left in reserve. And some of his pilots had been fighting for hours. He had to relieve them before he lost them. Fresher units could mop up around the planet. "Admiral, the surviving units of groups One through Four are to break off and return to the *Morocco*."

"Yes, sir."

#One TAAC.#

663-169.

#273 Wayholder reinforcements.#

663-442.

Wiegand leaped to her feet. "Over Com—"

"I know." He held up his hand and thought for a moment. "Admiral, accelerate the *Morocco* back to threshold speed while remaining within the deceleration lane. All hands to battle stations. The survivors from One to Four are to come alongside on matching courses as soon as possible."

#Three enemy.#

663-439.

"Are we pulling out, sir?"

"No." Sweat dampened his tunic and tainted the air with its acrid odor. He did not regard it as a sign of weakness, as he might have in his youth. Human physiological responses to danger evolved on African plains millions of years ago, and persisted despite their irrelevance.

#Fifteen TAAC; thirty enemy.#

648-409.

In the hologram, the lights representing destroyed units simply faded out. In Kajiwara's mind, ships burst with soundless fury, and occasional fragments traced fiery lines through the skies of New Napa. The hologram cleared.

Still in penta-flake formation, Five through Ten hit the battlesphere, lasers pulsing in unison. The searing blast obliterated the few remaining enemy. The formation kept going, clearly intending to collide head-on with

the two reinforcing fleets. The *Morocco* and sixteen
more ops groups followed close behind.

Kajiwara frowned. The latest waves of Wayholder
were not braking, even though they hurtled to intercept
a total force half again their combined size. Very stu-
pid. Or. . . .

Nothing would happen for a while. He had time to
think it through.

By the time the giant snowflake had come within
range of the Wayholder, Kajiwara's eyes had widened
with dismay. "Admiral, groups Five to Ten form Alpha
Force and maintain a straight-line course directly
through the enemy while accelerating to threshold
speed. They are not under any circumstances to loop
back. Hit and run."

"Ah . . . yes, sir."

Impatient now, Kajiwara chewed his upper lip while
Wiegand relayed the orders. The instant she looked up,
he said, "Groups Eleven through Eighteen form Beta
Force. Beta must accelerate to threshold speed on a
course parallel to the plane of the ecliptic going sunward. Groups Nineteen through Twenty-six form
Gamma Force and assume the exact opposite course."

Bewilderment crossed Wiegand's face, but she passed
Kajiwara's instructions on without question.

Alpha's snowflake—ten kilokay wide and one ship
deep—raced along the shaft of a spear eight thousand
kilometers long. Terran lasers stabbed through the alien
column, searching for gravity generators, finding whatever they could. The Wayholder threw everything they
had into Alpha's path.

#Four TAAC; seven enemy.#

644-402.

"Race the *Morocco* past New Napa, directly at the
Wayholder fleets."

"Sir."

Beta Force glided into a graceful arc toward the sun.
Gamma mirrored its move toward the outer planets. The
Morocco followed Alpha. Had the new directives
reached Alpha yet? Kajiwara clenched his jaw. Alpha's

commanders thought they would pass through the flames into safety. He knew better.

#Seven TAAC; twelve enemy.#

637-390.

Forty-eight megakay south of New Napa, a new constellation blotted out the stars.

#546 Wayholder reinforcements.#

637-936. If his flyers maintained their loss-kill ratio, the Wayholder would lose this battle—but Kajiwara Hiroshi would have lost almost his entire fleet. And if the Wayholder reinforced one more time, as they surely would . . .

Wiegand received the latest update and gasped. "My God, sir, where are they coming from?"

"From someone with more resources than I, Admiral."

The 157 survivors of Alpha accelerated. They held their penta-flake formation, though its center had utterly vanished.

#Twelve TAAC; twenty-three enemy.#

629-913.

Within seconds, Alpha would slam into the fifth wave, a hollow cube with a battle zone control craft at its center, and a full hundred units stronger. Whoever survived would almost immediately face the massive sixth, 546 fresh pilots arrayed in a sphere 41,000 kilometers in diameter. Kajiwara knew how few of his people would live through that passage.

The *Morocco* swooped past New Napa.

"Admiral, have OGs One to Four caught up with us yet?"

"Yes, sir."

"Have them form a mandala around us, 2,000 kilometer separation on all sides; they are to maintain threshold speed at all times."

"Sir."

"Twenty-seven through Thirty are to evacuate New Napa in this order: all wounded, rangers first, then civilians; all unwounded rangers; and finally, everybody else they can possibly fit on board. As soon as they're loaded to the limit they're to head for the Cheyenne, no looking back.''

"Sir.''

The *Morocco* and its outriders raced toward the splintered spear of the fourth wave. Alpha Force, badly outnumbered, smashed into the fifth. The physics of Alpha's flight precluded retreat, yet Kajiwara chose to admire his pilots' courage.

#One enemy.#

629-912.

#Five TAAC, eleven enemy.#

624-901.

He bit his lip. The snowflake fell through the cube. Pilots picked targets; computers manned weapon banks. Lasers cut wildly, invisibly. Metal glowed white-hot and vaporized. Bursting torpedoes sprayed an antimatter fog and the matter going through it raged, dying in the quantum light. Modules exploded with silent, incandescent fury. Entire warships shivered down to shrapnel.

#Nine TAAC; nineteen enemy.#

615-882.

Wiegand said, "Fifteen seconds to intercept.''

Kajiwara had time to wonder what the Wayholder commanders thought of his tactics. Did their culture have its own version of the kamikaze? Did they worry about their pilots' willingness to fly into the teeth of the foe?

The computer chattered constantly now, and the tallies flashed through his mind.

602-867.

592-846.

561-780.

551-760.

Eighty ships of Alpha Force emerged from their plunge through the cube. They raced headlong toward the sixth and largest wave. Seconds later the *Morocco* and her flankers met the survivors of the fourth.

And passed through them in less than one-tenth of a second.

#Twelve TAAC, ninety enemy.#

539-670.

"All three forces and *Morocco* at threshold speed, sir."

Alpha's battered circle disappeared into the world-sized formation of the sixth enemy wave. One half of one second later, six widely scattered carriers and twelve Zulus emerged on the other side.

#Sixty-eight TAAC; 130 enemy.#

471-540.

Yes. He would adopt Mikhailaivitch's tactics. No one should be so proud as to reject that which works simply because a subordinate developed it. "Tell Alpha to bounce back in front of the fourth wave and run the entire gauntlet again. *Morocco* does the same once we break through the sixth. Beta—"

The *Morocco* hit the fifth wave and tunneled through.

"—bounces back to the dark side of the sixth wave and passes through its vertical axis five seconds after we've gone through. Gamma repeats from the sun side five seconds after Beta's passed. All four to cycle until there's nothing left."

Wiegand's eyes widened. "Commander, the gravpipes can't take that much stress. They'll—"

"They will have to, Admiral."

"The pipes need a five-minute cooldown between bounces—you're not even giving my pilots five seconds!"

"Then give them six seconds."

#Four TAAC; seventy-three enemy.#

469-467.

She stood, her hands clenched at her sides, her shoulders stiff and her eyes afire. "Sir, if the pipes blow my pilots die!"

"Admiral—" He damped a flare of anger with icy self-control. "We are at war, Admiral. If we are to win, our pilots must take chances for which they would be cashiered in peacetime. You have your orders, Admiral."

"Sir!" Her salute insulted him with its perfection. She pivoted away.

He stared at the battle hologram. She was right, of course. TAAC regulations did require a five-minute cooldown.

Alpha Force completed its bounce. The battle command holo placed eighteen blue dots just before the fourth Wayholder wave.

The regulations stemmed from economics, though, not from tactics.

The battle command holo removed eighteen blue dots from the outskirts of the action as EM radiation from Alpha's former position ceased reaching the *Morocco*.

Soon Kajiwara Hiroshi would learn whether or not he should have followed the rules.

Ten seconds to impact with the sixth wave. Kajiwara shook his head. Granted the power of a fleetship, he was still going to attack 414 fighters with a mere five vessels. He suspected it might be his second court-martial offense of the day.

#Two TAAC; six enemy.#

467-461.

Power plants pumped energy; the overcommand's module's lights dimmed. The 3,400 lasers of the *Morocco* cycled two million times each. The telltales on Kajiwara's desk sputtered madly as instruments registered damage to struts and spars and life-support spheres.

And the calm voice said, #Two TAAC; ninety-two enemy.#

465-369.

Beta pounced on the fifth wave from the dark side.

#120 TAAC; 241 enemy.#

345-128.

The *Morocco* bounced to where the fourth wave would have been had it not been liquidated, and Kajiwara cursed himself for not amending his orders. Ahead, Alpha hit the fifth wave.

#Sixteen TAAC; forty enemy.#

329-88.

Alpha Force was gone. Completely. Not a single survivor.

Gamma came out of the sun to rip through the ribcage of the sixth wave.

#Fifty TAAC; eighty-one enemy.#

279-7.

The *Morocco* took out the last seven Wayholder with one swift pass.

279-0.

"We've won, sir," said Wiegand.

"Have we?" said Kajiwara softly. He felt drained, and dirty, as must a farmer who has spent the day smashing vermin.

"Yes, sir. Your tactic worked. We've won."

"I wonder . . ." He had won nothing. He had performed his duty, but gained no honor. Honor did not accrue to the slayer of the dishonorable. "Is there word from New Napa?"

"Yes, sir. Twenty-six brought up all ranger casualties. Twenty-seven took the unwounded. Both are on their way home. The civilian population refuses to evacuate."

Kajiwara said, "Get me their chief civil authority."

The computer said, #1,092 Wayholder reinforcements.#

279-1092.

A huge red spot exploded in the battle holo right in front of the *Morocco*. Wiegand gasped—but turned to Kajiwara for orders.

The over commander took a deep breath. So. He would meet his destiny here after all. He would die in battle, as a warrior should. Briefly, he wished he could respect this enemy, for he would lose face if he fell to inferiors. Still, it was his duty to protect the colonists to the best of his ability, and Kajiwara Hiroshi would do his duty.

Wiegand cocked her head and touched a finger to just behind her ear.

Kajiwara said, "Cancel that call, Admiral. Summon reinforcements from Octant Sagittarius. Send Beta—"

"Sir, priority-override message from USF HQ relayed from New Napa. Quote—"

"Later, Admiral. Send—"

"No, sir. Quote, 'Withdraw immediately—' "

"What?"

" '—under pain of arrest, trial, and public humiliation for you, your officers, and all your families.' " She spread her hands helplessly. "I'm sorry, Over Commander. That's the message."

He slumped in his chair. Icy shock percolated through him as he realized he had been relieved of command. He, Kajiwara Hiroshi.

His honor was gone no matter what. Could he strip his officers of theirs?

Unthinkable. "Home," he said tiredly. "All of us."

Chapter 4

The towers of the Unified Security Forces Headquarters cast shadows that darkened Howland Island's north shore and reached well into the bay. Kajiwara Hiroshi stood at a window in the tallest of those towers. Far below him, earthmovers spread shredded, treated refuse over the land reclaimed from the Pacific Ocean. New skyscrapers would rise on the landfill, and the bureaucrats in those buildings could take their turn watching the island bloat.

Kajiwara did not care whether the island grew or shrank. He did not care about anything. He had returned an empty man, bleak and dispirited. Only bushido—the Way of the Warrior—supported him. Without it, he could no more stand on his own than could the uniform he wore. Even with it, he feared that he would soon collapse.

Less than twenty-four hours earlier, the chairman had relieved him of command. Kajiwara had abandoned New Napa. He had left Octant Sagittarius. He had lost all claim to honor, and only one ancient ritual could expunge his disgrace.

Behind him, Raul Santiago, high commander of the Astro Corps, concluded his holophone conversation. "Hiroshi—"

Kajiwara turned and came to attention. "Sir."

Santiago waved his long, slender hand dismissively. "Not here, Hiroshi, not now. We have known each other too many years for such formality."

"As you wish."

Santiago frowned. "Why have you submitted your resignation?"

"I am no longer fit to command."

"Self-doubt, Hiroshi?"

"Self-knowledge." He would not make eye contact with his friend, his mentor. Instead he stared at the image of Earth that filled the floor-to-ceiling wallscreen behind Santiago. The silence lasted long enough for a sliver of the planet to slip into darkness.

Santiago finally spoke, in a low, wryly musing tone. "If you do, indeed, know such a thing to be true, then you have lost the faith in yourself that is essential to an officer's fitness to lead, thus vitiating any arguments I might offer to the contrary. But I must confess that I have difficulty visualizing you in your retirement, my friend. What does a samurai do when he lays down his swords?"

Onscreen, clouds shrouded the Japanese islands. It would be raining in Kyoto. Kajiwara wished he could go there again. "I will be a private individual, and my activities will be of no interest to those whom I have failed."

Scion of an ancient Castilian family, Santiago apparently understood Kajiwara's shame—and need. He fingered the plain silver crucifix at his neck. "I was educated by Jesuits, Hiroshi, and I remain too much the Catholic to condone your obvious intent, but I will accept this resignation if you feel you must tender it."

"I must." Now he met Santiago's gaze. The pain in his friend's brown eyes did not touch him.

Santiago gave a slow nod. "Then forgive me for sullying this moment with drably bureaucratic considerations, but I must ask you to be certain that all your papers are in order before you depart the island."

"I will."

The high commander came out from behind his desk, seized Kajiwara in a fierce Latin embrace, and pounded him on the back. Releasing him, he said, *"Vaya con Dios,* Hiroshi."

Kajiwara bowed. *"Arigato gozaimashita."*

An hour later, as he sat in a borrowed office filling out the myriad forms demanded by Personnel, a message arrived from Han Tachun, first commander of the Unified Security Forces. It said, "Resignation rejected. Under powers conferred by declaration of martial law, Over Commander Kajiwara Hiroshi confined to quarters until further notice. Kajiwara forbidden to commit seppuku; disobedience will result in death for all his living relatives and public humiliation for his entire ancestral line."

He stared at it, aghast. Never in his wildest dreams had he imagined that anyone could so coldly deny bushido while at the same time so cynically use it to manipulate him.

The fool. Did Han really not know that the only part of Kajiwara Hiroshi that mattered—his soul—had died in the bounce out of New Napa?

Or did Han take pleasure in keeping the rest of him alive?

It did not matter. He would obey. As a puncture does a pressure suit, disgrace had made him unusable without transforming him. Samurai in every cell of his being, he would heed his ruler until death released him from his duty.

For the next eight days he worked in the borrowed office, drafting a reprisal campaign against the Wayholder Empire. Planning such an expedition—or even commanding it—would hardly restore his honor, but he could not sit idle while barbarians savaged the borders. Forbidden to seek absolution in the time-honored fashion, he had to put his tarnished skills to the best possible use.

The data in the Association's bank disappointed him, for most of it came from debriefings of the linguists who had worked with the Wayholder thirty-five years ago. He would need much fresher information—and would gather it with the Astro Corps's 2,400 survey/reconnaisance vessels. Only the timing would present a problem, for the Empire would react quickly to intrusion into its territory.

So. One all-out simultaneous sweep would probe the 240 Wayholder star systems nearest the galactic rift. The spy ships would return at a prearranged instant and disgorge their data into . . .

He sketched a computer network architecture capable or receiving and analyzing information from that many sources. Yes. Child's play. The analysis program would then select the ten least-defended worlds; the fleets would strike at once.

No. Not ten worlds. The Wayholder used a base-seventeen number system, so TAAC would destroy seventeen worlds—retaliation one alien order of magnitude higher.

Crafting the plan did not assuage his shame. It merely occupied his time.

He took his meals in the tower's giant subterranean cafeteria. He sat alone, looking only at the simple food he permitted himself, all the while listening to the conversations that carried to him the hopes and dreams of Howland Island's finest.

". . . double the budget and—"

"The bank approved the mortgage, but—"

"Clearly, a separate administrative unit will be required—"

". . . to Proxy last year, but *this* year she wants something really primitive —without crawling things or slimy things. I ask you—"

". . . told her, I'm overdue for promotion and until it comes through—"

"God, I'm still hung over and it's been two days since the party."

". . . wounded in action, he says, and it's a damn paper cut, but he says there's this empty slot out in the Cheyenne, and how would I like it? And I say I'll have the papers done by close of business today. I mean, I *like* flying a desk, you know?"

Kajiwara Hiroshi ate alone, and listened, and wondered how Tokugawa Ieyasu would have reacted if he had overheard such discussions at his headquarters.

At night, with the silver glow of the star coral the

only light in his room at the transient officers' quarters,
he sat on the floor in the lotus position—hands on thighs
palms up, back straight, gaze focused far beyond the
chipped white paint of the wall. During those hours he
neither thought nor avoided thought. He sat. He was.
He waited.

On the tenth day after he ceded New Napa to the
forces of the Wayholder Empire, two sergeants escorted
him to the spaceport and put him on a suborbital flight
to Geneva.

Two more sergeants met him at Port Geneva, led him
to a groundcar, and drove him to the Corporate Chambers, the two-hundred-story office building that housed
the executive offices of the Terran Association.

A series of high-speed elevator rides brought Kajiwara Hiroshi and his guards to a gleaming white door
twice normal height and four times normal width.
Golden letters twenty centimeters high spelled out:

**Pierre LeFebvre
Chairman of the Board
Terran Association**

The over commander did not look around for a re-
ceptionist. Neither did he raise his hand to knock. The
news media had discussed that shimmering white door
so often and so thoroughly that the entire Association
must know how it worked. Certainly the sergeants did.
They stopped in their tracks.

Kajiwara walked straight into it.

Just before impact, the decorative hologram winked
out; the protective force field shut off. He passed
through an archway five meters high and five wide. The
door glittered back to life behind him.

Five people stood facing him. In the middle, the
chairman, fat, bald, and old enough to be Kajiwara's
great-grandfather. To LeFebvre's right, Han Tachun,
first commander of the Unified Security Forces. To
LeFebvre's left, Raul Santiago, high commander of the
Astro Corps. On either end, two Gurkha guards, each

of them young, well-muscled, and growth-accelerated to at least 240 centimeters tall.

So. The chairman's taste does truly run to the theatrical. Kajiwara came to attention, saluted, and waited for both Santiago and Han to return the salute. Ignoring the Gurkhas—LeFebvre's true guards had neither heart nor soul, but gallium brains, six dozen lasers, and reaction times measurable in nanoseconds—Kajiwara strode across the thick carpeting and stopped before the five men. He bowed. "Mr. Chairman."

Pierre LeFebvre inclined his head. Light glinted off his bare pink scalp. He sat. "Please." He waved to the armchair at Kajiwara's right.

"Thank you, sir." The over commander sat down, his spine stiff, his shoulders squared.

As Han and Santiago also took their seats, the chairman spread his hands on the top of his desk. "Do you like it?"

"Sir?"

He smiled. "My desk, Over Commander." He stroked its surface, a gravity plane seventy-five centimeters off the ground that provided him an invisible work area. He touched the arm of his chair. Equipment hidden from view projected a flawless hologram of the entire Milky Way into the desktop. LeFebvre could put his thumb on any star or planet he desired.

"Quite nice, sir." It did not move Kajiwara to envy, and he would not have commented if LeFebvre had not solicited his reaction. He did not care about such things, not anymore. He sat perfectly, inhumanly still, and waited for LeFebvre to speak.

The old man studied Kajiwara through cold brown eyes. After a long minute, he nodded. "Thank you for coming to Geneva, Over Commander."

"It was this one's duty."

LeFebvre's bushy eyebrows quirked. " 'This one'?"

Han Tachun said, "An archaic Japanese locution, Mr. Chairman, rather determinedly formal in nature. The over commander employs it as an acknowledgment of his personal insignificance in the presence of his superiors. The over commander is quite the samurai, you know."

"I see." LeFebvre turned to Kajiwara. "Is it that coming was not your desire?"

Kajiwara would not permit Han to provoke him to anger. "In time of war, the officer takes his ruler's desire as his own."

The chairman's lips thinned. "The first commander, he has said that you tried to resign."

"Yes."

"And that you had the intention to kill yourself."

Kajiwara bent his head a centimeter or two. "Death is preferable to a life without honor."

"He has said that he ordered you to stay alive."

"And this one obeyed."

"Then you will explain at once the meaning of this nonsense!" He slapped the arm of his chair.

The desktop hologram changed. The Milky Way vanished. The desk displayed the first page of a proposal Kajiwara knew well. "That is a portion of a strategic outline for a punitive campaign against the Wayholder Empire."

"This? No. This, it is a proposal for suicide." He dismissed it with a touch; the cold glory of the Milky Way blazed up again. "I have vetoed it."

Kajiwara swallowed sudden rage. *Calm.* "Sir, as stated in the preamble, this one calculated carefully the odds of success, and—"

"Your numbers are wrong." Leaning back, LeFebvre caressed his right cheek with a fingertip.

"You remind this one of his disgrace." He rose to his feet and bowed. "This one must respectfully resubmit his resignation, effective immediately."

"Oh, sit down, I do not accuse you of incompetence. Nor do I permit you to quit. I tell you your estimates of enemy strength are incorrect."

Kajiwara had taken the numbers directly from TAAC's databanks, and Intelligence had given them an accuracy assessment of 98 percent. Kajiwara looked at Santiago.

The high commander shrugged in apology. "We have

received more detailed information, my friend. I must tell you, I agree with the chairman's decision to cancel the expedition.''

''So.'' Kajiwara Hiroshi inhaled slowly, through his teeth. ''Is it the chairman's decision that no action will be taken against the Wayholder Empire? Or—''

''You have stated the matter correctly, Over Commander.'' LeFebvre leaned back in his chair and clasped his pudgy hands behind his neck. ''Such is my decision.''

''Sir.'' Kajiwara had trouble breathing. ''Respectfully. At the time of invasion, New Napa had a population in excess of 140 million people. An Intelligence survey completed after the Wayholder withdrawal reports that all of them are dead.''

''I know that.''

How could the chairman remain so placid—so smug? ''Slaughtered in cold blood, sir!''

''That, too, I know.''

He gripped the arms of the chair, at least partly to keep himself from leaping to his feet and pounding the desktop. ''And you will shame our race by permitting the Wayholder to go unpunished?''

Han Tachun said, ''You show disrespect to the chairman, Over Commander.''

An instant before Kajiwara could show disrespect to Han as well, LeFebvre waved his hand languidly. ''Enough. Both of you.''

Han grimaced. ''Yes, sir.''

The effort to remain civil nearly strangled Kajiwara. ''Sir—''

The chairman held up his hand. ''I am told that the Astro Corps of the Unified Security Forces of the Terran Association has eighty-three fleets at full strength, plus the remnants of the 79th.''

Kajiwara's cheeks grew warm.

LeFebvre shook his head slightly. ''No, no, Over Commander, this is not the criticism. The 79th, it destroyed almost eighteen hundred Wayholder ships.''

''At a cost of 741 of our own.''

"It was a miracle for any of you to survive. My point is that we have got, at most, seventy-five thousand warships."

"Yes, sir, but this one would only need seventeen fleets—"

"It is our belief, Over Commander, that the Wayholder Empire can field four million warships at any moment, and is either constructing or repairing two million more."

The numbers stunned Kajiwara. For a long moment, he sat motionless and searched his memory for the source of his miscalculation. Then he spotted it.

When he had asked for an estimate of enemy strength, he had believed the Empire to be invading the Association, and had assumed the foe had massed the bulk of its fleet in the sector abutting Octant Sagittarius. Astro Corps Intelligence had guessed there were 69,000 Wayholder fighting ships in that area. The number had stuck in his head. He had never, he realized, asked for an estimate of *total* enemy forces. He had committed a foolish mistake. He swallowed hard. "This one . . . sees."

"No, Over Commander, you do not see. Did you know the ambassador of the Wayholder had come to Terra mere hours before the fighting started?"

"This one has learned that, sir."

"It gave us the ultimatum."

He waited for LeFebvre to continue.

"In summary, any further attacks on Wayholder forces will constitute the *casus belli*. If we attack, the Wayholder will invade the Association and destroy each and every member planet in the same way they destroyed New Napa. If they invade, Over Commander, could you hold them off?"

"With 75,000 fighters? We would have to achieve a ninety-to-one kill ratio. Impossible."

"Then you see the predicament in which I find myself."

He nodded.

Wearily, the chairman massaged his bald scalp. "It is unfortunate, but there is more."

"Sir?"

"The Wayholder, they invaded New Napa as a training exercise for combat infantry fresh out of—call it boot camp. They have told us that they will continue to provide their forces with the similar combat experience on the other worlds of Octant Sagittarius."

Kajiwara's eyes widened. "Sir, we have a hundred separate colonies in the Sagittarius!" *Including,* he thought in dismay, *Longfall, where Michael O'Reilly, my great-grandchild, lives with his family.*

"And they will invade one planet every thirty-fourth week until they have desecrated all of them." LeFebvre gestured to Han. "The first commander will explain."

Han looked as though he resented having to explain anything to Kajiwara. "The Wayholder wage war with a species called the Korrin, who dwell on the other side of the Empire. The Wayholder say that veterans of ground combat survive a hundred times longer in battle than nonveterans. They say—" The acids of bitterness etched his voice. "They say we should sacrifice the colonies gratefully, because the Korrin will devour the entire Association if the Wayholder Empire falls."

Kajiwara straightened. "If they are already at war, perhaps—"

" 'The enemy of my enemy'?"

"Yes! Can we reach the Korrin?"

Santiago answered. "We sent a survey ship into Korrin territory the day before yesterday."

"I hadn't heard."

"Very few people have—or will."

Kajiwara narrowed his eyes. "What—?"

Santiago rubbed his crucifix. "The tag-behind observation robot came back with pictures of the survey ship's consumption. In this case, my friend, the enemy of my enemy is my enemy, too."

Kajiwara cocked his head. The high commander spoke English too well to have used the word "consumption" accidentally.

The chairman said, "The Wayholder ambassador likens the Korrin to an infectious disease. The ships of the Korrin travel through space vacuuming up the interstellar dust—"

"Apparently a variation of our dust-broom technology," said Santiago. "Instead of pushing it aside to clear the way, though, the Korrin gather it for its resource value."

"Yes." LeFebvre pulled slowly on his right earlobe. "And with their mastery of nanotechnology they manufacture . . ." He glanced at Han.

"Seeds." The first commander made a face.

LeFebvre shrugged. "That word, it is close enough. Each seed contains a unicellular embryo, a computer with software, and the basic tools of nanotech. A vessel makes billions of such seeds during its lifetime, and sows them each time it passes through a star system. Those that land on anything but the star itself burrow beneath the surface and—" Again he looked at Han.

The first commander spread his hands. "They germinate."

"This metaphor, it bothers me." LeFebvre rubbed the side of his face. "They hatch, like vipers. Or unfold, perhaps, like nightmares. That is irrelevant, though annoying. The computer then uses the tools to gather raw materials to make other tools, which build— or grow, or weave—a new ship, and an artificial womb. The embryo develops, the computer . . . untanks it, raises it, and educates it. When this . . . *thing* reaches sexual maturity, it mates. Not in our terms, but theirs. They exchange genetic material and need only do it once. The ship lifts, and heads outward from the Korrin's point of origin. At some point it begins manufacturing seeds of its own. The Wayholder say that deep within Korrin territory, there is nothing left but the stars themselves—no planets, comets, asteroids, or even dust. The Korrin have eaten everything that is not hot enough to melt them."

Kajiwara let out his breath. "That does not explain why the Wayholder attack our colonies."

The chairman laid his palms flat on his desk. "The Korrin breed only at a specific stage of their development—and that stage must, it seems, occur at the bottom of a gravity well. The Wayholder troops need the practice of locating and destroying aggressive, technophilic life forms. We are the only other race they have encountered. And, they say, we are nowhere near as formidable as the Korrin."

Kajiwara swallowed hard. "When do we commence evacuation?"

"Of the colonies?"

"Yes."

The chairman shook his head. "They have warned us not to. If they find the colony uninhabited, they will simply pick the closest populated one. If we interfere, they will destroy the Association planet by planet. Frankly, Over Commander, ours in not an estimable position. To resist them would be the foolishness in the extreme."

"But sir," he said in agony, "over ten billion human beings live in Octant Sagittarius!"

"I know. But there is nothing we can do."

He set his jaw. Ten billion people. His responsibility. And if he tried to save them . . . "Sir."

"Not at this moment, at any rate."

That piqued Kajiwara's interest. "Sir?"

"To attack the Wayholder Empire, it is necessary for us to have at least six million warships, and crews for all of them."

Kajiwara could not let that pass. "Respectfully, sir. This one suggests a smaller need. Surely the Korrin will keep many Wayholder fleets well away from our forces. Moreover, given our loss-kill ratio—"

"No, no, that is *your* loss-kill ratio, Over Commander, and who is to say it will be the same next time around? We take no chances with the survival of humanity, Over Commander."

Kajiwara could not fault the sentiment, so he said nothing.

LeFebvre's old brown eyes glittered. "I have vowed,

here—" he thumped his chest with his fist—"that we will build those ships. I have vowed that when we have built them, we will attack. And I have vowed that when we have attacked, Over Commander, we will eradicate the Wayholder from the galaxy."

Kajiwara leaned back in his chair. "When?"

LeFebvre's index finger doodled on the desktop. "It is within our capacity to build and staff one hundred thousand ships a year."

"Sixty years?"

The chairman of the board nodded.

Kajiwara closed his eyes in aching disappointment. Even with another organ rejuvenation he would lack the strength to command by then. "So the task of restoring my honor will fall to my successors."

"No, Kajiwara Hiroshi, it will fall to you."

"Sir?"

LeFebvre shot an amused glance at Han Tachun, whose set jaw and rigid posture suggested he had opposed the chairman's plan. Then he turned back to Kajiwara. "Listen."

Lieutenant Darcy Lee got her beer from the bar and looked through the haze for a quiet booth. She did not want to describe the battle yet again. She did not want to remind herself that of the thirty fighter pilots, 354 crew members, and 3,000 rangers aboard the *Kathmandu,* only she and 500 rangers had come home. She did not want any more of those goddamn speculative looks that wondered if she had stayed alive by staying out of it.

Darcy Lee wanted peace, and quiet, and a bartender who would fill her glass every time she raised it. She intended to raise it frequently.

She slipped through the crowd and dropped into the booth she had spotted. Only then did she notice its drowsing occupant. She started to get up.

"No, stay." The ranger captain lifted his head off the table. He had a two-day stubble, a red nose, and bloodshot blue eyes that focused slowly on her insignia. "I gotta talk. But only to shome—somebody who was there.''

"Excuse me, sir, I—"

"No sir. Mickey." He thumped his chest. "Mickey Barnard." He squinted through the gloom. Then he pointed at the name stenciled on her tunic. "Darcy Lee. I heard about you. You're the one saved our ass. Didn't know you're so pretty. Sorry." He waved a hand. "Didn't mean . . . you know. Too drunk anyway. Just wanted to shay—say thanks. You figured it out. Zapped those green knucklewalkers.''

"The what?"

"Wayhumpers. They're green. Well—" He held out his hand and waggled it from side to side. "Sort of. Sometimes they're blue. When they're dying they're blue. Af'er that they're green. Here." He dug into his tunic pocket for a holo that he spun across the table to her. "Ugly fuckers, huh?"

Trust a ranger to take pictures on the battlefield. She picked it up. It showed an alien corpse, its throat slit, lying supine on the tatters of its spacesuit. It had to measure three meters from head to toe. It was, indeed, green; its heavily wrinkled skin resembled elephant hide.

Atop massive shoulders and a bulky torso sat a large, spherical head with recessed ears and nostrils. Its coppery eyes bulged. Scales covered the skull, and seemed to splash down onto the shoulders.

She held it close, traced the line of a long muscular arm with her fingernail, then shuddered. "What'd you do, cut the fingers off?"

He shook his head. "They click in an' out. Like cat claws.''

"Toes, too?"

"Uh-huh.''

She tapped the short, extremely thick leg. "They can't move very fast on these piano legs.''

"You'd be shur—surprised. They run like g'rillas. Y'know? Knuckles on the ground? Faster'n hell.''

"Is this one male or female?"

He gave an elaborate shrug. "Who knows? They all looked the same. Didn't have *nothing* down there. Maybe it's somewhere else. I dunno. Didn't have time to look closer. Didn't *wanna* look closer."

"I can't blame you." She passed the holo back to him. She wished she had not looked at it. She knew she would dream of it.

"They don't—" he belched—"don't surrender."

"I heard."

He leaned across the table and breathed whiskey fumes in her face. "And they don't take prizh—prisoners, either." He dropped another holo in front of her. "Look."

She turned her head, but not before her first glance seared into her mind the image: a mound of headless corpses, none of them more than eight years old.

Chapter 5

Kajiwara Hiroshi sat in the backseat and scowled at the shaved necks of the bodyguards imposed on him by the first commander. Han Tachun had meant the escort as an insult. No one in the south of France had any reason to harm Kajiwara Hiroshi—except Kajiwara himself. Yet Han had already forbidden Kajiwara to commit seppuku, so assigning two men to guard him impugned his integrity more loudly than words alone could have done.

Kajiwara had come to expect such contempt from Han, a finance expert who had made a fortune in shipping before the board of directors appointed him first commander. Han had a strange traditional streak that included accepting, without apparent question, the old Confucian social order that viewed merchants as the lowest acceptable class. By his own belief system, Han the ex-merchant had less value to society than bureaucrats, farmers, and artisans.

Everyone needs someone to despise, and Han was no exception. The traditional Chinese social order gave him a target, for, unlike its Japanese counterpart, it placed no value on the military. An ancient saying that Han quoted with fondness put it most succinctly: "Good iron is not for nails, nor good men for soldiers."

Knowing this did not make Kajiwara feel any better, but it did help him understand what motivated Han. And it gave him something to think about on the drive from the Nice airport.

The Continuity Center complex appeared up ahead. It sprawled low and verdant beneath transparent force fields that made the grounds appear open to the ele-

ments. Kajiwara found the illusion disturbing. No un-
guarded structure could survive the random vandal, of
course, and the forcedome certainly appealed more to
the aesthetic senses than would a chain-link fence, but
it struck a false note. "We have nothing to hide," the
openness said, while the fields added, "Trust us."

The antigravity car turned into the drive, headed for
the main gate, and slid into the security lock. Red letters appeared on the windshield:

STOP
for identity verification

While the system read the car's ID beacon, Sergeant
Wilson looked back over his burly shoulder. "You did
say the Streeth Building, didn't you, sir?"

"That's right, Sergeant. Please use the parking garage."

A sentry peered into the lock. After a glance at the
flags on the front bumpers, he checked his screen, and
snapped a salute. The red warning faded; green letters
spelled out:

PROCEED

Wilson brought up a map of the complex on his dash-
board display. "We'll be there in two minutes, sir." He
spoke a command to the computer and settled back, as
much a passenger as the lieutenant beside him or the
over commander in the rear seat.

Kajiwara examined the one- and two-story buildings
as the car glided past them. *Shoeboxes,* he thought. *In-
nocuous, undistinguished, and dull.* Were he to design
a billion-dollar domed complex in a climate so temper-
ate, the lobbies would open into gardens, moonlight
would streak every desk with gentle silver, and the wind
would roam freely throughout.

He smiled. While he actually would lay the complex
out like that, he would have to build a tight little shoe-
box for himself. The former over commander of Octant

Sagittarius suffered from acute agoraphobia. He could endure it, or suppress it through electroneural stimulus, but he could not function to his full potential except in an enclosed space.

The car eased down the ramp of the Streeth Building's underground parking garage and stopped at the escalator. Kajiwara touched his implant. "Suppress phobia."

#Suppressing.#

Lieutenant MacNulty got out to open Kajiwara's door. "This way, sir."

"Must you accompany me?"

"I'm afraid so, sir. Wilson can stay with the car, though."

MacNulty stepped onto the escalator first, and half-turned to keep the over commander in view. Kajiwara gripped the handrail tightly. The escalator was open on either side, and the ceiling rose higher than he preferred. He studied his feet as an aid to breath control. The tiny current trickling from his implant eased the irrational fear, but made him feel insulated, cotton-wrapped. Perhaps he should seek therapy. Yes. When he had time.

The chairman had ordered him to come to the Continuity Center; he had obeyed despite his reservations about the wisdom of the procedure he would undergo. Modern medicine had already so lengthened the life span that many remained active and influential for nearly two hundred years. Did it truly benefit the world to permit the rich and the powerful to continue on for another two centuries?

Those who acquire power surrender it reluctantly, if at all, and rarely reverse their decisions. The young think new thoughts, not the old. Was it good for human culture to follow the same leaders—and by definition, the same course—for a hundred years at a time?

Kajiwara doubted it. But then, Kajiwara had lived his life within the Astro Corps, which mandated, with no exceptions, a five-year sabbatical for every twenty consecutive years of service. Only after completing the sabbatical could one reenlist, and even then one spent two years in refresher school before reassignment.

To Kajiwara's way of thinking, too few of the Terran Association's other major institutions had recognized the problem and dealt with it so well. Almost every other locus of power stank of ossification.

Some might think it odd for a man of Japanese ancestry to hold such views, but it was not. The Meiji Emperor himself had understood that while tradition can nourish, it can also strangle. Some things should remain constant. But others should change, for life is a process of continual change that can end only in death.

Had the chairman of the board not given him a direct order, Kajiwara would not have come to the Continuity Center. Not yet, at any rate. Not until he truly understood, at the deepest of levels, that continuity offered him his only chance for vengeance.

The escalator set them down a few meters from the door they sought. "Let me scan before you enter, sir." MacNulty turned the knob and stepped into a small office with green walls and no decoration of any sort. The room exhaled a whiff of disinfectant.

A short, middle-aged man in a white jacket stood up from a desk. He extended his hand. "I'm Doctor—"

"Wait." MacNulty took a card-sized electronic device from his tunic pocket.

"What?" The doctor started to step back but the chair blocked him. He tottered awkwardly as he tried to keep from falling over.

Eyes on the man in white, MacNulty pressed the device's RUN panel. The card turned green. He turned to Kajiwara. "All clear, sir."

"Thank you." Kajiwara entered. The room seemed even smaller with three people in it.

The doctor said, "Yes. Well." He held out his hand again and looked up into Kajiwara's face. "I'm Dr. Whittlesby. You must be Over Commander Hiroshi."

"Over Commander Kajiwara. Hiroshi is my given name." He shook the doctor's hand but said nothing to relieve his embarrassment. An educated individual ignorant of Japanese nomenclature deserved to blush. "My bodyguard, Lieutenant MacNulty."

"Oh." Whittlesby's brown eyes shifted left for a quick glimpse of MacNulty, then centered on Kajiwara again. "Uh-huh. I watched the reports on your defense of New Napa. Absolutely inspiring, Over Commander." He brushed a strand of graying hair off his forehead. "Uhm . . . if you'll make yourself comfortable?"

Stiffly, Kajiwara lowered himself into the indicated chair. MacNulty stayed by the door.

Whittlesby opened a cupboard. "I'll take the cell samples from one of your palms. Why did they attack?"

"They did not explain themselves to me." He raised his right hand from the arm of the chair. Wrinkled, liver-spotted, it trembled slightly. One hundred-sixty-seven-year-old hands will do that.

"People usually give a reason for starting a war." Glancing at MacNulty, and thereafter moving very slowly, Whittlesby slipped a levitating worktable under Kajiwara's hand. "Even if it's a self-serving justification." He touched an instrument to Kajiwara's skin. "There."

The over commander raised his eyebrows. "You're done?"

"Yes, completely. And it didn't hurt, did it, sir?"

"No more than a nip from a goldfish."

"Thank you." Whittlesby smiled briefly, tautly. "I'm worried. I've invested my life savings in mutual funds specializing in colonial development corporations, and if you could tell me—"

"Doctor, what I know is classified."

Whittlesby made a face. "I understand that. Half the people who come to me can't tell me what they do, it's so classified. So answer a different question, please—should I get out of the mutual funds, or stay in them?"

"Really, Doctor."

"Oh, well," He slipped the instrument into a carrying case, and locked the case. "I, on the other hand,

would be happy to answer any questions you might
have."

Kajiwara frowned. "Why does the popular press call
it immortality when it is not?"

"For lack of a better name, I'd guess. I'm glad you
recognize the distinction, though. I've had difficulty
making some magistrates understand it. To outsiders,
however, you *will* be immortal."

"Except *I*—" he touched his chest—"will die. This
person before you will not continue."

"Yes." He nodded with just enough solemnity to
show he understood how an old man, waking in the
middle of the night, could watch shadows flicker on the
ceiling and not know whether death attracted or re-
pelled him. "Yes, sir, you will die. But your knowledge, your experience, and your personality will
survive. In a body genetically identical to your own,
though a good deal younger."

"Surely—" His voice rasped slightly. "Surely it is a
mere copy of my personality that will endure."

"Yes, yes, but a good copy, a *true* copy, of who you
are at the time you make the recording. From your
clone's point of view, Over Commander, he will *be* you.
this is why it's called continuity. To you, everything will
end when you die. The clone, though, will believe that
he has lived your entire life *and his* without a break."

"I see." And perhaps he did. "How long to maturity?"

"Two years." He shrugged. "Oh, it's been done in
one, Jorgensen in Oslo and Nguyen in Hanoi, but
frankly, Over Commander, I think that's too fast. Force-
growing is, in effect, the stimulation of systemic cancers at the outset, and then their eradication at the end.
I think when you run them that fast you're planting the
seeds of serious trouble fifty years down the road."

"I see." He knew about cancer from three bouts with
it. Curable, certainly, but why cause unnecessary agony? "And you take them out of the development chamber at maturity?"

The physician's eyes widened. "Not at all. We don't

want them developing independent personalities. We want to lay the master recording down on clean tracks, so to speak.''

''So my—clone will stay in its artificial womb until I die.''

''Yes.'' The physician's voice softened. Again he seemed to comprehend how an old man could want not to meet himself.

Kajiwara levered himself out of the chair. He towered over Whittlesby. He made a sound of disgust for the stiffness of his joints.

''Arthritis?''

''Yes.''

''Sir . . .''

''Yes?''

Whittlesby took a deep breath. ''We've studied your files, of course, so we know that your height was artificially induced. We've been debating the, ah, the advisability of stimulating that additional growth. Again, the carcinogenic potential—''

''Make him every millimeter as tall as I.''

''Sir, the odds are you wouldn't have arthritis now if your parents hadn't subjected you to the hormone treatments. And they probably triggered your cancers, too. We checked with the environmental division. They couldn't find any significant environmental carcinogens in your background, which strongly suggests a genetic predisposition—''

''No.'' Kajiwara bent forward. ''If he is ever—activated, it will be in order to command the armed forces of the Association. Too often, the short must struggle for what the tall are granted. This can leave a bitterness, or worse, a desperation to succeed at any cost. Neither the bitter nor the desperate deserve to lead.''

The physician cocked his head. ''That sounds like an allusion to Napoleon.''

''Yes . . . the Russian campaign.''

''Okay.'' he sighed. ''We'll do it your way, sir. Tall it is.''

''Thank you.'' Kajiwara hesitated for a moment.

"You have access to my complete medical history. You know when each of my cancers was first diagnosed. You ought to be able to extrapolate backward to the approximate age at which each appeared. Perhaps if you were to examine my clone with special care during those time periods, he might be spared—" He could not finish the thought with words, but only with a gesture.

"I'll see to it myself, sir. And, uhm—" He glanced at MacNulty, then stepped closer to Kajiwara and dropped his voice to a whisper. "We'll preserve his sperm from the very beginning so that if the testicular cancer gets away from us anyway, he'll still be able to father children."

"Ah." Kajiwara nodded. "Yes, an excellent suggestion." Now that he thought back to it, he remembered mourning his infertility for a decade or two after the loss of his testicles. He was not sure that frozen vials deposited in a sperm bank would have made him feel any better, but they could hardly have made things worse. "Thank you."

"And now—" Whittlesby touched a glowing panel on his desk. The door opened to admit a slim boy who drew a hard look from MacNulty. "Nurse Herschel will escort you to the recording studio, and you'll be done for the day."

"Thank you." He bowed, and turned to MacNulty and the nurse. "After you."

The recording studio swallowed the sound of their footsteps. He looked around in surprise. "Anechoic chamber?" His voice sounded oddly thin.

Herschel said, "Sir?"

"Never mind. You may go."

"Yes, sir. Good day."

MacNulty found a place where he could keep his back to the wall and his eye on the door. "We should have brought the rest of the team, sir."

"You would have me feel even more self-conscious than I already do, Lieutenant?" He examined the banks of electronic equipment, the chair seemingly spun of optical fiber, and the honeycombed ceiling with its hundreds of recessed lights. "Embarrassment heightens my irascibility."

"Sir, wouldn't you rather be a little self-conscious than a lot dead?"

MacNulty was too young and too western to understand a truthful answer. "Who would want to kill me, Lieutenant?"

"Ah . . ." MacNulty colored. First Commander Han had obviously told him who posed the greatest threat to Kajiwara Hiroshi's survival. "Ah, sir, there are people who hate you because you didn't do more for New Napa."

"Ah, so." He nodded. "Stay alert for them, then." To fall to an assassin would salvage none of his honor. Only he could administer the cleansing death to himself. "Though I doubt we will encounter any of them here at the Continuity Center."

"No, sir, probably not. I'm just insurance, sir."

"Thank you, Lieutenant." Turning his back to cut off further conversation, the over commander considered the technology that could copy one's soul and press it on a body grown from one's own flesh. The result was neither a son nor a brother. What rules bound the new one? What shame would the old one bear if the new one lost face? He shuddered. He did not like this procedure that consigned his name and honor to another's care, but the chairman had ordered it. Though after New Napa, Kajiwara Hiroshi had no honor anyway . . .

The door whisked open. A black-haired woman wearing an unbuttoned lab coat over sweater and slacks entered. "Over Commander Kajiwara?" She had a brisk voice that nonetheless held a silent laugh.

"Yes. And my bodyguard, Lieutenant MacNulty."

"Janet Cerino." She looked once at MacNulty, then appeared to dismiss him as irrelevant. "I'll be ready to record in just a few moments. In the meantime, why don't you make yourself comfortable?"

"Very good." He sat. When he shifted his weight, the chair adjusted to his oversized frame. He relaxed.

Cerino flicked instruments on various panels and squinted at indicators, all the while humming a soft tune that the room devoured the instant it left her lips. He watched her, wondering her age, guessing her to be in that great thirty-to-ninety range. He wanted to touch her, but she would surely misunderstand.

"All ready, sir."

He spread his hands, his wrinkled, liver-spotted hands. "What should I do?"

"Relax. Close your eyes if you like—or keep them open, it doesn't matter. Try not to concentrate on anything in particular. The process will work despite anything you could be thinking, but why give the adjustment computers any chance for error?"

"Very well."

Lights flashed. The chair tickled him through his clothing. Digital readouts on the banked equipment flickered through mad numbers without surcease. Two minutes later she said, "It's over."

"That's all?"

"Yes, sir."

"I had expected—"

"Your life to flash before your eyes? Ancient memories to shake off the dirt of time and float to the surface?" She chuckled, and patted him on the shoulder. "Everyone expects that, Over Commander. It doesn't work that way."

"Obviously." He rose to his feet. "So now Kajiwara Hiroshi lives within your computers' recording medium."

She shook her head. "Now your mental image is frozen in the medium."

"But when you copy it back into the brain of the clone that Dr. Whittlesby is growing, you will have Kajiwara Hiroshi, yes?"

She spread her hands. "An exact replica of your mind will exist within a body genetically identical to yours. Why do you ask?"

"Kajiwara Hiroshi has obligations, Doctor." He smiled down at her. He could smile, now that he had been freed. "I merely wished to ensure that he could fulfill his obligations."

She nibbled on her lower lip for a moment. When she spoke, she chose her words with care. "The Association is paying for the procedure. I infer from that that it wishes to retain your talents and your experience after you have . . . passed on. Is this correct?"

He nodded.

"I further assume—and if I'm breaching protocol or security, please say so—that at some point in the future your clone will replace you."

"You may assume that."

"Then a word of advice, Over Commander." She ran her gaze the length of his body, then peered up into his eyes. She did it dispassionately, professionally. Her irises were the green of old jade. "You appear in excellent health with many decades of useful life left to you. Please remember, though, that accidents do happen."

"Yes?" He waited.

"Some continuity candidates don't update their recordings as often as they should. Then something happens. They die, and their clones don't know anything that's happened since the last update. Bringing them current can waste time. To avoid significant discontinuities, you should update your recording every two weeks, and immediately after achieving any important insight."

He could not say *But I have done my duty!* as he wanted to. Instead: "Is it necessary to return here for the recordings, or can the equipment—"

"I'm afraid you'll have to come back here, Over Commander. Will that cause a problem?"

Not if I still live. To return would only entail leaving Howland Island for a few hours. He had lost the entire New Napa system in less time. But then, now that he was over commander of Room B87Q, and not of Octant Sagittarius, he had no systems left to lose. Or honor. Just Room B87Q and his life. Yet why give warning? He smiled again. "No problem."

"Good." She caught her lower lip between her teeth, worried it a bit, then said, "May I ask a question, Over Commander?"

"One may always ask."

"There's a rumor circulating that the Unified Security Forces will begin drafting medical personnel in the very near future. Is that true?"

"I don't know. I have not seen or heard of any plans for such an action, but that does not mean the plans do not exist. I regret that I cannot be more helpful."

"Thank you anyway." She looked embarrassed for having asked.

"I'll see you in two weeks, then."

"Yes." He paused. "Unless something comes up, of course."

Darcy Lee entered the small room deep beneath one of Howland Island's tallest towers, and came to attention. "Lieutenant Darcy Lee, reporting as ordered, sir."

The dark-haired officer standing by the coffee maker straightened his tie self-consciously. She took in the vitals with a swift glance: name, Abu Beri; rank, captain; unit, Intelligence. Fifty, maybe sixty years old. His brown eyes were exactly on a level with hers, which put him at the same 168 centimeters tall. He probably did not weigh more than her sixty-two kilos, either. He had a sleekness to him, a smoothness that almost concealed the ambition beneath. "At ease, Lieutenant."

"Thank you, sir." She looked around. Bare green walls, two chairs, and a card table on which rested both a red rose in a bud vase and an electronic device. She narrowed her eyes at that. A mind probe? Uneasiness stirred within her.

Beri sat in one chair, and waved to the other. "Please, Lieutenant."

"Thank you, sir." She took it and faced him.

"I see you're curious, so allow me to explain. Rumors have reached us concerning the possibility that the Wayholder implanted posthypnotic suggestions in cer-

tain individuals involved in the battle of New Napa.
We're investigating this carefully, for understandable
reasons.''

She stiffened. She had never heard this rumor before,
and Darcy Lee had better connections to the gossipnet
than most. Could it be another way to deny her valor?
Oh, Lee? They let her go, she was a Trojan Horse.

Beri continued. "Now, from the flight recorders of
the Catman 18 I can tell you that if the Wayholder did anything to you, it had no effect on your performance." He
lowered his voice just a touch. "You do know you're
up for a commendation, eh?"

"No, sir." She had *assumed* she was—she had, after
all, taken out fifteen Wayholder fighters and a skirk
single-handedly, a count surpassed only by the *Morocco*
itself—but until now, no one had confirmed her expec-
tations. "That's nice, though."

He tapped the probe. "Do you know what this is?"

"Yes, sir."

"You sound less than pleased to see it."

"One was used on me before, sir, on Rubio. It gave
me a migraine."

He frowned. "Were you convicted? I saw nothing in
your file—"

"As a witness, sir, not a defendant."

His frown deepened. "Lieutenant, probes aren't
forced on witnesses in criminal cases."

"Captain, they're optional for eyewitnesses to capital
crimes, at least on Rubio."

"Perhaps you'd better tell me about it."

"Yes, sir." She sighed. She never liked recalling
this. "I was at a bar. Unquestionably under the influence.
Coming out of the john I went through the wrong door,
into the alley behind the bar. Two rangers were out there
raping a Rubian girl. Ten years old. She died of head
wounds. At the trial, they denied assaulting her; they
claimed they were trying to resuscitate her. I had already admitted my intoxication, so the court questioned
my reliability in regards to the position of their pants."

Beri said, "Beg pardon?"

She stared at him without expression. "The rangers said they had them on; I said they had them off."

"Ah. Continue."

"The court probed me—with my permission—to establish grounds for forcing a probe on the rangers. They were convicted, sir. And hung."

"I see." He folded his hands, and studied them. "Thank you for clarifying that, Lieutenant."

"You're welcome, sir."

"I'm afraid, though, I'm going to have to probe you again. And this time, you won't have a choice." He lifted his eyes. Suddenly he smiled. It took twenty years off his age. "I have aspirin in my briefcase."

His smile proved contagious. "Thanks for coming prepared, sir."

"All right. First, though, let me check—your native language is the Hsing P'ing dialect of Mandarin Chinese, isn't it?"

"It is."

"For once the files have their facts straight." He took a cartridge from his briefcase. "So let's do it, eh?"

Nodding, she held out both hands. He opened the probe up and passed her the headset, a mesh of soft wires that fit like a skullcap. She pulled it over her short-cropped black hair and adjusted it at her temples. Donning his own set, he turned the control unit on and plugged in the cartridge. Her entire head began to resonate. The last time the sensation had become intolerable within minutes.

"All right. We're recording." He closed his eyes and propped his head on his upraised left hand. "What surname do you use?"

"Lee."

The probe's theory of operation was simple. An inquiry stimulated the area of the brain containing the answer. Her headset read the response and fed it to the control unit, whose computer analyzed it, consulted the native-language cartridge, and relayed a translation to the operator's headset. The first few questions of any session allowed the operator to fine-tune the reading program to the respondent's individual parameters.

The hardware to achieve all this was, of course, considerably more complex.

Beri whispered an instruction to the set. "What given name do you use?"

"Darcy."

He scowled, then touched a button on the probe's panel. "What given name do you use?"

"Dar—" She realized the problem. "In the service I use the name Darcy. At home I'm called Mei-liang."

"My mistake." Opening his eyes, he flashed her that smile of his. "My friends from the Academy still call me Razz."

"My sympathies. But better Razz than Goose."

Beri chuckled, then relaxed and closed his eyes again. "What is your serial number?"

"0181-988-438."

"What is your specialty?"

"Fighter pilot."

"And your command?"

"The *Kathmandu 18*." A dull ache throbbed just behind her eyes. She massaged the bridge of her nose. It did not help.

"Were you engaged in the battle of New Napa?"

Billy Wong's quick smile flashed in the back of her brain, but Beri could not have meant that, for he could not have known, so the smile went out and darkness took its place.

Beri said, "Lieutenant?"

"From the very beginning till the very end." Pricked by the probe, memory stirred. She tried to ignore it because she did not want to remember a second more of the battle than she had to.

Some of it must have seeped through anyway. Sweat popped out on Beri's forehead and his shoulders stiffened. He took a deep breath. "At any point in that engagement did the Wayholder communicate with you?"

"You mean verbally?" The probe touched *"Mayday, mayday!"* "No, sir."

He inched forward on his chair. Excitement touched his voice. "How about nonverbally?"

Electronic hum and *a blur across her bow biting down burning air gone.* "No sir."

Eyes still closed, he leaned toward her, half rising from his chair. "There *was* something! What was the message?"

Pain behind the eyes a *flare! But faceplate mirrors black inside and pain and blind?* "No message, sir." Memory pulled on her like a gravity well. She tried to break free—

"Don't lie to me, Lieutenant. What—"

Fields swirling in her skull blew the pipes halfway to escape velocity and she tumbled into free fall lost as the nightmares shouldered their way into daytime past overlaying present and she whimpered as—

—the alarm whooped. The ship lurched left. Straight ahead loomed the massive Wayholder mothership. Behind it hung blue New Napa. #Dustbroom down,# said the computer. The Catman 18 began to spin on its long axis. #Enemy aft scoring lasers on hull.#

"Corkscrew!" she shouted. *Her mouth had dried to leather. The ship pitched. She floated free of her couch until the webbing contracted. She ran on reaction mass now. The mothership would ravage her grav generators if she switched them on. Her lasers chewed steadily at alien metal. An enemy torpedo burst to port and overloaded the hull sensors; the port screens went black. "Fix that!"*

#Impact with compressed dust in twenty seconds.#

"Use a torp, blow a hole." She slapped the button to arm and fire just in case the processor was tied up. *"Drop a seeker mine off the rear."* The biogauge on her faceplate reported a pulse rate of 173. But she knew that already. If her heart beat any faster it would break through her ribcage.

#Torp away.# The Wayholder mothership eclipsed New Napa. *#Mine away.#* Planetshine slipped through

the cracks. Catman 18's spin made the view kaleido-
scopic. Suddenly everything bucked. #Explosion aft; hull
breached. Fuel running low.#

"Keep the lasers—"

"Lieutenant!"

Her cheek stung. Beri must have slapped her. She
moved her jaw experimentally. It worked fine. Her head
throbbed, though.

"Lieutenant?"

"Sir?" Her voice came out weak and hoarse.

One white-knuckled hand gripped his stomach; the
other wiped sweat off his pallid face. A haunted look
filled his eyes. "A simple 'no' would have been enough,
eh?"

"Sorry, sir." The migraine squeezed her temples hard;
she had to blink to clear her vision. "The probe—" She
gestured vaguely. "Jesus Buddha, that hurts."

He took a deep breath, held it, then let it out slowly.
"I've never flown a fighter."

"Really, sir?"

"I think—" He tried a grin; it came out shaky and
uneven. "I think maybe I'll need the aspirin as much
as you."

"Not likely, sir."

"Let's proceed. And let's keep the reenactments to a
minimum, eh?"

"I can't control them, sir. It's the probe, it just—can
you maybe turn it down some?"

He nodded, and touched the controls. "Did you
emerge from the battle feeling anything you had not felt
beforehand?"

"Yes, sir." The pain continued to mount. She
clenched her jaw and hoped she could keep from vom-
iting.

Again his dark eyes widened. "What was that, Lieutenant?"

"Confident that I could fly against the best and beat
them, sir."

"Ah, of course." He sank back in his chair. "During

the battle, did any thoughts occur to you that had not previously occurred to you?"

"Yes, sir."

He looked warily interested. "And they were?"

"One concerned means of destroying a Wayholder mothership without dying in the process, sir. Another concerned the nature of the Wayholder, whom I had previously believed to be good neighbors. A third—" She stopped.

"What, Lieutenant?"

"A third reflected—" she swallowed hard—"my astonishment at surviving for so long when so many people I admired had been killed."

He switched the unit off. "You can remove the headset, Lieutenant."

She did. The reverberations ceased. The pain did not. "Well?"

"Well, what?"

"Did they implant a posthypnotic suggestion?"

"Not unless they wanted you to want to kill more of them." He packed the unit up. "That's it from my end. Do you have any questions?"

"As a matter of fact, yes." She leaned across the table. "But first, would you please break out that aspirin? And I dare you to wear the probe while I'm asking the questions."

"No way." He put a small bottle into her hands. "You get migraines; I get temporary paralysis. What are your questions?"

She swallowed the capsule dry. "Okay, first, the media have nothing about preparations for an attack on the Wayholder Empire. Why?"

"Tight security, Lieutenant. And I won't break it, either. I enjoy my prefrontal lobes, and I want them to stay right where they are, eh?"

"Okay. Number two. My home planet is Hsing P'ing—"

"Yes, I know."

"Oh, sure. Anyway, my family just wrote me a letter.

They were going to come visit me when I go on sabbatical.''

"That's right, this is your nineteenth year, isn't it?"

"Yes, sir."

"Any idea what you'll do on your sabbatical?"

"I had been planning on getting my Ph.D. in lepidopterology, sir, but with this Wayholder thing—'' She shook her head. "Frankly, sir, I'd rather stay in the service. Do you think they'll relax the rules?"

"Not a chance. At least that's what I hear. As I understand it, there's a severe shortage of equipment, but a surplus of people. So you're a butterfly hunter. Tell me—''

"Sir, my next question?"

"I'm sorry, Lieutenant. Go ahead."

"Well, Hsing P'ing has four ships with bounce capabilities, and my family had booked passage on one scheduled into L5 with a load of industrial diamonds, but the Association has commandeered them.''

"The diamonds?"

"No, sir, the ships. All four of them. It's really disrupted travel out there, sir. Do you know why they did it?"

"Sorry, Lieutenant." He spread his hands. "I don't know a thing about it—but frankly, given the situation out in Octant Sagittarius, I'm not sure you should try to find out." He gazed directly into her eyes. "If you know what I mean, eh?"

She nodded thoughtfully. "Yes, sir." But she would be damned if she took *that* for an answer.

Chapter 6

"I apologize, Mother, but these men are my body-guards, and they must accompany me wherever I go." Kajiwara Hiroshi coughed. The March wind blew thick with demolition dust that darkened the gravel footpath and stained the emerald moss beneath the bamboo. He wondered how she would remove the grit without bruising or uprooting the moss. Not if she could, but how she would. The old woman had nursed the one-hectare garden through wars, typhoons, and earthquakes for a century and a half; surely she would not let the dust of urban regeneration defeat her. But the grim air suited the mood of a man who had come home to kill himself. "This is Lieutenant MacNulty and Sergeants Wilson, Iovini, and Redstar."

Oh Mitsuko, a tiny woman in a somber yukata, drew down her gauze mask as she tilted her head back. She squinted at the four guards, each of whom dwarfed her son, who himself stood 220 centimeters tall. Then she let out a laugh, high and harsh, like the caw of a crow. "The over commander of all Octant Sagittarius needs to be protected from his withered old mother? What fun you must have when you are with a younger woman! Do they taste your food for you, too, Hiroshi?"

"No, Mother." Ah, she hadn't changed a bit. Despite his misery, he nearly smiled. Instead, he raised one eyebrow to silence Sergeant Wilson, who was about to describe the microsensors destined for the kitchen and dining areas. "Personally I prefer to visit alone, but the chairman refused to let me leave Howland Island without an escort."

"Is that so? Do they—" An office building imploded two hundred meters away. The roar of its collapse obscured her words. The dirty wind gusted, rattling the bamboo. Annoyance flicked her face; she folded her arms and waited till the noise had faded. "I'd hoped they'd engage Masutori Construction, but no. Though they *said* Ginahara submitted the low bid, everyone knows the district director went to Tokyo U. with Ginahara's CEO. When Masutori tore down Osaka, they used sound domes; your cousin Kenji's son said he didn't even know it had started until he woke up one morning and the block of flats across the street had already been plowed under. Well, are you just going to stand there on the porch? Come in, Hiroshi, *with* your gaijin guards—and Hiroshi, tell them to take their shoes off. Oh. Make sure they know the proper manner and frequency of bathing, too."

Following her through the doorway, Kajiwara made a face. "Mother, these officers speak excellent Japanese, and are more than conversant with our customs."

"Gaijin soldiers speak good Japanese?" She widened her eyes and rolled them back to gape at the ceiling. "I would be astonished, Hiroshi, if men so overgrown could speak at all."

"Do remember, Mother, that you fed me the growth hormones, too."

"The doctors injected you at your father's command. I had nothing to do with it. Nothing!"

"Of course, Mother. But my point is that even after all those treatments, I am at least marginally articulate, and so are they—in the language you and I are speaking as well as their own. Isn't that right, Lieutenant?"

MacNulty, his cheeks red, looked up from unlacing his shoes. "Ah . . . well, sir, 'excellent' just isn't the right word, not for me—I expect my accent's bad enough to hurt your ears."

"It is," said the old lady.

"Mother!"

"No offense taken, sir," said MacNulty with a grin.

Kajiwara gave him a small bow, and a weary smile.
"And she wonders why I come home so rarely."

Despite her nearly two hundred years, she insisted on
serving the tea herself. When she finally settled to the
tatami, with many a creak but nary a groan, she gestured to the four grotesque shadows on the rice-paper
screens that served as the room's walls. "Are they conversant enough with our customs to pretend that sound
does not pass through shoji?"

It would have delighted Kajiwara if MacNulty had
said, "Yes, ma'am," but the lieutenant kept still. "Yes,
Mother."

"What brings you here? This is your first visit in
thirty years. What prompts it?"

"Hearing that Tokyo was to be leveled for rebuilding—"

"Don't play the fool with me, Hiroshi. You know any
garden over fifty years old is exempt."

"Ah, so. I am reassured." He sipped politely at his
tea. The cups and the pot dated from his childhood,
and that pleased him. He wished to look on familiar
things one last time. "But will it survive? The rubble,
it is said, will raise the city by four meters. I suspect
that runoff from the first rain will make a pond of your
garden."

She scowled at him. "You ask me to tell you things
you surely know. They will slide giant sheets of metal
beneath my hectare, and hoist it high in the air to permit
underfilling with the pulverized rubble. When they have
added four meters' worth, they will set my garden back
down and remove the metal." She snorted. "If you ask
me, Ginahara's incompetent engineers will ruin the
drainage, the giant bamboo will all die, and the moss
will brown and blow away as soon as the sun strikes it.
They will have spent all that money in vain." She
shrugged. "Although Ginahara will not think so." She
took a greedy gulp of tea. "The truth, now, Hiroshi."

He sighed. "To tell you that you have another—son?
Grandson? Descendant."

She leaned her head to one side, narrowed her eyes to slits, and stared hard at him. "You have been continued."

"Your shrewdness never fails to surprise me, Mother."

Her time-rounded shoulders rose and fell. "You gave it away." She studied him for another long minute. "I knew you had money, Hiroshi, but I did not know that in your 167 years you had acquired overweening vanity as well."

He brushed off her accusation as though shooing a fly. "The decision was not mine. The chairman himself made it. I thought you should know."

"Must I acknowledge your clone as a son?"

"No. Although you may if you wish—it will have, at least for a short while after decanting and imprinting, the same charming personality as I."

She grimaced. "Thank you, no."

"As you wish."

She looked from his face to her cup and back again. "That's not it, either," she said abruptly. "The truth, Hiroshi. On your father's grave."

He met her gaze for what seemed like years. "I have quarters on Howland Island, well-guarded quarters at the heart of the base."

"Have you been relieved of command, then?"

"Promoted." He took a breath. "I command a large desk and an empty office at the chairman's express orders. He wishes me kept . . . from harm."

She said nothing.

He lowered his voice. "So I have returned for great-grandfather's swords."

"His daisho are safe here, where they belong. You know this. Why do you ask for them?"

He closed his eyes, bowed his head, and then said, simply, "I lost my honor at New Napa."

"Ah." The length of her exhalation detailed the depth of her understanding. "Kajiwara Hiroshi, who as a boy yearned to become the last true samurai, has lost his honor and still lives?"

"The chairman forbade me to do otherwise. And—" he indicated the shadows on the shoji—"I am . . . protected, as well."

She sucked air though her teeth. "Thus the small devices in my kitchen."

He nodded placidly despite a spark of irritation. He would have to have a word with Wilson; the technician must be growing careless. Unless . . . "Have you had new eyes, Mother?"

"Could I see to weed if I had not?" She sniffed loudly. "So why do you come to me? I am a very old woman; I am not samurai; I do not walk bushido. Explain this to me, my son."

"Because you're the oldest person I know." He did not bother to keep the exasperation from his voice. "Our concept of honor confounds my acquaintances, who are all, with the exception of the chairman himself, much younger than I."

"And you think I can assist you."

"I *hope* you can assist me." He finished his tea and set the cup down gently. "Will you?"

She stared past his shoulder. She rocked minutely back and forth once, twice, three times. "You are my son," she said at last, in a voice like bird feathers rustling. "Yes. I will."

They walked on the gravel, beneath the giant bamboo. They wore masks against the haze of dust that filled the air. It choked the sun, even now, at noon, so a moonball floated two meters above their heads and followed them as they crunched along. Two bodyguards led them by ten meters, and two trailed at the same distance. MacNulty was cautious, but not paranoid. From beyond the ancient garden's walls came the steady, mind-numbing rumble of giant machines devouring the city Kajiwara Hiroshi still loved. "How can you stand this, Mother?"

"One adapts."

"To this?"

"In time. The noise has no meaning—it does not

shout, 'I am Mitsukoshi's, and I am crumbling!'—so the mind ceases to puzzle over it after a while. I was born in a farm village, remember, and when your father brought me to Tokyo I thought the clamor would drive me mad. Cars and buses, trains and trucks, cranes and planes, and over it all the sirens and the hiss-hiss-hiss of tens of millions of people talking. My first night I said, 'I'll never sleep a wink,' and I didn't, but my second night I did, and my third morning, well, the noise still bothered me, but I knew I would grow accustomed to it in time. So it is with this.''

"And the air? The darkness?''

After a judicious pause, during which she squinted up at the bamboo canopy, she said, "Well, it is gloomier than usual.'' She took a remote-control device from the pocket of her yukata, pointed it at the sky, and touched a button. Eye-searing light burst from a score of lamps suspended just beneath the canopy. "Ginahara installed them for the moss, but I don't like them.'' She tapped the button again; darkness returned. "I suspect there are clouds above the dust, and if there are, it will rain, so I'd better get busy.''

"Doing what?''

"Cleaning the moss, of course.''

"I don't understand. Won't the rain—''

"No. It falls black, soiling all it touches. A long, heavy thunderstorm, of course, will end clean, and wash away the filth that drifted from the air earlier, but anything less merely moistens the grime so that when it dries, it sets like concrete. This is living moss, not synthetic. It thrives between stones, or atop them—never beneath them.''

"So how do you do it?''

She looked embarrassed. "Ah. Come.'' She led him to a shed screened from view by lacy ferns. The moonball bobbed along behind them, its tiny propellers inaudible beneath the tumult of Tokyo's death. "I had to consult more than a dozen mechanics and engineers before we finally came up with this.'' She pulled out perhaps the most awkward-looking device Kajiwara had ever seen.

"Filial though I am, Mother, I can only assume that you asked each of your consultants to design one-twelfth of this . . . this *thing,* and did not tell any of them what the other eleven were doing."

She wrinkled her nose at him.

"Please don't keep me in suspense. What is it?"

"A vacuum cleaner."

"What?" He appealed to the guards who stood a discreet five meters away. "Does this look like a vacuum cleaner to you?"

MacNulty coughed into his half-closed fist.

Wilson's brown eyes lit up as he stepped closer to examine the machine. "Now that is one ingenious sonofabit—sorry, ma'am."

Hands on her hips, she gave her crow-laugh again. "In two hundred years, soldier boy, I have heard, used, and forgotten epithets that would shrivel your balls, so—"

"Mother!"

She winked at her son. "So don't worry that the coarseness of your speech might offend me. I expect no sophistication from a gaijin soldier."

Wilson screwed up his face while, apparently, he reviewed her comments to make sure he had understood. Then he flashed his teeth and said, in English, "Hot damn, mama, you all right!"

"Numba One, Wi-son-san," she said, also in English. "Numba One!"

"Are you two finished?" said Kajiwara Hiroshi.

Wilson drew himself up to attention. "Sorry, sir."

She said, "Hiroshi, you have no sense of humor."

He sighed. "Explain this—this *mechanism* to me."

"It's a vacuum cleaner." She tapped the canister. "I had it mounted on balloon tires to let it ride lightly over the moss. Its wheels are driven by this second motor, here. The steering is remote-controlled so that I may guide it from the path. The blue sensors measure distance from the top of the moss to the bottom of the

cleaner. They connect to the computer, which directs
the worm screw to raise and lower the cleaner so as to
maintain close contact. This miniature gravpipe—''

"As she touched the glittering tube, Kajiwara gasped.
"Mother, for a civilian to own a gravpipe is illegal."

"And expensive, too," she said. "It provides negative buoyancy to a degree determined by the computer,
acting on input from those green sensors underneath.
The assembly gets heavier as the collection tank fills
up, you see, so the tank rests on scales which weigh it
constantly and report to the green sensors. Feedback
circuitry adjusts the antigravity as necessary. The ane-
mometer outputs to the red sensors, which tie into the
computer and thus to the gravpipe, so that when the
wind picks up, it does not carry my moss cleaner to
Yokohama. Have you got all that?"

"Ah . . . I think so. Does it work?"

"Most of the time, yes." She unplugged the power
cord from the onboard battery pack and released it; an
automatic reel wound it back into the wall of the shed.
"Watch." She turned it on. The gravpipe began to
whisper. "Ideally, suction alone holds it to the ground—
and then only lightly. It sucks up everything that is not
actually rooted. Unfortunately, when the winds achieve
great strength, I must select the alternate programming,
which stabilizes it, but which leaves tire marks in the
moss."

"No wonder you needed so many subcontractors."

She flashed him an angry glance that softened as she
absorbed the compliment implied by "subcontractors."
"It's ready to go. Will you ask—ah, I forget. Gaijin,
get out of the way."

The four guards backed off to appropriate distances.

As the gravpipe powered up, the bottoms of the balloon tires unflattened.

She said, "So. The media called you the Hero of New
Napa. Did they lie when they said you destroyed twice
as many ships as you lost?"

"No."

"How is it, then, that you think you lost your honor there?"

"An entire world died because I retreated."

"What do you mean, 'an entire world died'?"

"I mean the Wayholder forces landed and murdered every human being they could find until there were none left to die."

"Did you know this would happen?"

"I suspected it might."

"Why, then, did you retreat?"

He glanced away. "I was ordered to."

"And why were those orders issued?"

"The chairman traded New Napa . . . for Terra."

"Ah." She reached inside the shed and retrieved a remote-control unit. "Watch." At the touch of a button, the cart began to move.

He said, "Hmm."

She said, "The hardest part was adjusting the feedback loop for the separation sensors. First the vacuum rode too high, and failed to remove enough dust, and the next rain damaged great patches of moss. Then the vacuum rode too low, and the very act of cleaning killed. I destroyed over two hundred square meters of moss before I finally hit upon the right setting."

He looked at her. "You're trying to tell me something."

"If you had not retreated, could you have saved the lives of the people of the New Napa colony?"

"In war," he said, "all things are possible."

"Oh, don't be a sententious fool. Could you have done it?"

He inhaled, held it for a long time, and let it out slowly. "Not all of them."

With a gentle twist of the controls, she urged the cart along the edge of the path. "But some?"

"Perhaps. We might have been able to evacuate a good number of colonists, with enough time, with enough ships."

"Did you have either?"

He shook his head. "The Wayholder kept coming,

each wave twice as large as the last, and I could barely protect our shuttles as they lifted off the planet. Had they boosted two minutes later, they would all have been lost.''

"What if you had been given adequate reinforcements?''

He looked up at the moonball, at the undersides of the bamboo leaves above it. ''All the ships of the Terran Association together would not have been even two percent of what I needed for victory.''

"You exasperate me, Hiroshi. You could not possibly have won, yet you claim your honor has been lost.''

"Yes.''

"How?'' A squirrel descending the trunk of a bamboo stopped to chitter accusingly at the vacuum cleaner.

"Those it was my sworn duty to protect died even as I was fleeing their star system.''

"But you could not have saved them.''

"I could have made the Wayholder Empire pay more dearly!''

"At what cost? Your life?''

He nodded.

"And the lives of all your crew?''

"Yes.''

"You are a deeply disturbed man, Kajiwara Hiroshi.'' She tapped the remote lightly. The cart rolled left and circled the base of the bamboo to which the squirrel clung. "Tell me this, then. How many ships do you think you would need to defeat the Wayholder?''

"Three million—half as many as they have,'' he said. "Our tactics are superior.''

"So any Terran admiral could beat them, given that large a fleet?''

"Well . . . perhaps not *any* Terran admiral.''

She smiled. "How many have the gift to do it?''

"Two.'' He shrugged. "Perhaps three.''

"You said you had been continued at the chairman's orders.''

"Yes.''

"Before or after New Napa?''

He swallowed to clear his throat. "After."

"Because of what you had done—or because of what you might do?"

"Perhaps both."

"You think of yourself as samurai, but what you know, you learned from books. Romantic tales of Edo and the Shogunate. I tell you this." She faced him, now, put her hands on her hips and lifted her chin so she could look into his eyes. "When the world grew so complex that a warrior with two swords could no longer master it, the true samurai became generals of industry. They formed and guided the zaibatsu, the real armies of the industrial era, the ingenious regiments of men and machines that made our land powerful far beyond its size."

"I know my history—"

"Do you? Then you know that the best ceased to value themselves so worthless as to throw their lives away when they failed. The more complicated life is, the more likely failure. Have you forgotten the Prince of Mito who said, 'It is true courage to live when it is right to live, and to die only when it is right to die'?"

"But they slaughtered 140 million people!"

She did not answer that. She turned away from him, aimed the remote at the vacuum cleaner, and directed it into an ever-widening spiral. "Why does dust blanket my moss, Hiroshi?"

"Because they're tearing down Tokyo, Mother."

"And why are they doing that?"

"Because it doesn't work anymore."

"Ah!" She bobbed her head several times. "Once I was offered fifty billion yen for this hectare. I turned the offer down. I felt I had a duty to the moss, to the bamboo. Now they are 'regenerating' Tokyo. The dust is killing the moss; Ginahara will kill the bamboo. Have I failed in my duty?"

"Of course not."

"Good. Please. Around this bend."

He followed, the gravel crisp and firm beneath his shoes. The land fell away in a gentle slope, as so much

of her garden did; here, though, only a light gauze of
green covered the soil. "Yes?" he said, allowing impatience to ring in his voice.

"This is where I killed the moss."

"But it's not dead, it– hmm."

"Yes." Grunting, she bent over, and reached behind
a large chunk of obsidian. Up and down the slope,
sprinklers popped out of the ground and sprayed the
young moss with a fine mist. She straightened, and
rubbed the small of her back. "Moss is tough, Kajiwara
Hiroshi. So is bamboo. Given half a chance, they will
recover from almost anything. Given proper care, and
adequate protection, they will prevail." She took his
arm. "Come."

"Where?"

"Just follow." She led him and his guards around three
small pine trees and past a spring-fed pool to a teahouse
on a slight knoll. She clicked yet another remote control
at the security plate; the door latch released. "In here."

"Why?" He moved out of Redstar's way—the sergeant had to inspect the premises before Kajiwara might
enter.

"Because your mother has told you to." Within the
teahouse, something beeped softly.

"Yes, Mother." Kajiwara knew what had beeped, and
why, and kept his face impassive while his last hope
shattered like a Tokyo office building.

Redstar came out. Pocketing his flashlight, he nodded
to MacNulty. Oh Mitsuko stepped forward; the giant
lieutenant blocked her path. "Sorry, ma'am. Unless you
want us in there with you."

"I do not." She paused, considered, and said, "You
will let my son go in alone?"

"If he's ready, ma'am." MacNulty turned his calm,
measuring gaze on Kajiwara. "With High Commander
Santiago's respects, sir."

Kajiwara let nothing show on his face. He slipped off
his shoes, ducked his head, and entered the dim room.
Lest he blunder into something breakable, he sat cross-

legged on the tatami till his eyes adjusted. Only a scroll in an alcove took form among the shadows, a scroll of Fujiyama, serene and irreproachable.

Then a relay clicked. The scroll—no, the entire back wall of the alcove rose into the rafters. He blinked, and caught his breath.

On a black lacquered stand rested his great-grandfather's two swords. The long—and the short. He knelt before them, touched his forehead to the rice-straw matting, and knelt up again, his spine erect, his shoulders square. He lifted the short sword with both hands, eased it halfway out of its sheath, and laid it on the tatami before his knees.

So Raul Santiago had understood, after all, that the true Kajiwara Hiroshi, the essence of Kajiwara Hiroshi, had died at New Napa, and that what filled out the uniform now was only a dishonorable shadow.

Slowly he unbuttoned his shirt, his gaze clinging to the pale gleam of fine steel. Voices drifted in to him— MacNulty and his mother, discussing the absence of birds in the garden. She seemed to be saying that they would return when the dust and the noise settled.

After wiping his palms on his thighs, he raised the sword to eye level. *I am samurai.* He drew it from its sheath. *This is the way.*

Light glittered on the point of the sword. He saw in that sparkle New Napa, and all the other stars he had sworn to defend.

His arms grew tired; his chest ached from holding his breath.

All the stars he had sworn to defend. . . .

And the soft moss, green on the slope.

He sheathed the sword, then bent at the waist to brush his forehead against the tatami, and returned the weapon to its place of honor on the katana kake.

Buttoning his shirt, he rose and went outside.

Oh Mitsuko turned as he emerged. She held his gaze for a moment. She bowed deeply to him. As she straightened up, the tiniest trace of relief—of respect— flickered on her face, and was gone. ''I was telling your lieutenant that I am not the owner of this garden, I am just the caretaker. As, I think, are all of you.''

''Yes.'' He returned her bow. ''Thank you, Mother. I must go.''

''I will be here when you return.''

He grinned. ''I'm sure you will be.''

Chapter 7

Start with a single human cell—a fertilized egg. Give it any nucleus you want, because you can use anyone's DNA. Kajiwara Hiroshi's, for example.

Immerse the egg in rich nutrient broth and it will divide. And divide again. And again and again and again, while you, watching the clump grow, monitor the soup's quality and regulate its temperature.

Things quickly get interesting. The ball of undistinguished cells hollows out, then begins to lengthen and curl. Each cell knows its place and its destiny, and divides again. Cell lines form; minuscule bumps appear here and there. Five of the bumps swell into arms and legs and a tail (yes, a tail like that our ancestors the fish used to drive themselves through the briny birth seas, but it usually disappears before it can cause any embarrassment to the mother, father, grandparents, or, in this case, the machine). One end folds over to become a head, with loosely shut eyes and a mouth and ears (no teeth, not yet, for obvious reasons).

In the normal course of events, the process runs for nine months, the product hits the womb's maximum capacity, and another tiny, fully formed human being pops into the world.

However, Kajiwara Hiroshi's clone grew in a glass tank. Well, not wholly glass, and not truly a tank, but close enough on both counts.

An artificial environment. With sophisticated plastic and throbbing pumps. (They could have made them quiet, and in the beginning they did; in the beginning, the pumps ran without any sound at all, and the clones who tumbled out ran psychopathic from the word go. They never did figure out why; theories flowered like ragweed in autumn and all revolved around the notion that a child grows to a beat, the steady thu-thud of the mother's heart, the rhythmic whooshing of blood surging through her veins, and if a child grows in silence, a child grows insane. Only a theory, mind you, but three hundred clones pace the cells of a Cambridge asylum in support of the theory. There used to be five hundred, but that was before the head shrink recognized the necessity for solitary confinement.) Behind the scenes, coolly cycling microprocessors listen, taste, adjust. . . .

Now, in that nurturing soup drifted hormones milked from cultures of cells carefully crafted to produce a great excess of those hormones. And what they did, those hormones that claimed naturalness because they came from real tissue but were every bit as mass-produced as soyburgers, what they did was pick up the pace a bit.

Rather as cancer does.

By the sixth month the nucleus of one cell plucked from the millions lifted off Kajiwara's palm—transplanted into an average, ordinary, fertilized human egg— weighed in at about four kilos. Everything was going just fine.

On 15 July 2348, Kajiwara Hiroshi, over commander without a command, sat at his desk in Room B87Q and contemplated war. He had sworn to defend the colonies. He would keep his word, no matter what the chairman said.

The key problem remained TAAC's ignorance about conditions within the Wayholder Empire. How many planets did the aliens inhabit, and did each of their worlds devote itself to the production of certain specialized items, as many Terran colonies did, so that the destruction of a breadbasket planet could starve a dozen factory worlds into submission? What about their early-warning systems, their antimissile defenses? Kajiwara knew none of the answers. He needed to know all of them.

Clearly, he must send out agents to obtain the facts, fresh and unambiguous. The risk was that the Wayholder might react to a reconnaissance run by sacking even more colonies than they had planned to.

Now, if TAAC could manage to disguise a survey/reconnaissance vessel as a Wayholder. . . .

Yes. Any astroyard could stamp out a replica, if its CAD-CAM system had accurate holos to use as a guide. The Battle of New Napa had provided TAAC with more than enough holos. And surely Frank Munez had retrieved some derelicts, so—

His desk buzzed, derailing his train of thought. "Display." A memo appeared, announcing the latest version of TAAC's implant operating system, and requesting him to install the update as soon as possible.

Since the memo had disrupted his concentration anyway, he took the interface cable from the center drawer, stuck its self-adhesive contact to a spot just behind his right ear, and jacked the other end into the desk itself. "Install operating system software."

After verifying his identity, the desk printed silver letters on its surface: "Installation under way." It flashed the letters three times, then changed them to "Installation complete."

Kajiwara returned the interface cord to the drawer. "Track the Corps-wide rate of the installation of this new operating system." He touched the spot where he wanted the desk to post the numbers. "Display as an integer percentage."

Letters and numbers immediately formed beneath his finger. "Installed—5% Uninstalled—95%"

He shook his head, wondering how long the Corps would take to switch completely over to this release of the operating system. Last time, a week had passed before even half of TAAC carried the new software. Some people *still* had not upgraded. He did not understand how their COs could let them get away with it.

The desk chimed an incoming holo.

"Accept."

A dark-skinned face formed in the cube. "Good morning, Over Commander. My name is Steven Cavendish, from Longfall, and I'm a researcher with the EGB Network's Octant News Tonight. May I ask you a few questions about the announcement the USF made this morning?"

"From Longfall? Perhaps you know my great-great-grandson, Michael O'Reilly?"

Cavendish gave a charming smile. "As I'm sure you know, Over Commander, the planet has more than its share of O'Reillys, so—"

"He's the associate director of the colonial police."

"That Michael O'Reilly? Oh, of course. That is, I've met him on several occasions—press conferences and the like—but I can't say we know each other personally." He glanced down, presumably at his notes. "About the USF's announcement?"

Kajiwara spread his hands. "I am afraid that I know nothing about it."

Cavendish raised his thick eyebrows. "I see. To summarize it for you, First Commander Han announced that TAAC will be forming 115 new fleets every year. He's also launched a drive to recruit crews for all the new ships, and says that preliminary indications are that enlistment applications will pour in by the millions."

"Thank you," said Kajiwara. "What did you wish to ask?"

"To begin with, sir, can you tell me why the USF waited two entire weeks after the Battle of New Napa to come to this decision?"

"No." He raised his shoulders slightly, and let them fall. "I did not participate in the decision-making process. The normal procedure, however, calls for the Corps high commander to present a proposal of such magnitude to the USF's first commander, who would present to the chairman, who would in turn seek the approval of the entire board of directors."

"Were you, as the Hero of New Napa, consulted in any way?"

Kajiwara assumed that Cavendish meant the epithet as a compliment, and did not realize the pain it actually caused. "Yes, of course."

"And what did you tell them?"

Before Kajiwara could even begin to reply, his implant said, #Classified.#

Astonished by the interruption, Kajiwara tried hard to keep his face expressionless. "The discussions were private, Mr. Cavendish."

The researcher frowned. "Uh-huh. Perhaps you could explain why the latest industrial capacity data don't jibe with First Commander Han's announcement."

"Pardon?"

Cavendish looked down, then up again. "I won't go into all the details, Over Commander, but we've noticed a small discrepancy. TAAC's astroyards can launch, at best, only 107 complete new fleets a year."

#Classified.#

"Your question, Mr. Cavendish?"

"First Commander Han insisted that we would be adding 115 new fleets a year. Where are the extra eight fleets coming from?"

#Classified.#

"Many decades have passed since my last tour as a procurement officer, Mr. Cavendish. I cannot resolve your discrepancy."

"Surely, Over Commander—"

#Terminate conversation.#

This time Kajiwara could not control his surprise—or his anger at being addressed so contemptuously by an operating system.

Cavendish must have thought Kajiwara's brief scowl directed at him, for he said, "Please excuse me if I've given you any offense, Over Commander—"

"You have not, Mr. Cavendish." He placed his right hand on his stomach. "Growing old occasions a surprising variety of aches and pains, most of which strike when one would wish to focus his attention elsewhere. Our bodies were not meant to last this long, and they do, I fear, insist on being pampered. If you'll forgive me, please.'' He inclined his head gravely, and tapped the holo's off pad.

So. Eight ghost fleets. And an implant that now doubled as a full-time, live-in censor. Most interesting.

He had his desk get Raul Santiago on the holo. "There is a problem with the new implant operating—''
#Classified.#
"—system.''
#Classified.#
From the expression on Santiago's face, his implant was also speaking up. Gingerly, Kajiwara said, "I find this . . . distracting.''

"You are not alone, my friend.''

"Will something be done about it?''

Santiago shrugged. "I attempted to send a scathing memo to software development—''
#Classified.#
Kajiwara winced just as Santiago flinched. The implant's "voice" seemed to be getting louder.

"—but found it impossible to finish dictating the memo.'' He ran a hand through his hair. "If you would like to write such a memo yourself, you have my blessings. But be careful. Trying to complete a forbidden thought provokes a great deal of pain. I must go.''

The cube emptied. Random colors swirled in it for a moment, then dimmed and were gone. Kajiwara stared at it until even his memory of the colors had faded to black.

"I'm speaking purely for myself, Over Commander, but I got to tell you, I resent your insinuation that a Wayholder spy has somehow disguised himself as a member of the North American Bankers Association.'' The crowd applauded. The lights tracked across the darkened auditorium until they focused on a fast-talking man with a Philadelphia accent and a bald spot on the crown of his head. "Our aggregate loan exposure in Octant Sagittarius averages out to ten trillion dollars per planet, and only half of that is insurable. That gives us a right to know what you're doing to safeguard our depositors. So how about you stop saying 'That's classified' and start telling us what's going on.''

Kajiwara Hiroshi waited for another round of applause to die down. He wished he were back on Howland Island—or better yet, out in the Cheyenne System. Thirty-four weeks had passed since the Battle of New Napa. If the Wayholder launched their second training exercise on schedule, they would be attacking a colony at that very moment. He should be there, not here in New York with a group of Association executives, attempting to pacify some very nervous interstellar bankers. Why had the commander sent him, rather than someone knowledgeable about finance and comfortable with financiers?

The balding man had stretched out his hand and was pointing up at him. Kajiwara stayed silent, letting the crowd quiet and the man's arm sag slightly. Then he leaned forward. "Excuse, please. I did not mean to imply that one of you was in costume—" a few people chuckled—"or in the pay of our enemies. However, the chairman of the board, my commander in chief, has issued an order requiring all news of a military nature to be channeled through his office. Put most simply, I will not disobey my commander in chief. Please remember that it is still possible to discuss any information already divulged by the chairman's office.''

"All right, then.'' The man had lowered his arm, but had not sat down. A low buzz arose at the back of the room. He spoke louder. "The colonies have to export if they're going to earn enough foreign currency to make their loan payments on time, but you people took away their bounce ships eight months ago, and haven't given them back yet.''

"Excuse, please, but in matters like this it is important to maintain factual accuracy.'' Kajiwara paused to let the crowd absorb his meaning, and to arrange his thoughts while they did. The muttering at the rear of the auditorium increased; he trusted that the public address system would adjust its output accordingly. "Yes, TAAC has taken control of all interstellar transport vehicles belonging to Octant Sagittarius colony worlds. Yes, those ships are now based at Octant Headquarters in the Cheyenne System. Yes, tourism has been suspended for an indefinite period of time. But, trade continues without significant interruption. Perhaps someone at this table more versed in commerce than I could provide the relevant statistics?''

The pudgy commander at the end of the table, an economist who had flown in late from Howland Island, said, ''Yes, Over Commander, having most fortuitously brought with me the very latest trade data, I think that I can shed more than a little light—''

''It's Gandhi!'' The shout came from the middle of the room. ''They're hitting Gandhi right now!''

Without warning, the screen behind Kajiwara lit up, and filled with the face of a frightened woman speaking into a microphone. ''At 0449 GMT this morning, 24 February 2349,'' she said, ''a skirmish control craft of the Wayholder Empire coasted into orbit around our planet, Gandhi. Sixteen of its fighters took control of the ac/decel lanes. The skirk itself has started to drop landing craft. The first one down was full of combat infantry. Help us, please! This is Shuttle Control, Indira, out.''

The scene cut immediately to the street outside Corporate Chambers in Geneva. A network newscaster gestured to the building behind him. ''The tape you have just viewed arrived by SitUp capsule at Octant Sagittarius Headquarters in the Cheyenne System some forty-five minutes ago. At this moment, we can add nothing to the information it contained. Pierre LeFebvre, chairman of the board of directors of the Terran Association, will address the entire Association momentarily, in a live broadcast from his office on the 200th floor. Informed sources do tell us that Over Commander Franklin Munez has dispatched four fleets to the scene—the 124th, the 132nd, the—''

''No!'' The uniformed economist leaped to his feet and screamed again, so loudly that he drowned out the newscast. "No! The 124th—" He stopped. "It's—the 124th—" He grabbed his head. "Oh my God. The one twenty—the one—the—" He shrieked in anguish and fell across the table.

Others rushed to the economist's aid. A babble of alarm spread throughout the auditorium.

Kajiwara Hiroshi collected his notes and departed. On his way out, he did not speak to anyone except to say, "Excuse, please." It occurred to him, as he walked in the lee of his bodyguards, that he was afraid to speak. He understood too much, now.

The ghost fleets, for example. The 124th did not exist, except in computer memory. Nor did the 132nd. Yet both had "responded" to the invasion of Gandhi.

The implant operating system, too, made sense. The unfortunate economist had tried to expose the chairman's hoax—and his implant had stopped him cold. Dead cold.

And finally, he realized just why the chairman had commandeered the colonies' bounce ships. Now based in the Cheyenne, and now piloted by TAAC officers wearing TAAC implants, those ships would not be carrying the real truth anywhere.

Kajiwara slipped into the rear seat of the car and Lieutenant MacNulty shut the door. Kajiwara laid his hands on his thighs, palms down. He closed his eyes. He controlled his breathing.

"To the shuttleport, Sergeant," he told the driver. "Lieutenant, please arrange immediate priority air and ground transportation to the Continuity Center in Nice. I must update my recording without delay."

On 17 March 2349, the Wayholder ground troops shuttled back up from the surface of Gandhi, their mission accomplished. Fighter pilots bored nearly to alien tears by three weeks of routine patrolling returned to their berths about the mothership, which then accelerated to threshold speed and bounced home.

On the ground 192 million headless corpses gave the local scavengers their greatest feast of all time.

The chairman of the board, in a speech taped and shipped to every outpost of humanity, saluted the valiant heroes of the Battle of Gandhi. He reported the complete and total destruction of six Terran fleets and more than thirteen thousand Wayholder vessels. Regrettably, he said, Gandhi fell because the Association could not reinforce its doomed warriors as quickly as the Wayholder Empire reinforced its barbaric troops. But next time! he promised. Next time would be different!

Millions of families gave thanks that their relatives serving with the armed forces had survived the slaughter, and prayed for the souls of those who had died.

Since no next of kin anywhere received notices, personal effects, or survivors' benefits, however, the only ones who did die must have been single, friendless orphans.

All very easy to arrange, when radio waves take years to cross the interstellar gulfs, and almost all bounce ships remain in private hands.

In its twelfth month of life the clone of Kajiwara Hiroshi massed fifty kilos, though its brain remained strangely primitive. Selective hormone application works in mysterious ways its wonders to perform. . . .

The folks running that high-tech high-price version of the birds and the bees decided it was time to decant the child and move it into the development tank.

There they strapped the child into an exoskeleton, which would promote growth of bone and muscle through an automated but well-scrutinized program of exercise.

The exoskeleton pushed and pulled the child's little muscles through the motions of crawling and walking, of running and jumping, of climbing and throwing and catching. The child grew in bulk, stature, and dexterity. The exercises increased in complexity.

Of course, such massive physical stimuli triggered the firing of millions of synapses in that undeveloped brain, which stimulated the development of the primitive centers for motion, balance, and control. But the higher brain, the cerebral cortex—who needed it? Indeed, who wanted it? Imagine the sort of personality that would develop in such an environment—dwarfed and warped, surely, by the soundless, lightless fluid whose only constant was pain.

What higher functions did form presented no problem. The staff of the Continuity Center knew just which tracks to wipe, just how to clean the slate. The equipment for that had been kicking around a *long* time.

Between 20 October and 3 November 2349, the defense of New Dublin consumed five entire fleets, and cost the Wayholder Empire over twelve thousand fighting ships.

So the Association said.

New Dublin did fall, its hastily organized militia proving no match for the superbly armed survivors of Wayholder boot camp. The planet's 88 million human inhabitants did fertilize its soil over the next few years (while simultaneously poisoning an ungodly number of indigenous carrion eaters). The Wayholder Empire, though, did not lose a single ship.

Despite all its precautions, TAAC lost one, a fighter, piloted by an impetuous New Dubliner with an outdated implant operating system. When the news reached Liam McCorcoran on 22 October, he deserted his post and bounced home. He thought he would lend whatever support he could.

Instead of the Armageddon for which he had braced himself, he found sixteen Wayholder fighters and their mothership orbiting a dying planet. He considered making a grand gesture, but decided the truth was more important than any damage he could do. He turned on all the Zulu's sensors and recorders, then flew past at threshold speed. When enemy fighters rose to challenge him, he bounced out.

But not back to his carrier. Oh, no. His commander would turn him over to the fleetship's psychiatrists, who would scrub his mind clean and iron out the wrinkles.

TAAC shrinks always did that to deserters—and would probably, McCorcoran suspected, do it extra-carefully to a deserter who had just caught TAAC in the biggest lie of all time.

McCorcoran had a triple-great-uncle, the wisest man he knew, who manned a solitary observatory in the comet belt of the Jayarr System. Uncle Mitch also distilled his own whiskey, and McCorcoran badly needed a drink.

He set the coordinates and bounced.

Using hormone overloads to accelerate clone growth is like unleashing Dobermans to chase the kids out of your garden. It works just fine, if you stop them in time.

The technicians suspended the exercises. They changed the composition of the nutrient fluid that bathed the clone. They tickled some glands, pumped drugs and other hormones into the bloodstream, raised the temperature to 38.8 degrees C, and monitored everything very, very carefully.

And they did it all long before the clone had reached full growth, because the process acquires the same sort of inertia that a cancer does, and it would take months to revert all the cells of the already impressive body to normal. Like stopping a ship moving at threshold speed—you power up the rear pipes *here*, but you just do not stop until *there*.

Everything seemed to work as planned. They heaved a sigh of relief. What they had never told Kajiwara Hiroshi was that sometimes they lost control, and when they did, they had to begin the whole process again.

On 24 June 2350, Darcy Lee sat in her living room. She wore a dirty bathrobe and her throat ached, but she had finally stopped crying. She ignored the voices that muttered outside her apartment door. The doorguard had its instructions: Do not disturb except in extreme emergency.

Four days of mourning had drained her. Her entire

family, gone. Her entire *world,* gone. She could hardly believe it.

If only I'd been there! In January of '49, she had hit the twenty-year mark; regulations required her to take a five-year sabbatical. She had requested exemption, been denied, and appealed that denial all the way to the top. Howland Island had upheld it. The brass was not about to set any precedents, not even during the Battle of Gandhi. They cut the implant out of her skull and sent her home.

A twenty-year stretch is long enough, they had said. Take the five years off, then re-up. You won't miss anything—this war will run a century, at least. You'll do more for us if you come back refreshed. By then we'll have a wonderful new implant—smaller, faster, better all around. You'll love it. See you in five. Goodbye.

A display case of—call them alien butterflies; they were certainly exo-lepidopterons—filled the wall above her desk. She had collected each and every one on Hsing P'ing. She wondered if any of the species had survived. Or did the Wayholder massacre only humans?

The doorguard buzzed, surprising her. She sat up. Hesitantly, she touched the intercom button.

A metallic voice said, "A Mr. Steven Cavendish to see you, Ms. Lee. ID verified. Unarmed. Probe reads negative for drugs, alcohol, and hormonal disturbances."

Cavendish? "I don't know him." It hurt to talk. "Tell him to go away."

"He insists it's urgent."

"What's the emergency?"

"He says only that it concerns your family."

She gritted her teeth. "Is he a memorial salesman?"

"He says not. The polygraph confirms him in all respects. Awaiting instructions."

"Oh, Jesus Buddha." But in the end, what did it matter? She glanced in the mirror. Limp black hair, dark-smudged eyes, but her appearance did not matter. Nothing mattered much anymore. "Oh, all right." She refastened the belt of her bathrobe. "Let him in."

The door opened as she rose. A middle-aged black man came through, ducking his head to avoid hitting it on the lintel. She thought him vain until he straightened up, and then she realized he did stand a few centimeters over two hundred.

He looked down at her. "Lieutenant—" he took her hand and touched her shoulder—"I'm so very sorry." His voice rang like a gong, deep and comforting.

Dully, she said, "For what?"

"For what you have lost—and for what you are about to lose."

He had the huge dark eyes of a deer, and they mesmerized her. "I don't understand."

"Please." Leading her to her own sofa, he gently pushed her into a sitting position. He set his briefcase on the floor, and sat beside her. When he enveloped both her hands in his, a portion of her mind found it odd that she did not mind the contact. "Ms. Lee, you've heard the Association's reports about the Battle of Hsing P'ing, yes?"

"Yes."

"The reports were all lies."

That took a moment to sink in. Then she blinked. "What?"

"The Association did not defend your planet." His grip tightened.

"But—" Her voice broke. Her vision blurred as she looked over to the holovision. "But I watched, they said seven whole fleets, twenty thousand Wayholder ships—"

"Zero fleets. Zero Wayholder ships. Just 240 million dead civilians—and perhaps a few score Wayholder infantry."

She absorbed the pronouncement numbly. She sat in silence for a long time, a silence he did not shatter, though he held her hands and gazed at her somberly. A single phrase chased its tail through her mind: *Zero fleets.*

At last she said, "No. I won't believe it. I *can't*. Why would they lie?"

He lifted his shoulders, and let them fall again. "We don't know."

She stiffened. "Do you have proof?"

"Of a sort." He released her hands and reached into his briefcase for a packet of holos. "Here."

She flipped through them reluctantly. First the close-ups. The familiar outline of Pei Ta Lu, the largest of the four continents, wrung a sob from her. She had grown up on a farm right *there,* two kilometers from the shore of Shan Hu, the mountain lake. Tears streamed down her cheeks. From slightly farther away, a holo with Hsing P'ing a disk in the center, and Wayholder fighters everywhere. Rocking back and forth, letting her grief flow again, she could barely focus on the last, taken from perhaps a megakay, showing the besieged planet but absolutely nothing in the way of relief. Gasping, she had to try three times before she could say, "Forgeries."

"They could be." His strong bass voice soothed her, supported her. "But they aren't. A young pilot risked his life to take those. He took identical holos at New Dublin."

"No. . . ." Cavendish had to be lying. TAAC did not abandon colonies to monsters. She knew. She was TAAC. TAAC fought and its people died in the cold of space to save the helpless innocents below. He had to be lying. Her family was dead and she was TAAC and if TAAC stepped aside to let aliens slaughter humans then she bore the blame, she had helped kill them, and she didn't, she hadn't. "Oh, Jesus Buddha, you bastard! Why are you lying to me?"

"I'm afraid it's the truth." He handed her a thick stack of printouts. "These could also be forgeries, but aren't. They show how money supposedly spent to build and staff eight new fleets a year disappeared, trickled into the account of the company that insures loans to colony worlds, and was eventually paid out to settle the banks' claims. . . ."

"Why are you telling me this?" The words came out

a shriek, and that startled her. She sank back on the couch. "Why?"

"I'm from the Sagittarian Guard. We're colonists. We've decided that if the Association won't protect us, we're going to have to protect ourselves. And we will."

"What does that have to do with me?" She held the closeup of Hsing P'ing in cupped hands. A tear, dropping from her cheek, fell on the holo's casing. And she had thought she had shed her last a day ago.

"We need you."

"I'm a TAAC officer. I took an oath—"

"The Wayholder have not returned to the New Napa system. We've been salvaging derelicts there and repairing them. We're putting together a space force. We need veteran officers to fly our ships, to teach our recruits how to fly them, to form the nucleus of something that will save our worlds. TAAC won't give us any. We have to find them on our own."

It was that which convinced her. She saw her old comrades regularly, at bars and parties, at weddings and funerals, and she would have heard about a program to train a colonial space force. She wiped her cheeks with the sleeve of her bathrobe. Suddenly her TAAC oath seemed a fragile bond indeed. Cavendish offered vengeance on the Wayholder. TAAC didn't. "And you want me?"

"Oh, yes. Very much. Will you come? Will you help?"

"Yes" Her eyes had dried. Her voice had steadied. "Yes!"

In the twenty-fourth month after the Battle of New Napa, the clone of Kajiwara Hiroshi measured 220 centimeters in length and 125 kilograms in mass. Just as big as Papa. All ready to go.

And just in time.

Chapter 8

For Kajiwara Hiroshi, 29 January 2351 began like every one of the 931 preceding days. Awakening before dawn, he lay motionless so that sleep would not relinquish him. While it still controlled him, its magic put him where he most wanted to be, where he most truly belonged—in an overcommand module in the Cheyenne System.

For the 932nd day in a row, sleep departed, stranding him in a small flat in the Howland Island transient officers' quarters.

Moonlight spilled through the bedroom window and splashed on the parquet floor.

He hated moonlight. Its color, so like that of his own hair, symbolized age and weakness and death. Damn the moon, all pockmarked and cold. It could not look away from its ruler; it knew its place and stayed there, bound by laws that proscribed its every move. It could not even claim its light as its own, for it merely reflected the glory of the sun. It could only say, "I do my duty."

He rose from his futon and put it away. He forced himself through a rigorous series of calisthenics. After showering, he ate breakfast. Then he stepped out of his flat, bowed to his bodyguards, and with them took the underground slideway to Room B87Q of TAAC Headquarters.

There, as he did every day, he went "swimming." He linked his implant to his desk, and used that as an interface to the giant databases containing every drop of knowledge the human race had poured into its computers.

Great silver schools of data coursed through that electronic sea. He tracked them, observed them, and tried to determine if their ranks had swelled since his last long soak. If they had, he investigated more closely.

Despite the chairman's ban on intrusions into Wayholder territory, even in the disguise of a Wayholder or a Korrin, TAAC Intelligence still found it possible to pump many reports on the Wayholder Empire into the system every day. Kajiwara considered most of them worthless—the imaginings of mindless illiterates striving to justify their employment. He read everything, however, from the lab teams dismantling and analyzing the derelicts Munez had recovered in the New Napa system. Those teams worked at a maddeningly slow pace, but their sporadic reports often enlightened him.

This latest, for example. TAAC software translators maintained that a Wayholder's on-board computers did not check bounce coordinates against a catalog of known hazards. Kajiwara found himself almost admiring that. If a TAAC pilot tried to bounce to a point that happened to lie at the heart of a star, his OBCs would rescue him from his own incompetence. An equally inept Wayholder pilot would burn. The Wayholder Empire must be very rich, Kajiwara decided at last, if it could afford to replace so many ships simply to guarantee that its pilots paid attention to detail.

He could not linger over the report, though. An entire oceanful more awaited him. Keeping current was almost impossible, but he had to make the attempt. Someday a man with the mind and the body of Kajiwara Hiroshi would sail against the Wayholder Empire once more. These waters would support him if he knew them, or drown him if he did not.

A hand touched his shoulder. He sputtered to the surface. "Yes?" Sergeant Iovini stepped back a pace. "Beg pardon, sir. Holo."

An image formed in the cube; Raul Santiago smiled

out. Kajiwara got to his feet despite the hot ache in his arthritic knees. He saluted.

The high commander touched his right hand to his right temple, then waved Kajiwara back into his chair. "No formality today, Hiroshi. We must speak privately."

Kajiwara glanced at Iovini, who nodded and said, "I'll wait outside, sir."

"Thank you, Sergeant." He waited for the door to slide shut before looking back to Santiago. "So. You have called to stare at the caged animal?"

Santiago shook his head. "We have a problem in Octant Sagittarius."

Surprised, he straightened up. "With Frank Munez?"

"No, no, my friend, Munez is doing an excellent job."

As he should, considering his trainer. "Then why do you call me, Raul?"

"Captain Beri from Intelligence made a disturbing report, which I wished to talk over with you before I brought Munez into it. I'd like Beri to come on line with us, if that's acceptable."

Kajiwara gestured agreement.

The holo clouded. The image of Santiago's head shrank; Abu Beri's round dark face came into focus beside it. Beri saluted the over commander. "Sir. I'll keep this short."

Kajiwara Hiroshi rather doubted he would. "I listen."

"At random intervals, we have bounced reconnaissance drone ships with ultrasensitive scanners into the New Napa, Gandhi, New Dublin, and Hsing P'ing systems, to see if the Wayholder are modifying the environments or exploiting the systems' resources. Our last probe of New Napa revealed a great deal of activity. But it's human activity, sir."

Kajiwara abruptly forgot his joints. "Did someone survive after all?"

Beri shook his head. "No, sir. At least I don't think

so. I believe I know what's going on. My scenario is based on three facts, and fleshed out with rumor and conjecture."

"Ah, so. What scenario have you developed?"

Beri looked pained. "Sir, if I might do this in my own way?"

"I apologize. Please, go on."

"Thank you, sir." He took a breath. "Fifteen months ago, during the invasion of New Dublin, Liam Mc-Corcoran, a native of that planet, deserted with his fighter and has not been heard from since. After that invasion, and after the invasion of Hsing P'ing as well, the Wayholder Empire requested an explanation for the presence of an observer on the scene. An observer we had not posted. Finally, our probe spotted at least thirty operating gravpipes in the New Napa system. TAAC gravpipes, sir."

Kajiwara fingered the control pad of his holo. Santiago's image swelled, pushing first chin and ears, then forehead and nose, beyond the cube into invisibility. Only the brown eyes remained, giant and weary. "Raul, have any TAAC units at all conducted maneuvers in the New Napa?"

"No." Santiago's eyes stayed calm, unflicked by the whip of an implanted censor.

Kajiwara therefore believed him. "What is your conjecture, Captain?"

"First the rumor, sir. An organization called the Sagittarian Guard has been formed out in Octant Sagittarius." Beri stopped.

"Go on." He shrank Santiago's eyes until all the man's face appeared.

"That's the whole rumor, sir. The name does seem self-explanatory."

"Do we come now to the conjecture?"

"Yes, sir. I believe McCorcoran bounced to New Dublin to help fight the Wayholder, discovered that no bat—" Grimacing he touched the side of his head. "Yes. Well. Then he fled. He made contact with a person or persons unknown and apprised them of the truth. With a Zulu-class fighter, sir, he had cameras, flight recorders—''

Kajiwara held up a hand. "Please forgive the interruption, Captain, but it is puzzling that with such a quantity of evidence in his possession, this deserter has not created a public uproar.''

"It puzzles me, too, sir. Personnel records indicate that McCorcoran never updated his implant's op—'' Beri's eyes squeezed shut. He took a deep breath. "I think you understand what I mean, sir.''

Kajiwara said, "Yes, yes, of course. Go on.''

"My suspicion, sir, is that McCorcoran's superiors intend eventually to blackmail the Association. The information's release will cause panic—''

"If believed,'' said Kajiwara.

"Yes, sir. But I think some people have heard it and believe it already, because of the rumor concerning the formation of the Sagittarian Guard. I conjecture that if the Guard really exists, then it is the Guard which has established a base on New Napa and is now salvaging the wreckage of ships lost in the battle. Naturally, its actual intentions are unknown, but I've narrowed down the plausible assumptions. Either the Guard intends to rebel against the Association, or it intends to defend an Octant Sagittarius world against the Wayholder Empire.''

Kajiwara groaned, but silently, to himself. On 8 February, assuming they held to their schedule, the Wayholder would sack another world. If some ragtag force attempted to stop them in space, the entire Association would find itself at risk. "Your assessment of the danger, Captain?''

"At the present time, the Sagittarian Guard presents no significant threat to the Association—or to any Wayholder invaders. The sole danger at this moment is that by interfering with the Wayholder, they might trigger reprisals against the Association.''

"So. Your recommendations?''

The Intelligence man pronounced his words carefully.

"To my way of thinking, sir, our best option is a surgical strike on their base."

Kajiwara's heart sank. The Guard were preparing to act without true knowledge, a foolish path for warriors to walk, but he acknowledged the rectitude of their willingness to die in defense of their people. To slay them without trying to win them over would be dishonorable. "Before even talking to them?"

"Sir, they have gravpipes, so we cannot quarantine the system. Any call for negotiations will tell them we have discovered them. They will, I believe, immediately distribute their information to as many media outlets on as many worlds as they can reach. This will provoke precisely the turmoil—"

"Oh, come," said Kajiwara impatiently. "Small children have the equipment to generate false holograms. Media which support the chairman politically will ignore the alleged evidence. Media which oppose the chairman know better than to engage in yellow journalism while martial law is in effect. Only if this Guard could convey media representatives to the scene of a battle and demonstrate the lack of debris—"

#Classified.#

"—would media of any political orientation consider commencing an investigation. Since TAAC can prevent the Guard from hosting battlesphere tours for the media, there is no cause for alarm."

"Nonetheless, sir, I formally recommend against attempting to open negotiations."

Santiago looked down at something out of camera range. "The chairman orders us to exterminate these rebels, Hiroshi."

So. His old friend would not offer even moral support. Kajiwara's heart sank further. He breathed three times to calm himself, then focused his attention on the high commander. "So. This one has heard the report, and asks again, why do you call the over commander of Room B87Q?"

"Frank Munez has a distinguished record, my friend,

but you are TAAC's premier strategist. I'd like you to
plan this campaign.''

Kajiwara Hiroshi closed his eyes for a moment, and
inhaled through his teeth. ''Captain Beri has made a
rational recommendation which the chairman seems to
have accepted, yet this one would prefer a better solution, a more ingenious solution, one that would not require us to pit human against human in the very system
where so many TAAC forces died in defense of their
own. Therefore, High Commander, this one must ask
if the Association has decided beyond chance of appeal
to shed human blood.''

Santiago frowned. Kajiwara's determined formality
must have stung him. ''No. Not beyond chance of appeal. Not if someone were to suggest a less . . . costly
solution.''

A lifetime devoted to the study of military history
develops strategic instincts, tactical reflexes. A possibility glimmered in Kajiwara's mind. ''So. A few questions, if you would be patient with an old man.'' He
cocked his head and glanced from one holographic image to the other. ''The Association does control every
shuttleport in its sphere, yes?''

Beri and Santiago looked puzzled, but nodded.

''We also control every cargo ship, with the exception
of any derelicts that might remain in the New Napa
system, yes?''

Santiago said, ''We thought we did.''

''And I presume that the Sagittarian Guard is based
on New Napa itself, and depends on the planet for food,
water, and the like, even if they actually conduct repair
and reconstruction in orbit.''

Beri said, ''That's my conjecture, sir. I don't know it
for certain, but a recon run or two would settle the matter.''

''You will find that out, Captain. And if the situation
is as I have outlined, then we will apply classic strategy—cut their supply lines.''

Four eyebrows went up. Beri looked at Santiago, and
then at Kajiwara. ''Sir?''

"So. I will explain." He felt pleased with himself for finding a solution that would not entail the death of a single human being. Still, wistfulness mingled with pleasure, for the planet called New Napa would pay a heavy price. "We will require several million megatons of nuclear explosives. . . ."

The machine shop module had once hung from a strut of the TAAC *Peking*. Now, its punctures patched and its generators lovingly overhauled, it bobbed in geosynchronous orbit high above New Napa. Components of vessels both Terran and alien floated near the walls and ceiling, held in place by short tethers. Most of the mechanics had suited up and jetted over to the barracks, to grab some sleep before starting another sixteen-hour shift.

Two men remained behind, hovering over a cluttered lab bench in the micro-electronics section.

The short brown man, Ramesh Boripartya, brought up onscreen the schematics of a device found in the wreckage of a Wayholder ship. "Now I cannot guarantee that it will function as I am about to outline to you, because I am not a physicist of the first rank nor am I even a competent engineer, but I am all we have at this moment, so if you will listen closely I will tell you to the best of my poor ability what tricks I think this little intricacy performs."

Even though he had, for the last six months, shared a barracks room with the Guard's self-deprecating technical genius, Mitchell T. McCorcoran was still not fond of Boripartya's loquacity. McCorcoran had enjoyed two solitary decades in Jayarr's comet belt before his nephew Liam showed up in his airlock demanding he save Octant Sagittarius. By the time a bachelor hits 122, he has pretty well determined what he likes and what he dislikes, and Mitch McCorcoran did not like constant chatter.

But from Ramesh, he would tolerate it. Maneuvering to get a better view, he hooked the bench's edge with his bare toes and anchored himself. "Okay. Fire away."

"Believe me, please, when I stress the hypothetical nature of this explanation. It appears, though, based on the reactions of the parts and the current flow through the various circuits, that this is a tracking device, probably the kind that enabled that first Wayholder ship to follow the *Cheng Ho* back to Octant Sagittarius headquarters all those years ago."

McCorcoran squinted at the screen. Just a lot of little lines and circles to him. Fortunately, he did not have to feign comprehension with Boripartya. "*This* is what lets one ship bounce to coordinates only the other ship knows? Are you sure?"

"No, no, Mitchell, have I not just been telling you of the extent of my uncertainty? If I had not been examining the larger system in which it is embedded at just the moment that Darcy Lee test-bounced her Zulu, I might never have noticed. But it appears the only plausible explanation for this here—" the Gandhi native tapped a point onscreen with his finger, drifted away, and pulled himself back—"which imposes a distinct modulation on the current when exposed to the gravity waves emerging from a singularity, and for all this microcircuitry that seems inexorably to produce a set of coordinates at this end." He touched the bottom of the picture. "The only way to be sure of course, is to attach it to a fighter and try it out."

"Uh-huh." He rubbed his lantern jaw. "Will you take the test flight?"

"Me? Oh, no, my friend, no, indeed, I am a timorous soul who vastly prefers to putter quietly about his laboratory, and to whom the idea of testing this device in action appeals not at all."

The schematic disappeared from the screen. The face of a young black woman replaced it. "Mitch, if you're there, it's an emergency."

"Camera on," said McCorcoran. "Two-way comm." The lens swung to cover him. "What is it, Beth?"

"We have unidentified decelerating objects in the system, lots of them, headed for the planet. A SitUp capsule bounced in along with them, two minutes ago, and broadcast the following message on all frequencies. The tape of the full transmission is in the banks. I'm sending a copy to your screen now.'' Beth Scones bent her head to her right and touched a button.

''Thanks, Beth.'' He nodded to her. The screen cleared and then displayed the message.

> To the Commanding Officer, Sagittarian Guard:
>   The Terran Association cannot permit an independent armed force to exist within its borders.
>   We do not wish to engage in armed conflict with you.
>   We must, therefore, cut your supply lines.
>   We trust none of your people will come to any harm.
>   Surrender at any shuttleport anywhere.
>   Kajiwara Hiroshi
>   Over Commander

Boripartya had read the message over McCorcoran's shoulder. ''Surely this Kajiwara must be playing some sort of practical joke upon you, Mitchell my friend, for it is clear to the smallest of minds that we have no supply lines to cut, and—''

''Shh.'' He pushed off the deck, shot across the hangar-sized room, and landed on the wall above the system monitor console. He clambered down. His fingers rippled over the keys. Eight wallscreens lit up, each with a satellite view of a different area of the planet's surface. ''Oh, God.''

''What?''

He pointed to the rightmost screen, which displayed the entire continent of San Jose. Bright flashes winked all across the continent, each obscured almost instantly by a growing black puffball. He understood it all with a glance. He trembled. ''They're nuking it.''

Boripartya shrugged. ''But we have no one on San Jose.''

''Precisely.''

"Mitchell, my friend, I do not understand."

"It's all loess, Ramesh. Three, four meters deep in places."

"Loess?"

"A kind of soil—or soil structure, I'm not sure which—extremely light, laid down by wind that picked it up from somewhere else. They're blasting it up into the sky. And look!" Flares went off on the screen in the middle. Nausea welled up in him. How could they do this? "They're hitting the Andries, too."

"But why vaporize a desert and a ring of volcanoes?"

"The volcanoes because the bombs set them off; the loess because the nukes blast it up into the stratosphere. The dust stays there, Ramesh, stays there for years. It blocks out the sunlight."

"But—"

"Kajiwara is trying to plunge New Napa into nuclear winter. The temperature drops, there's not enough light for photosynthesis—we just lost our agricultural base. That's what he meant by saying he was going to cut our supply lines. He's trying to starve us out."

"So?" The smaller man seemed unconcerned. "We decided to farm our own food only to maintain secrecy. Let us go buy what we need—we have the ships for it, and we have the robot mines to produce the precious metals to pay for it."

"Where do you load a shipment of food, Ramesh?"

"At a shuttleport, of course."

"And where does he want us to surrender?"

"Ah . . . I begin to see our quandary. . . ."

McCorcoran floated free of the console. The Sagittarian Guard had come a surprisingly long way in a very short time, but Kajiwara had just delivered a masterstroke. Unless . . . He tapped into the main computers for information. "We have about two months' worth of food in orbit."

"You are forgetting the warehouses on New Napa."

"And you're forgetting the radioactivity."

"Ah, yes, although in an emergency—"

"Ramesh, do you think that Wayholder tracker will work?"

"As I said before, it must be tested, but if I am translating the output correctly, yes, it will work for us as it did for them. A ship with this installed in its controls will be able to follow any other bounce ship anywhere."

"Then I think it's time to test it."

Darcy Lee still had trouble believing that she was about to lead a pirate raid. Her pre-Guard life would hardly have qualified her for sainthood—and perhaps not even for heaven—but she had proudly upheld the values and traditions of the Corps, and the Corps did not tolerate any interference with interstellar commerce. TAAC had actually deposed governments for attempting to meddle with another planet's trading patterns. But that was the old Corps. The new Corps . . .

Five weeks earlier to the day, on 8 February 2351, the Wayholder Empire had invaded the colony world called Pasteur. TAAC had done nothing to stop them. In fact, it had not even announced the invasion until the last Wayholder ship had pulled out. When the Guard arrived, Lee and her comrades found 72 million corpses, and lakes still stained red.

Hsing P'ing must have looked a lot like that, once the Wayholder were gone.

Clearly, TAAC had turned coward.

She could not change the past—she could not bring her family back to life—but she could damned well change the future. The Wayholder Empire had to pay for what it had taken. If the Corps lacked the balls for the job, at least the Guard didn't.

Hence this mission. The tracker had worked perfectly in every trial. The Guard needed food. The Association *deserved* to lose its grain.

So she felt disbelief, but no remorse at all.

Hiding in the shadow of Dakota's moon, she and Liam McCorcoran focused their ships' most acute sensors on Dakota's orbiting starport. The onboard computers spared her the need to monitor the radio traffic, but she kept the video on because she liked to watch good pilots at work.

A swarm of tugs, ugly but graceful, like stevedores performing zero-G ballet, hauled three grain bins out of the cavernous warehouse and into the void. Each hundred-meter-long bin held ten million liters of grain—more than enough to feed the Sagittarian Guard for months.

The cargo ship resembled a box kite on a long string. Since it would never touch atmosphere, it needed no streamlining. It consisted of two small, heavily reinforced cubes—a drive unit forward and a life-support module behind it. From the rear of the life-support module jutted its tow bar, a two-kilometer-long piece of rigid, heavy-gauge monomer.

The tugs dragged the bins into position. Robot arms with built-in cameras reached out of the tugs' tool bay to lock the bins onto the bar in a long train. The tugs backed off to inspect their handiwork, then veered away and headed back to the warehouse.

A whisper hissed into Lee's implant. #Departure clearance granted. Generators cycling up.#

For a few moments the cargo ship hung immobile above the starport, then slowly, almost imperceptibly, began to pull away.

Lee took a deep breath. Time to see if this crazy scheme would work. She called her companion ship on the scrambler.

"Liam, remember not to—"

"Darcy. How many times have we practiced this?"

"Sorry. Nerves. Dinner's under way. Let's do it."

They tailed the cargo ship from a megakay back, matching its pace as precisely as their OBCs could manage.

After twenty minutes of acceleration the freighter disappeared from their screens.

In less than an eyeblink, they bounced, too.

The cargo ship, already beginning to decelerate, lay about a quarter million kay ahead.

"Darcy! It works! Sonovabitch!"

She shook her head. He must have been more nervous than she was. Oh, well. She had met a lot of pro-pilot-amateur-persons in the Corps. Eventually they grew up. Most of them. Billy Wong had, and—

The unexpected, unsolicited memory stung. She pulled her attention back to the present. "Sure, Liam. Be cool, now."

Their OBCs analyzed the rate at which the grain ship slowed, waited a short while, then decelerated at 110 percent of rated maximum. In less than four minutes, she and Liam caught up with the rearmost bin. To their delight, their velocity was only half a meter per second faster than the grain ship's.

Now for the tricky part. McCorcoran headed for the life-support module of the ship. Darcy Lee said a quick prayer that she hoped somebody, somewhere, would hear. Despite the deceptively static scene on her screens, she could not forget that the cargo vessel a few meters away was traveling in excess of sixty thousand kilometers a second.

Do it! She swooped down to snag the tow bar. From the shuttle's cargo bay came the whine of gears. The computer whispered, #Grapples attached.#

"Cut the bar and lift immediately." The laser-control lights on her panel flashed briefly.

The computer said, #Tow bar severed. Lifting.#

She was no longer decelerating—but the cargo vessel was. As she separated her prize from the chain, she passed over the cut end of the tow bar, which made for the grain bin like a lance seeking a target. "Vaporize more bar."

The laser-control lights winked again. An incandescent line leaped from just below her bow to half a kay in front of her. The bin ahead swelled in her screen as she closed in on it. She could not burn a path through that much mass, nor would she survive a collision with it. "Lift, dammit, lift!"

The lasers melted more tow bar. She had pulled her bin maybe five meters out of line. A hundred meters ahead, the next bin grew like an insane anti-tunnel—a solid plug of matter in a mountain of vacuum. And she raced right toward its mouth. Sweating, she said, "Come on!"

The computer said, #Eleven meters separation.#

She had cleared it. As she accelerated back to threshold speed, the long dark bulk of the bin slipped beneath her like a silent freight train. "Jesus Buddha." She shook her head. The muscles on her back quivered, as though they had provided the muscle power to pull her into a new line of flight. She called McCorcoran.

"Pay the nice man, Liam. And explain to him what's going on."

A kilometer and a half ahead, McCorcoran's ship paced the life-support module. At her signal, he ejected a coffin-sized parcel and pulled away. Inertia drove the parcel into the side of the life-support module; powerful magnets in its casing held it there like a limpet mine.

"Attention, grain ship outbound from Dakota. The Sagittarian Guard has just paid you two million in gold for grain we could have stolen free and clear." McCorcoran accelerated as he talked, not to catch up to Lee, because he could not, but to get out of the system himself. "The payment is not meant for the USF, and especially not for the Astro Corps, but for the merchants who own the grain. We apologize to them for any inconvenience we have caused. End transmission."

Lee activated her radio's scrambler. "Very nice, Liam. Congratulations."

"I just read what Uncle Mitch wrote."

"Sure, but you didn't add 'Nyaa-nyaa!' "

"I wanted to. . . . Geez, Darcy, Blackbeard must be spinning in his grave. Pirates are not supposed to pay."

#Threshold speed,# said her computer.

"Bounce!"

She fell into the artificial singularity, and emerged a heartbeat later in the New Napa system. She commenced deceleration at once.

Relief at surviving washed over her, along with astonishment that it had been so easy. She tried to visualize the cargo pilot's face, tried to imagine his reactions to Liam's announcement. She grinned then, and chuckled once, and grinned some more all the way home.

Interstellar piracy—who'd have believed it?

"I had ordered the eradication of the rebels, Kajiwara," said Pierre LeFebvre. "You have failed me— you did not launch the attack irresistible, you did not even impose the blockade. Why?"

"Either course of action would have cost TAAC lives and equipment, sir. Acting in what this one thought to be the best interests of the Association's shareholders, this one selected what appeared to be the most cost-effective tactics." Kajiwara Hiroshi sat stiff-backed across from the chairman of the board. He kept his hands in view at all times because the Gurkha guards preferred it that way. "This one concedes that he has failed you, for when he cut their supply lines he did not anticipate their response. This one humbly submits his resignation with the request that it be speedily accepted."

"But no." LeFebvre waved a fat hand. "To accept your resignation would be the reward, and I do not reward failure. I do not accept this, your latest plan, either."

"Sir." His boyhood dreams of bushido had never pictured the Way of the Warrior leading him to a moment like this. "This one knows exactly where the Guard is and exactly how to eliminate it without needless bloodshed."

"But of course you know, my dear Over Commander." LeFebvre stroked the transparent surface of his desk. Below his hand hung a holo of the cargo ship with the abbreviated tow bar. "Just as you know that we cannot afford to lose you."

"Mr. Chairman, this one has sworn to defend the worlds of Octant—"

"Octant Sagittarius belongs to your successor—you

have the greater responsibility now, Over Commander.''

Room B87Q was a greater responsibility than Octant Sagittarius? LeFebvre's mockery kindled Kajiwara's anger. He tried to keep the rage, and the frustration, from his voice. ''Mr. Chairman, even First Commander Han has approved the plan—''

LeFebvre slapped his desktop. ''Over Commander, I have vetoed Han's approval. I have reprimanded both Han and Santiago for accepting your plan. And I will not argue this decision of mine with you. Is that clear?''

''Yes, sir.''

He peered at Kajiwara through cold brown eyes. ''Howland Island says that we should send you because you are the best we have, and that I should not worry no matter what comes, because you have the backup clone.''

''Exactly, sir, if you would—''

The chairman half rose from his chair. The Gurkhas stirred. ''Quiet!''

''Yes, sir.''

''You are without peer. I know that as well as anyone. Therefore, I will not risk your life and your immense talents in a battle with pirates! But you have said it exactly when you say that these pirates might involve us in a crisis with the Wayholder Empire. So I will tell you my decision. If this clone they have made of you is as capable as you are, wake him up and send him out.''

Kajiwara took a breath. So. His punishment for failing. LeFebvre had no concern for Kajiwara's life—so long as misery filled it. ''Sir—''

''You have heard me. Surrender command of the task force to your clone. You will remain on Howland Island, where the safety of your person can be assured, until your clone has liquidated the pirates.''

''Yes, sir.'' He began to rise, slowly, lest a quick motion release his fury at the monstrous old man who ran the Association.

''Oh, Over Commander?''

''Sir?''

LeFebvre waited for him to get to his feet. "It is possible that ill fortune might befall this clone of yours, no? Start another. Dismissed."

Kajiwara met the chairman's gaze. For that one split second, he let his hatred show. LeFebvre flinched. Kajiwara bowed. "Yes, sir," he said, and left.

On 3 April 2351, Kajiwara Hiroshi dreamed of the woman who had left their marriage while he was recovering from the surgery that cost him his fertility. A disloyal woman, but a beautiful one, with high firm breasts and wet fire between her legs. He awoke still throbbing, still missing her, though he had long since expunged her name from his memory.

He lay on his back a moment or two longer, postponing the moment when motion would rekindle the arthritic flames in his joints.

But no, he could not linger, he had to review the plans one more time, then activate the clone and turn command of the task force over to him. He just hoped he could conduct the briefing by holo. He did not want to have to shake his own hand.

He sat up, swung his legs over the edge of the bed, and stepped quickly toward the bathroom. Then he stopped. Odd. Something felt wrong. No, not wrong, different. As though he had lost weight overnight.

Ah, of course, he had turned down the gravity generators and forgotten to turn them back up again.

But no. He was on Earth. One did not use gravity generators on Earth.

What, then?

"Lights!" he called peremptorily. The overheads hummed to golden brilliance.

He looked at his hands. His smooth, strong, unspotted hands. And then he knew everything. Except who he really was.

Chapter 9

Sitting cross-legged in midair, holding a squeeze bottle of raspberry juice, Darcy Lee looked around the enormous gymnasium module and tried not to remember too much, or too deeply. Back when the module hung off the *Morocco,* she and Billy Wong had spent a lot of time in the hike booths. Together they had treadmilled through all the parks of North America, oohing at the holoviews and gasping at the grades the smart gravity generators created.

A booth wasn't as good as the real thing, of course. You couldn't stop for some fun in the sun, because the deck still felt like a deck even when hologuised as Sierra meadow, and because your time would surely expire and the next hikers enter at precisely the wrong moment. Still, a hike booth looked right, and smelled right, and you could get sunburned. In some very interesting places, if you were daring enough.

Below, an airjet hissed. She looked down. An older man was rising toward her. He waved, switched the jet off, flipped it upside down, and turned it back on again. She returned his wave, but waited for him to come to a full stop before she said, "Hi, Mr. McCorcoran."

"Darcy, please. Call me Mitch." He smelled of coffee; tiny beads of epoxy glinted in his red hair. "It depresses me when pretty girls go all formal on me."

She raised an eyebrow. " 'Girl'? I turned forty a couple of weeks ago."

"Yeah? Well, I'm a hundred twenty-two, and any female less than a third my age is *ipso facto* a girl. Is that really Liam over there?" He pointed to one of the men standing on the track that clung to the bulkhead high above the deck and circled the entire gym module.

"Sure." She smiled. "Liam has a bet with the guy in the scarlet shoes. Loser has to make the next Longfall pickup." She smiled again, more broadly than before. "They think it's a ten-kay race. What they don't know, and what no one's told them, is that some of the gravgens in the track are toggling from positive to negative and back again. I can't wait."

"Neither can I." Mitchell McCorcoran chuckled softly. "What's the problem with the Longfall run?"

"It'll pucker you." She nodded to the track. "There they go."

Liam jumped out to a five-meter lead. His uncle said, "Care to wager?"

"No point—they'll never finish. Anyway, to pick up the Longfall volunteers, you have to come in behind Sisyphus, the gas giant, so it occludes you from the TAAC ships at the spaceport. That means going along the plane of the ecliptic, instead of perpendicular to it. There's more junk in the plane. It's not really dangerous, but . . ." She spread her hands. "It's just not as safe. Riding the plane makes the hairs rise at the back of your neck."

Liam hit the quarter-kay mark ten meters ahead of his opponent. Both ran with easy, graceful strides that flashed in near unison, but Liam had the longer legs.

Mitchell McCorcoran stroked his lantern jaw. "Ten laps?"

"That's the plan." She scratched her nose. "You know, Mitch, I hate to be gloomy, but sooner or later the TAAC CO in the Longfall is going to notice that more 'miners' are slowboating out to Sissy's moons than are coming back."

McCorcoran shrugged. "When that happens, we'll figure something else."

"I was talking to a guy from the last batch," said Darcy Lee. "The Neue München Group?"

"Uh-huh?"

"Well, he knew what he signed up for, but he thought

we were TAAC auxiliaries—that TAAC would resist the next invasion, and we'd be there to help TAAC. What I mean is, even a Guard recruit didn't know the truth.''

"Not many people do."

"But why?" She took a sip of raspberry juice. "Why keep it a secret? Let's tell the whole Association that TAAC is *not* defending Sagittarian worlds, that instead it's letting the Wayholder wipe them out!"

"We have good reasons." McCorcoran held up three fingers. "Dissemination—" he bent one finger over— "disbelief—" he bent a second—"and disaster."

A droplet of syrup leaked out of the squeeze bottle; she caught it with a finger before it could stain Mc-Corcoran's blue tunic.

"Thanks," he said.

"You're welcome."

Liam shrieked as a malfunctioning gravgen threw him away from the track. He twisted in midair to face the direction of his "fall." Then he sailed into the domain of the next gravgen. He yelped again, reoriented himself once more, and hit the track running.

Darcy Lee clapped her hands. "Now that's slick."

"That's my nephew. What I was saying—"

The man in scarlet shoes had slowed down when Liam fell off the track. Now he had apparently figured out the problem, and left his feet like a long-jumper as soon as he entered the bad gravgen's domain. The gravgen had, however, toggled back to positive. The resulting long jump would have earned middling marks at a track and field meet, but did the man no good.

Mitchell McCorcoran laughed. "I think we have our pilot."

"Liam's got a real good lead on him now. Let's see if it holds up."

"Hmm. I was saying, we have a dissemination problem. We own the only bounce ships left in private hands. Before New Napa, we could simply have told our story to a news agency; it would have investigated, found we were telling the truth, and then spread the word for us, using its own SitUp rockets and bounce ships. But now

TAAC controls all that. So we would have to sneak into each system in the Association, contact the local media, persuade them to come back here with us to see for themselves, get them home again, and hope over and over again that TAAC wasn't closing in on us.''

"Sure, but—"

"Wait." His blue eyes held more weariness than Darcy Lee would have thought possible. "Why should any media rep believe us when the Association has inundated them all with holoclips of the savage battles TAAC fought?" He frowned suddenly. "For that matter, why did you believe us?"

She looked away. "Steve Cavendish was . . . very convincing." Through her shivered an echo of the despair—and the rage—she had felt when he had shown her the holos. "I believed. I can't really say why."

"Yes, well. . . . Finally, if we do get the word out, and if people do believe us, what next? Panic and rioting on all the Sagittarian worlds, that's what. People will be desperate to flee, but TAAC won't let them. Dozens of our worlds are so new that a civil war, say, could leave most settlers dead. Think what would happen if rioters disabled the landing platform on Eisenplatz."

"Jesus Buddha, they'd starve!" Her hand tightened on the bottle; a globule of raspberry juice shot straight out and broke on McCorcoran's forehead. "Oh, I'm sorry!" Leaving the bottle floating, she held his head with her left hand and rubbed her right sleeve across his forehead.

"If you were really sorry—" he winked—"you'd lick it off."

"Would you like the rest of the bottle in your hair, Mitch? It would cover the gray, restore the natural red."

The man in scarlet shoes bellowed as he fell away from the track. Liam did not even look over his shoulder, but kept running, although with perhaps a bit less abandon than before.

"He's got fifty meters on the guy," said Mitchell McCorcoran.

Darcy Lee snapped her fingers. "If we can't tell the colonies, then spread the word in the inner system! The Association's a democracy, isn't it? The next election—"

"The chairman's already imposed martial law. He'll suspend the next election indefinitely if he thinks there's any chance he'll wind up with a hostile board of directors." His wristlet beeped; he glanced at it. "Duty calls. Come along. It's time you met Ramesh."

"Sure, I'd like that." She had heard of the chief engineer, of course, and had seen him when his crew had installed the tracking device in her shuttle, but she had never spoken to him. "Think Liam will let us know how the race turns out?"

Mitchell McCorcoran grinned. "If he wins." He jerked his head toward the exit, and switched on his airjet.

She followed him to the hatch; they left the module on foot. Gravgens lined the floor of the linktube, so they walked that stretch, not resorting to the jets again until they entered the hangar.

McCorcoran put his hand on his stomach. "Zero G, full G, zero G again—it's starting to get to me."

She patted his shoulder. "Just think of poor Liam."

He laughed, and launched himself into the air. They crossed the hangar behind a boy with tonsured blond hair who was guiding a bin of salvaged sensors. At Ramesh Boripartya's work area, the boy tethered the bin to the wall, saluted, and swam away.

As McCorcoran and Lee alighted, Boripartya held out his hand. "Thank you, Mitchell. I appreciate your coming so quickly." He looked down at Lee's sleeve. "Has she injured herself? There are first-aid kits at every workbench, we—"

"Easy, Ramesh." McCorcoran touched the technician's hand, but did not shake it, not in zero G. "It's just a spilled soft drink. Darcy, may I introduce Ramesh Boripartya; Ramesh, Darcy Lee, once a TAAC lieutenant, now a Guard pirate. Ramesh, you beeped me— what's up?"

"Two thousand three hundred sensors are running outside as we speak, and you have sent me even more." Boripartya gestured to three full bins. "Are you certain you wish for these to be refurbished and put back in operation?"

"Yes." McCorcoran frowned. "Why?"

"Because it is so depressing, Mitchell. The greater the volume of space we scan, the more evidence of intrusion we find. Here, look." He took McCorcoran's arm and pulled him toward a holotank. He spoke a few words to the computer, then said, "The last twenty-four hours compressed into a minute, Mitchell."

A yellow globe marked New Napa's sun; green beads, the innermost planets of the system. Here and there stretched tiny red threads, each lasting but an instant before it disappeared, yet so many that as soon as one faded in one area, another blinked alive elsewhere.

McCorcoran rubbed his big jaw thoughtfully. "Recon drones?"

Boripartya shrugged; Darcy Lee said, "Absolutely."

"Wayholder or TAAC?"

"Ah, that is indeed the question, Mitchell. They drop in, maintain threshold speed as they streak through the system, and bounce out. Every time we extend our detection range, we find more of them."

"But you don't know whose they are."

Lee said, "Ramesh, how long do the drones stay in the system?"

"Twenty to thirty minutes."

Her heart sank. "I think they're TAAC. And if they are, then this—" she tapped the face of the tank—"is a standard pre-attack recon pattern."

Boripartya made a noise of dismay. "I am thinking, Mitchell, that if these do presage an attack on our base, it would be a very good idea for us not to be home when the attack begins."

McCorcoran's red eyebrows rose. "Move the base?"

"Why not? We no longer have a reason to orbit New Napa."

"But only half of what we have is bounce-capable."

Darcy Lee said, "Tow the rest."

McCorcoran nodded. "Any ideas as to where we should go?"

Boripartya waved a hand expansively. "The nearest star is twelve light-years away. Let us move the base to some arbitrary point on a line connecting the two stars—say, four point eight light-years from New Napa. We will know its location, but it is unlikely that anyone will stumble over us."

"And we'd have nearly five years before our EM radiation reaches the system. Yes, yes, I like that, Ramesh. We'll do it."

"Soon?"

McCorcoran flashed a tight smile. "Now."

Kajiwara Hiroshi pressed a chrome circle on his desk. "As soon as he arrives, show him in, please."

"Yes, sir." The desk did not mind in the least that Kajiwara had issued that command four times in the previous fifteen minutes.

If Sergeant Redstar, standing guard by the door, minded the repetition, he gave no sign of it. Kajiwara had never seen a more impassive face, not even in a mirror.

He attempted to organize his thoughts, but an odd lack of self-confidence interfered with his concentration. Meeting this . . . this *other* would be like his first time with a woman. Well, not quite, or at least he hoped it would not turn out the same, but the sense that he would be without secrets before this person disturbed him greatly.

The door opened. Redstar pivoted, relaxed, and resumed his stance. Kajiwara Hiroshi as he had been in the early twenty-third century entered the office. Kajiwara Hiroshi as he was in the mid-twenty-fourth rose to greet him.

The two ages of one giant bowed to each other, then straightened. Kajiwara studied his clone, whose muscles stretched the fabric of a bright yellow shirt and dark blue pants. He had hair the color of midnight, and skin that glowed with youth. Kajiwara envied the young-ster—and quelled the envy by remembering the arthritis and cancers that would torment that magnificent body in the decades to come. "So."

"So." An echo, but an echo without apparent mock-ery. "What is my name?"

"I am to brief you on the plan of attack—"

The clone waved a massive hand. "The latest record-ing dates from 2 April; today is only the 4th. I need no briefing—I developed the plan."

"No, I—" He inclined his head. "Very well. You will command—"

"The *New Zealand.*"

"The other fleets of Octant Sagittarius will be at—"

"My disposal, I know all that."

"The goal is—"

"To capture the rebels while killing as few of them as possible. I know all that, Kajiwara Hiroshi." Impa-tience hardened his voice. "What I do not know, and what I insist upon knowing, is my name. Am I Kajiwara Hiroshi?"

"No!"

"Kajiwara Hiroshi Model Two?"

"When I die you may have my name. Until then we will call you—" A translingual pun occurred to him then. As it did not happen often, he relished it. "Dai-taku."

The clone blinked. "Daitaku? 'Dai' meaning big, of course, but 'taku'?"

"TAAC'er," said Kajiwara.

The clone broke into a smile. "Big TAAC'er? Dai-taku? I like it, Kajiwara Hiroshi, I like it."

"I hoped you would."

"Our tastes have not diverged sufficiently for some-thing to appeal to one of us and not the other."

Kajiwara nodded. "Soon, though."

"Yes," said Daitaku, suddenly thoughtful. "Yes, we must begin to grow apart almost immediately."

Still savoring his earlier pun, Kajiwara said, "And now we must *go* apart."

Daitaku winced. "I am not very good at plays on words, am I?"

Kajiwara shook his head. "Sayonara."

"Hai!" he bowed. "Sayonara."

As Daitaku headed for the door, Kajiwara's desk murmured, "You have a visitor, Over Commander."

"Who?"

Daitaku hesitated for a moment, then continued onward. The door closed behind him.

"One Michael O'Reilly, from Longfall."

"My great-grandson!" Unexpected pleasure surged through Kajiwara. He glanced at the star coral glowing like burnished silver in their case on the wall. It would please Michael to see his long-ago present on such prominent display. "Show him in."

The boy—well, a grown man, now, with a full family of his own, but Kajiwara would never cease to think of him as 'the boy'—looked over his shoulder as he came through the door. He jerked a thumb toward the reception area. "Great-Gramps! Who was that who just left? He stopped, stared real hard at me, then . . . *twitched*, I guess is the word, and walked out."

Kajiwara smiled. "A relative. Of a sort. What brings you to Earth?"

"Politics. Stopped in—can only stay for a couple of minutes—to say hi and to get your advice about this Wayholder situation. We're sitting right on the edge of the fire, there—what should we be doing?"

Kajiwara sat behind his desk and steepled his fingers. "Are you truly in that great of a hurry, Michael O'Reilly?"

" 'Fraid so, Double-Gee. Since we have to use TAAC ships, I gotta be there when they say, and they've cut me a schedule so tight I'll miss the ship back if I stop to brush my teeth. Can you point me in the right direction?"

Kajiwara let out his breath with a sibilant hiss. Would his implant interrupt? "Briefly, then, Longfall must raise and train as large a standing army as possible, as quickly as possible, but should not build a space fleet."

"That's the same advice we got from the chairman's office."

"It is good advice, Michael."

"But it's odd to hear it coming from an over commander of the Astro Corps."

"Michael, security seals my lips. Even this is too much, but . . ." After all, the Wayholder had told the Association the Empire was training combat infantry, not pilots. "Should you be invaded, and should you defeat the ground forces of the Wayholder Empire, they will not be reinforced."

"But a few orbital fighters would—"

"They would doom your world, Michael. Do not build them. If you have them, do not use them."

"That won't be an easy sell back home, Double-Gee."

"Perhaps not. But you *must* sell it."

"Why?"

#Classified.#

Kajiwara shook his head slowly.

O'Reilly stood. "Big tough army, no space force." His shoulders rose and fell. "I'll give it a shot. I have to go now, but I do appreciate the advice. I'll keep you posted."

Kajiwara rose as well. "TAAC Intelligence will handle that for you, Michael. Please give my love to your family."

"And they send theirs to you." He seized Kajiwara's hand and pumped it. Then slapped the side of his own head. "Sorry, I forgot." Stepping back two paces, he crossed his hands in front of his chest and gave a low bow. Then winked. "Bye."

"Sayonara, Michael." He waited till the door closed before sinking back into his chair. He would have to warn TAAC Intelligence to monitor developments on Longfall closely. If only he could have given his descendant a tape of the Wayholder's warning to TAAC not to intervene! One gravpipe vessel looked, from a distance, much like another. What if the aliens mistook local ships for TAAC ships?

* * *

The 78th Fleet, with Daitaku in command, bounced into the New Napa system at every point of the compass, with every ship aimed directly at New Napa itself. They braked hard, alert for strays and attempts to escape. In a marvel of coordination, the last fighter arrived in position barely two tenths of a second after the first.

They achieved total englobement without needing to fire a shot.

Then they looked around and discovered why. The Sagittarian Guard had gone.

Daitaku growled deep in his throat. TAAC Intelligence would hear about this. "Search the system from the comet belt in."

Two days later, a holo of Admiral Leo Duschevski, commanding officer of the *New Zealand,* fleetship of the 78th, appeared in the corner of Daitaku's overcommand module. The old man looked haggard. "Is no joy, sir."

"Nothing?"

"Nothing, sir. If they are still in the system, they are either hiding underground on one of the planets, or they have discovered a most miraculous way to mask thermal radiation, because nothing in this system is radiating above 3 degrees Kelvin except natural objects. What I am concluding is that since they were not having the time to dig in thoroughly enough to hide all traces of their operations, and since even the Wayholder Empire has not been insulating its spacecraft *that* well, they cannot possibly be here, and are going somewhere else."

"Agreed." He glared at the battle command holo, in the middle of which spun the golden ball of New Napa's sun, smug in its secrets. He wished he could put out that light—it had illuminated the only three failures of his career. Then he shook himself. The first two failures belonged entirely to Kajiwara Hiroshi; the third, they shared. "Call all ships back to the rack. Prepare to return to the Cheyenne."

"Aye, aye, sir."

"Wait."

"Sir?"

"SitUp Over Commander Munez. Ask him if his investigation teams require any more of the debris from the battle of New Napa. If they do not, locate all of it, and destroy it."

"Sir?"

"The Sagittarian Guard will surely come back for it."

Duschevski's brown eyes gleamed. "Then let us be leaving it, sir! If we are going to catch them, perhaps to bait a trap with the debris—"

Daitaku said, "No."

"Sir?"

"Off the top of my head I can imagine at least two ways in which I could retrieve that matériel without falling into your trap—any trap at all. Let us not underestimate our opponents too severely. Destroy beyond hope of repair every piece of scrap which Over Commander Munez does not require."

"As you are wishing, sir."

"Thank you," he said dryly.

Chapter 10

Darcy Lee meandered past the rice paddies of her home village, down the path to Smoothstone River. Early-morning sun slanted onto seedlings, ricocheted off flooded paddies, and angled up into the mist swaddling the round hills beyond the river. Butterflies danced on the breeze, monarchs and viceroys—how could they fly here, so many light-years from Terra?—but she had not brought her net so she could not ask them, she could only marvel at the rich orange chocolate of their wobbling, fluttering wings.

A child ran past her, laughing and skipping and reaching for the wedges of color that careened just above his head, reaching with pudgy hands that grasped in vain, in fun.

"You won't catch them that way," she called.

The little boy turned, brushing silky black hair from his eyes, his small white teeth flashing in a dazzling smile. "I know, I know! But I don't want to catch them, I want—"

The green thing rose up from the paddy, muddy water sluicing from its elephant-hide skin. One giant hand seized the boy by the hair and lifted him. The other drew a glinting knife.

The boy tried to scream, but the knife cut too quick, cut the scream out of his throat before it reached his mouth. The plump young corpse dropped headless to the path. Vivid red jets spattered the rice, stained the brown water.

She gagged.

The green thing spotted her.

She backed away.

It straightened to its full three meters and bounded toward her, vaulting off its impossibly long arms like a hideous parody of a gorilla. She shrieked, spun, began to run—

A hand closed on her shoulder.

She yelped. She twisted. Sun dazzled her eyes. She found the stance, the strength, the seething hatred to kill the huge green thing with nothing but her stiffened fingers and callused feet. She lashed out. She blinked.

She stood beside a metal cot on a metal deck in a small metal room. Butterflies banked and wheeled through the air; she tensed, and then recognized them as a holographic projection she herself had programmed. Liam McCorcoran lay in a heap by the hatch, hands to his belly, blood trickling from his smashed lips.

"Jesus Buddha!" Darcy Lee crossed the room and dropped to one knee. "Liam." She smoothed his hair back from his forehead. "God, I'm sorry, Liam, I was having a nightmare and—"

"'Sokay." He groaned. "Help me up, huh?"

She caught his wrists and helped him lever himself to his feet. He doubled over immediately, gasping for breath. Cool air wafted from the ventilator to dry her sweaty skin. Her bare skin, she realized. Grabbing her robe, she slipped it on and belted it. "Liam, what are you *doing* here?"

"Uncle Mitch sent me. They want you—in control room. ASAP." He staggered to the straight-backed metal chair, wrapped both hands around its top rail, and tried to unfold himself. He failed. "Heard you yelling—coming down the hall. Didn't know what—" This time he succeeded in lifting first his head, then his shoulders. "—what was wrong. Tried to wake you. Dumb move." He forced a smile. "Next time—Uncle Mitch can get you." Squeezing his eyes shut, he forced back his shoulders until he achieved a posture approximating the vertical. "Damn, you're tough!"

"Sorry." This time she did not mean it. He *had* made

a dumb move—he should have *known* not to grab her. They taught that in basic training. "Wait for me outside."

"Huh?"

"I have to get dressed."

"Oh, yeah. . . ." Palm against his solar plexus, he hobbled to the hatch, and through it, and pulled it shut.

For a moment she merely stood and looked at the sheet of metal, wishing she could sleep like that, all flat and strong and dull. Then she shook her head. Only death would grant her that kind of sleep, and death would come eventually. Before it did, she had family and friends to avenge.

She dressed, doused the lights and the butterflies, and stepped into the passageway.

Liam McCorcoran leaned against the bulkhead, his cheeks still pale. As she closed the hatch, he straightened up. "Ready?" He tucked a crimsoned handkerchief into his pants pocket.

"Readier than you are, I suspect." She started walking.

He grinned as he fell in beside her. "You suspect right. Where'd you learn to wake up so ferociously?"

Memory flashed: a child's head swinging in a huge green fist. Involuntarily, she shuddered.

"Darcy, are you okay?" He put his arm around her shoulders.

"Don't." She pulled away.

"Ah—right." He dropped his arm and moved to his left, opening a meter-wide gap between them. "I didn't mean to offend you. You just seemed . . . like you needed a friend."

She took a deep breath. "I do." She looked at the height of him, at the breadth of him, and thought for a moment how safe it would feel to be enclosed in those arms. Only for a moment, though—because if she, seven centimeters shorter, fifteen kilos lighter, and nightmare-befuddled to boot, could knock him down and practically kill him, his arms did not, in all probability, offer a great deal of safety. "What I don't need is to be touched."

He gave a slow, thoughtful nod. "To be perfectly honest—" turning his head, he winked with his unswollen eye—"I didn't much need it, either."

Embarrassment heated her cheeks. She looked away. "I am sorry, Liam." Now she meant it. "It was this horrible dream—"

"We're here." Hand on the hatch to the control room, he paused. "If you'd like to talk about it afterward—across a table in the mess hall, you understand—just let me know, okay? I make a good friend, Darcy Lee."

"Thanks." She almost touched his arm, then, but did not want to do anything he could misinterpret. "Let's go."

He jabbed the controls and the hatch swung open.

Inside, Mitchell McCorcoran and Ramesh Boripartya sat at a table, cups and saucers before them. Their rumpled hair and bloodshot eyes told how long they had gone without sleep. McCorcoran lifted his head. "Darcy! Thank you for coming. We need another TAAC'er's opinion on this." He pointed to a hologram near the wall to his left.

She approached the holo. "What is it?"

"Playback from probe runs through the New Napa system. See what you think."

The cubical projection contained the entire system, with all the objects in it grossly enlarged for visibility. Thousands of—

"Ships, I presume?" she said.

Boripartya said, "Yes, of the 78th fleet, we believe, if the decoding equipment has translated properly."

"The *New Zealand*?"

Mitchell McCorcoran nodded.

"Admiral Duschevski in command?"

Boripartya slapped the tabletop. "Bloody hell! Everything *else* decodes into comprehensible English, why does the damnfool machine *insist* that the name is Daitaku?"

"Who?" said Darcy Lee.

Mitchell McCorcoran gestured to the holo. "According to the decoder, an 'Over Commander Daitaku' is running the show there."

"Daitaku? Never heard of him. Or her." She frowned. She could have sworn she knew the name of every over commander in the Corps—High Commander Santiago kept the Astro Corps leanly staffed, especially in the upper echelons. She peered at the projection once more. "So what's going on?"

Boripartya said, "Center on the planet New Napa; magnify one hundred times."

As the holo blinked from one configuration to another, small dots of light flared like fireflies on a summer's night. Now she understood. "A debris sweep."

"That's what I told them," said Liam McCorcoran.

His uncle said, "We just wanted a second opinion, Liam."

Darcy Lee said, "Are they taking out everything?"

"So it seems," said Boripartya. "Coffee?"

"Is there juice?"

"Of course there is." He rose from the table and crossed to the dispenser. "Orange? Apple?"

"Cranberry?"

"Artificial only, I fear."

"That's all right."

"Please, please, take a chair, be comfortable."

"Be depressed is more like it."

"Perhaps, perhaps. Here." He set a tumbler down in front of her.

In the holo, the ships from the *New Zealand* methodically searched out and destroyed every scrap of derelict larger than a football.

Then the screen blanked. Mitchell McCorcoran said, "Dammit!"

"I'll second that," said Darcy Lee.

Ramesh Boripartya shook his head. "Why do they do it? What is wrong with them that they so carefully destroy everything that might be of use?"

Liam McCorcoran said, "C'mon, Ramesh, they're afraid we'll get our hands on it, you know that."

"Not necessarily." Darcy Lee tasted her juice. Definitely artificial. Sour, too. "I helped conduct sweeps off Rubio, after the civil war there. Orbiting scrap metal's a navigational hazard. This might mean that the Association's planning to recolonize New Napa."

"Oh, yes, yes, but that is not what I meant, not at all. What I do not understand, in light of the fact that the Wayholder Empire holds a significant technological edge, is why TAAC has chosen to destroy rather than to salvage and to analyze."

She looked closely at him, but he seemed serious. "Ramesh, they've salvaged. They've got, ah, three whole ships and parts of others back in the Cheyenne."

Boripartya's eyes widened. "Why didn't you tell us?"

"I thought you knew. I mean—" She gestured with her free hand. "It's classified, and the media must never have gotten hold of it because I've never seen anything about it there, but all of TAAC knew. I just assumed—" she nodded to Liam—"that he'd told you. Or that somebody else had. Since you never asked me about it."

Boripartya closed his eyes and breathed deeply through his nose. Eyes still closed, he said, "Our entire strategy for survival has been depending upon their inability to follow our pirates back to base after a raid, and now you tell me that they might soon possess that ability?"

She made a rude noise. "No. Not soon. Not soon at all. For something like this, they go by the book. The standard development cycle for a new guidance system runs eight years from initiation to deployment. You wouldn't believe the number of checkpoints along the way, the number of offices that have to sign off on it. Assume they found the tracker the day they brought the first derelict back to the Cheyenne. It'll still be eight years before they issue the manufacturing release and start installing it."

Mitchell McCorcoran said, "But this Daitaku's come out of nowhere to command the 78th. That kind of rapid rise suggests special qualities. Can you be sure *he'll* go by the book?''

"Can you be sure it's a *he*?'' said Darcy Lee. "Sorry, that's irrelevant. The thing is—'' she held out her hand, palm parallel to the table, and waggled it a few times— "Han Tachun is such a traditionalist that I swear he's a relic from Confucian China. The way he looks at things, if nobody did it before, nobody's ever going to do it. With him in charge, Howland Island has gotten so ossified that it defines a maverick as an officer in scuffed shoes. I wouldn't worry about innovation from someone Han promoted. If Han could figure out how to do it, he'd force both Santiago and Kajiwara to retire.''

"But what do *we* do?'' said Ramesh Boripartya.

"About what?'' she said.

"About obtaining more ships, of course.''

She shrugged, and looked around the table.

Liam McCorcoran said, "More ships won't help. We already have eighteen—but only fourteen halfway qualified pilots. Let's use 'em.''

"What?'' said his uncle.

"The next time the Wayholder attack, let's hit em!''

Darcy Lee choked on a mouthful of juice. Gasping, she said, "Liam, that's crazy! The Wayholder lost skirk after skirk at New Napa, and just kept reinforcing. Boom, boom, boom! Until we finally had to cut and run.''

"C'mon, Darcy! We went to Pasteur—''

"Which was a mistake. We were damn lucky the Wayholder were gone. We never should have risked it.''

"But with what we've got—''

"Liam, we need fourteen *thousand* fighters, and qualified pilots for each, before we can even *think* about defending a besieged world. And I'm not sure even that'd be enough.''

He made a face. "So what do you suggest?''

"Carry the attack to them. Get more Zulus, lots of them, then launch a series of hit-and-run engagements that damage Wayholder Empire resources at little or not cost to us.''

Hotheaded he might be, but even Liam McCorcoran saw the sense in that. "That means we need more ships *and* more pilots."

"Pilot trainees have been flocking to our standard since we began recruiting," said Ramesh Boripartya, "but with the derelicts gone, the only source for additional spacecraft is the Astro Corps itself."

"So." Darcy Lee smiled. "We steal them from TAAC."

Mitchell McCorcoran said, "How?"

"Well, I've got a few ideas. . . ."

The last line of text on the screen read, "Ordered by Kajiwara Hiroshi, Over Commander, Long-Term and Special Strategies, Room B87Q, Howland Island, 8 April 2351."

Kajiwara nodded at the screen, then rolled the ball of his thumb across its lower right-hand corner. He considered the gesture a useless, almost dangerous successor to the signature, but the book called for thumbprinting orders, and one ignored the book at great peril to oneself. During a revision cycle, one might urge replacing thumbprinting with voiceprinting, arguing that anyone could press a dead and/or detached thumb to a monitor, but only the owner of a voice could make it work right. Howland Island permitted debate over the *next* book—but the current book had the stature of Holy Writ, and one did not risk charges of sacrilege.

Not unless one rode the ebon sea aboard a fleetship, light-years and light-years from home.

He blanked the screen. Daitaku now held the responsibility to respond to sightings of the Sagittarian Guard. Daitaku, and Daitaku alone.

1500 hours. The chairman had requested him to call at 1515 hours. He went into the attached bathroom, where he rinsed his face, brushed his hair, and made certain that his uniform looked crisp. Emerging, he asked Sergeant Iovini to wait outside. Then he ordered his desk to place the call.

After only a short delay, the corner of the office

formed an image of the chairman, rooted behind his desk like an ancient tree stump. "Ah, Over Commander, I appreciate the promptness. I have the desire to brief you on a meeting that we have just held with the ambassador of the Wayholder Empire."

Police in forty-five cities were still quelling devastating riots triggered by the ambassador's visit, but Kajiwara knew better than to mention it. He laid his palms on his thighs and waited quietly.

The chairman, perhaps flustered by Kajiwara's silence, cleared his throat. He shoved a piece of paper under his desktop scanner. "Here."

Kajiwara touched a portion of his desktop; almost before he had lifted his finger, the desk displayed the document. "And what is this?"

"It is the text of our message. I will make the summary for you, yes? We have notified the Wayholder Empire of the existence of the self-styled Sagittarian Guard. We have disclaimed all responsibility for the actions of this Guard. We have requested the Wayholder to destroy the Guard on sight." He folded his hands across his paunch and smiled smugly. "Well?"

"Sir?"

"What is it that you think?"

"That the matter, being settled, requires no further comment."

"Surely the Over Commander of Long-Term and Special Strategies has more to say than that."

Kajiwara had a great deal more that he wanted to say—but to dispute one of the chairman's *faits accomplis* would ruin him. Instead he mustered his softest voice. "Mr. Chairman, it is this one's duty to execute policy, not to review it. Will there be anything else?"

"No." The chairman sank back in his seat. "Thank you, Over Commander. That will be all."

He rose and bowed. "Good day, sir." He stood motionless until LeFebvre's image disappeared and the indicator lights on his own cameras went out.

Then he stripped off his tunic. From the cupboard he took a short gray hapi coat and a candle. He donned

the coat. He lit the candle and set it on the floor. He
knelt.

The flame shivered in air disturbed by his motion. He
watched it carefully, focusing all his attention on it,
inviting it to fill his mind with its light and its heat. He
looked inward.

He found Pierre LeFebvre's jowly face instead. The
fool. The sheer, absolute fool. How could he do such a
thing without consulting the man charged with devising
a defense for the star systems of Octant Sagittarius? Kajiwara would have objected strenuously, would have insisted that such notification would help only the enemy,
would have fought against the proposal with every ounce
of logic and persuasiveness he possessed.

So. A small enlightenment, a fractional satori—the
chairman had excluded him from the discussions concerning the message to the Wayholder precisely because
he would have opposed it, and might have been able to
sway the board. Pierre LeFebvre did not appreciate
challenges to his authority.

The fool.

Kajiwara stared into the candle flame once more.
Technical and scientific training let him understand that
drop of fire more concretely than any Zen master of the
shogunate ever could have, yet they had all grasped the
essence of the flame in ways that still eluded him. They
had been able to take it into their souls, to mimic it, to
make their minds and bodies act with the same airy
grace, the same outspreading of warmth and illumination.

If he had studied with them, he could truly have followed bushido, instead of merely groping, sightless, for
a path through the dark.

Ah, but if he had studied with them, then his lord
would also have walked the Way of the Warrior, and
Kajiwara Hiroshi would not have found himself in the
impossible situation of serving a man with no honor,
and no comprehension of it.

The fool.

His desk interrupted. "The delegation from the Longfall army is here to see you, sir."

"Wait." He snuffed the candle. After returning both it and the *hapi* to the cupboard, he put his tunic on. He glanced in the mirror to check the smoothness of his uniform, the blankness of his face. "Send them in."

Sergeant Iovini led two men and one woman into the room. The woman, red-haired and blue-eyed, threw him a casual salute. "I'm Colonel Megan O'Flaherty, Over Commander, and these are Major Toole and Major McWillis."

"I am most delighted to meet you." He waved to a row of plush chairs. "They are not, perhaps, very comfortable, but please, sit. Tea?"

"No, thank you, sir," said O'Flaherty. "Our shuttle leaves in forty minutes."

He sighed. "To business, then. I had intended merely to repeat, for your benefit, the advice I gave my descendant. The situation, however, has changed . . . in ways I am not at liberty to discuss. Therefore—" He went to his desk and removed a small box. Holding it, he hesitated, wondering if this was an honorable thing to do. But then, could a man condemned to a life without honor possibly do anything honorable?

So he handed O'Flaherty the box. "These are copies of chips recovered from the ruins of New Dublin. During the ground phase of that battle, the New Dublin militia recorded the patterns of the communications traffic of the invading Wayholder infantry. Even after two years, the Army Intelligence team which analyzed the data has yet to agree on a reliable interpretation, and has therefore not released a report. These chips may prove useful to the Longfall army. As I said, they are copies. There is no need to return them. In fact—" Pausing, he cocked his head and stared into the woman's lake-blue eyes. "In fact, there is no need to acknowledge their existence, or your possession of them, if you understand me."

Abruptly, she winked. "We understand, Over Commander. We need all the friends we can find these days; the last thing we'd do is jeopardize one we have found.''

"Thank you, Colonel.''

"No, sir. Not at all. Thank you."

Daitaku prowled the 78th Fleet along the face of Octant Sagittarius, where it looked into the rift. Bouncing the fleet into one randomly chosen border system after another, he aligned it each time in system reconnaissance formation.

They arrived six gigakay out from the star, roughly five megakay above the plane of the ecliptic, with the *New Zealand* at the center of a line six billion kilometers long. The 1,981 warships swept over the system at threshold speed, and scrutinized the EM spectrum for signs of the Guard.

Exactly twenty-one hours later, they bounced to a reformation point, where the computers aboard the carriers debriefed the OBCs of the shuttles, fighters, and survey/recon vessels, and the fleetship's OBCs subsequently riffled through the carriers' databanks.

Then on to another system, for another twenty-one-hour high-speed run.

Alone in his overcommand module, Daitaku did not grow impatient. Finding one small, presumably disguised base in such a vast volume was a near-impossibility, but until he received a report that someone had sighted the Guard, his only other option was to lie to and wait.

Constant movement made communications with Howland Island difficult, however, and diminished the chance that news of a sighting would reach them in time to react.

Admiral Duschevski had thought the problem soluble. Now his spare, wrinkled face filled the holo. "Over Commander.''

"Admiral.''

"Is good news, sir. Lieutenant Trinh is working already a deal with Howland Island. They've given us our own SitUp channel. Software here on the Enzi and back on Luna are synchronized so that as we are bouncing, we are sending a SitUp capsule back to Luna. That is getting there just as we are reaching our destination, and is telling Luna where we are going to be twenty minutes later, so that they can send any messages to the appropriate coordinates.''

"Impressive, Admiral." He nodded respectfully. "Please convey my compliments to Lieutenant Trinh. Have you tested this yet?"

"We are just getting ready to test, Over Commander." The old man glanced to one side, then back to Daitaku. "Bouncing in five seconds."

Daitaku held his breath, then let it out as they finished the bounce. The sun that shone on the colony world Liberdad appeared as a tiny gold coin on several of the screens in his module.

Lights flashed. Gongs chimed. Duschevski scanned his own boards, swiveled about, and said, "Wayholder ships, sir. Enveloping Liberdad."

Daitaku's consoles told him everything he needed to know. The planet lay 30 degrees to port. Six billion kilometers ahead. After waiting for the gravpipes to smooth out, the fleet could bounce to the top of the decel lane and take up defensive positions around Liberdad twenty minutes later.

Daitaku had orders to avoid the enemy, though, and the way to acquire honor did not lie in ignoring specific instructions.

Besides, the Wayholder were not due to sack another Sagittarian world until 4 October.

"It is not an attack, Admiral. The aliens hunt the same prey we do. All units are to bounce to the reformation point in—" he queried his implant; the transmission would take two hours and forty-seven minutes to reach the ends of the fleet's immense line—"two hours fifty minutes."

Duschevski looked at him as though he had gone mad. "Sir, we could—"

"But we won't." Hot ire surged through him, surprising him with its intensity. He had not been so angry

with a subordinate's suggestion since . . . ah. Since his
last bout of cancer. He would have to remember that he
was not Kajiwara Hiroshi anymore, that testosterone
could again cloud his judgment. "Prepare—"

The console bleeped. The display showed the Zulu
nearest the *New Zealand* pulling ahead of the rest and
angling for Liberdad. Daitaku's temper flared. He would
not tolerate insubordination, and he *could* not accept
incompetent piloting. He made his voice like ice. "Recall the deserter. Patch me into the comm line. I wish
to hear him explain himself."

The crew in the admiral's module carried out the order; twenty seconds later a distant voice said, "With all
due respect, sir, this is *Seoul 6*, telling you to stuff it.
My family's down there. Over and out."

Duschevski's gaze measured Daitaku.

Daitaku checked his boards. They had been in the
Liberdad system for well over a minute. A pilot impetuous enough to break formation might not wait for his
gravpipes to unwrinkle. If he bounced now, into the
midst of the Wayholder forces . . . Daitaku concealed
a shudder. "Burn it."

The admiral raised one eyebrow, but otherwise made
no move.

Daitaku understood that Duschevski was offering him
the chance to recant a rash decision. He closed his eyes.
He sorted through the fury within, assessed his own
motives. No. The pilots of the fleet—and by extension,
of the Corps—must never forget that they were the instruments, and he was the surgeon. One could not allow
his scalpels to cut on their own. "I repeat. Burn it."

Now Duschevski's jaw muscles bulged as he glowered
at his superior officer.

Daitaku said, "Now."

Duschevski turned his head and spat on the deck. "Do
it."

Twelve seconds later, two hundred laser beams con-
verged on the aft end of the *Seoul 6*. The little craft
vaporized almost immediately.

Duschevski's head pivoted 90 degrees to face the

cameras. The hatred in his dark Slavic eyes stabbed out of the holo projection. He blinked once, slowly, contemptuously. "You are wanting anything else? Sir?"

To provoke a crew to mutiny is to lose all honor forever. "I repeat. All units are to bounce to the reformation point in two hours fifty minutes. Inform them, Admiral. Out." He switched off the holo and looked for his calligraphy brush.

Chapter 11

On the first of June, 2351, Darcy Lee came openly into the Huksung System. As soon as the tug she was piloting materialized at the top of the decel lane, she hit the transmitter button. "TAAC *Madison Avenue*, Lieutenant Michelle Chou commanding, inbound from the Cheyenne with a delivery for Shin Chosun Incorporated's orbital facilities. Over."

There. The message would reach Huksung Spaceport Control just as HSC's sensors reported the arrival of her ship. The controller would log her in. The spaceport's computers would radio her onboards a delta-vee schedule to route her to Shin Chosun's mini-mill. No one would pay any more attention to her unless HSC's sensors decided her electromagnetic emissions were the wrong patterns or strength for an Astro Corps tug.

But since the ship she commanded had once served the *Morocco*, she figured she was safe.

She switched the transmitter off and her receivers on. She did not expect to hear from Huksung Spaceport Control anytime soon—her message and their reply had a *long* way to travel—but her duties on this run included recording all broad- and narrowcasts possible.

An hour-deep cross section of the entire broadcast spectrum would answer almost all the Sagittarian Guard's questions about the political climate, commercial conditions, and popular mood planetside. If their man on the ground still had his freedom, the Guard would also pick up specific tips for future operations within the Huksung. Like her current mission, for example. He had given them all the details they needed during their last raid.

A white dot formed in the center of her screen—Huksung, a world of rocky ridges, fertile valleys, and broad shallow seas. She and Billy Wong had spent a leave there once, but the planet had no butterfly equivalents for her to hunt, and the humidity turned even the simplest hike into a trek through a steam bath. They had wound up drinking *makkoli* in *seul chips* and scorching their tongues on the local version of *kimchi*. and at night— she winced, coughed, and turned her thoughts away from the memories.

The control board offered distraction. She assumed the instruments worked, but the console was so shabby, so worn and scratched from years of use, that she distrusted it. Before she took the Maddie Avvie out again, she would watch the maintenance crews test each of its controls.

She settled back in her chair. With nothing to do until she reached the mini-mill, she could relax. If she could get used to all the extra room. Years in the cockpit of a Zulu had warped her. Unless one shoulder brushed the inside of a fuselage every time she shifted her weight, she had a hard time getting comfortable.

She linked the board's largest monitor to the receivers, then hopscotched through the video spectrum, looking for an English-language broadcast, or, failing that, a *taekwondo* movie.

Studio interview, in Korean. *click* Baseball. *click* Sit-com, from the laugh track, also in Korean. *click* A tearful woman's face—soap opera? *click* A news program. The announcer was saying, ". . . skirmish today in an uninhabited system along the rift. A TAAC spokesrep put Association losses at 473 vessels, and Wayholder losses at 618. The spokesrep said the aliens beat a hasty retreat 35 minutes after the skirmish began." Behind the announcer's head, a crippled skirk slammed into an asteroid and disintegrated.

Darcy shook her head. Would anybody familiar with TAAC buy that story? Yes, the cameras on TAAC ships ran all the time, so if the incident had happened, a clip of it would exist, but post-engagement debriefings ran a long time at fleet, longer at Octant HQ, and even longer at Howland Island. And *then,* before TAAC Intelligence could release clips to the media, it had to get Geneva's permission. Which took a full day, at the least.

Propaganda, she decided, and wondered why the station had fallen for it.

"In other news, panic swept Park City today when a rumor broke out that Wayholder ships had arrived in the Huksung. Despite quick, official pan-media denials of the rumor, terrified residents clogged major traffic arteries as they attempted to evacuate the city. Fastway 792 remains closed at this hour due to an eighteen-vehicle pileup near the Taehan interchange." The announcer looked directly into the camera. "Please, folks, if you hear a rumor, tune us in right away and we'll let you know if it's true or not. It's a serious loss of face to flee to the countryside for no reason—and on a day like today, it's an exercise in misery. Coming up next, Im Chae-il tells you about the temperatures broiling those Park City panickers."

A Korean-language commercial for either new cars or disposable diapers came onscreen. Darcy Lee damped the volume.

Somewhere behind her, Liam McCorcoran should be entering the system, disguised as a TAAC trainee on a familiarization flight. She hoped he had remembered to bring the gold.

An accentless voice rolled out of the console's speakers: *"Madison Avenue,* this is Huksung Spaceport Control. We are uploading vectors and delta-vees to take you to Shin Chosun Incorporated's orbital facilities, repeat, Shin Chosun Incorporated. If another destination is desired, please advise; otherwise, expect arrival twenty-two minutes and eighteen seconds after your bounce-in. Out."

She queried her onboards, then thumbed the transmitter button. "Huksung Spaceport Control, this is

TAAC *Madison Avenue,* acknowledging receipt of the delta-vee schedules. Out.''

Her assigned route eased her from the bottom of the decel lane and into a polar orbit, then brought her to a halt in the shadow of the orbiting mini-mill, a tangled cluster of huge modules surrounded by enough solar-cell arrays to power a city. To port lay the planet itself, its spiny terrain gauzed over with clouds. A kilometer to starboard, reaction-mass tugs strapped bundles of structural alloy to the tow bar of a boxy cargo ship. The oreboat wore the TAAC insignia stenciled on a field of white, which she guessed concealed the original scarlet logo of InnerSys Lines. According to the Guard's local agent, the ship would be carrying ten thousand tonnes of alloy. If the original schedule still held, it would depart in less than half an orbit. From the looks of its tow bar, it was ready to leave.

So she had to hurry. ''Shin Chosun, this is TAAC *Madison Avenue,* Lieutenant Michelle Chou commanding. I'm returning another of your tow bars; we found this one adrift in the Beaujolais. Over.''

The comm monitor displayed the round, sallow visage of the elderly Asian whose family owned Shin Chosun. He smiled. ''Ah, Lieutenant Chou, how nice to see you again. And how thoughtpul ob you to return tow bar despite our message.''

Something's wrong here. She swallowed hard, but kept her face still, ''It's good to see you again, Mr. Paik. What message?''

''After last pirate attack, we notipied Octant Sagittarius Headquarters that ip they pound stolen tow bar, they should keep it. But neber mind, I'm sending a tug out to pick it up now.''

''Really, sir?'' Her screen centered on a small craft that moved away from the cargo ship and headed in her direction. ''Apparently your message is still going through channels, because it hasn't filtered down to us yet. Why don't you want the bar?''

''Insurance company.'' Shaking his head, he inhaled through clenched teeth, making a sharp hissing sound.

"They rebiewed situation, and determined prebious tow bar design too likely to result in high liability claims. Made us adopt quick-release bar that practures at pirst touch of pirate laser. When bar breaks, ship automatically accelerates at max por one second, to widen gap between ship and cargo. You TAAC'ers don't like to gib up cargo so easily, but without insurance, we can't ship, yes?"

"Of course not." After double-checking that she did, indeed, lie motionless with respect to the steel mill, she opened the tug's grapples and released the tow bar.

"New bar is bery expensib to install, but ip it sabes libes. . . ." He shrugged. "Bery bad time to be in business. Economy out here has gone to hell. Obercapacity eberywhere you look, and nobody's buying, not anymore. Plus whole lot of receibables went south when Wayholder killed our customers on Pasteur." He blinked. "I know you TAAC'ers want to smash all pirates, but we business people, we say whoeber wants to pay por our steel can hab it. And these pirates pay good, you know?"

She suppressed a smile. "So I've heard, sir." A gentle touch on the thrusters sent her rising from the tow bar. She kept a camera trained on it so that she would notice immediately if her maneuvers jostled it.

"Terrible times to be in business, Lieutenant Chou. We mine ores, smelt them, and alloy them. We're running at 70 percent ob capacity, hab maybe pibe thousand tonnes in pinished goods inbentory, and about a month's worth ob orders booked. Maybe ten percent ob those orders call por delivery in next quarter. Pirates hit us three times in three weeks, pay good gold each time. And customers still need their steel, so we replace shipment. To the bottom line, it's like sales hab jumped. Seems like salbation, yes?"

"From your point of view, sir, sure." The tug Paik had dispatched slipped beneath the Maddie Avvie and snagged the bar without even slowing down.

"So what happens? TAAC decides that starting next week, it is going to escort ebery shipment leabing Shin

Chosun mills. Ten Zulus per shipment. You think pirates will take on ten Zulus just to get our steel? No, they'll go steal somebody else's steel. Bery sad.'' He glanced to his right, then nodded. "Ah, we got it now. Tug pilot sends his compliments. You opp-duty? We got a nice restaurant here, and a better bar. Come on in.''

She checked the screen showing the cargo ship. Only a few tugs still fussed over it. The bar looked fully loaded. It would take the next ramp onto the acceleration lane. "No, thank you, Mr. Paik. I have to get back to the Cheyenne. I'll relay your message to my CO, though.''

"Leabing so soon? You depribe an old man ob an enjoyable meal, Lieutenant. But I understand. Maybe you can do me one small pabor—keep an eye on cargo ship, please. It's a Class VI ToyoMack, but its maintenance log says it's been habing problems with its onboards. Sometimes they all crash all at once, and—'' His shoulders rose and fell. "I worry.''

"Jesus Buddha. . . .'' She would worry too. A multiple systems crash. Outbound for elsewhere and your ship-handling systems freeze. Everything locked in an endless loop that refuses to let you regain control.

What do you do? Besides pray, that is. Because the factory's probably not expecting you, personally, to return at all; the factory's just expecting the dispatcher at the freight lines to send another cargo ship about the time the next shipment's ready to go. The buyers expect you, but they won't even start to fret till you're forty-eight hours late, because minor delays often crop up in the loading process. So say after sixty hours the alarm goes out.

She touched her implant. "Subject, mathematics; query, how far will a ship travel in sixty hours at a constant velocity of—'' she picked a number at random— "a thousand kilometers per second?''

#Two hundred sixteen million kilometers.#

So you're this luckless pilot, 216 megakay from port, with even your emergency beacons frozen mute. What does that mean?

It means everyone ramping up that port's acceleration lane will watch for you, just in case.

Because instead of a thousand kps, you might have been doing fifty thousand kps when your systems crashed, in which case you'd be ten *giga*kay from port.

Search parties tend to fail over astronomical distances. . . .

She shivered, and looked back into the screen. "I'll stay behind it all the way, Mr. Paik. If anything goes wrong, I'll take it in tow."

Paik blinked. "Good. Thank you. Ip you need to radio the pilot, his name is Paik Mun Tang."

"Paik?" She cocked her head. "Would he be a relative of some sort?"

"My son." He chuckled. "It's a pamily tradition to do twenty, thirty years in the military bepore going into the pamily business. Por one thing, it guarantees us pensions in case company goes belly up."

"But he's a native of Huksung."

"Yes, why?"

"How did he get assigned here, then? Isn't that—"

"That? Certain people on Howland Island are more than willing to waibe regulations like that por anyone with adequate, ah, wealth."

"You *bribed* a TAAC officer?"

"A pile clerk, actually. You don't think the Ober Commander, Personnel, makes the assignments herselp, do you? But enoup. I think your ramp is approaching."

And indeed it was. She said goodbye and readied the tug for insertion into the acceleration lane. The cargo ship slipped into the lane first; she told her onboards to accelerate at exactly the same rate it did. Almost immediately, a TAAC fighter left orbit to pull into the lane behind her. She hoped it was Liam McCorcoran in the ersatz *Rome 12*. She set the tug's sensors to maximum sensitivity, and warned the onboards to stay alert for any other TAAC craft in the vicinity.

Darcy Lee began to get suspicious within three minutes. The oreboat ought to be doing better than six thousand kilometers a second by now, but she was pacing it, and her readouts held steady at 750 kps.

Her comm line crackled alive; the ultralow-power-transmission light blinked on. "Darcy, it's Liam."

She gritted her teeth. Even after thirty missions together, her partner continued to unnerve her. Why was he breaking radio silence? Sooner or later his impulsiveness would endanger them, might even cost them both their lives—but the boy did fly as if he'd been born with wings.

Finger to her implant, she said, "Select ultra-low-power transmission; focus on the *Rome 12.*"

The onboards gauged the distance between the two vessels. Setting the tight-beam dispersal factor so precisely that when the cone-shaped beam reached the other ship it would be no wider than the cross section the other fighter presented, it cranked the power down to the minimum necessary for reception at the other end. A third vessel, a kilometer beyond the second and listening on that frequency, would hear nothing but static.

#ULPT selected.#

"What do you want, Liam?"

"I think the ToyoMack's systems glitched. It's not accelerating."

"Don't worry about it. Mr.—"

"Dammit, look for yourself!"

"I know what's happening here, Liam. Mr. Paik—"

"Do they have a mayday out?"

"No, they—"

"Darcy, it's not a glitch, it's a trap! He's keeping velocity low on purpose. So we come in, match velocities, snatch the cargo—and still have a twenty-minute run up to threshold. So another ship that's already doing sixty or seventy kilokay comes zipping in from behind."

"Liam, listen to me! I'm pretty sure he's faking it. His family owns the mini-mill, and would really like to sell us another load of alloy."

"Are you serious?"

"Yes." Quickly she reprised her conversation with

Paik. "Let's let him get farther out and then, um, do our thing."

A few minutes later, they crept up on the giant ToyoMack. A whispery voice, all popcorny with static, filled their speakers: "Greetings. Please switch immediately to ultra-low-power transmission."

Automatically, she instructed her onboards to comply. "What?"

"Lieutenant Paik Mun Tang, reporting intermittent but complete systems failure. I suspect the gravpipes are working too hard, and generating radio-frequency interference that's crashing the onboards."

"I think we have a solution for that." Smiling, she focused her laser sights on a stretch of tow bar just aft of the life-support module. She fired. The bar separated at once. The LSM leaped ahead.

"You've confirmed my suspicion," said Lieutenant Paik. "I guess you'll have to take the bar in tow while I return to the mill and have the mechanics go over the gravpipes again. Got enough room to latch on there?"

She eased the Maddie Avvie into the widening gap. "Yes, thank you." She directed her onboards to latch on to the tow bar.

"Ah . . . I'll bet you've got something you'd like me to carry back to the mill for you."

"Sure do. Liam, give the lieutenant the package."

The *Rome 12* sidled up to the cargo ship's LSM, ejected a magnetized container, and eased away again.

"Thank you," said Paik. "Listen, something you should know. Huksung can't get high profile, but we'll do anything we can to help anybody willing to defend Octant Sagittarius. Christ, there are four generations of my family down there on Huksung; I know what'll happen to 'em if the Wayholder show up. So good luck. And goodbye." Paik switched on his gravpipe and turned into the long slow circle back to his planet.

"Goodbye," said Darcy Lee. "And . . . thanks."

Forty-five minutes later, while construction crews swarmed over the load of stolen alloy, Darcy Lee and

Liam McCorcoran went to Conference Room A to make their report to Mitchell McCorcoran.

The older man rose as they entered. "Greetings!"

"Hi, Mitch. Excuse me, I'm dying of thirst." She crossed to the autobar and ordered a glass of strawberry syrup. Just as the machine cut off, Steven Cavendish walked into the small room. "When did you get back?"

"Last night." He groaned as he eased his long frame into a chair. "Twelve passports, twelve worlds, twelve days—I do not recommend that kind of trip for anyone in need of relaxation. Oh, the controllers at Tuscania Orbiting Port are about to go on strike; TAAC's berthing the *Ghana* there, and lending the port authority a full crew."

"But we were supposed to go in for those chips next week!" She set her glass down and rubbed her temples. Civilian controllers, especially in the Sagittarius, did not bother to confirm that a ship of the name they had just been given actually existed. TAAC controllers, implanted and possibly on-line to their fleetship's databanks, cross-checked reflexively. So the Guard would have to use the names of ships actually in service, but that had its own danger—TAAC controllers could find out, almost instantaneously, the assigned duty station of any ship in the Corps. And they took a very dim view of pilots who left their posts without authorization. "Steven, this really complicates things."

"I know, I know. We'll figure something out. A cover story, better documentation, I don't know. But we'll do it." He scowled at the holo projection of the M51 galaxy on the wall. "I'm awful tired of stars, folks. Would anybody mind if I changed it?"

She liked the holo, if only because it had no soundtrack. "Go ahead."

"Thanks." He thought a moment, then pressed the projector's viewchange button as he said, "Vermont foliage in October."

Hills of flame rolled across the wall—sugar maples at the peak of their autumn color, beneath a high blue sky.

A breeze rustled their leaves; birdsong and squirrel calls rose in counterpoint.

"Ahhhh," said Cavendish, visibly relaxing.

Liam McCorcoran said, "Did you find us some pilots?"

"Recruits, yes; about a thousand, anytime we want them. Pilots, only a few TAAC'ers on sabbatical. We'll have to train most of these people thoroughly before— Oh, another news item. Wayholder skirks are paying surprise visits to the colonies—not attacking, mind you—they just show up, orbit for a few hours, then take off."

Darcy Lee swallowed a mouthful of strawberry. "Recon?"

"Possibly," said Cavendish. "They're not explaining anything, but the folks on Liberdad think they're trying to flush us out—that they're hoping somebody will cut and run when they arrive. So if they show when you're on a mission, don't try to escape. Act normal and innocent. Wait till they go before you strike. And how *did* your mission go?"

Lee set her glass down with a thump and summarized the action.

He took the news in stride. "That's the third raid today that's turned out that way. In fact, one TAAC pilot, a native Gandhi, claimed his gravpipes were so bad that he needed a tow, too."

"What puzzles me," said the elder McCorcoran, "is that none of the other pilots offered anything more than token resistance."

"Of course they didn't," said Darcy Lee. "They're warriors—or at least that's what they're trained to be— and they're not fighting. If they believe the propaganda, they think *TAAC* is fighting, but they know damn well that they themselves are just marking time. So their contribution to the war effort is to let us arm ourselves."

McCorcoran shook his head. "I can understand them sympathizing with a force actively fighting the Wayholder—but we're not. We're *creating* a force that *will* fight back, but we haven't gone into action yet. So why—"

"Because," said Cavendish, "they believe we're going to do something as soon as we can."

"And one more thing, Uncle Mitch," said Liam McCorcoran. "It might be different if we weren't paying for the stuff, but we are. They can see that we're not hurting the local exporters, so what does a TAAC pilot care if we take delivery instead of somebody forty parsecs away?"

"But why no escorts? Why is TAAC letting us get away with this?"

Liam McCorcoran said, "Munez."

The older man blinked. "What?"

"I disagree," said Cavendish. "I don't think he's letting us help ourselves. LeFebvre and Han would cashier him as over commander of Octant Sagittarius if he were. More likely, TAAC's stretched too thin to cover all strategic shipments. Sooner or later, some of our pirates are going to see action."

Liam McCorcoran made a face. "If we don't go into action against the Wayholder soon, we're going to start losing the pilots' sympathies, so shouldn't we be getting some ships and attacking the Empire?"

Now Mitchell McCorcoran smiled. "Actually, Steve and I just finished arranging an intricate plan to acquire the ships we need, and we'd like to run it by you two for your reactions."

Liam's eyes brightened at once. "A plan?"

Cavendish reached for the controls of the holo projector. "There's a gravpipe factory operating off Longfall. . . ."

A week later, two Sagittarian Guard fighters and one shuttle bounced into the Longfall system. They braked to a halt one kilometer away from the factory's loading dock.

In Room B87Q of TAAC HQ on Howland Island, a holographic image of Frank Munez shimmered still and motionless, like the ghost of a statue. Kajiwara Hiroshi stared through it thoughtfully while he finished dictating. "Do not overestimate a planetary administrator's influence with Geneva, Frank. The chairman is not likely to reprimand you for refusing to send troops to help colonial forces quell panics. He is more likely to chide the administrator for losing control of the citizenry."

A voice sounded in the anteroom; Kajiwara tapped his desk's PAUSE button. He nodded to Sergeant Wilson. The bodyguard opened the door a crack, peeked through it, and stepped outside.

Kajiwara faced the camera once more and touched RESUME. "Frank, if the Wayholder keep searching Octant Sagittarius for the Guard, they will continue to provoke panic in every system into which they bounce. The panic will be short-lived. Unless actual rebellion occurs, your best course of action is to do nothing. By the time your crowd-control specialists reach the ground, most of the panic will have died down. Use your own judgment, of course.

"Please extend my congratulations to your investigative team for their success with the Wayholder holograms. I intend to view the recordings you sent as soon as possible." He inclined his head a centimeter or so, then touched END. "Dispatch this to Over Commander Franklin Munez via the next available Sit-Up."

"Yes, sir," said his desk. "Commander Abu Beri to see you, sir."

"Tell Sergeant Wilson to bring him in."

"Yes, sir."

Wilson came into the room, scanned it quickly, then, stepping aside for the intelligence officer, took up his post by the door.

The short, black-haired Beri snapped off a perfect salute. "Good morning, Over Commander."

Kajiwara gestured to the new silver spheres on Beri's shoulders. "Congratulations seem to be in order, Commander."

"Thank you, sir."

"Please, sit." He knew why Beri had come, but that

could wait. "You may find this interesting." He cued
the first recording. "Over Commander Munez just sent
several holos transcribed by his Wayholder technology
team. The team is not certain whether these are docu-
mentaries, propaganda, or entertainment—and, if entertainment, whether comedy, adventure, or drama. The
first, though, features the Korrin." He touched PLAY.

Above Kajiwara's desk formed a planet with a point
of light orbiting it. The dot expanded into a gray spaceship shaped like a manta ray. It left phosphorescence in
its wake, as a sea vessel does when it sails through
tropical waters.

The scene shifted. The desktop became a stretch of
flat land where a hoarse wind rustled through clumps
of bluish vegetation. Silver motes dropped from the sky
like a light rain; birdlike creatures burst into the air with
a rattle of wings. When the motes hit, some stayed put,
while others rolled in apparently random directions. By
the time they all stopped moving, they had distributed
themselves into a precise grid.

Abu Beri coughed into a half-closed fist. "Over Commander, this is all very interesting, but—"

"These are the seeds of the Korrin, Commander.
They will mature into the enemies of our enemy. Let us
watch."

The bright sparks of life became disks whose center-
points stretched upward into cones. The soil level
around them began to fall, revealing gleaming metal
cylinders with ever more elliptical cross sections, until
at last the entire manta-ray shape of the ship appeared.

Kajiwara quirked an eyebrow. "Not a documentary,
then."

"Too much nanotech for one afternoon?"

"Just so, Commander."

"Over Commander," said Beri quickly, "copies of
highly classified data chips have fallen into the possession of the Longfall army. I'm trying to determine how
that happened, and I would like to ask you a few questions."

Kajiwara touched PAUSE. "Would those be the chips recorded by the New Dublin militia?"

Beri blinked, "Why, yes, sir."

"Ah, *so desu.*" He touched RESUME. "Look."

Hatches opened in the bases of the evenly spaced ships. Small copper-colored beings stepped out of them. The cameras zoomed in on one until it stood on the desktop a meter tall.

"Is that their actual size?" said Beri.

Kajiwara only shrugged.

The Korrin had pipestem arms and legs, a head like a tangerine, tiger-slit eyes, and a toothless mouth. The mouth opened wider; a wail shivered the air. The ship extruded a tube that found the Korrin's mouth and filled it. The Korrin sucked lustily on the tube.

"An infant." Kajiwara glanced at Beri. "I gave Longfall the copies."

For a moment, Beri's dark eyes widened. The tip of his tongue touched the middle of his upper lip. He had the look of a man who has found a treasure—and wonders if it is booby-trapped. "Why did you do that, sir?"

"To have them analyzed, of course." He pointed to the holo. "Watch."

The cameras drew back. The Korrin began to stagger around the bases of their ships. They wailed; they fed; they grew. They bumped into one another. Sometimes they paused; sometimes they continued on. They began to move with grace, and their meetings lasted longer, involving speech and gestures. They grew more, and now when they met, they mounted each other.

"Propaganda," said Beri.

"Perhaps. Although we cannot yet rule out entertainment."

The Korrin disappeared into their ships, which trembled, and rose in soundless waves toward the sky. Each trailed a phosphorescent wake.

The cycle began again.

As silver rain fell on the desktop, Kajiwara Hiroshi looked at Beri. "One cannot, in good conscience, develop a strategy for reprisal without comprehending, thoroughly, all available Order of Battle Intelligence. I had waited eighteen months for your department to submit its analysis of the New Dublin OBI data. I could wait no longer." He leaned toward the holo. "Tell me, Commander, is TAAC Intelligence understaffed?"

Beri licked his lips again. "Sir?"

Kajiwara tapped his index finger on his desktop. "Commander, it is a simple question. Your people have now had the New Dublin chips for twenty months, and have produced nothing. The Longfall army has had them for two months, and has generated reams of useful analysis. Why did you fail me?"

The round-faced intelligence officer paled. His voice shook when he answered. "Over Commander, I'm not at liberty to answer any questions concerning those chips."

Hoping to rattle him, Kajiwara narrowed his eyes to slits. "At whose orders?"

A bead of sweat rolled down Beri's cheek. "I'm not at liberty to say, sir."

Kajiwara froze his features, steepled his fingers, and leaned back in his chair. "Commander—"

"Sir—"

"Ah!" He pointed to the desktop.

Wayholder shuttlecraft tore through the air. The Korrin ships spat light, sound, and solids at them. Ships both grounded and aloft began to explode.

"Now," said Kajiwara, "we see how they represent what they do."

A squad of Wayholder combat infantry tumbled down the ramp of their shuttle. A laser sliced their leader into top and bottom halves, but a sizzling beam from the shuttle put the Korrin ship's lights out. The squad blasted open the Korrin ship's hatch, and stormed inside. The camera followed. They cut through another hatch. They charged into a room with padded orange walls and floor, where an infant Korrin sat with a rattle in its hand. Laser beams slashed down from the ceiling. The infant gaped. Wayholder soldiers fell in slices. A beam licked out. The Korrin's head bounced on the floor. The ceiling went mad. The troops retreated as one fired a bazookalike weapon at the ceiling.

The camera drew back to a bird's-eye view of the Korrin settlement. Wreckage littered the gridwork; bodies and body parts lay everywhere. Slowly the Korrin weapons sputtered out. Wayholder soldiers marched through the settlement, waving boxy devices whose orange lights glowed brighter when aimed more directly at a surviving Korrin.

"A life detector of some sort?" said Kajiwara.

Beri shook his head. "I think it's a rangefinder."

"Also possible." He touched PAUSE. "You report to Admiral Graysun, is that correct?"

"Yes, sir."

"And she reports to Over Commander Forwood?"

"Yes, sir."

"Who reports to High Commander Santiago, who reports to First Commander Han, who reports to the chairman of the board."

Beri nodded.

"Then I shall speak to each of them in turn, Commander, until I find the cause of your division's failure. For your sake, Commander, I hope that Admiral Graysun admits that she ordered you to ignore those chips. Because if she denies responsibility, Commander, I will see to it that you are transferred to ground duty on whichever world of Octant Sagittarius the Wayholder Empire seems most likely to attack next." He tapped RESUME.

As the Wayholder consolidated their hold, fewer and fewer orange lights flashed. When the last light blinked out, the soldiers formed up on one side of the settlement and began to march toward the horizon.

The camera drew back even farther. Smoke rose from a dozen, a hundred, a thousand Korrin settlements. Wayholder troops marched north from each, scouring the land for more Korrin to kill.

"Propaganda." Kajiwara hit PAUSE. "Do you have any questions, Commander?"

The man looked pained. "Sir, you weren't authorized to release those chips to anyone."

White-hot rage seared Kajiwara. He kept his voice as steady as possible. "Dismissed, Commander."

Beri hesitated a moment, then rose, saluted, and departed.

Once the door had closed, Kajiwara took a deep breath, and then another, but calm stayed at arm's length. How could Beri sit on those data for twenty months and then have the audacity to be offended by their dissemination? The man wore a TAAC uniform, drew a TAAC paycheck—did he not realize he had a duty to defend the worlds of the Association? Did he think that information about Wayholder tactics had no value?

Kajiwara squeezed the edge of his desk until his knuckles ached from the strain. As soon as he could speak without fury, he would call Graysun—

His desk chimed; the words INCOMING, FIRST PRIORITY, and ACCEPT/STORE glowed on its surface. He touched ACCEPT. As the desk began to display the message, he scanned it quickly.

Then smiled a cold, wolfish smile.

He touched a chrome circle on his desk. "Urgent message for Over Commander Daitaku," he said crisply. "Record and transmit via next SitUp out of Luna." He paused a moment to suppress his elation. "Daitaku. The Sagittarian Guard is attacking Kao-Hsiung Gravpipe Limited's assembly plant off Longfall. Proceed immediately to the scene, capture them, and interrogate them until they have revealed the location of their base. Strike at the base immediately after you learn its location.

"The Guard surely expects to be in and out of the factory before you arrive, but they do not know that the Longfall army has posted troops on all its satellite installations. The garrison at that factory should be able to hold off the Guard long enough for you to get them.

"Go. Strike. Win."

So. He wished he could lead the strike force himself,

but he could trust his clone. By the end of the day, the Sagittarian Guard would cease to exist as a threat to the survival of the Association.

One down, one to go.

He touched the holo controls. "Get me Admiral Graysun immediately."

Daitaku scowled as Kajiwara Hiroshi's message sounded through the speakers of his overcommand module. "All ships in and on Yellow Alert," he told Duschevski. "Bounce for Longfall ASAP. We must make fastest possible rendezvous with a factory in high-altitude polar orbit around the planet."

The holographic admiral saluted.

And Daitaku fumed. He did not disagree with Kajiwara's orders—rather, he felt them unnecessary. The over commander could—no, should—simply have said, "The Sagittarian Guard has attacked KaoHsiung Gravpipe Limited's assembly plant off Longfall. The Guard do not know that Longfall has posted troops on all its satellite installations." Daitaku needed no additional information. Kajiwara Hiroshi had not. And were not Kajiwara Hiroshi and Daitaku the same person?

The *New Zealand* bounced. Daitaku said, "Locate the KaoHsiung Gravpipe assembly plant. Stop the *New Zealand* within one ship's radius of it. Carriers are to move in and land rangers on its surface. Fighters englobe from two kilometers back."

While Duschevski scrambled to carry out his orders, Daitaku fiddled with the battle command holo's magnification and resolution. He picked out Longfall immediately, but the fleetship was still too far away to discern the details of the orbital installations.

Five minutes later, from 23.5 million kilometers out, he could read the orange signboards of the resort hotels orbiting Longfall. A moment later he picked up the KaoHsiung logo. Yes. Two Zulu-class fighters, one standard shuttle. He thought of attempting to disable the vessels with the lasers, but decided to wait. Any or all of the Guard ships might explode, damaging the plant.

No hurry. The 78th would strike within minutes, anyway.

The *New Zealand*'s velocity had dropped to below a thousand kilometers a second when the Guard craft separated from the assembly plant's locks.

"They flee," he said to Duschevski. "Wait until they are two hundred kilometers from the factory, then lase off their gravpipes and overtake."

"Aye, aye, sir." The admiral bent his head and spoke to someone off-camera.

Five seconds passed, and another five, and the rebel ships still accelerated away from the factory.

Daitaku raised his voice to a roar. "Admiral!"

The figure in the holo shot him a baleful glance. "Is problem. Wait." Duschevski turned back to his crew. "Fire, Lieutenant! Or by God—"

#All rebel vessels' gravpipes disabled,# said Daitaku's implant. #Inertial velocity—#

"Overtake those ships, Admiral," said Daitaku, "and have that coward of a weapons officer court-martialed."

Duschevski said, "He is no coward, sir. He is New Dublin boy, and—"

"No excuse. Charge him with desertion in the face of the enemy."

"Sir, I must recommend against that."

"Oh, really?" He glared at the holo of the *New Zealand*'s commanding officer. "And why?"

Duschevski ran a hand through his thin hair, but he held his ground. "Because you are not going to get conviction, sir, not from officers aboard this ship. I am recommending ignoring incident entirely—"

"No."

"—but if you going insist to discipline him, insert reprimand into file and let it go at that."

"You risk a great deal by addressing me like that."

"I am knowing exactly my risk, Over Commander. Perhaps before you are committing yourself irrevocably, you should consider the strength of feelings of myself and others."

"This is not a democracy."

"No, sir." His gaze flicked sideward as action on a screen Daitaku could not see caught his attention. "Is capture, sir. Pulling them in now."

"Excellent. Throw them in the brig. Separate cells—they are not to speak to each other prior to interrogation."

Duschevski grimaced in distaste. "Aye, aye, sir."

"Sarcasm, Admiral?"

Duschevski spoke to his computer implant; his projected image shrank to permit a new scene to form beside it. "Is lock they are entering through. Already fifty crew members are waiting for them. They—"

The hatch swung open. Into the hallway stepped two burly rangers. Behind them came someone wearing a gold skinsuit. One ranger turned, took his prisoner's right arm, and raised it high in the air.

The assembled crew members cheered.

Daitaku said, "I see." He thought a moment. "Triple security in the brig area. Call all ships back to the rack, and bounce us to the Cheyenne System as soon as we reach threshold speed."

"Aye, aye, sir."

Chapter 12

Three hundred thousand kilometers behind the *New Zealand,* and maintaining exactly the same course, Darcy Lee fought off the nausea of fear. The plan scared her a lot more out here, in execution, than it had back at base, on a computer screen.

Soon the *New Zealand* would bounce out of the Longfall System. The Wayholder gadget would translate the waveforms thrown off at the bounce into coordinates. Darcy Lee and her eleven companions, each in a Zulu-class fighter, would then follow.

She squinted at the screen, waiting for the Enzi to disappear.

#Bounce complete,# said her onboard computer.

She made a face. Even after all the pirate raids she had led, she kept expecting her quarry to vanish from her viewscreen, but the tracker read the waves, derived the coordinates, and bounced the ship in less than one screen refresh cycle. So without ever losing sight of the Enzi, twelve Sagittarian Guard fighters had entered the Cheyenne System—home port to every fleet of Octant Sagittarius.

Her sensors spotted the Enzi eighty kilokay ahead, and decelerating at the maximum allowable rate.

She gritted her teeth, counting seconds to herself while her onboards did the same, though rather more accurately.

After a precisely calculated delay, the computer kicked the gravpipes into braking at 110 percent of max. Warning lights bright as arterial blood flared across her control panel. She gulped. Her knuckles whitened as

she gripped the arms of her chair. She hated this part.
Her every instinct screamed that she should override the
computer, brake more slowly, put less strain on unver-
ified welds, and plates scavenged from the graveyard of
a shattered fleet.

But if she did, she would shoot past the *New Zealand*.

#Two minutes twenty-five seconds to intercept,
mark.#

For the next 145 seconds, then, she would ride an
overstressed spaceship down a high-traffic decel lane
toward the largest cluster of warships in the entire octant. For 145 seconds, she and her companions would
inch closer and closer to the *New Zealand*. For each of
those 145 seconds, she would hope they had figured it
right.

A fleetship did not expect to be mugged by friendly
forces. When its sensors detected a handful of TAAC
Zulus closing in from the rear, its programming should
assume them to be friendlies looking for berths.

Through her earphones came a female voice, clear
and articulate with faint musical overtones: "This is the
New Zealand, calling the wing plus two fighters riding
our wake back to base, identify yourselves."

She swallowed hard. At a button tap, the onboards
squawked out the FM pulse that vouched for her ship's
identity. If TAAC had changed signals since Steven
Cavendish's visit to the *Portugal* . . .

Flicking her microphone on, she let fright control her
tongue. "Survivors, Enzi! *Ottawa 32* in command. Out
of the badlands. Got an eyes-only for your admiral.
Duschevski, right? Please direct us. Please!"

At their current separation, the time lag lasted just
long enough to irritate. "What unit are you with, *Ottawa 32*?"

"Late—" She meant to force a sob, but it came easily. "Late of the *Portugal, New Zealand*. Aren't you
taking our pulses?"

This pause lasted longer. The comm officer must have
hesitated. "What are Octant Auriga fighters doing out
here, Oh Three Two?"

"Trying to get a message from our admiral to yours before it's too late, Enzi."

"And the message is for Admiral Duschevski?"

"For the first admiral or over commander we encounter, Enzi."

"Read it to me, Oh Three Two."

"That's a negative, Enzi. The personal portion is paper-based and signet-sealed for admiral or higher in a do-away pack; the data are on a Solarflare-class codechip. I open the personal, it burns on me, and they don't give courier pilots Solarflare codechip readers. Besides. Even if Dark Bart *is* gone, I know what orders he gave, and I'm not violating 'em."

The time lag had shriveled to the barely perceptible. "What kind of data, Oh Three Two?"

"OBI, I guess. God knows Dark Bart waited till the damn battle was pretty much over before he kicked us off the Porch."

"What kind of shape is the *Portugal* in, Oh Three Two?"

" 'Bout a zillion shapes, Enzi. Small shapes. Twisted and sorta scorched. Now, you gonna direct us to your admiral, or what? We're about to penetrate your aft fields! I'd hate like hell to wind up escaping the whole goddam Wayholder space force only to get fried by TAAC fields."

"Fields off, Oh Three Two. Weapons systems nulled, but keep your IDs pulsing." New respect filled the woman's voice. "Standard layout; Admiral Duschevski's in Command Module Four today. We are carrying an over commander, though. Daitaku's his name. He's in CM 5."

"Thank you, Enzi. Out."

"Out, Oh Three Two."

The twelve Sagittarian fighters held formation while they slipped into and through the giant latticework. Then they paired off. Each pair headed for one of the six modules from which the fleetship could be controlled. The plan called for Darcy Lee and her winger to take

Duschevski, while Liam McCorcoran and his would capture the mysterious Daitaku.

The *New Zealand*'s current nerve center looked like any of the life-support modules scattered throughout the vast framework—except for modest stenciling that read "CM 4." While her winger positioned his craft so its main lasers pointed at the module's gravity generator, she snugged up to the com-mod's airlock and waited for the hatches to cycle open.

Standard-issue courier satchel in hand, she stepped into the lock. The pressure hatch to her ship closed behind her. The one to the interior of CM 4 opened so slowly she could have screamed. In less than sixteen minutes, the fleetship would coast to a halt in the heart of Octant Sagittarius Headquarters. She had to get it done before then.

Barely moving her head, she scanned the room as she entered. Jesus Buddha, being back in a real TAAC ship felt weirdly comfortable. Like coming home, sort of, or like pulling on a custom-tailored glove.

She took a quick headcount. Four men, three women, officers all. Two lieutenants sat at the boards; a commander stretched out on the couch; two captains stood by the galley talking, beverage mugs in hand. A gaunt, elderly admiral and a thin-faced lieutenant approached her. Drawing herself to attention, she snapped off a salute. Reflexes.

The admiral returned it. "Is okay to crack helmet now, Lieutenant." He reached for the sack.

Instead she triggered her external speakers and drew the dart gun from the satchel. "Hands in the air and freeze!"

Seven faces gaped at her, eyes wide, mouths open.

"Away from the boards, now!" She leveled the gun at the lieutenants manning the controls. Everything depended on whether the pilot would try to shut down the gravpipes—and if she could kill him before he succeeded.

The communications officer pushed her chair backward; after the slightest of hesitations, the pilot followed suit.

"My winger's lasers are trained on your gravity generator, and he's plugged into my circuit. Anybody moves, your generator's gone. At max decel, we'll all wind up on the forward bulkhead looking like raspberry jam. Do I make myself clear?"

The white-haired admiral raised one eyebrow. "Sagittarian Guard?"

"Yes, sir." She had to smile at the way familiar surroundings triggered old speech habits. Or old conditioning. She wasn't sure which.

"Duschevski, commanding officer of the *New Zealand.*" He spoke to his crew without turning his head. "We are doing what the Sajjer says."

"Thank you, sir. All of you, step to the rear of the module, and keep your hands in the air, please." Courtesy couldn't hurt, she figured.

The crew balked, but at the brusque gesture from the admiral, they raised their hands and backed away.

"Please sit against the bulkhead, legs straight out before you, ankles touching, hands clasped behind your necks."

They slithered to the deck and sat as she had ordered.

"Thank you for your cooperation."

Duschevski shrugged. A difficult motion to complete, considering his position, but he managed it nicely. "Is not attractive proposition, dying at human hands, if you understand me. Now, if we die at Wayholder hands, that means we must be doing our job, but Sajjer hands? No."

She faced the admiral. "Sir, the Sagittarian Guard is requisitioning the *New Zealand*. For the moment, I'm afraid you and all your crew must consider yourselves prisoners of war."

"To be treated in accord with all conventions?"

"Of course, sir!"

"Very well, then, Lieutenant ah, Lieutenant?"

"Lee, sir."

"Lieutenant Lee. *New Zealand* is, apparently, in your hands now."

An alarm whooped; a red light flashed on the board. Darcy Lee pointed to the comm officer, a tiny oriental woman whose name badge read Trinh. "Quick, see what it is."

Trinh scrambled to her feet. Halfway to the board, she said, 'Gravgen failure in CM 3." She tapped the controls twice. The alarm shut down; the light blinked out. "Life-sign monitors zeroed out."

"Jesus Buddha!" She motioned Trinh to rejoin the others. "Admiral, I . . . it looks like some of your officers tried to be heroes. Please let's not let that happen here, sir."

"It won't." Duschevski glanced toward the consoles, then looked back at her. "You are trained in fleetship handling?"

"As I understand it, the OBCs do the work."

"For most part, yes, but why take chance? Lieutenant Corzini, my weapons officer—" he nodded to a thin man with cropped black hair—"is native of New Dublin. I am thinking he is delighted to serve as Sajjer fleetship pilot. Is right, Zi?"

"Betcher ass, skipper!"

The admiral suppressed a smile. "Rest of us are lacking Zi's partisan fervor, but not one of us is going to commit suicide to keep Enzi flying TAAC colors. Except, of course, for almost-heroes in CM 3. And Kid Kaji. Since CM 5 still has gravity, I am trusting your colleagues have already dealt with him."

"Who?" She bit her lip as she remembered the passing seconds. "Wait. Lieutenant Corzini—"

"I'm Zi and you're Lee, all right?"

"Fine, Zi," she said faintly, holding out the satchel. "There's a chip in there with coordinates. Get us to those coords ASAP"

"In a flash, Lee." He grabbed the sack and scurried over to the boards.

Her winger's voice crackled out of her suit speakers. "The other com-mods are under control, Darce."

"What happened in Three?"

"Two of them jumped her and took her gun away. Her winger pulled the plug on 'em."

"Any other trouble?"

"Some. You want a replay?"

"In a minute," she told her winger. "Tether on."

"Aye, aye. Liam's coming in."

"Thanks. See you later."

Frowning, she turned her attention back to Duschevski. "Admiral, who is Kid Kaji? I thought I knew all the fleet admirals, even by nickname, but—"

"Is Kajiwara Hiroshi's clone."

"What?"

Now he looked surprised. "You are not knowing? I am thinking he is surely reason for your, um, expropriation of *New Zealand*. Over Commander Kajiwara Hiroshi has undergone continuity. His continuation is commanding fleet."

"This is crazy." Behind her the airlock door motor began to whine. "Is that you, Liam?"

"Yes. Undamaged, thank God." He came up to stand beside her.

"What happened?"

Corzini said, "Hey, Lee! We've resumed acceleration. Threshold speed in five minutes thirty seconds, mark!"

"Thanks, Zi," she said. "Liam?"

McCorcoran pointed to the communications officer. "Is the flight recorder in CM 5 running?"

Lieutenant Trinh nodded.

"Replay it, please, starting from, uh, four minutes ago."

Trinh rose from the floor and walked to her station. She touched a few spots on the panel before her. A hologram took form in the corner.

A spacesuited figure moved into a small room, helmet turning like a turret, handgun at the ready.

A door hissed open. A deep, hard voice cracked through the module like the sound of a whip. "Treason."

Liam McCorcoran spun just as the speaker charged.

Across the floor dove a huge man, black-haired and handsome and impossibly young for the over commander's uniform he wore. McCorcoran's trigger finger squeezed. The gun chattered. The giant went down in a spray of blood.

McCorcoran stood above the body for a moment, hands on his hips, shaking his head. Then he bent, seized the still form under the armpits, and dragged him across the floor to a hatch marked with a large red cross. As soon as the hatch cycled open, he fed the young giant in headfirst.

The holo ended.

Darcy Lee took a deep breath. "Admiral Duschevski, was that Kajiwara Hiroshi's continuation?"

"*Da.*" The old man's narrow face had gone white. "Is he—"

McCorcoran said, "No, he's alive. The aid chamber said he'll be fine."

Duschevski passed his hand over his dark eyes. "Good. Good."

Darcy Lee said, "What is Kajiwara Hiroshi's clone doing in command of the *New Zealand*?"

"His mission is—*was*—to search out and destroy Sajjers." For a moment he looked thoughtful, then he leaned back against the bulkhead and gave a slow smile. His teeth flashed in the fluorescent light. "I am thinking you have really turned table on him."

"Yes," she said slowly, "yes, but . . ." She shook her head.

"Yo, Lee!" said Corzini. "Two minutes to bounce, mark!"

"Thanks, Zi."

The admiral said, "Yes but what?"

"What are we going to *do* with him?" she said plaintively.

"Dear girl—" He chuckled. "I am not having faintest idea. But you start planning something, because Kajiwara Hiroshi original is going be furious."

* * *

Kajiwara looked up at Admiral Maria Graysun, a ninety-three-year-old woman with faded blue eyes and gray hair cropped recruit-short. "I want an explanation for your behavior, Admiral." His anger did not show on his face, or in his voice, except perhaps to someone who had stood beside him through dozens of fleet maneuvers, but inwardly he raged.

"Sorry." She paused just long enough to stoke his fury. "Sir."

"Your division had custody of the New Dublin chips and did nothing with them, even though the information they contained might have saved tens of millions of lives. Why?"

"It's classified. Sir."

A silver light flashed on his desk. He reached, noticed that she watched intently, and pulled his hand back. "Dismissed, Admiral." He would get nowhere with her anyway. He would have to take it up with her immediate superior, Over Commander Forwood.

"Thank you." She did an about-face. "Sir."

He waited till the door had closed before he activated the message display.

Frank Munez's voice filled the room. "Sir, the *New Zealand* just returned from Longfall—it entered the system roughly forty minutes ago, began to decelerate, then changed course and ramped back up to threshold speed. It bounced out without explanation. Is there something going on that I ought to know about? Please advise. Thanks."

Silence fell as Kajiwara Hiroshi stared at his desktop. In and out without a word of explanation? Something stank here.

He imagined himself in Daitaku's position, and mentally retraced his clone's steps.

Bounce to Longfall. Kajiwara checked the summary of message traffic on the special channel set up for the *New Zealand.* Yes, the fleetship had announced its intention of going there, and then had confirmed its arrival.

Capture the pirates. Back to the summary. Indeed. Two fighters, one cargo ship, captured with all hands unharmed.

Bounce to the Cheyenne. And again, the summary recorded the message.

Dock at base, and interrogate the prisoners. No messages to that effect, though.

What would have caused Daitaku to change plans without informing Kajiwara or Octant Sagittarius HQ? An incoming message?

Not if Kajiwara could believe the summary. Luna had neither originated nor relayed any messages to the *New Zealand* in over two hours.

Something the prisoners had said?

He pondered that for a moment. Eyes closed, seat tilted back, he visualized one of the Intelligence staff calling up, bursting with news, news so urgent that the fleetship could not stop, but had to bounce back out without delay.

News so urgent that Daitaku would not drop a SitUp? Kajiwara shook his head and sighed. No, that he could not accept. Perhaps a Wayholder attack on the fleetship could justify that sort of silence, but Munez would have reported a firefight in the Cheyenne.

What, then? What could cause him, Kajiwara Hiroshi, to execute that sort of maneuver without informing anyone of what he was doing?

His blood ran cold. He *knew* what had happened.

Mutiny. Flight. And, probably, desertion to the Sagittarian Guard. Nothing else could explain the silence.

How dare they? To mutiny against his continuation was offensive enough, but to hijack the ship he controlled vicariously through that same continuation—it was as though the mutineers had stolen a fleetship from beneath Kajiwara Hiroshi's own feet.

He touched the chrome circle on his desk and the microphone came alive. "Message for Frank Munez, Over Commander, Octant Sagittarius. The most probable explanation for the mystery is mutiny and desertion to the Guard. Dispatch ten fleets in search of the *New Zealand* and Daitaku. Rotate fleets, but keep ten searching until they have found the *New Zealand* and destroyed the Guard. It would be preferable if they were to retrieve Daitaku alive. Preferable, but not mandatory. Ah. And warn the COs to be alert for any sign of incipient mutiny. If it can happen once . . .'' He touched the circle again and the microphone lapsed into somnolence.

For a long time he sat motionless, brooding, wondering how it had come to pass that nearly everyone, it seemed, both above and below him, had turned against him. The chairman. Forwood, Graysun, Beri. The mutineers! The sun faded. The room darkened. The only light came from the star coral display case.

Silver flashed on his desk. A chime sounded. A memo from First Commander Han appeared. He snapped out of his brown study and leaned forward eagerly. Had they found—

The message dismayed him to the point of dizziness.

Howland Island had told the Wayholder Empire everything! More, it had requested that the Wayholder destroy the fleetship on sight.

Kajiwara's jaw worked, but no sound came out. He had hardly expected Han Tachun to hew to the Way of the Warrior—but this! It had never occurred to him that Han might display such craven cowardice, such disloyalty to any concept of military honor.

All his fury concentrated into a single burning point, like the flame of a candle. It soiled him to be subordinate to a man like Han; it shamed him. Yet he had no choice! Forbidden to resign, forbidden to die—ah, the terrible irony of losing honor precisely because he tried to uphold it.

Yet he, Kajiwara Hiroshi, samurai in disgrace, did not matter. All that mattered was the chance that someday he, or his continuation, would redeem his name. And he, or the other, could do that only by saving Octant Sagittarius from the Wayholder Empire.

If the chairman and the first commander would ever permit it. . . .

He slapped his desk and demanded direct connect to the chairman. The holo formed almost immediately.

At a murmur from one of his guards, LeFebvre looked up. "What is it?"

"Kajiwara Hiroshi requests permission to return to Octant Sagittarius."

"Is this in regard to the mutiny aboard the *New Zealand*?"

"Yes, sir."

"The permission is denied," said the chairman in a bored voice.

"Sir. In a situation of this gravity, this one ought to be present in the flesh."

"Perhaps. But you will remain on Earth, Over Commander. You are the Association's best hope against the Wayholder Empire, and until your next clone has achieved the maturity, you will not be permitted to risk your life. Dismissed."

He stared at the man a moment longer, as if through telepathic assertion of will he could force the fat idiot to change what passed, in LeFebvre, for a mind—but the chairman merely glanced at Kajiwara's holo image, narrowed his eyes slightly, and shut his cameras off.

Daitaku awoke on the oversized bunk installed in the command module especially for him. He wore bandages, tubes up his nose, a thumb-sized monitor on his left nipple, and a pair of boxer shorts through the fly of which another tube rose. A one-meter-tall orange robot scurried to him as he stirred.

"Do not move," said the robot.

"Release me."

Could robots shrug, it would have. "Lie still. Anesthetic field on." It touched a limb to his skull and a pleasant fuzziness filled him, a fuzziness through which he barely felt the tubes retreating from his orifices. "Field off. You may move."

Now it stung when he breathed, and it ached when he moved, and dizziness carouseled his brain when he forced his throbbing body into an upright position. He filled his lungs for a shout. "Hello!"

The robot said, "You are alone."

How nice, he thought, grunting as he planted his bare feet on the cool metal and levered himself erect. He took a step. A micronova of pain burst within his right knee, and the joint gave way. He fell forward, and threw his hands out just in time to break his fall before the fall broke his nose. Sweat stung his eyes as a whole new flood of torment washed over him. "Help me up!"

The robot moved behind him. Plastimetal claws, heated to human body temperature by internal elements, slipped under his armpits. A motor purred, then whined for an instant as the claws hoisted him off the deck.

He let his legs dangle until the big toe on his right foot grazed the deck plates. "Set me down slowly." He gritted his teeth as his legs took all his weight. "All right. Let go."

The orange claws slipped away.

He wobbled, and reexperienced the vertigo, but he did not try to move and so he did not cause his body to fail. He inhaled deeply once, and again. Fine, he could do it. He had proved his point—though he was not sure to whom. "Adjust the controls to zero gravity."

When his weight disappeared, so did a great deal of his pain. "Sso," he said to the robot, "I am alone here."

"Yes."

"Do I receive visitors?"

"It is permitted."

A gentle push with his good foot sent him drifting toward the control panels. One look was all he needed—the Sajjers had disabled the controls.

And, he realized a moment later, as he opened the compartment by the airlock, they had taken his spacesuit as well. But why not? The module made a conve-

nient prison cell, especially with a robot nurse to tend
his wounds.

He hung in midair by the lock, wondering if they had
programmed the robot against letting him leave. To
space himself would be an honorable, if hardly traditional, course of action.

A yellow cube took form in the middle of the room,
then faded away as the face of an oriental beauty coalesced within it. A familiar beauty with high cheekbones in a heart-shaped face, full red lips beneath a
delicate nose, and eyes so large and warmly brown that
something caught in his chest and *ached*.

He knew her. No, not he Daitaku—he Kajiwara Hiroshi. He had met her . . . where? Her name trembled
at the top of his throat but would come no further.

Her dark eyes flickered, probably across the equivalent cube at her end, and concern filled them. "Over
Commander Daitaku?"

Futile to hide. He could avoid the holocameras, but
not the robot or the humans they would send to double-
check. He pushed away from the wall and floated into
the focal region. "Yes?"

She inclined her head gravely. "It's a pleasure to meet
you, sir. I am Darcy Lee, formerly a TAAC lieutenant
and pilot of a Zulu racked on the *Kathmandu* of the
79th Fleet. I served under your—ah, ancestor?—at the
battle of New Napa."

He sucked air sharply through his teeth. "Of course.
I knew your face, but could not name you." With memory thus jogged, he recalled a great deal about her. Facts
culled from personnel files, mostly. No, entirely. That
startled him. Why had he, Kajiwara, never met this
woman in person? He, Daitaku, would have. "Now that
I can name you, I am much less surprised that the *New
Zealand* is no longer mine to command."

Again she gave that slow, gracious head movement
that lay somewhere between a nod and an abbreviated
bow. "You honor me, sir."

"Do you command the *New Zealand*, then?"

"In a manner of speaking, yes. Although we have rechristened it. We call it *Empire Bane*."

He stared into the holocube, willing his face to remain impassive, his tone of voice to remain idle. "A fleetship requires many trained hands—more than TAAC Intelligence believes the Guard to have. How are you managing to cope?"

The corners of her lips twitched. "TAAC Intelligence's estimates may have been accurate prior to, ah, our acquisition of *Empire Bane*, but we've had quite a rash of enlistments recently. As we modify the operating systems of their implants, we once again find ourselves in the extremely frustrating position of having more personnel than ships."

"My entire crew defected?" He could not keep the bleakness from his tone, no matter how he tried. "All of them?"

"All but a handful, sir."

He dropped his gaze to the deck. All but a handful! Then a thought occurred to him, and immediately he wondered why it had taken so long. "How long have I been unconscious?"

"Nine days, Over Commander."

"Has the *New*—the *Empire Bane* seen action yet?"

She shook her head. "We're still finalizing strategy, sir." She chewed her lip as she stared thoughtfully at his replicated image. "Several of your officers have suggested that you could, if you were willing, give us better advice than anyone alive."

He blinked. "They said that?"

"Yes, sir."

He clasped his hands behind his back. "They spoke truthfully."

"You will advise us, then?"

"Oh, no, Lieutenant." He put steel in the words, tempered steel suitable for a samurai sword. He did not know why, but he expected her, perhaps more than anyone else, to understand the importance of walking bushido. "I will not advise rebels, except to this extent: Bounce the *New Zealand* back to Octant Sagittarius

Headquarters at once, and you might escape with your lives.''

She smiled sadly. "Thank you anyway, Over Commander. Good day.''

The holocube dwindled into a dazzle of gold, then vanished.

Chapter 13

The fleetship hung high above the desolate system; the sun of the world called Gandhi spun directly below. Three years earlier a steady stream of freighters and liners and scarred orehunters would have been rolling down the decel lane toward the colony, an inflow balanced by outbound traffic ramping up the accel lane. Three years and one day ago, the Wayholder still kept to their side of the rift.

Now only lazy comets blipped incoming on the surveillance screens. Ten carriers from the *Empire Bane* and all their fighters formed a torus of EM noise at about the 1.5-billion-kilometer mark, as widely spaced Sajjer trainees practiced "riding the plane."

"Run a simulated engagement?" In Command Module Four of the *Empire Bane*, Darcy Lee looked at Anatole Corzini and did not disguise her skepticism. "Why?"

"Because." He ran a hand through his thick black hair, then gestured to the control panels. "The machines can fix almost everything that breaks. Everything except hearts." He gave her a rueful smile. "The thing is, people fix it quicker. Not better, necessarily, but quicker. And if, in the middle of an engagement, a chunk of flying titanium wipes out a bank of lasers, you want it fixed *right now.*"

"But TAAC mech-mechs *are* fast." She wondered about that smile. He couldn't have a crush on her, could he? She hoped not. Things were sticky enough. "I've watched them in the hangars, and—"

"Watch closer sometime. Each motion is fast, but

they don't skip any steps, no matter what. They don't take chances—they're programmed to go by the book. The book calls for constant quality-control checks, and the mech-mechs won't certify something if it doesn't measure up. Hell, they won't even turn the thing on.''

''If our lives depend on a system not failing—''

''When you need oxygen, you need it now. A flawed system pumping in five seconds is better than a perfect one in five minutes, yes?''

''Point taken. Can we reprogram the mech-mechs?''

''Not anytime soon.''

She frowned, disturbed—and abashed—that she knew far less about the operation of a fleetship than she had thought nineteen years in uniform had taught her. Thank God Duschevski and his TAAC'ers wanted to cooperate. ''So the main reason the *Empire Bane* has a crew is to make emergency repairs during a battle.''

''You got it, Lee.'' He winked at her. ''The machines handle everything except quick fixes. Those, people handle—*if* they're properly trained. Which is why TAAC runs simulated engagements. The main computer generates the enemy's likely behavior, probable damage to the ship, the works. Let's do it. Your Sajjers are never going to survive a real—''

An alarm chimed; a red light blinked on-off-on three meters down the control panel. ''Sure, and it's my board,'' said Lieutenant Peter Connaught, the surveillance officer. ''We've a visitor.'' The pudgy SO glanced at Admiral Duschevski.

''Who?'' Duschevski moved to that end of the module.

Connaught began to translate the numerals on his screen. ''No ID beacon. It was 111 minutes ago that it bounced in, two gigakay out from the sun, four kilokay high. No initial decel apparent. So far it's on a straight-line trajectory for the sun. Assuming it maintains its current speed and heading, it will be passing one of our vessels in—'' He pressed a finger to his implant. ''Wait. *Did* pass, probably.'' He glanced at another screen and touched a button. ''That'd be the *Rio de Janeiro*, Liam

McCorcoran commanding. We can expect datatrans
from *Rio* eighty-three minutes after it sighted the visitor, call it seventy-six minutes from now, give or take.
Still no decel or course change on the stranger.''

Darcy turned to Corzini. ''Is this your simulation?''

''Uh-uh.'' He licked his lips. ''Simming without telling the CO is a court-martial offense, Lee—assuming
you survive the CO's wrath long enough for someone
to bring charges against you. Whatever it is, it's real.''

She touched the red-haired surveillance officer on the
shoulder. ''When will it make its closest approach on
our position?''

''Six and a half hours, if it doesn't brake or bounce.''

''We got here four hours ago.'' She spoke slowly because she was calculating the varying time lags the *Empire Bane* and the stranger faced. ''Our EM radiation
shell had expanded past its bounce-in point before it
showed up. So it knows where all of our ships were at
that instant—it knows where *we* are—and more important, it probably knows *who* we are.''

''Assuming it's a TAAC vessel,'' said Corzini,
''sure, because every fleetship has a unique emissions
pattern, and every flight computer has the patterns in
memory. But what if it's Wayholder?''

''Then the situation could be even worse. Zi, take us
up to threshold speed. With your permission, Admiral.''

Duschevski inclined his head slightly. ''Is wise.''

Corzini touched his implant without taking his gaze
from her face. ''Are we going home?''

''Not just yet. Let's investigate the stranger.''

His eyebrows arched. ''Twenty minutes to threshold
speed.''

The alarm chime sounded again; the surveillance officer said, ''Uh-oh. Either our stranger's just bounced,
or another one's come for tea. Thirty seconds ago it
appeared nine megakay away from us, our height above
the ecliptic, initial trajectory indicates intercept attempt, no decel apparent yet, intercept in seventy-five
seconds—mark!''

Darcy Lee spun to examine the monitors.

Connaught said, "Jesus, Mary, and Joseph! *Rio*'s on its tail."

"So there's only one stranger?"

"I've not decided yet." He pointed to two screens mounted in the bulkhead above him. "Visuals for you. Our own, and a broadcast from *Rio.*"

Darcy Lee looked—and flinched. "That's a Way-holder skirmish control craft." On the third anniversary of the desperate battle off New Napa, she still shuddered as though she had just fled the system. The sweat of fear, of hate, dampened her armpits and the skin between her breasts.

Corzini slipped past her to stand beside Connaught. "A skirk's smaller than a carrier even. We don't need to worry about it."

She tapped Connaught's shoulder. "What the hell is Liam doing?"

The SO said, "Attacking, if you believe my boards."

A wave of pure panic pulsed through her. Had McCorcoran left the skirk alone, it might have passed straight through, letting the Guard quit the system without incident. The impulsive son of a bitch had ruined that chance. But if they could destroy the alien before it called for reinforcements. . . .

"Take it out! Now!"

Corzini raised his hand to his implant.

A smile spread slowly across Duschevski's gaunt face. Though it deepened his wrinkles, it so enlivened his features that he seemed years younger. "Is one thing certain now, Lieutenant—Wayholder tracker is working for carriers as good as for fighters."

She paused, considered that, then asked Connaught, "Have you decided yet whether it's one ship or two?"

"I'd wager one," he said. "There's the similarity of the emission patterns, you see. And *Rio* bounced in as though hotly pursuing, for another. It's a mystery, though, why they let their EM radiation reach us before they made their move . . . which of course means that it might after all be stranger number two we've turned

our lasers on, and the matter won't be a definite thing
unless the first one drops off the screens and the times
check out.''

White light filled the monitors. When they went to
black, Corzini said, ''All gone.''

''Are we still accelerating to threshold?''

''Yes, why? Change your mind?''

''No, no, but—'' The immensity—the impossibility—
of the task ahead nearly crushed her spirit. She clenched
her teeth and took a long slow breath. ''We all have to
be back at base within twenty minutes.''

''Why? We just—''

''Because, unless we got very lucky, that skirk will
be reinforced by two more.''

''So?'' Corzini shrugged.

''So twenty minutes after we attack them, four more
show up, then eight, then a battle control craft.''

His brown eyes narrowed. ''How can you be so
sure?''

''Kajiwara Hiroshi spotted the pattern at New Napa,
and the Wayholder held to it through the whole battle.''
She strode over to Lieutenant Nguyen Trinh, the communications officer. ''Message the *Rio*, tell Liam to
bounce out to a gig and a half and then bounce around
the system clockwise, moving from one ops group to
another, ordering everyone back to base instantly.
Fighters currently off the rack bounce home on their
own. Reassemble at ba— Oh, Jesus Buddha!''

Duschevski narrowed his eyes. ''Lieutenant?''

''They'll track us!''

''Not if we're gone,'' said Corzini.

''You're wrong, Zi. Admiral, if they come into a part
of the system that all our EM radiation hasn't passed
yet, they'll see us bounce. Their tracker will read us.
And they'll follow us home.''

The old man stared at her for a long moment, his
eyes soft with thought. He stroked his chin with the tip
of his index finger. ''Only alternative is remain here and
wait for them, *da*?''

Unable to speak, she nodded.

"If we are doing that, and they attack, and we defend ourselves, they are going reinforce over and over and over until they erase us, *da*?"

She bobbed her head up and down.

"Then recommendation is continuation of original plan. Please, finish issuing your orders. I'll have suggestion for you after."

"A suggestion? Can we use it now?"

"No. Unfortunately." He sighed. "Please, hurry."

"Yes, sir." She turned back to Trinh. "Reassemble at base, and—dammit!—prepare to defend it against a major assault; they must inform base all Guard vessels should start accelerating to threshold speed at once because we're going to need a new place for base. Tell Liam to bounce at one-minute intervals, circle the system twice, and then go home himself."

At that, Duschevski paled. "Lieutenant! According to regulations, a five-minute cooldown between bounces is—"

"Death for our outlying units, Admiral." She straightened to look him in the eye. "We have less than twenty minutes, and nine separate carriers to contact, plus all their individual fighters. The gravpipes can take more stress than the book says they can."

Corzini gaped. "How can you—"

"Run the numbers, Zi. After a sixty-second rest, there's only five chances in twenty thousand a pipe'll blow."

He touched his finger to his implant.

She waited till his lips stopped moving. "As soon as we hit threshold speed, we bounce out to the same distance, and travel in the same direction delivering the same message. We have *got* to get our asses out of here."

Corzini said, "You're right about the odds."

"Thanks for the vote of confidence. How long till threshold?"

Again he queried his implant. "Sixteen minutes."

"Damn! Bounce at *thirty*-second intervals." She spun on her heel to confront Duschevski. "Sir, the *Morocco* stood the strain, and the *Empire Bane* can, too. And we just don't have much choice, sir.''

He glared at her. ''Is my ship at stake.''

''I know, Admiral.'' She spread her hands in a gesture of helplessness. ''But we don't have any alternatives. . . . You said you had a suggestion?''

''Yes.'' He shook himself, once, as though throwing a weight off his back. In the background, Corzini was calling all hands to battle stations. ''If I am understanding correctly, tracker takes hunter to exact same point in space to which hunted bounced.''

''That's correct, sir.''

''*If* gravpipes can take strain of repeated bounces—hypothesis which we seem going to test—then, on future maneuvers, designate random point in space as intermediate rendezvous.''

''Sir?''

''Use forward gravpipes to bounce in. On instant of arrival, flip ship end over end with reaction mass. Immediately use aft pipes to bounce to final destination. Pursuit is going wind up *inside* our EM shell, which is expanding *away* from hunter at speed of light. Their trackers are finding nothing to read.''

''I like that, sir.'' Then she cocked her head. ''Of course, if they knew the time lag, they could jump that many light-seconds ahead of themselves, and get on the outside of the EM shell. . . .''

He ran his finger along the side of his jaw. ''Perhaps two intermediate stages, then. A common rendezvous, and then pilot's choice, so entire series of wave fronts spreads from given point. Might confuse them, *da*?''

''Ye-e-es, yes, it might at that, sir.'' She looked up suddenly, into his brown Slavic eyes. ''Are you trying to distract me, sir?''

''Me, Lieutenant?''

''You, sir.''

''Threshold speed,'' said Corzini in a bored tone.

Duschevski said, ''Just trying to break tension, Lieutenant.''

"Thank you, sir." She patted his shoulder. "You know what to do, Zi."

"Doing it." The displays changed. The message went out. The displays changed again.

In the next four minutes, the *Empire Bane* bounced eight times. All the while, Duschevski stared so intently at the systems status boards that he seemed not to blink.

"We're back to where we started from," said Corzini. "Don't you think the message has gotten through by now?"

She scowled at him. "Two carriers were still more than three light-minutes away. The damn Wayholder are probably in already. If they—"

"Sure and they are here," said Connaught.

"Oh, Jesus Buddha, they sent a battlebox!"

In the screens loomed a battle control craft—a hexahedron twenty-five kilometers high and wide, and twelve deep. Its black struts bristled with lasers. As it decelerated, four skirks launched off its forward face. Each of them appeared to brake slightly, and launch its fighters.

"Lee, got a lot more than two skirks here," said Corzini.

"Sure. They've changed tactics. But—" The *Empire Bane* alone had three or four times the firepower of the battlebox and all its complement; they could handle it easily. But what would the Wayholder reinforce it with? "Connie, what are they doing?"

Connaught looked up. "They're after the *Ontario*. It's accelerating, but won't hit threshold for . . . eleven minutes."

"Zi, bounce us . . . two seconds ahead of the ship closest to Ontow. Then slow us down. Let the battlebox catch up. When it gets in range, shut off all gravpipes, and laser in on its gravity generators."

Corzini relayed her orders, then took his finger off the implant. "Lee, you're crazy."

She just *looked* at him while the *Empire Bane* bounced.

"Shit." He shook his head. "I'm sorry, it's not insubordination, just I don't think—"

"Commo!" said Darcy. The lights dimmed slightly as the *Empire Bane*'s lasers pulsed. "Make sure Ontow knows it's supposed to go home."

"Aye, skipper." Touching a tiny finger to her board, Trinh whispered urgently into a microphone.

The systems status panels began to flicker as damage reports flowed in. A lot of pinpricks, apparently. Nothing to fret about. Over on Weapons, the readouts tallying the number of remaining available targets counted down steadily. Satisfied, Lee turned to Corzini. "Mr. Corzini."

He held up his right hand, palm facing her. "No need to say it. I was wrong. If you'd like to confine me to my quarters, I'll go quietly." He tried a nervous grin.

At the boards, Duschevski said, "Get them!"

Lee stared at Corzini. "Once more and I *will* confine you."

"Thank you."

"Yes!" said Trinh, in a voice much larger than she.

Lee looked over to them. "Connie?"

"The good news," said Connaught, "is that there are no functional enemy left in the system. The bad news is that one fighter bounced out, presumably for home."

"Commo," she said, "has *Ontario* confirmed receipt of its orders?"

Trinh bobbed her head. "They say nine minutes to threshold."

She felt helpless. The *Empire Bane* had already shot past the Ontow. They could make repeated bounces to a point just behind the carrier, and shepherd it until it had fled the system, but that would put even more stress on the gravpipes. Yet until both craft traveled at approximately the same velocity, the fleetship could not pick the carrier up. The same with . . .

"Which other group might not have gotten the word?"

"*Hanoi*," said the SO.

"Take us to where it ought to be, Zi."

"You got it, Lee."

The scenes on the monitors appeared not to shift, but the numbers shivered and came up different. Connaught scanned the surveillance boards. "No sign of them."

"Could we have possibly missed anybody?"

"I'd not think so." His shoulders rose and fell. "At this point, we and *Rio* have been around the system so many times so quickly that our own ghost images pop up just about anywhere we go. The message must have gotten through by now."

"Rio? Is it still in the system?"

Lieutenant Trinh said, "It shouldn't be, because they confirmed two laps and out, but the only way to tell for sure is to go home and see if they're there."

"Not yet. Zi, take us just far enough behind Ontow that we'll be right on their tail when they bounce."

"And scoop them up coming into base?"

"Sure."

They bounced. Then they stood looking at each other, wondering what they would find when they returned to base, until finally Connaught said, *"Ontario's* bounced."

"Home, Zi," Darcy said.

"Home it is."

They began to relax as the sensors located the base, but after only a few minutes Connaught said, "Um . . . Skipper? It's a Wayholder that's coming in, a megakay aft, no decel. A big guy, it is. I think it's a zoner. A warnut. Has the shape of a doughnut with a hole a hundred thirty kay across."

Her heart sank. Hot on her trail roared a war zone control craft—the largest vessel in the Wayholder Empire's navy. It carried sixteen battleboxes, each of which held sixteen skirks, which in turn bore sixteen fighters each. Four thousand ninety-seven enemy ships. And all of them almost within laser range. "Maximum acceleration, Zi. Commo, warn base what's coming at them. Weapons, let's drop some pinwheels aft, cancel as much of the pinwheels' forward momentum as possible. Zi, scramble all ops groups—they're to brake relative to us and form directly to our rear. Commo." She stopped abruptly.

Four concerned faces turned to her.

"Commo. Get me Over Commander Daitaku."

The pale light of power poured out of the hologram, into Room B87Q. Kajiwara Hiroshi bowed. "Mr. Chairman—" He paused to select his words with care. As commander in chief, LeFebvre had the power to charge him with a court-martial offense—and any court-martial the chairman called would surely convict the defendant. "Mr. Chairman, it has come to this one's attention that TAAC Intelligence failed to release vital data analysis at your personal—"

"You speak of the New Dublin chip, no?" said LeFebvre.

"Yes, sir."

LeFebvre leaned back in his chair and laced his fingers across his belly. "The chip that you have given to the army of Longfall?"

Kajiwara inclined his head a few centimeters.

"You have thwarted me, Kajiwara Hiroshi, but me, I am a man of magnanimity." He gave a smile placid on its surface, implacable below. "I will explain to you, just the one time, the rationality of my decision, and I will expect you to observe the spirit of my decisions henceforth." He raised one eyebrow.

It occurred to Kajiwara that if the chairman would not let him die, nor let him leave the Corps, then the chairman had very little hold on him. LeFebvre could hardly disgrace him more than he already was. Nonetheless, he bowed slightly. "This one awaits the chairman's explanation with great interest and attention."

"You walk on the thinnest of the ice, Kajiwara Hiroshi." LeFebvre pursed his lips, then shook his head. "The landing parties of the Wayholder, though heavily armed, are quite small. They are also composed in the entirety of recruits just out of the basic training. If they encounter defenders who have the good idea of what they were likely to do, they might lose.''

''Yes, sir, and a planet would survive—''

''Quiet! Have you noticed, Over Commander, that colonists are in many ways the citizens most militant of the Association? I do not mean that they submit well to military discipline, because they reject it. No, my meaning is that they are quick to take offense, and even quicker to defend themselves.''

''Taming a new world forces them to develop self-reliance, sir.''

''Yes, that is true.'' He lifted one finger and looked to his right; the Gurkha guard on that side saluted, and went out of camera range. ''Yet if they develop the sufficient self-reliance, Kajiwara Hiroshi, they might prove too formidable for the Wayholder recruits. And therefore the Empire might decide to find the other worlds for training exercises. The worlds more mature. The worlds more soft.'' The guard returned bearing a cup and saucer, which he set down on the invisible desktop. LeFebvre nodded, lifted the cup, and took a sip. ''The worlds like Earth, Over Commander. I will not have that. To assure the survival of Earth, it is my responsibility, and I will make sure that it does survive. My policy, therefore, is to withhold all information with the military value from the colonists. We will have the knowledge in reserve for our own moment of need.''

''But, sir, Earth has so many more military personnel—''

''The clerks! The deskbound data-dorkers! The gray-haired, fat-bellied over commanders staining their noses brown as they jockey for that final promotion. My God, Kajiwara, Howland Island could not beat back the junior high school—'' His desk became a ruby slab.

Kajiwara's desk chimed and flashed its silver light.

LeFebvre and Kajiwara leaned forward simultaneously to cut the holo connection. Kajiwara then told his desk to deliver the message.

An agitated voice said, ''Over Commander, the Wayholder ambassador has just stated that the *New Zealand* attacked a Wayholder ship in the Gandhi System. As a result, the Gandhi System has been declared off-limits to the Terran Association for all time. Further, they have traced the *New Zealand* back to the Sagittarian Guard base. They will shortly eliminate the Guard. They demand that no TAAC forces approach within 1.6 parsecs while they do."

Kajiwara blinked. "We are hardly in a position to argue with their demands, are we?" And yet . . . and yet if they did destroy the fleetship, Daitaku would die with it. He, Kajiwara Hiroshi, rightful over commander of Octant Sagittarius, would remain a prisoner of Howland Island until the next clone had reached maturity.

He almost hoped the Guard won. He thought that he, perhaps, could get Daitaku back alive.

"Over Commander, there's a second report, from TAAC Intelligence, that makes things much, much worse. Our recon drones have spotted gravpipes in operation in and around Longfall, gravpipes that do not belong to our forces. Since the planet's entire gravpipe output is supposed to go to TAAC, Intelligence suspects that Longfall might be the new home base of the Sagittarian Guard. And if it is . . ."

"So." Kajiwara closed his eyes. Michael O'Reilly had not listened. Or else O'Reilly's comrades had ignored Kajiwara's warnings. In either case, a good many of Kajiwara Hiroshi's descendants might die horribly in the very near future. "Tell me."

"Yes, Over Commander?"

"Has the chairman been informed of the Wayholder demand?"

"Moments ago, sir."

"Has he responded?"

"Immediately, sir."

"And what was the chairman's response?"

"He acceded to it."

Kajiwara had expected nothing different from Le-Febvre. Once again he wished for a ruler worthy to walk bushido. "You paraphrased the demand for me.

Did the Wayholder state the location of the Guard base?''

"No, sir."

Kajiwara Hiroshi sighed. "Has anyone asked the Wayholder how we are supposed to remain 1.6 parsecs away from a point whose coordinates they have not seen fit to give us?''

"Ah . . . no, sir, apparently not."

"You might suggest to the chairman's office that this be done immediately. If the chairman fears that such a query might be taken as temerity, point out to him the incalculable harm that will occur if the fleets of Octant Sagittarius should happen to be on the scene when the Wayholder attack.''

"Yes, sir. At once."

"Thank you." He shut off his desk. And prayed silently that TAAC Intelligence had made a mistake about Longfall.

"Over Commander Daitaku?"

He turned. A holo of the woman called Darcy Lee stared at him. She looked frightened, which explained why the lights had been dimming. The *New Zealand* must have come under heavy attack. Nothing else would cause a woman like her to show fear. Nonetheless, she seemed in control of herself, and he admired that. "Yes?"

"I don't quite know how to put this, sir. The *Empire Bane* and the Guard are facing a Wayholder war zone control craft. We don't have anyone capable of commanding, not against a force like that. Would you take command for the duration of the battle?''

"No."

She blinked. "Sir, it is obvious that the welfare of the Guard is of no concern to you—"

"False. I would gladly help the Wayholder Empire defeat you."

Her jaw sagged as though he had punched her. It angered him that she should display such weakness—and that her weakness should inspire guilt in him. Then she cleared her throat; she shook her head briefly. "And the shanghaied crew of the *Emp*—the *New Zealand*? Would you gladly see *them* die?"

He shrugged.

"They are TAAC'ers; they are your crew."

"So?"

"Do you deny responsibility for them?"

"As they denied their oath to me, so I deny mine to them."

Her lip curled at that. "Have you no honor, then?"

He closed his eyes. "Kajiwara Hiroshi left his honor at New Napa."

"You are not Kajiwara Hiroshi. You are Daitaku."

"I am his continuation."

"No. You are his second chance."

He took a breath. A deep one. He took it all the way in, all the way to the bottom, and behind his closed eyelids, tears stung. "I wish you had not said that, Lieutenant."

"You will lead us?"

"No."

She closed her eyes and ran her hands through her short black hair in apparent exasperation. He found himself wondering how that hair would feel against his fingers. He concentrated on the featureless orange robot in the corner so that he would not have to acknowledge her distress.

"There is a legend, Over Commander, of the great Kenshin, who warred against Shingen." Opening her eyes, she drew his gaze, swallowed visibly, and went on. "The provinces that Shingen ruled obtained their salt from the Hojo prince. The prince was not at war with Shingen, but wanted to weaken him, so he stopped the sale of salt to Shingen's provinces. Kenshin found this repugnant. 'I do not fight with salt, but with the sword,' he said, and ordered his own people to provide salt to his enemy." She stopped.

He stared at her image. "What has that to do with me?"

"Are you warrior enough to defeat us yourself? Or

will Kajiwara Hiroshi decide, afterwards, that you did your duty by permitting us to fall to the murderers of children?''

''You seek to shame me into saving you.''

''What I seek, Over Commander,'' she said through gritted teeth, ''is to force the Wayholder Empire to pay the highest possible price for Terran lives. If it is right to die here and now, then so be it, but I refuse to be mocked as a fool for not offering Earth's greatest tactician the chance to command.''

As I will be mocked for not taking command. He looked around the module. He did not want to die a prisoner. The woman was right—no, the *women* were right, for had not Kajiwara Hiroshi's mother also quoted the Prince of Mito?

To die now would be to fail.

''I have no choice, it seems.'' He turned away from the cameras and wiped his eyes. ''Enable my controls at once.''

The consoles glowed golden for one long moment, then subsided into a shifting mosaic of white, yellow, and red displays. Lieutenant Lee said, ''Enabled, Over Commander.''

Touching his implant, whose familiar mutter thickened as it tapped into the main databanks for the first time in weeks, he crossed the command module. ''Activate battle command holo.''

The module's fluorescents dimmed; motes of symbolic light flared to brilliance all through the small chamber. He studied the formations carefully. He might *be* a second chance, but if he initiated hostilities incorrectly, he would not *have* one.

How much had the Wayholder Empire learned at New Napa?

How much had *he* learned at New Napa?

He spoke to the Sajjers assembled in the—now—secondary command module. ''We will endure the smaller enemy ships while concentrating on the war zone control craft. Ops groups One through Eight form Strike Force Alpha. Nine through Sixteen, Beta. Seventeen through Twenty-four, Gamma. The rest remain in reserve.'' He touched his implant, obtained the data he needed, and issued instructions to the fleetship's computers.

Then he hurried to the toilet. Certain things were best done before battle. . . .

#Software distributed.#

He spoke to Lee and Duschevski again. "The reserve force will maintain threshold speed on the current heading, and all bounces away from the action will be to the reserve force for reinforcement. Each strike force is to form a circle. The diameter of Alpha's will be 123 kilometers. Beta, 125; Gamma, 127. All onboard computers have been supplied with the requisite tactics. We go—now!''

Alpha Force bounced. The formation materialized parallel to the giant foe, and 320,000 kilometers in front of it. Each fighter dropped two pinwheels. Each carrier dropped four. All ships immediately flipped end-over-end and bounced away, less than one second before the force's brief burst of EM noise—its heat and its signals and the whispery chatter of its onboards—would fall on the warnut like blue-shifted hail.

Beta Force darted, dropped, and departed.

One second later, Gamma Force repeated the same maneuver. Even as Gamma's pinwheels began to unfurl, Alpha's metal spiderwebs tore into the zoner.

Chain met strut at a closing speed of 160,000 kilometers per second. Gigajoules of energy burst loose. Metal, plastic, and ceramic vaporized. Hell lights flared. Pinwheel pieces that met nothing blew silently through the fifty-kilometer length of the warnut in three ten-thousandths of a second.

The Wayholder vessel had sustained, at most, minor structural damage. A million pinwheels woven into one giant ring would not quite cover the warnut's forward edge. . . .

Daitaku assumed that they were beginning to react to the sighting of Alpha. The battleboxes docked with the torus on the forward side of the zoner should be strain-

ing at their moorings as the Wayholder computers
flashed command after command.

Now the *New Zealand* materialized eight thousand
kilometers away. She would speed through the hole in
the torus, her gravity pipes shut down, her lasers aimed
and firing at the zoner's gravity generators.

Ahead of her, in a circle 125 kilometers wide, Beta's
pinwheels chewed through the enemy's intricate girder-
work.

Three ten-thousandths of a second later, the *New Zealand* came out the far side, and Daitaku did not know
if the Wayholder had even noticed her onslaught.

Gamma's pinwheels hit just as eight battleboxes pulled
away from the mother craft.

An eyeblink later, Alpha Force bounced again. Two
fighters exploded because their gravpipes had not quite
smoothed out. The survivors appeared eight thousand
kilometers in front of the battleboxes, ignored them
completely, and raked the main ship's gravity generators with every available laser. By the time the Wayholder computers noticed, Alpha had swept past
unscathed. The Wayholder lost five generators.

The battleboxes began to spit skirks in all directions.

Beta struck as the skirks were clearing the rack. But
Beta flew *toward* the warnut, and the skirks flew *away*
from it, so Beta blurred through the torus untouched.
Untouched by the enemy, that is—three of its fighters
never came out of the bounce.

Gamma followed a tenth of a second behind.

Then the *New Zealand* roared down the middle again.

At T plus six seconds, the Wayholder computers had
discerned a pattern, and had already redirected the zoner's lasers to cover a circle 180 kilometers in diameter
at a point eight thousand kilometers away.

Alpha, Beta, and Gamma dropped pinwheels from
320,000 kilometers instead.

And the Wayholder were shifting the mirrors on their
lasers when the *New Zealand* burned down its middle.

Five cycles. Thirty seconds all told. On the *New Zealand*'s last run the enemy did not fire. Its transmitters

had gone off the air. It had perished. Only its children survived.

Fifty-five TAAC vessels had vaporized due to gravpipe distortion.

Daitaku wiped his brow, and immediately regrouped his forces. Fourteen battleboxes, and most of their attendant skirks and fighters, still filled space with their fury, but to no effect, as long as they lacked nearby targets. "Let all pipes cool for sixty seconds. Then take the battleboxes, Ops groups One and Two together, and so on. The computers will tell you which target is yours. Twenty-nine and Thirty, come back now, we shall need you." He was afraid to take the time to plan a more conservative attack. He expected the enemy fleet to be reinforced soon, and if the Wayholder maintained their pattern of sending twice the strength of the previous detachment, he would confront *two* zoners.

Carriers and fighters coasted while onboards assigned targets and commanders picked tactics. Ops groups coalesced into angry swarms. Blasting skirks and fighters out of the way, they struck the battleboxes. Eliminating the highest link in the chain of command paid off. The Wayholder forces, disorganized, succumbed within two minutes.

"So. We have endured." It did not surprise Daitaku that he still lived. What surprised him was the relief that flooded through him. "Two war zone control craft will arrive soon. The base must move at once."

The Lee woman said, "It's already under way, Over Commander."

He checked the battle command holo. Yes, it did show the motley collection of vessels that composed the Sagittarian base accelerating for the bounce. "Keep the *New Zealand* at threshold speed."

"Aye, aye, sir," said Lee.

"How much time do they need?"

She touched her neck. "Twenty-five minutes to get them all off."

Too much time. If he could liquidate a zoner and all

its complement so quickly, what could two of them do to his wayward sheep?

Sixteen minutes later, it seemed he would find out: two huge ships appeared, one behind the other, half a million kilometers aft of the slowly accelerating base vessels.

Hoping to distract them so the base could flee without being tracked, he told Duschevski and Lee, "We will run the cycle again, beginning with the ship in front. After the destruction of that warnut, we will ignore its small craft and go immediately for the second warnut. We must fully expect to die. Most of us will die. But we shall, I trust, inflict a humiliating defeat on the Wayholder Empire." *And ensure the survival of the Sagittarian Guard,* he thought sourly. "We go on five."

The original kamikaze—the divine wind—drove Mongol fleets to ruin off the coast of Japan. Its heirs sorely bothered the Americans five hundred years later. Its latest incarnation—the *New Zealand*—blew faster and bit harder.

In less than one hundred seconds, Daitaku's plan had turned the two zoners into scrap. The "victory" cost four hundred fighters, six carriers, and 30 percent of the *New Zealand*'s functionality.

The last of the base vessels bounced away. Daitaku's implant relayed the glad news. As the battered strike forces met on the rendezvous trajectory, he gave the order to run.

Twenty-eight Wayholder battle control craft pursued.

Chapter 14

Every light on the control consoles in Command Module Four burned red. Every siren shrieked. Admiral Duschevski, fingers pressed to his implant, roared at the computer to deactivate the audible alarms.

Voices began to drop out of the chorus of doom. Before long, the module rang with silence. Exhaustion rippled over the admiral's thin face; he looked his full 131 years.

Darcy Lee let out her breath and uncovered her ears. Restless, jittery, burning with excess adrenaline, she needed to act—to battle the enemy, to bed Billy W—Jesus Buddha, why did her memory *do* that to her?

She forced herself to study the swirl of activity around her. The command crew moved with such practiced economy that even standing still she felt awkward. That they would prove equally inept at the controls of a Zulu did not comfort her. She wanted to help, but could not. The mere offer might distract them, and a break in their routine could lead to disaster. So she stayed in the corner, back to the bulkhead, and vowed not to get in anyone's way.

Hand on a chair as if to support his weight, Duschevski was turning to the holo of Daitaku. "Your boards are telling you same thing mine are, Over Commander." The words came out tired, raspy. "We can run awhile longer, but damage to another major system is going to shut us down completely."

Anatole Corzini stopped at Darcy Lee's side. Squeezing her shoulder, he put his face too close to hers. "Are you all right?"

"Sure." Giving him a slight frown, she eased out from under his hand. The module seemed to tilt. Problems with the gravity generators? Her heart beat faster. She wiped cold sweat off her forehead, and nodded, more to herself than to him. Shock. She ought to lie down, but she would be damned if she gave Corzini any reason to hover over her. He did too much of that as it was. "Relieved. Dismayed." She gestured to the flashing control panels. "How could the ship take such a pounding?"

"Fleetships are tough." He seemed not to have noticed her reaction to his touch. "Although I confess I had no idea they were *this* tough."

"So how do we fix it? We can't stop at a shipyard, not with the Wayholder hot on our tail."

His look mingled amusement and scorn. "Haven't you ever been in a repair drill before?"

She winced. "Sure. But remember that during a drill, all fighter pilots do is fly cover. You don't think they'd let us get our hands on anything we could break, do you?"

"Good point. On the other hand, you're not a fighter pilot anymore, you're a . . . hmm. What are you? Daitaku commands the fleet. Duschevski's in charge of the *New Zealand*. But they both take orders from you. So that makes you . . ." His eyebrows scrunched together, and he nibbled his upper lip.

He looked so perplexed that she had to smile. "Someone who'd better let them do their jobs, I think."

He considered that a moment, then nodded. "So listen—"

"Don't *you* have a job to do, Zi?"

He brushed his hand past his implant. "I'm ready if they need me."

"When do they start the repairs?"

"They already have." He wore the earnest expression of an economist at a podium. "The main brain started running Program Perfix—as in, a *per*son *fix*es what's broken—as soon as we got hit. Now that everybody's back on the rack, the program should really hit its s-s-stride.''

The stutter abruptly enlightened Darcy Lee. Anatole Corzini wore his pedantry like a mask. Underneath it, he was frightened to the marrow. He talked to keep fear at bay—no, more than that, he *lectured* because the terror made him feel inferior to his shipmates. He had to balance the scales, to prove to himself that while they had bravery, he had brains.

It surprised her to find that she felt truly sorry for him. Not because he was afraid, but because he did not understand they were *all* afraid, or at least all the sane ones were. She looked into his brown eyes. ''Why don't you tell me about Perfix?'' she said gently. ''It's been a long time since my last refresher course.''

He relaxed a little, and brightened a lot. ''The computer prioritizes damage as it occurs. It accesses personnel records to determine the crewmembers most capable of making the most urgent repair, while at the same time it maps their locations through the ship to figure who's closest. It assigns the closest of the most capable to that problem, along with as many assistants as the job demands. Then it does the same for the number-two task. And so on until either all damage sites have been covered, or all crewmembers have been assigned. Simple?''

A voice spoke inside her head: #Lieutenant Darcy Lee, report to Dock One Four Nine Three by Command Module Four for shuttle pilot duty. Software downloaded. Parts and tools on board. Technicians en route.#

Corzini said, ''Lee? Your eyes j-j-just unfocused. Are you all right?''

''Sure.'' So much for calming him down. ''Program Perfix gave me a job, that's all.'' She licked her lips and stepped out of the corner. ''Admiral!''

Duschevski scowled. ''What?''

''I have to go fly a shuttle—''

''So go! Fly!''

She held up a hand. ''Of course, sir. But first—'' she inclined her head to the holo of Daitaku—''if the over commander attempts a bounce to the Cheyenne system, please disable his controls at once.''

Daitaku's dark eyes brightened with anger, as smoke does when flames burn behind it. His jaw worked but no words came out.

#Lieutenant Darcy Lee, report to Dock One Four Nine Three by Command Module Four for shuttle pilot duty. Software downloaded. Parts and tools on board. Technicians boarded and waiting.#

She touched her implant, said ''Coming'' in a whisper, then met the heat of Daitaku's gaze. ''Sincere apologies for any offense, Over Commander, but this ship *must* rendezvous with Guard HQ. Will it?''

His nostrils flared as he drew in a deep breath. He exhaled, inhaled again, and spoke in tones as cold as ice. ''I agreed to command the *New Zealand* in its moment of need, Lieutenant. I have made no other promises.'' He snapped his fingers. The holo dissolved into a shimmer of scarlet dots, which dwindled down to one hot red point and then vanished.

Duschevski looked at her, shook his head, and walked away.

Corzini patted her on the shoulder. ''Well done, Lee! Twenty-eight battleboxes on our tail, and you piss off the one man aboard who might be able to s-s-save our asses. Thanks loads.''

#Lieutenant Darcy Lee, report to Dock One Four Nine Three by Command Module Four for shuttle pilot duty. Software downloaded. Parts and tools on board. Technicians boarded and waiting.#

Finger to her temple, she said, ''Coming,'' then brushed past Corzini without a word.

TAAC Intelligence had pinpointed the Longfall System as the focal point of Guard activity in Octant Sagittarius. Kajiwara Hiroshi's objections to that conclusion were melting like snowbanks in spring, yet he continued stubbornly to search for proof of Longfall's innocence.

It mattered to him that Longfall be exculpated. If the

Guard had originated there, or was based there, then his great-grandson Michael O'Reilly would be heavily involved in it, and Kajiwara bore shame enough without the additional disgrace of a foolish descendant.

Wearily, he massaged his temples. He felt old, worn-out. He had succumbed to emotion. He had abandoned rationality to defend his family, and that disavowed everything he had believed about himself. How could he call himself samurai when he could not look the truth in the eye?

Even so, he understood himself. Did not bushido say that "to know is to act"? Admitting that he knew would force him to act, and he did not want to do that just yet.

In Michael's defense, no competent surveillance officer could miss the emissions patterns of a fleetship, but no one had sighted the *New Zealand* in the Longfall.

More tellingly, the Wayholder claimed they were attacking the Guard base. Had they invaded the Longfall, the colonists would have reported it, and begged for military assistance. Neither report nor plea had arrived.

Therefore, the Guard base lay elsewhere.

Unfortunately, that did not exonerate Michael. Colonists might deserve their reputation for bullheadedness, but only holocoms perpetuated the myth of colonial stupidity. Longfallers would know that basing the Guard in their system—as opposed to directing it from there—equated to painting a bull's-eye on the planet.

With great reluctance, he scanned again the initial results of the Longfall investigation, written by an admirably terse Captain Mueller:

1 July 2351

(1) Output of Longfall gravpipe factory, as reported to TAAC: 2000 units/month.
(2) Actual output of Longfall gravpipe factory, as recorded by surveillance equipment: 2100 units/month.
(3) Discrepancy: 100 units/month.
(4) Output of Longfall fighter fuselage assembly

    plant, as reported to TAAC: 1240 units/month.

(5) Actual output of Longfall fighter fuselage assembly plant, as recorded by surveillance equipment: 1340 units/month.

(6) Discrepancy: 100 unit/month.

(7) Conclusion: Longfall is adding 100 gravpipe fighters a month to unregistered forces (Longfall Astro Corps or Guard or both).

(8) Supporting evidence:
    (a) Detection of unidentified gravpipe wavefronts. (Appendix 1: Sensor Readings from the Longfall System)
    (b) Imposition of Universal Military Service. (Appendix 2: The Creation and Operation of the Longfall Ready Reserve)
    (c) Adoption of resistance (if and when) as formal government policy. (Appendix 3: Transcripts of Longfall Council Proceedings)

(9) Recommendations:
    (a) Seizure of gravpipe factory and fuselage assembly plant by TAAC forces. (Appendix 4: Surgical Seizure—A Tactical Outline)
    (b) Subsequent operation of factory and plant by TAAC forces (Appendix 5: Military as Manufacturer)
    (c) Disarmament of LAC by TAAC forces. (Appendix 6: Enforced Demobilization—A Plan)
    (d) Arrest and confinement of Longfall public opinion leaders. (Appendix 7: Snuffing the Spark)

Kajiwara stared at the white glow spilling from the star coral case. He admired the citizens of Longfall. Though skeptical of their chances for survival should the Wayholder Empire attack, he respected their re-

solve. He understood their refusal to submit meekly to
the demands of interstellar politics. But . . .

On a personal level, they had requested his advice
and assistance, which he had given gladly. Then they
had ignored his advice. More, they had done exactly
what he had told them not to do. That showed contempt. It hurt. He owed Longfall, and Michael, no further consideration.

Professionally, Kajiwara Hiroshi had sworn to defend
not just the worlds of Octant Sagittarius, but of the entire Terran Association. He did not dare allow one planet
to jeopardize all the rest.

Perhaps the time had come to admit that he knew.

Twenty-eight Wayholder battle control craft, strung
out like obsidian chunks on a chain, chased *New Zealand* through the dark between two yellow stars. The
nearest battlebox ran 160 kilokay aft—almost close
enough for its lasers to singe.

Still smarting from the Lee woman's outrageous behavior, Daitaku paced Command Module Five. It upset
him that he could not put the scene out of his mind. He
should have been concentrating on tactics, but every
time he began to evaluate scenarios, her words "please
disable his controls at once" echoed through his head.

He hungered to bounce out of danger. Were he the
enemy commander, he would already have closed in on
his crippled prey, and probably dispatched it by now.
He expected a wall of ships to appear in front of the
New Zealand at any moment; it puzzled him that they
were taking so long to arrive.

How could she have tied his hands like this? Granted,
she had only forbidden a bounce to Cheyenne, but if
Duschevski misinterpreted and killed his controls at the
wrong moment—or if, to avert that possibility, he had
to take the time to clear his movements with Duschevski
first—he could lose the ship and all her crew.

Perhaps the Wayholder had chosen to run him to
death. Certainly he could not hold the lead forever. Interstellar dust was slowing the ravaged fleetship; it had

to keep accelerating just to maintain threshold speed. Battered nearly beyond belief, the *New Zealand* could not continue much longer before something, somewhere, burned out.

He sniffed the air. Something had already burned. Insulation, perhaps, charred by a short circuit. A small one, though, with its odor faint and fading fast, so he would not have to devise a scenario that included abandoning his module.

Apparently she had been devising scenarios, too. He stopped pacing, and stared through the battle command holo without seeing it. He tried to put himself in her place, tried to view the situation through the eyes of a fighter pilot entrusted with a command but unused to it. He grunted softly. At her age he might have been as tactless. Would he have been as foresighted? He could not say for sure. Perhaps he should respect her rather than resent her.

Perhaps he should get them out of this mess. He wanted to bounce, but the last one, instead of widening the gap, had narrowed it. He had gone into the bounce 760 kilokay ahead of the Wayholder—and lost 600 of them. Why?

His implant proved no help. He opened the line to Command Module Four and asked Duschevski.

"Is function of Wayholder tracking device, Over Commander. Pursuer bounces to exact same point to which target has gone, arriving there as long after target did as pursuer's trackers took to notice target's disappearance and perform appropriate calculations. So last time we bounce, they see we're gone two seconds after we go, they bounce, here they are now, two seconds' travel time behind."

Of course. "Thank you, Admiral." He closed the line, and made a sound of disappointment. He should have deduced that for himself. Then he shook his head. The source of an answer did not matter, so long as it came correctly, and on demand.

So. If he bounced now, how close behind would the Wayholder be?

The computer said, #0.421 seconds; 67,360 kilometers.#

They would cut his lead to less than half a second. And another bounce after that would narrow the gap even more. Until finally they would be on him, despite Zeno's paradox of Achilles and the tortoise. How could he possibly shake them?

He asked the computer how long the repairs would take.

#78 percent functionality within forty-eight hours. 92 percent within seventy-two hours. 100 percent requires drydock.#

The gravpipes could not run for three days straight. Period. Even if they could, and even if the Wayholder let them run through the interstellar night without ever driving in for the kill, 92 percent functionality would not permit one fleetship to defeat twenty-eight battleboxes.

Half a second behind . . .

He snapped his fingers. A few months ago, he-Kajiwara had read a report from the lab teams analyzing the Wayholder derelicts; the report claimed the enemy's onboards did not check bounce coordinates against a table of known hazards.

The Wayholder would follow him to any point in space. Arriving there, next time, 0.421 seconds after he did.

New Napa. How utterly appropriate. Destroying a force nearly fifteen times stronger than his own would not erase the dishonor of having been relieved of command, but it would cast serious doubt on the competence of those who had lost confidence in him. Smashing that force on the shoals of New Napa itself would only drive home his point.

A few succinct queries to his implant drew the data he needed. He gave the onboards their orders.

#Prohibited destination. Too close to planet.#

"Prohibition overridden."

#Acknowledged.#

He caught his breath. He got Duschevski on line. "Admiral, we bounce to New Napa—now!"

The planet appeared off the port bow, impossibly huge, impossibly near, lumbering along at a stately thirty-one kilometers per second. The *New Zealand* dashed across its orbital path—and for one-ninth of a second, blazed through the fringes of its ionosphere.

Less than half a second later, a battlebox materialized—thirteen kilometers deeper in the atmosphere. It emerged a glowing hulk. A like time after that, the next reached space as a mass of orange and yellow sparks. The following twenty-six did not come out of the atmosphere at all. They simply vaporized.

Daitaku shuddered. He told Duschevski, "To the rendezvous," and wondered, despite himself, whether Lieutenant Lee would see the victory as his, or hers.

Chapter 15

Palms flat on the shuttle's command console, Darcy Lee stared numbly at the monitor. The five spacesuited technicians she had ferried to the bank of lasers had just become glowing red clouds. On the panel before her, five life-support-system monitor lights burned scarlet; the readout beneath each read, CATASTROPHIC SUIT FAILURE.

She touched her implant. "Replay from just before the suits failed," she told the shuttle's onboards. "Super slow motion. Visuals only." She did not want jagged echoes of agony lingering in her mind.

The monitor fuzzed over, then sharpened as the onboards began to replay the recording.

Against a star-pierced ebony backdrop, a tech shone her headlamp beam on a box at the junction of six girders.

Blackness blinked into bright blue and white.

The tech's spacesuit lost its shine, and then its definition. It swelled. Gauntleted fingers blurred into each other; legs melted together. The tech and her tools and the girders all blushed. As the red brightened, the tech dissolved into a column of cherry smoke.

"Oh Jesus Buddha . . ." Darcy Lee pressed her implant again. "Subject, location; query, where are we?"

#New Napa System.#

She rubbed her eyes. Phosphenes flared the same red as the wraith outside. She yanked her fingers away and jabbed a comm-link button. "Come in, bridge. This is Lee."

230

"Z-Z-Zi here, Lee. Go ahead."

"Did we just go through atmosphere?"

"Yes. S-s-skimmed the top of New Napa's atmosphere. Overloaded the dustbroom for a sec. Lotta damage. The Wayholder followed us in. They bit deeper—they're gone. All twenty-eight of 'em."

"All of them?"

"Yeah. Incinerated to a crisp. One helluva fireworks show . . . a s-s-shame no one was on the ground to see it."

At the reminder, she gritted her teeth. And hoped that New Napa's air had cremated some of the aliens who had once spilled blood on its soil. Or on Hsing P'ing's soil. But twenty-eight battleboxes, zap! And all their skirks and fighters and shuttles and landing forces . . . they deserved it, the bastards. She wished they had died more slowly. "Zi, we lost five technicians."

"How?"

"They were on the girders when we hit air."

"Oh, shit! Do you have a fix on their positions?"

"No joy in that, Zi." Calmly at first, because five techs for some fifty thousand aliens seemed a good trade, she said, "At threshold speed, an air molecule cuts through you like a laser beam. We hit enough air to—" She stopped because now the acids of nausea were biting the back of her throat. "Oh, Jesus Buddha, Zi, it's like they were forced through a sieve, but they're still here. Just floating in position, puffing out, getting fainter and oh, damn, Zi, I can see a star through one of them."

"Oh my God."

"Tell Daitaku." She tried to find professional dispassion, but could not. "Tell him for Buddha's sake to warn us if he's going to pull that kind of stunt again."

"Will do, Lee." Corzini's voice shook. "Don't worry about a replay right n-n-now, though. That gas pass cut us to eighteen percent functional. I hope you take well to fatigue blocking. The Admiral says nobody sleeps until we're bounce-capable again."

"That makes sense. How long—"

#Lieutenant Darcy Lee, return to Dock One Four
Nine Three by Command Module Four for further shuttle pilot duty. Software downloading. Parts, tools, and
technicians waiting at gate.#

"Lee? Lee? Are you—"

"I'm fine, Zi. Just Program Perfix giving me another
assignment. On my way back now."

"Oh."

"Later, Zi."

She checked the monitor one last time. The five
corpses had expanded into even greater evanescence,
but still glowed as they radiated back the energy they
had absorbed. No honor guard could bury those five.
They would have to spread their own ashes through
space. She saluted them.

Putting the controls on automatic, she let the onboards guide the shuttle through the maze of struts and
girders to the dock. The running lights of other shuttles
shone all around her as the fleetship fought to heal itself
before the Wayholder found it. Eighteen percent functional. If a skirk came along at that moment, the *Empire
Bane* would die.

No, not the *Empire Bane*, but the *New Zealand*. An
ironic smile twisted her lips. With Daitaku in command, it was, truly, a different ship altogether. And a
very dangerous ship, to the Wayholder Empire.

The dock loomed before the shuttle; the onboards requested permission to mate with it.

"Sure," she said absently, her mind on the matter of
Daitaku. She *must* recruit him to the Sagittarian Guard.
They needed a leader like him.

The meditation exercises were neither calming Kajiwara Hiroshi's impatience nor easing his dread. He kept
listening for his desk chime; he kept glancing away from
the flame to see if any new message lights had come
on. Tension forged a steel bow from the muscles atop
his shoulders. His heart pounded, and he could not slow
his breathing down.

At last he gave it up. Perhaps the old Zen masters

would have done better, but he doubted it. Had they
been waiting to learn whether or not their families had
triggered the extermination of the human race, they too
would have found concentration almost impossible.

Extinguishing the candle, he returned it to the cupboard, hung the hapi on its hook, and went to his chair.
He touched the desk.

The holo cube flashed the image of a young woman
wearing the uniform of TAAC Intelligence. She was
bent over her desktop, apparently reading something on
its display screen.

"Lieutenant," said Kajiwara.

She looked into the cameras. She had short brown
hair, enough freckles for two people, and the name
"Roddle" on her badge. "Yes, Over Commander?"

"Have the Wayholder provided the coordinates of the
prohibited area yet, Lieutenant Roddle?"

"No, sir." She held up a finger, leaned to her left,
and inspected something on a secondary screen. "We
have no report on whether or not the chairman's office
has asked for them, sir."

"Inquire, please. It has been two hours."

"Yes, sir." She reached for her holo's controls.

"Before you do that, have we received any word from
Longfall about Wayholder activity in that system?" He
held his breath.

"No, sir," she said. "No word at all."

He inclined his head, forcing his joy to stay within,
forbidding it to touch his cheeks, his lips, or even his
eyes. "Thank you, Lieutenant."

"My pleasure, sir."

He switched off the holo and swiveled his chair to the
right, so he could stare at the tray of star coral. That
his great-grandson possessed the insight to realize that
Kajiwara would treasure such delicacy of form, pattern,
and color almost swayed him, almost convinced him
that he did not really know what he thought he knew.

But he did know, and thus he must act.

He swiveled back and slapped his desk. Abu Beri's

round face blinked out of the holo cube. "Good afternoon, Commander Beri."

"Yes, Over Commander, what can I do for you?"

"You have certainly read Captain Mueller's report, Commander."

Beri nodded. "Of course."

"Then you will understand why I wish to speak to Michael O'Reilly—of Longfall—immediately."

Beri's brown eyes narrowed in thought. "Your grandson, is he not, sir?"

"My great-grandson, yes."

Hesitating, Beri seemed to pick his words with care. "Do you think he—"

"I wish to question him about precisely that, Commander. Now if you would be so kind as to bring him to Howland Island—"

"Of course, Over Commander. How soon do you want him?"

"I said immediately."

"Yes, sir." He pressed his finger to the black hair above his implant, then tapped his desk. The cube swallowed his image. It went dark.

Kajiwara let his attention drift back to the white luminescence of the star coral. Was it wise to pick up O'Reilly? Could he really reason with his great-grandson better in person than through the available media?

He was not optimistic, but he was determined. If, through this small action, he could convince Michael O'Reilly of the wrongness of Longfall's plans, then he would never have to take greater, more terrible action.

Daitaku stood in the center of his command module, right hand holding his left wrist behind his back. The air still smelled of burned insulation, a smell which the ventilators would not soon remove, as they ran at half power or less. The light had dimmed to twilight levels. A most romantic setting, were he not alone. He inhaled through clenched teeth.

The orange robot nurse made a questioning sound.

Daitaku shook his head slowly. "I am just thinking."

The absurdity of his stunt still unnerved him.

Five technicians, lost in an instant. Granted, they fought for the Guard, which he had been ordered to eliminate, but he needed them. They kept the *New Zealand* running. He could hardly put down their rebellion if the Wayholder destroyed the fleetship first.

Next time he would need better tactics. A black hole, perhaps. A bounce to the appropriate distance outside its event horizon would place the pursuit inextricably inside the horizon . . . not all, though, not if he fled a number of enemy vessels, unless the black hole was truly immense.

A star? Too unpredictable, even the familiar yellow ones.

A gas giant? But they had so much debris around them.

An airless planet might be better. Something on the scale of Mercury. If he skimmed its mountaintops, practically grazing them . . .

He frowned. The hunters would materialize *inside* the planet. The explosion would never reach the *New Zealand*, which would be moving away at threshold speed, but the mining conglomerates that owned the planet would object strenuously to his destroying their expensive extraction equipment . . . although perhaps not to his pulverizing the planet itself.

The black hole offered elegance, though. The navcomp had millions on file, and could locate any of them instantly, to within ten or twenty meters. Still, the notion of dancing on the rim of an infinite pit disturbed him. No. He forced himself to be honest. The notion terrified him. He would not try it unless circumstances forced it.

Daitaku cocked his head and stared hard at the bulkhead. It looked incomplete without the tray of star coral. Another idea came to him then, an idea based on an antimatter torpedo with a timed fuse.

The distance between predator and prey determined

how much time would pass between the fleetship's bounce and the Wayholder's. Call it Time T.

Let the Fleetship bounce to Point A, adopting any trajectory, then immediately to Point B, T seconds' travel at threshold speed away from A, oriented in exactly the opposite direction. At Point B the fleetship drops the torpedo, which inertia will carry to Point A.

Hastily, the fleetship bounces well out of the way. Once it has, the antimatter disperses in a deadly cloud.

The first Wayholder pursuer would materialize at Point A just as the expanding sphere of antimatter arrived there.

Mass would transmute to energy in an insanely violent explosion, one more than powerful enough to demolish the enemy, even a warnut. It would vaporize a great deal of the vessel, and probably exert enough force to cancel the inertia of the rest of the vessel's fragments. Pieces as large as an ocean liner would hang motionless in space—and then the next Wayholder would bounce into the cloud of death.

Also traveling at threshold speed, it would scorch itself on the superhot metallic vapor. Then it would collide with the solid fragments, sweeping them out of the bounce area but gutting itself further, and losing even more velocity in the transfer of kinetic energy. The third craft would appear at full speed. Unable to decelerate quickly enough, it would ram the second from behind.

As would all the rest. Even those that survived collision could not bounce—the series of rear-end impacts would have jammed what remained of each ship's framework into the one before and the one behind.

The fleetship could then return to the scene, and flash past the long daisy chain of wreckage, firing as many antimatter torpedoes as time would permit. The Wayholder would be too crippled to defend themselves.

When the *New Zealand* next bounced out, no one would follow. . . .

Daitaku smiled. Humanity could defeat the Wayholder Empire after all. It would mean adopting a hit-

and-run-and-trap style of warfare utterly foreign to TAAC, which in previous engagements had always had both the quantitative and the qualitative advantages, but it would work.

He had to let Kajiwara Hiroshi know about this at once.

Chapter 16

As she stepped into the cool, crisp brightness of Command Module Four, Darcy Lee kneaded the small of her back with both hands. Fatigue blockers kept pain at bay, but twelve hours in the pilot's seat, shuttling technicians from one damage site to another, had left her spine so stiff she could hardly walk upright.

Granted that the onboards had done 99.9 percent of the work, she had done all of the worrying. The computers had not been running on adrenaline and Over-Time™, twitching at every new blip on the screens, and praying that the crews would repair the *New Zealand* before the Wayholder found it. Nor, presumably, had tension frozen their every major and minor muscle group.

From his post by the control panels, Anatole Corzini began to wave, then used the hand to cover his mouth as he yawned. He pushed himself out of his chair and walked over to her. Dark circles underpouched his bloodshot brown eyes. "Hey, Lee. You look like you could use a back rub." He tried to smile, but succumbed to another yawn instead.

"And you could use a shot of OT."

"Makes me giddy. Then I throw up. And I'd hate to do that around you. I'll bet you need a cup of coffee."

She wished that for just once he would keep his distance. She liked him well enough, but no more than she liked anyone else in the command crew, and his constant hovering had begun to get on her nerves. At least he seemed to have mastered his fear. "What I need is to hear that we're functional enough to get out of here."

He shook his head slowly. "Eighteen point two percent, that's all."

"What?" She frowned at the status boards against the left bulkhead. "Why so slow? That's not much better than when we started."

"It's a big ship! It took some major hits during the battle, and then the gas pass scraped it raw. Serious damage takes time to repair, Lee. And for obvious reasons, we start with power and life-support systems."

"Sure, but—"

"Further, in case you haven't noticed, we're still on Red Alert—all hands remain at battle stations." He jerked his thumb at the consoles.

"Why," she said wearily, "are we still on Red Alert?"

"A precaution against being taken by surprise by the Wayholder?"

"That's absurd!"

"You don't think they could jump us?"

"Sure, sure, they *could*, if they knew where we were, but it's been twelve hours since Daitaku burned them, and we've traveled three or four billion kilometers since then. Jesus Buddha, we're practically out of the New Napa. How are they going to find us?"

Corzini shrugged. "By spotting our EM emissions."

"Oh, right." Her last dose of OverTime™ must be wearing off. Fretful fatigue tripped a pulse of pain in her right temple. Squinting, rubbing that temple with the fingers of her right hand, she raised her voice. "Admiral Duschevski! Could we bounce now if we had to?"

The old man, gaunter than ever from his own vigil, raised one eyebrow and twisted his lips. "We could try," he said after a moment. "Is very dubious proposition, though. If I set odds, I will be giving us sixty percent chance of bouncing out . . . and perhaps thirty-five percent chance that we will actually be getting to selected destination. In other words, Lieutenant Lee, Leo Duschevski will not be giving order to bounce."

"Thank you, sir." Her eyes wanted to slip shut; she stopped resisting them so she could think.

The *New Zealand* coasted through the dark outskirts of the New Napa system at nearly threshold speed, with all hands manning battle stations against the possibility of attack. At 18.2 percent functionality, it might have the resources to fight off a skirmish control craft—if it also had a lot of luck.

She forced her eyes open again. Corzini had moved closer in the interim. Annoyance flared quick and hot. He made her feel so damn *at risk*. An exhausted, not-quite-controllable portion of her mind wondered if butterflies felt like this when she pursued them with her net. After all, she kept trying to sneak up on them, in order to catch and mount them. . . . She must have given him a strange look, because he took an immediate step back. "We have to stand down, put everybody on repair duty, and get this ship fixed *right now.*"

"I agree, but—" he spread his hands—"I'm not exactly on top of the chain of command here, Lee."

She stepped past him and approached Duschevski. "Admiral?"

"Is exactly how I feel, what you have just said."

"So—" She gestured to the controls."

The admiral shook his head. "Is responsibility of Over Commander Daitaku, who is commanding entire fleet."

Both officers looked expectantly at her.

After a moment, she got it. As ranking representative of the Guard, she was in nominal command of Daikatu. "I'll talk to him. Can you raise him on the holo?"

Corzini turned his head to the console. "Lieutenant Trinh—"

Before the young communications officer could respond, a new light flashed rhythmically on the board.

Darcy Lee pointed to it. "What's that?"

Corzini stroked his chin. "Daitaku's just launched a SitUp capsule. I wonder why."

"Oh, Jesus Buddha," she said in a whisper. "Admiral! Disable the Over Commander's boards *immediately.* Zi, get us on a new heading—*any* new heading! Commo, order that SitUp to self-destruct."

Trinh touched a button, studied the dials, then jabbed the button repeatedly. After a moment she shook her head. "Sorry, Lieutenant. It's ignoring the command."

"Wonderful." She took a deep breath. "Friends, if that SitUp contains the message that I think it contains, every damn fleet in Octant Sagittarius is going to be paying us a call forty minutes from now. Anybody have any ideas?"

Kajiwara looked up as the door to Room B87Q opened.

Sergeant Redstar ducked his head and entered. "Visitors, sir." Straightening, he came to attention beside the door.

Michael O'Reilly came into the room with Abu Beri hard on his heels. Beri stopped and saluted. "Your great-grandson, Over Commander, as requested."

Kajiwara said, "Thank you, Commander. If you'll wait outside, please? Michael, please, be seated, Sergeant—?"

Redstar nodded, and glided into the far corner, his face impassive, his eyes alight.

O'Reilly grasped the back of a chair and leaned on it. The stance gave the short, burly man an air of immovability. "What's going on here, Great Gramps?"

"Please, sit." He pointed to the chair. "Coffee?"

"No." He narrowed his green eyes to slits, an effect enhanced by the epicanthic fold bestowed on him by his Asian forebears. "I won't sit. I don't want coffee." Exasperation sharpened his tone, tautened his gestures. "I want to know what the hell's going on."

"Tea, perhaps?" He touched the chrome circle on his desk and ordered a pot for himself. "Or some other beverage; we are adequately provisioned here on Howland Island."

"Dammit, Double-Gee! All I want is answers. A squad of uniformed goons snatched me out of bed and threw me on a military shuttle. Nobody explained *nothing.*"

Kajiwara let his shoulders rise and fall. "Actually,

Michael, we also desire answers.'' Steepling his fingers, he sought to achieve a self-control devoid of emotion, a calm that would well up and out from his center to impose itself on his descendant. "Answers from you.''

"Christ, what's wrong with the mails?''

"Their security leaves something to be desired.''

O'Reilly jerked his head at Redstar. "Yeah? What about him? Is he deaf?''

"No. Sergeant Redstar is loyal.''

O'Reilly's nostrils flared. "You're insinuating something about *my* loyalty. What?''

Kajiwara blinked. Tea arrived. "Excuse me, please.'' He lifted the teapot's glazed lid and glanced inside to get an idea of how long it should steep. The water was nearly transparent. A few minutes, then. He sighed. "Michael, TAAC Intelligence maintains that Longfall is attempting to develop its own space fleet.''

O'Reilly set his jaw and said nothing.

"Surveillance suggests that your factories are producing one hundred more gravpipes and fuselages each month than your records acknowledge.''

Now O'Reilly scowled. "Those are Kaohsiuing Gravpipe Limited's factories, not Longfall's.''

"Never mind who owns them. Are the reports true?''

The younger man merely shrugged.

"Michael, I speak not to you, but through you, to the government of Longfall. Your planet is not permitted to have a space force.''

O'Reilly gave an unpleasant smile. "Since we're keeping this impersonal, the government of Longfall informs the Terran Association that it will not permit the Wayholder Empire to destroy it.''

The sadness of certainty grew in his soul. "Michael, did I not advise you to strengthen your army?''

"We have. But why should we let the Wayholder land unopposed?'' His knuckles whitened. The chairback creaked. "Why shouldn't we burn them when they enter the system? Why should we *wait* for them to get down on the surface—so they can slaughter more children?''

"If you attack them in space you're doomed, you—"

"From space they can do to Longfall what you did to New Napa!"

Kajiwara stood because if he sat any longer he would explode. "They will not."

"Bullshit! If they want the damn planet—"

"They do not."

#Classified,# said Kajiwara's implant.

"Fine, then they want us *off* the damn planet—"

"Michael—" He made his voice as soft, as reasonable, as *convincing*, as he possibly could. "I assure you, they do not."

#Classified.#

"How the *hell* do you know that?"

"Because—"

#Classified.#

"Because *what*?"

"Michael—" The boy's emotions ran too high; Kajiwara had to pause lest his great-grandson's anger swamp his own small preserve of calm. He lifted the lid on the teapot. Done. He removed the perforated silver ball that held the tea leaves. Carefully, almost ceremonially, he poured a cup "Michael, they invade in order to—"

#Classified!#

A needle of pain flared in his skull. Trying to ignore it, he took a sip of tea. "If you defeat their ground forces, they will depart. If you attack their space vessels, they will reinforce again, and again, and again, until they have crushed you."

"How can you feed me such garbage? It's *me*, Great-Gramps, Michael O'Reilly!"

"Who can profess to understand their motives? Consider, though, the hypothesis that the Wayholder Empire has a greater need for spaceships than for combat troops. TAAC does not know whether this is due to a shortage of ships or to a surplus of soldiers. What TAAC does know—"

#Classified!#

"What?"

The pain faded more slowly this time. He took a shallow breath, then a deeper one. It infuriated him that by silencing him the implant's operating system might cause the very tragedy it was designed to prevent. "Michael, defeat them on land and you will survive. Attack them—"

"Holding the high ground is a basic military tactic, Double-Gee, and—"

"You speak to me of basic military tactics?"

"I do." His green eyes blazed.

The insult lodged in Kajiwara's skin like a barbed hook. "To defend the heights against attack from below is easy. To sweep down from the heights to attack a force massed at the base of the heights is also easy. But if the attacker must descend to the base and then cross level territory, he has forfeited all his advantages, and weakened himself by tiring his troops. Apparently, the tacticians of Longfall have such faith in their genius that they prefer to fight the enemy where he is strongest, rather than where he is weakest. I would follow developments with the greatest of professional interest were the lives of my great-great-grandchildren not at stake!"

The door opened. Redstar moved, then stopped as Beri stepped inside. "Apologies, sir. A message from Over Commander Daitaku. Your eyes only."

Kajiwara made a face. "Return this fool to the family which will die because of his foolishness."

Beri said, "Yes, sir. Mr. O'Reilly?"

O'Reilly spun and marched out, his shoulders square, his back so stiff he nearly quivered.

So. Once more I have failed. Depression settled onto him like a yoke. With an effort, he set it to one side, knowing he could—and would—pick it up at every available opportunity.

He touched a white panel on his desktop. Daitaku's message, decoded by electronics keyed to Kajiwara's finger- and voiceprints, appeared on the surface of the desk, silver on emerald. After changing the colors to a more readable combination, he skimmed the document.

Then he frowned. Daitaku had discovered two ways

to destroy a pursuing enemy. Valuable. Perhaps crucial. But nowhere did the clone mention the location of either the *New Zealand* or the Guard base.

Kajiwara stroked the slick desktop with an idle finger. The message raised unsettling questions. For example: Was it true?

Obviously the rebels had censored the report prior to transmission—why else did it not contain the data TAAC needed to recapture the fleetship? But had Daitaku himself actually written this? Or had the rebels forged it in its entirety?

If it were true, it would give him an enormous advantage in his next encounter with the aliens. Were it false, and were he to adopt its tactics in the event of an attack, the entire Terran Association would fall.

He wanted to believe it. But why were the Wayholder so easily gulled? Why did they leap without looking? No Terran of any experience would pursue so blindly. No Terran *could,* unless he had first rewritten his onboards' software.

Could it be that Wayholder commanders lacked experience? Could it be a blindness in their tactical perspective? Or could it be that they and their systems were optimized to track and destroy invading Korrin regardless of the danger?

That last thought gave him some unease. A willingness to defend the Empire at whatever cost beat in the heart of every samurai. Could these alien monsters have their own version of bushido?

In any event, Kajiwara's commanders needed to know of this at once. Just in case they— He froze. If he told his forces of Daitaku's discovery, would it seep back to the Wayholder Empire?

Yes, it surely would, if the politicians learned of it.

He would have to hold the information in reserve, ready to be communicated the moment hostilities broke out, but not until then. If the Terran Association and the Wayholder Empire ever went to war, TAAC would need every advantage it could possibly find.

The desktop chimed; a disembodied voice said, ''The

chairman of the board wishes to speak to you at once, Over Commander.''

He grumbled to himself, but not to the voice. ''Coming on line now.''

What the hell does he want?

The holo formed. LeFebvre's image flashed a ghastly smile. ''You find yourself in the interesting position, Over Commander.''

''How do you mean, sir?''

''The reports reaching my desk insist that the clone of yours has gone over to the pirates. Another series of reports maintains that one of your descendants seems to be engaging in the activities that could be considered the prelude to the armed revolution.''

''Sir—''

''The question that must be answered, Over Commander, is this: Just how loyal to the Terran Association are *you*?''

Daitaku paced the length of Command Module Five, sidestepping the orange robot, struggling with his own soul. TAAC had entrusted the fleetship *New Zealand* to him, and charged him with the responsibility of smashing the Guard. Then the rebels had stolen the fleetship from under his very nose, and blundered into a situation in which it and all its crew could have—should have—been destroyed.

He had, therefore, agreed to direct the skirmish against the Wayholder in order to preserve the tool he needed to put down the rebellion, and, at the same time, to protect his own honor.

Now his command consoles no longer functioned. He had, once again, lost the fleetship, without which he could not extirpate the Guard. Had he any honor left?

He had saved a TAAC fleetship from certain destruction.

He had saved rebel lives.

He had wreaked astonishing destruction upon the Association's true enemy, and in the process defined tac-

tics that would strengthen the Association on the field
of battle.

He had kept the Wayholder from crushing the
Guard. . . .

Yet he could not have done the one without the other.
And he would not have had the opportunity to do either
if Darcy Lee had not given him the chance to die with
honor. How very odd that the Sajjers seemed to understand honor, while TAAC Command did not.

Oh, it claimed that it did. But consider the way TAAC
had abused Kajiwara's honor during the battle of New
Napa. Consider the Association's abandonment of a
hundred worlds, of ten billion people.

He reminded himself that he was samurai, pledged to
his lord, capable of understanding that one must be prepared to accept small defeats if those are the required
costs of the greater victory. But *were* they actually required, or had Pierre LeFebvre merely succumbed to
cowardice?

And why had he not told Kajiwara where to find him?

Chapter 17

To Darcy Lee, the command module lights burned too strongly for someone under the synergistic influences of anxiety and OverTime™. Brilliance filled the small cabin, leaving no room for friendly shadows. Fluorescence bleached already pallid faces. Relentless lumenfall gave the surface of the control console the sort of greasy shine that warned her not to touch, and to wash well afterward if she did.

She ran her fingers through her hair. They came away damp with sweat. She wiped them on her pants. Just a few more minutes, and the fatigue blocker's side effects would fade away. "Commo, is he answering yet?"

Trinh touched a spot on the comm panel, which glared bright red when she lifted her finger. "No, Lieutenant, not yet."

Sickness hollowed the pit of Lee's stomach. Why had Daitaku severed communications with the rest of the ship? "Admiral, assume he told them where we are and what kind of shape we're in—would they come after us?"

"Like wolves after sick rabbit they come."

"What would they send?"

He shrugged. "If *I* am Over Commander, Octant Sagittarius, I am sending two, maybe three fleetships. Just in case. I would think is maybe trap, is best be ready."

"How long would Munez take to scramble three fleetships?"

Duschevski stared solemnly at her. He lifted his right hand, and snapped his fingers. "That long."

"Then if they're coming, they're already here." She turned to Connaught. "Surveillance—"

"Nothing, Lieutenant. And it's a scrupulously careful job I'm doing here, I assure you, seeing as how it's my life in the balance, too."

She smiled at that, but the smile faded quickly. She had to decide soon. The fleetship—call her *Empire Bane*, now that Daitaku no longer commanded her—had not decelerated since sliding across the face of New Napa, but neither had she accelerated, and the pressure of interstellar hydrogen smashing into the forward shields was slowing her perceptibly.

The *Empire Bane* was too beat up to stand and fight. If TAAC ships arrived, she would have to bounce to safety, which she could not do at her present velocity. "Admiral, how long would it take us to get back to threshold speed?"

He touched his implant; his lips moved soundlessly. Then he winced. "We have chance that gravpipes do not blow up diminishing in proportion to acceleration we are demanding from them. Is very good chance at one percent operating maximum, so we make threshold in forty-nine point nine minutes."

"That's too long!"

"At thirty-five percent op max, we have one chance in ten thousand that the gravpipes are not blowing up. This is becoming one chance in ten million at fifty percent op max."

So. Using the pipes could destroy them. Waiting for a TAAC task force to show would give the repair crews that much more time. If the crews fixed the pipes before the task force arrived, then the wait would have proved worthwhile. But if they failed, the *Empire Bane* would lie as helpless as a bleeding swimmer in a shark pool. Incapable of either fight or flight, it would suffer a quick and very messy death.

Duschevski regarded her in silence. Sympathy shone in his dark Slavic eyes, but he did not offer advice.

She shook her head. "I have to talk to Daitaku."

Trinh said, "He's still not answering, Lieutenant."

"I'm going over in person."

Without looking away, the admiral raised his voice. "Zi! Assign four sergeants to security escort for—"

"No." She raised a hand. "We need them on repairs."

Though Duschevski pursed his lips, he said nothing.

She threw him a sketchy salute. "The ship's in your hands now, Admiral. If TAAC pays a visit while I'm out, use your best judgment."

He returned the salute with greater formality, then walked over to where Corzini sat at the boards.

Darcy Lee slipped into her spacesuit, took a broomstick from the rack, and programmed it for Command Module Five. She carried it through the lock, and out into the darkness amidships. Straddling it, strapping herself onto it, she touched the GO button.

The stick leaped forward. It carried no gravity generator, so the three-G force shoved her back against the passenger harness. The violence of it frightened her. A long time had passed since she had accelerated without a compensating gravfield to cancel the unwanted G-forces, and she had almost forgotten the sensation.

The stick reached its cruising speed of 160 kilometers per hour in one and a half seconds. The weight lifted from her chest. She double-checked that the pilot switch still tilted toward AUTO, then gripped the handles and enjoyed the ride.

Like an eel through a coral reef, the stick slipped over, under, and around wires and cables and struts and modules. The gravpipes of a passing shuttle slowed it down and rolled it on its back, but in space, where up and down are conveniences rather than fixed frames of reference, this made no difference. Darcy Lee hardly noticed.

Instead she focused on the damage that surrounded her: the twisted microwave receivers, the structural framework with a hundred square meters missing from the middle, the ruptured life-support modules . . . red emergency lights still burned in one of them, and their glow fell on a corpse half-zipped into a spacesuit. She closed her eyes and said a silent prayer for all who had died in the battle.

Then, opening them, she cursed every soul within the Wayholder Empire.

Outside Command Module Five, the stick slowed to a halt. It extruded its recharger cord, which rose like a tentative cobra, turning this way and that, until it located the socket and plugged itself in.

Darcy Lee dismounted and went into the airlock. After orienting herself properly, she tapped the cycle button. Artificial gravity clapped her feet to the deck. Her stomach queased. The inner hatch opened.

Daitaku waited for her inside. He wore a plain gray yukata and soft leather sandals. He bowed, a graceful unhurried incline of the head and shoulders, then straightened to his full 220 centimeters. His brush-cut black hair made him a good five centimeters taller.

She had holoed him often enough to know the set of his jaw when he was being stubborn, the timbre of his voice when decisive, but holo technology stripped reality down to audiovisual information, and then compressed that into a small colored cube.

The sheer height and breadth of him jarred her. So did his aura—his presence, the impression he radiated—part power, part danger, and part pure animal masculinity. She had not expected this at all. She had expected Kajiwara Hiroshi, fresh-faced to be sure, but still wrapped in the original's great age, the century and two-thirds that transmuted immediacy into timelessness, vitality into endurance.

This man before her—this was a young lion, and she had just walked into his cage.

Instinctively she retreated half a step, but she stopped her foot before it touched the metal deck. Almost defiantly, she brought it forward again.

He raised one eyebrow. His lips quirked slightly.

She popped her helmet. The module's humid air smelled of fresh male sweat and rose-scented soap. She pulled off the spacesuit and hung it on the rack by the airlock.

He motioned her to the chair beside his desk.

She took it, glanced meaningfully at his empty chair, and waited for him to be seated.

When he had settled himself, he made a small sound, almost but not quite a sigh, tapped his fingers on his desktop, and cocked his head.

She frowned. "I have to speak first, is that it?"

He nodded.

"Over Commander, I have no time for games."

A smile touched his eyes and his lips and was gone. "Whereas this one has more time than he can fill."

"Then let me help you fill it. Please tell me the message carried by the Situation Update capsule you just sent out."

With apparent sadness, he shook his head.

"Jesus Buddha! Over Commander, you're putting me in a situation that could cost a lot of TAAC lives."

"How is that, Lieutenant?"

"You bounced a SitUp back to Octant Sagittarius HQ. You either did or did not reveal this ship's location. If you did, Munez will send a task force to recapture it. If the task force appears, we will have to fight—and we will lose. Our alternative is to attempt to bounce out ourselves, but we can't trust the gravpipes. They could—no, they *will* explode if we ask too much of them, and if *that* happens, this ship and its crew are stranded out here. And you're stranded along with us."

He shrugged. "That is hardly this one's concern, Lieutenant."

"Your survival isn't your concern?"

His shoulders squared just a little bit more. "I am samurai, Lieutenant. My mission was to destroy the Sagittarian Guard, not to keep myself alive. I have failed to complete my mission, but should the *New Zealand* find itself marooned off New Napa, or destroyed by a TAAC task force, I will at least have prevented the Guard from acquiring her. So . . ."

She took a breath. This would be very tricky. "I see.

You are samurai. Therefore shame affects you not at all.''

"Shame?" He said it lightly, disbelievingly.

"Loss of face, Over Commander. Dishonor."

"You see a way hidden from this one's view, Lieutenant. Please, enlighten me."

"TAAC gave you a fleetship and a mission. You lost the ship. You did not complete your mission. Moreover, you destroyed three Wayholder war zone control craft—and all their lesser ships, and all their crew. The Wayholder Empire will seek revenge. Thanks to you, Sagittarian suns will rise over lifeless worlds whose soils are drenched with human blood."

"How could this one have done all that without a ship?"

"Very simply, Over Commander. You did *not* lose the ship. You turned traitor. You went over to the rebels."

"You know better, Lieutenant."

"Oh I do, Over Commander, and you know better, and all the crew of the—the *New Zealand* knows better, but TAAC does not. TAAC will *never* know the truth, if the *New Zealand* dies."

He shifted his weight a centimeter forward in his chair. The fabric of the yukata strained as his muscles tensed. His voice acquired a new hardness. "What will TAAC know, Lieutenant?"

"They will intercept a SitUp from the *New Zealand* requesting the Sagittarian Guard to send emergency assistance. They will see your face, and hear your voice. Who will ever believe you didn't really record the message?"

"Kajiwara Hiroshi, for one."

She shrugged. "He has already been dishonored. Who at TAAC High Command will believe his defense of his clone?"

Suddenly his cheeks reddened. He slapped the top of his desk. "I will not betray the Association!"

"I am not asking you to do that. All I want to know is, did your SitUp message give our location?"

254 Kevin O'Donnell, Jr.

He looked at her for a long moment. Then he shook his head.

She had not felt so relieved in a long time. "Thank you, Over Commander." Rising, she strode to the holo. "With your permission, sir?"

He waved a hand.

"Thank you, sir." She flicked the holo on, and stepped into the focal area of its cameras. "Admiral?"

Duschevski's face formed in the cube. "Yes, Lieutenant?"

"Lieutenant Connaught can relax. We all can. Over Commander Daitaku did not tell TAAC where we are."

Skepticism slipped across Duschevski's wrinkled face, but he nodded. "Thank you."

"You're welcome. I'll be back soon." She switched off the holo. Then she turned to Daitaku. "Sir—why don't you join us? You're a charismatic leader and a tactical genius. You have more experience than any five of us put together. We need someone like you."

"Of course you do," he said quietly. "But I wear the uniform of the Terran Association Astro Corps."

"Sir, you've proven that TAAC is mistaken. We can defend ourselves against the Wayholder Empire. Don't you think it's wrong to let slaughtered innocents go unavenged? Sir, it's *right* to fight, even if that means calling ourselves outlaws and running from TAAC while we do so."

"I bear TAAC's commission, Lieutenant. Can I keep my honor if I disavow that commission?"

"Do you think, if you return, that you will keep your commission?"

"No." He gave her a sad, haunted smile. "I am a disposable over commander." His gaze met hers; pain burned in it, and pride, too. "Should I return from this— this fiasco, I suspect that TAAC would first record my memories, for judicious editing and subsequent transfer to other clones, and then either execute me or turn me over to the Wayholder Empire for whatever punishment the Empire deems appropriate."

"In that case—"

"No." He said it firmly, and set his jaw. "Go. Leave me in peace.'

She did.

The moon rode high above Howland Island, but the drawn shades of Room B87Q barred its silver beams. The holo display in the corner threw light enough. It held the faces, some scowling, some impassive, of the thirty members of the emergency committee of the board of directors of the Terran Association. At the moment, the chairman's head appeared full-size in the middle of the display; reduced images of the others surrounded it.

To Kajiwara Hiroshi, only three directors mattered. He knew what they thought of him, and hoped to use their preconceptions to his advantage.

If he read Pierre LeFebvre correctly, the chairman of the board and commander in chief viewed Kajiwara Hiroshi as the Association's best tactician—and its most influential potential traitor. LeFebvre had proved that though he did not himself walk bushido, he understood it, and would manipulate the samurai code to achieve his ends. Like a warrior with a double-edged sword, he would wield Kajiwara carefully. He would try to keep Kajiwara in a position where the over commander had to defend the Association and could never attack it.

Han Tachun, first commander of the Unified Security Forces, hated Kajiwara. He would like nothing better than to ruin the over commander, but he burned to succeed LeFebvre, and could not hope for the chairmanship if a rebellion succeeded, or if, failing, it nonetheless triggered war with the Wayholder Empire. Unfortunately for him, he was an indifferent general who lacked the insight to suppress the Sagittarian Guard quickly, surely, and with a minimum of casualties. A bloodbath would puncture his ambitions for all time, because the board would never elect one accused of genocide. Han would prefer to have the blood tarnish Kajiwara's reputation.

Elizabeth Jones, high commander of the Air Force,

planned to take Han's seat when the first commander moved up to the chairmanship, and considered Kajiwara Hiroshi her most serious rival. The woman had the look of a grandmother and the soul of a politician. She would, he thought, want him to undertake something essential, and to fail miserably.

He would need masterful tactics to defend himself against three powerful enemies approaching from different directions. Defeating them one at a time seemed impossible, for he would have to bare his back to two while dealing with the first. Therefore, he thought, they must run side by side. Convince them to approach from a single direction, and then strike all three with a single blow. He rubbed his jaw with the tip of his index finger. He must appeal to the prejudices of all three simultaneously.

LeFebvre said, "Fellow directors, I thank you for joining me in this conference on such short notice. We have received the communication outraged from the ambassador of the Wayholder Empire. This communiqué, it accuses the TAAC fleetship *New Zealand* of conducting the hostile operations in the Octant Sagittarius. We must first discover exactly what it is that has happened, and then decide what steps to take. I—"

"Mr. Chairman." Kajiwara kept his voice level, while inwardly he exulted. *So. The moment comes so quickly, so effortlessly.* "If you will forgive the effrontery of this interruption, some light can perhaps be shed upon the situation."

LeFebvre nodded. "But of course."

He took a moment to scan the holovised faces, but kept his own as blank as slate. In thirty other displays, he would appear at the center, greatly enlarged. It would not do for him to have any expression which Han or Jones could read.

"To begin. This one's primary continuation was dispatched to lead TAAC forces in pursuit of the Sagittarian Guard; the clone was, instead, captured by the pirates." Ah. Triumph had flickered through Elizabeth Jones's gray eyes.

Leaning forward, she waved a hand at the camera controls. The display blinked, and she held the center. "Would you tell us how that happened, Over Commander?"

Raul Santiago answered for him. "The Astro Corps has received no official information, High Commander. We're forced to assume a mutiny in the ranks, but we won't know until we've recovered the ship and its datacorders."

"I see," she said.

And she thinks she sees even more, thought Kajiwara. A younger, stronger version of Kajiwara Hiroshi had fallen into a Sajjer trap. In similar circumstances, the aging original would embarrass himself even more thoroughly. High Commander Jones would, therefore, do her best to get the original back into the field, and let his own ineptitude block his rise to the top.

Kajiwara addressed the board again. "The chairman has mentioned the complaint filed by the Wayholder ambassador. The Empire has not reported the destruction of the *New Zealand*, so we may assume that the fleetship defeated the Wayholder in battle. Given the strength of the Empire, that implies a commander with great tactical ability—that is, this one's continuation."

Han spoke up. "Are you calling your clone a traitor?"

He shook his head. "Without better information, First Commander, any allegation of impropriety would be inappropriate." He gave what he hoped was a rueful smile, and brushed his fingers through the white hair above his right ear. "It is, of course, common knowledge that a certain dossier contains more than a normal share of reprimands for exceeding authority, so one could postulate, perhaps, a genetically determined character flaw. . . ." He sighed. "It is, however, apparent that of the two foes the Association faces, one is well led, and the other is well armed."

LeFebvre flicked a finger. His image popped up in the middle of the display. "Are you leading to a rec-

ommendation in the roundabout way so typical to you,
Over Commander Kajiwara?''

"Yes, Mr. Chairman.'' He blinked slowly. "Eventually. But one more observation, please. If the continuation known as Daitaku does indeed direct the
Sagittarian Guard, then we cannot assume that the Empire will crush the Guard in the course of its training
exercises. Rather, we must assume that the Guard will
cause so much damage that the Empire will hold the
Association responsible and strike out at it.''

LeFebvre controlled the muscles of his face, but could
not prevent himself from blanching.

Kajiwara thought, *So, Mr. Chairman, now you comprehend the fire on the border, and the smoldering em-
bers at the core. You must somehow put both out—or
stand back and let each extinguish the other.*

The chairman cleared his throat. Brusquely he said,
"Your recommendation, Over Commander.''

"Mr. Chairman, fully three continuations of this one
are physically mature at this moment; each is ready to
have my memories implanted and to don my uniform
whenever you require it. This one humbly requests that
you permit him to return to Octant Sagittarius today. If
anyone can, ah, anticipate the logical processes of Daitaku, it is this one. Let this one destroy the clone before
it provokes the Empire into invading the entire Association.''

LeFebvre turned his head from side to side, as if
searching for opposition.

Kajiwara said quickly, "Sir. To crush an insurrection
of this sort before it brings on Armageddon might require measures the Association has heretofore been reluctant to adopt. The board might wish to empower the
commander of such an expedition to take any and all
steps he deems necessary, and to demand of him that
he stand before it in judgment when the mission has
been accomplished.''

Han Tachun immediately said, "Yes. Over Commander Kajiwara makes an excellent point, and I move

that the board adopt his recommendations without amendment.''

Elizabeth Jones said, ''Second the motion.''

Subsequent debate was perfunctory and pro forma. Within twenty minutes, the board of directors of the Terran Association ordered Over Commander Kajiwara Hiroshi to return to Octant Sagittarius and to do whatever was necessary to put down the rebellion.

Daitaku paced the small module, from one end of the mute, dark console to the other, from there to the galley, to the desk, and back to the deactivated control panel again. He moved slowly, his eyes nearly closed, his feet finding the way on their own. The orange robot followed in his wake, ready to render whatever medical or psychopharmaceutical assistance he desired.

The disposable over commander.

He gritted his teeth. If *she* had called him that, he would have erupted in fury, but he had coined that phrase himself.

He had touched the truth without even reaching for it.

So. To return would be to die. A fitting end, for one who has failed. A fitting end for any samurai. ''The Way of the Warrior is death,'' Yamamoto Tsunenori had said in *Ha Gakure*. Why, then, did Daitaku shrink from death?

He looked to the wall where his star coral should hang, but the wall stared back blankly, because the star coral belonged to Kajiwara Hiroshi, not to Daitaku the disposable over commander. He shook his head.

Ha Gakure cited the Four Oaths—''Never be late with respect to the Way of the Warrior. Be useful to the lord. Be respectful to your parents. Get beyond love and grief: exist for the good of man.''

And yet how could he apply those oaths to his situation? Each canceled another out.

Seppuku would end his usefulness, except perhaps as an object lesson.

Must he accept the chairman as his lord? He thought

not, but could not name another to whom he owed allegiance. In any event, to attempt to obey LeFebvre now—to try to destroy the Guard—would mean deceiving those who had respected his honor, thereby forfeiting it, and retroactively shaming them for having respected that which he did not have. Yet not making the attempt also sacrificed honor.

And who were his parents?

He frowned over that one for a long time. Kajiwara Hiroshi? Kajiwara's parents? The technician who stimulated that first cell into dividing, and the mechanical womb that nourished him as an embryo?

Exist for the good of man. So very easy to say, but who could tell good from bad? The Wayholder said protect yourselves and we will destroy you; leave yourselves naked and you will survive. The chairman said kill these rebels so their children can die at alien hands.

The children of man said save us from death.

The Way of the Warrior is death.

Never be late with respect to the Way of the Warrior.

Be useful to the lord.

Be respectful to your parents.

Exist for the good of man.

Exist.

Chapter 18

On 6 July 2351, five days after the catastrophic battle with the Wayholder, Darcy Lee was feeding a set of forged IDs into the slot of the card reader at Port Long-fall's Customs and Immigration booth. She held her breath. The uniformed official in the C&I booth gave the reader's screen a bored glance, gave her tight-fitting flight suit an interested one, then waved her through the gate with a sigh. She smiled at him as she left.

Outside the customs area, hundreds of colonists, some holding placards with names printed on them and others carrying flowers or children, looked at her briefly and blankly, then shifted their attention back to the sliding doors she had just come through. She stopped to wait for Steven Cavendish.

A moment later, the tall black man worked his way through the crowd to her. Tucking his red leather card-fold inside his suit jacket, he scanned the lobby. "She ought to be here somewhere, but this place is a mad-house."

"If she knows your face—"

"Oh, she knows it, all right."

"Then she'll spot you." Darcy glanced at him curiously, hoping he would explain the ruefulness in his voice.

He buttoned his jacket. "Let's just hope she doesn't call me by name."

A female voice said, "Dr. Loagheris!"

"Wake up." Darcy Lee elbowed Cavendish gently. "I think she just called you by an alias."

"Oh. Right." He straightened his tie. "Colonel O'Flaherty!"

A woman in uniform stepped forward. No longer young, but not yet middle-aged, she had observant blue eyes and windblown red hair. "How very nice that you could come yourself . . . Doctor." She hesitated, then extended her hand.

Cavendish's cheeks twitched. He took her hand in both of his, and held it. "The honor is all mine, Colonel." He sounded as if he was trying not to laugh at a private joke. "May I present Lieutenant, er, Chou, my pilot?"

Lee came to attention and saluted.

O'Flaherty slipped her hand free of Cavendish's grip to return the salute. "At ease, Lieutenant. I have a car out front. Follow me, please."

Soon the three sat in the back of a staff car, with a plasglass barrier between them and the impassive sergeant who drove. The spaceport dwindled behind them. O'Flaherty unbuttoned the collar of her tunic and made herself comfortable. "Steven, when did you become a lepidopterist?"

"It was Darcy's idea." He flashed a dazzling grin and stretched his arms across the top of the seat. His left hand fell on O'Flaherty's shoulder. She did not seem to mind. "Butterflies are her hobby; we figured she could cover for me if somebody questioned my credentials."

"Then what really brings you to Longfall?"

"Gravpipes."

O'Flaherty's eyebrows rose. "Why?"

"We have a fleetship. The *Empire Bane*."

"AKA the *New Zealand*?"

"Right. She made it back to base after knocking out three Wayholder war zone control craft, but she's disabled. Over two hundred of her gravpipes are down, and we can't repair them. We can't replace them, either—we've used up all the pipes we salvaged from the wreckage off New Napa, and we don't have the facilities to make more."

"Go on," said O'Flaherty.

"We thought we'd try to get them direct from KaoHsiung Gravpipe Limited. They have that factory up there—" he pointed to the roof of the car—"and we hoped we could strike a deal."

"I'm afraid you wasted a trip, Steven. KGL has a long-term contract with TAAC for all of its output. Under different circumstances, I'm sure they'd be willing to come to some sort of arrangement, but—"

"But," said Darcy Lee, disappointed in O'Flaherty for not leveling with them, "the Longfall Astro Corps already has first claim on what KGL's quality control inspectors reject, yes?"

O'Flaherty's head turned as if on a ball bearing. Her lake-blue eyes chilled into frozen pools. "May I ask why you said that?"

"We came in on the *Cuyahoga*, a Lewisanclark-class surv/recon vessel formerly attached to the *New Zealand*. The only thing with better EM sensors is a fleet-ship. You have 273 one-bod fighters parked at the inner edge of your Oort cloud; not one of them shows up in TAAC's registry of fighting ships." She sat back, pressed her shoulders into the upholstery, and stared straight ahead. "If a fleetship drops in to pay you a visit, you're going to have some explaining to do."

"Lieutenant Chou—"

"Lee."

"Pardon?"

"Lee. Darcy Lee. 'Chou' is to me as 'Loagheris' is to Steve." A plantation of southern pine bordered the highway. Cardinals flitted from branch to branch. She wanted to get out of the car and run down those perfect rows of conifers, feet springing off the thick bed of needles beneath the branches. "Could we open a window, please? I've been breathing recycled air for so damn long. . . ."

O'Flaherty touched a button on her armrest. The windows hissed down; thick resiny humidity gushed in. "Is your rank as fictitious as your name?"

She breathed deeply, coughed, and inhaled again.

"Jesus Buddha, that smells wonderful. . . . Steve, have we gotten around to formalizing ranks?"

"Not really." He gave O'Flaherty a lazy smile. "Yesterday Darcy was in command of the *New Zealand*—and of Over Commander Daitaku, the clone of Kajiwara Hiroshi. I think that means she ranks you, but military protocol has always eluded me."

"What is she doing as your pilot?"

Darcy Lee answered that herself. "With the *Empire Bane* out of commission, I don't have much to do except fret. Steve needed a pilot. So here I am."

"Trying to blackmail us."

Cavendish sat up straight. "No!"

"Why not?" said Darcy Lee.

O'Flaherty scowled. "Make up your minds." She brushed Cavendish's hand off her shoulder.

Darcy Lee said, "We need gravpipes. Lots of them. You produce lots of them. You need a defense. A good one. We provide a good one. Let's deal."

The long columns of ten-meter-tall southern pines ended in a lawn, smooth enough for a putting green, that ringed a small office building. The car turned into the building's drive and stopped before its lobby.

A burly sergeant opened the car doors and directed them up an escalator to a sparsely furnished conference room, where two elderly men sat at a round table, clearly awaiting them.

O'Flaherty said, "Mr. Prime Minister, allow me to present Mr. Steven Cavendish and Lieutenant Darcy Lee of the Sagittarian Guard. Mr. Cavendish, Lieutenant Lee, our prime minister, Sean Padraic Flynn, and his first assistant, Stanislaus Wochny."

Flynn came barely to Darcy Lee's shoulder. Balding, with a frizzy white beard that hung below his collarbone, he had faded blue eyes and the deep suntan that comes from years of work in the open air. He did not offer to shake hands, but waved them into chairs. "We can only spare you the couple of minutes," he said in a soft tenor voice. "Which is why I hope you'll be forgiving us for having the audacity to listen to your conversation with the good colonel here on the way over."

Cavendish looked startled, but said, "That will save us some time, sir."

"Fine. Then I'll first be asking after the truth about the Wayholder invasions."

"The truth, sir?" said Cavendish.

Wochny leaned forward. A thin man, with strong high cheekbones ad shoulder-length gray hair, he had a voice like gravel in a mixing bowl. "Why are they attacking?"

Cavendish gestured to Lee. "Darcy?"

She raised her shoulders and let them fall again. "To be honest, gentlemen, we don't know. For one thing, we don't have much intelligence on the Wayholder Empire. We've concentrated on acquiring the equipment and personnel to fight back."

Flynn combed his beard with the fingers of his left hand. "One of our people, you see, a certain Michael O'Reilly, who has family within TAAC at the very highest of levels, is after telling us that the Wayholder won't be reinforcing their infantry if the invasion goes sour on the ground. Now what, if anything, do the two of you know about that?"

"Not a thing." She frowned down at the wooden table, and traced its grain with a fingertip. "What kind of losses will they take before they retreat?"

"We don't know for sure they're going to retreat," said Wochny. "O'Reilly's high-muckety-muck relative at TAAC clammed up. The picture O'Reilly got was that the Wayholder spacecraft would watch us slug it out on the ground, and not butt in."

Darcy Lee rubbed her temples. "That doesn't make sense. To ferry troops across a galactic rift, shuttle them down, and then not support or reinforce them— Unless," she said slowly, her mind awhirl with improbable possibilities, "these aren't real soldiers. I mean, if they're condemned criminals, and their sentence is to go conquer a world or die trying . . . or religious fanatics who won't go to Wayholder heaven if anyone helps them fight, or adolescents doing a rite of passage, as African boys used to hunt lions, or any of a thousand other scenarios. Jesus Buddha, who knows why aliens do anything? So O'Reilly could be right. Did he have any other information?''

"It's advice he's pressing on us, not hard cold data, more's the pity. It's his contention that the way to protect ourselves is to raise and train a large standing army capable of meeting the foe at the drop site and defeating them on the ground. And what would you be thinking of that, now, Lieutenant Lee?''

"Sir, if what O'Reilly told you is true, it's the only thing to do. The Wayholder haven't occupied any of the worlds they've taken. They've landed, slaughtered the inhabitants, and departed. They haven't left guards, monitor satellites, mining operations, *anything* behind. Just . . . corpses.''

"We know that,'' said O'Flaherty. "We managed to obtain some OBI chips of the New Dublin massacre from TAAC.''

A finger touched Lee's elbow. "OBI?'' said Cavendish softly.

"Order of Battle Intelligence.'' She scratched the tabletop with a fingernail for a moment. "Colonel, can we get a copy of those chips?''

"The chips and all our analysis, of course.''

"How did it sound to your people? Was the landing party made up of seasoned vets? Did they mention being on their own? Was there any clue in the comm at all?''

O'Flaherty shook her head. "There's too much we can't translate. Where we understood it, though, they were using comm channels like real pros—minimum talk, maximum information, with no gossip, backchat, or bullshit—but the individual squads seemed to need an awful lot of guidance. One of our analysts insists that no one below their equivalent of company commander had ever seen combat before, but she's eccentric at the best of times.''

Flynn said, "Mr. O'Reilly is also advancing the argument that defending ourselves in space would be a catastrophic mistake, that the aliens will forgive us for beating their infantry, but not for damaging their space forces. Would you be having an opinion on that subject, Lieutenant?''

"No, sir. Intuitively . . . I reject it." She closed her eyes, thought back to the holoclips Liam McCorcoran had taken of the invasions, and tried to remember how things had gone. "And yet—'' she opened her eyes to gaze right into Flynn's— "and yet aliens don't react in the ways my intuition says they will. I honestly can't tell you, sir.''

Cavendish touched her again, and bent over so his lips brushed her ear. "Do you think Daitaku could?''

A mixture of embarrassment and annoyance shot through her. She should have remembered Daitaku herself. "Sure. Of course he could. If anybody out there can.''

"The key question, Mr. Cavendish, Lieutenant Lee,'' said Wochny, rising to stand beside Flynn's chair, "is, can you guarantee to protect us?''

Darcy Lee winced. "No. We guarantee to come to your aid if you call, not to defeat the Wayholder. I can promise that we'll make any attack costly for them, but not that it will be so costly that they'll break off.''

Someone knocked on the door; Flynn called, "Come in.''

The barrel-chested sergeant stepped inside. "A SitUp from Octant Sagittarius just reached us; the *Morocco* will pull into parking orbit in approximately twenty minutes.''

Darcy Lee glanced from one Longfaller to the next before asking, "The *Morocco*?''

Wochny made a disgusted sound deep in his throat.

Flynn said, "Yes. The *Morocco* will be making a . . . courtesy call. Intended, I believe, to acquaint us with her commanding officer, Over Commander Kajiwara Hiroshi.''

* * *

Kajiwara Hiroshi emerged from the shuttle into the hot wind and white light of Longfall. Involuntarily, he recoiled from the thousands of acres of concrete that surrounded him.

He wished he were back in his command module. There he could pace the perimeter in fourteen strides—three forward, four to the left, three, four. This emptiness, though, this openness oppressed him. Not even a mobile walkway to link ships with the terminal buildings. *Ah, colonists. So parsimonious with their hard currencies; so reluctant to invest in the niceties of civilization.*

Still, one must show the flag. He straightened, breathed deeply. Despite his best intentions, his nose wrinkled. *On my next sabbatical I should submit to analysis, and discover why my nose prefers recycled air to fresh.*

Yet he knew the answer: A fleetship smelled like home.

Two men approached. From TAAC Intelligence summaries of Longfall politics, he recognized them both. Prime Minister Flynn and his first assistant. Wochnowicz? Wochny. Stanislaus Wochny. He waited for them to come all the way to him before he gave the appearance of noticing them.

Flynn nodded, but neither offered his hand nor showed any other sign of respect. "Over Commander Kajiwara, welcome to Longfall. Your first visit here, is it?"

"Actually not." He bowed despite Flynn's lack of courtesy. The warrior must observe the rituals even in the midst of barbarism. "I am delighted to have returned, though, for Longfall is a most interesting system." He smiled down at the two colonists. "Perhaps more interesting than even you who share its bounty realize. For example, the area beyond your system's last planet contains 273 single-person fighter craft, none of which the registry could identify." He squinted into the sunlight. "One would inquire about them, but of course no one on Longfall would know anything about them."

"Of course not." A pallor developed beneath Flynn's sun-leathered skin. "Are you thinking that they're Wayholder, sir?"

"One would doubt that, Mr. Prime Minister. Their emissions patterns clearly identify them as Zulu-class fighters, similar to the ones assembled in the Kao-Hsiung Gravpipe Limited factory. Definitely not Wayholder."

"I see," said Flynn. "Well. Then it's our great good fortune that you've arrived at our fair world before those—those—" He gestured toward the sky.

"Bandits?" said Kajiwara politely, helpfully.

"Sure, and if that isn't exactly what they must be! Bandits here to intercept our exports and use them for their own nefarious purposes." He stepped forward, reached up to take Kajiwara's left arm just above the elbow, and pointed to the terminal building. "If you'll be coming with us, Over Commander, there's a long line of citizens awaiting the opportunity to shake the hand of the Hero of New Napa." He seemed not to notice the sudden bunching of Kajiwara's jaw muscles. "They're just inside there, as they've repaired the air conditioning in the terminal, you know. And I believe there's more than a few of them whom you'll be recognizing as soon as you lay eyes on them. The O'Reillys, I mean."

A spark of surprised pleasure ran through Kajiwara, not displacing his anger, but mellowing it, gentling it. He liked seeing his family, though he preferred it if he chose when and where to meet them, and reserved the right to depart whenever he wished. Families often reminded him of large knapsacks—durable, safe to fall back on, holding all a man needed to survive, and with a weight that would drive you to your knees if you tried to carry it too far, or too long.

Aloud, he said, "The O'Reillys. What an excellent welcome for a traveler, Mr. Prime Minister. But first I must have a word with the security detail." He half-turned to the shuttle; Sergeant Iovini appeared immediately. Kajiwara spoke loudly, wanting Flynn and Wochny to hear every word. "Sergeant, tell Admiral

Wiegand to send ops groups One through Twenty out to destroy the Zulus we detected on our arrival."

"Yes, sir."

"Also, the bandits certainly have spies here. Obtain a full squad and inspect the documentation of all ships and crew." Wagging his head from side to side with apparent sadness, he watched Flynn and Wochny out of the corner of his eye. "Since no loyal Longfaller would assist bandits, the spies must have entered the city using false papers. One assumes they intended to eavesdrop on communications concerning export schedules. Arrest anyone with inadequate identification. Shoot them if they resist." He nodded, and turned back to Flynn and Wochny. "And now, my most honorable hosts, let us go into your newly refurbished terminal building, for the sun, I fear, has brought excess perspiration to all three of our brows."

* * *

Ponds mirror crane wings
And iridescent carp scales.
The hatchlings exult.

Daitaku laid the calligraphy brush aside. Holding his hands before him, palms down, he flexed his fingers. No pain. None at all. Not even the faintest pinprick in a single knuckle.

He shook his head. *How odd,* he thought, *to remember, with a brain rather less than four years old, 110 years of never-ending pain. How frightening, to comprehend my destiny.*

He suspected that arthritis would settle in no matter what he did, but he hoped that this time, the doctors would catch the cancers early enough to preserve his virility. Although if he never got an opportunity to exercise it, he would lose it to atrophy anyway.

He rose, paced the module, told the orange robot to return to its recharging station. The bulkheads gleamed. The deck shone like the sun. The top of the writing desk sparkled under the fluorescent lights. He opened the closet and closed it again because nothing within re-

quired attention; because, in fact, if he shined his shoes
one more time they might blind anyone unlucky enough
to glance at them.

He had too much energy—or at least so much more
than he-Kajiwara had that he-Daitaku had not yet grown
accustomed to a body that begged to be used rather than
spared. But the thought of doing his calisthenics a fourth
time in one day did not appeal at all.

For a moment he considered spilling the ink, just to
give himself something to do. *Ah, disposable over commander to samurai maid. . . .* He laughed, not happily,
but because no other reaction seemed appropriate.

And then he frowned. These people—these Sajjer rebels—appeared to understand him in ways that the Corps
did not. Perhaps they would comprehend his needs—
and trust him. He activated his holophone. "Mr.
McCorcoran?"

A surprised look passed over Mitchell McCorcoran's
long-jawed face. "Over Commander?"

"Yes. Empty time weighs more heavily than full; one
must be a true Zen master fully to appreciate its
weight."

McCorcoran smiled. "Bored, eh?"

"To tears, Mr. McCorcoran, to tears." He sighed.
"Perhaps, though, boredom might be alleviated through
the pursuit of knowledge. Such would require your permission."

"My permission?" McCorcoran blinked. "Has your
library terminal been disconnected?"

"No, Mr. McCorcoran, no it has not. Yet to my
shame I grow weary of the reflections of reality. I wish
to perceive it at first hand."

"With all due respect, sir, you've lost me completely." He scratched his jaw. "What can I do for
you?"

"Lend me a fighter."

"What? Let you escape? Come on, Over Commander, Darcy would—"

"I seek to escape nothing but tedium. If you will
permit me to borrow a fighter, I will use it only to

investigate the Korrin, and then return it to you afterward.''

McCorcoran cocked his head warily. "The who?"

"The Korrin—the other enemy of the Wayholder Empire.''

McCorcoran stared down, presumably at the holo of Daitaku. "And you'll come back here afterward?"

Daitaku gritted his teeth. Did even these people doubt his honor? "I will return, Mr. McCorcoran, either at a specified time if you prefer, or when I have satisfied my curiosity.''

McCorcoran's lips pursed, then relaxed. "Do you think these Korrin might have something we could use?''

"In all honesty, Mr.McCorcoran, I cannot say. I know only that—''

#Classified.#

"Over Commander?"

"My apologies, Mr. McCorcoran. It seems that I am barred from speaking freely.''

Mitchell McCorcoran nodded. "We're familiar with that problem. New software is available to you anytime you want it.''

"I think not, but thank you."

"Your word of honor?"

"Yes.''

"Well, then—" Now worry flitted across McCorcoran's face. "The thing is, our onboards don't have charts for Korrin territory, Over Commander. I don't even know where it is. If you bounce into a dust cloud or an asteroid belt—''

"I understand, sir, but consider the odds."

McCorcoran exhaled loudly. "You're right. Space is awfully empty.''

"Then—''

"Take a surv/recon vessel." He held up a hand. "One minute." He glanced to one side, reached to touch something, presumably a display screen, and nodded. "The *Rhone*'s at a hundred percent and no one's using her. She's got much better sensors than a fighter does.''

It took Daitaku a moment to realize the enormous compliment McCorcoran had just paid him. He bowed toward the holo image. "Thank you, Mr. McCorcoran."

"And take my nephew."

Daitaku stiffened. "I have given you my word—"

"Sir! That's not what I meant! Just get him out of my hair. Please?"

Daitaku paused while he searched his memories. McCorcoran, McCorcoran . . . "Your nephew's name is Liam?"

"Yes, Over Commander."

"Now I understand. Yes, of course he may come. Have him meet me at the dock in five minutes."

Mitchell McCorcoran broke into a broad smile. "Thank you, sir. Thank you very, very much."

Thirty minutes later, the *Rhone* bounced four thousand parsecs toward the center of the galaxy. It materialized in Korrin territory, a full light-year from a Sol-type star. "Why so far out?" said Liam McCorcoran.

"Before intruding—" Daitaku whispered rapid instructions to the onboards—"let us examine the system for objects which would dismay us if we were to collide with them."

"And then we'll bounce in?"

"Just so, Lieutenant." Ah, it felt good to be on the move again, to be in command again, even when the command consisted of a very small ship and one impetuous lieutenant. He gave the onboards their last orders.

Immediately, all of the *Rhone*'s alarms sounded. "Silence them!" said Daitaku, as he queried the computer for the cause.

#Three hundred seventeen unidentified objects approaching in ovoid formation with a major axis of 2 million kilometers. Range, 90.2 million kilometers and closing.#

"Now what?" said McCorcoran.

"We wait for them to react. They will notice our

presence in three and a half minutes. They will do something then.''

''What?''

''The answer to that question is precisely what we seek, Lieutenant.'' Quickly, he ordered the *Rhone* to focus all its sensors on the star system beyond the on-coming formation, and to estimate the orbits of all detectable objects within it.

It did not matter that the information would be a year old. He no longer had any intention of venturing into the system. He simply wanted to verify the claims the Wayholder had made three years earlier, when they explained their attack on New Napa.

As the data scrolled up on the screen, he conceded the truth of the Wayholder assertions.

The system had a star, six planets, and nothing else in natural orbit. No comets, no asteroids, no dust particles large enough reflect light or to absorb and re-radiate heat . . . just thousands of small, unidentified objects on artificial trajectories away from the star and toward Wayholder territory.

McCorcoran let out a yelp. ''Sir!''

''Yes, Lieutenant?''

''We're accelerating!''

''Remarkable,'' said Daitaku in a murmur.

''But, sir, the pipes are off.''

''Of course they are.'' He told the onboards to measure stress patterns on the hull. ''Are you ready to bounce, Lieutenant?''

''You don't want to stick around and find out why we're picking up speed, and what it is that a surv/recon ship can't identify?''

''This monitor—'' he tapped it—'' displays the gravitational forces impinging on our fuselage. Those forces originate from the objects ahead of us—the Korrin. Please recall that gravity strengthens in inverse proportion to distance. Then tell me if you think that we will last long enough to learn the Korrin equivalent for 'We come in peace'?''

McCorcoran stared, his blue eyes gradually widening

as he absorbed the information on the computer screen. "Can we learn a new language in less than three minutes, sir?"

"I doubt it, Lieutenant."

"That's all the time we've got before we're torn apart."

"Say 'Sayonara,' then." Daitaku told the onboards, "Bounce!"

#Bounce.#

Liam McCorcoran let out a loud sigh of relief that tickled the hairs on the nape of Daitaku's neck. Then he asked, "So where are we now?"

Daitaku checked the readouts before answering. "Two hundred lights deeper into Korrin territory. One light out from another small yellow star. This time, however, we have put the star between us and the Wayholder Empire. Interesting. The onboards detect no orbital bodies of any significance. We must get closer."

"What an incredible coincidence."

Daitaku looked back over his shoulder into the young man's face. "The lack of orbital bodies?"

"No. Dropping into the middle of a fleet on maneuvers. When you calculate the odds against that—"

"A phrase more accurate than 'fleet on maneuvers' might be 'flock in migration,' Lieutenant."

"Sir?"

A yellow warning light began to blink.

"One moment, Lieutenant." Daitaku asked the onboards why the light had come on.

#Inexplicable deceleration of one meter per second per second. Dustbroom sensors report hydrogen density of zero point one molecule per cubic meter. Observed density does not correlate with observed deceleration.#

"Sir?" McCorcoran spoke at a higher pitch than usual.

"Yes, Lieutenant?"

"Could this deceleration be caused by the, um, 'flock' thirty megakay aft?"

Daitaku smiled to himself. "How large is the flock?"

"Five hundred ninety-eight, um, sheep?"

"Ships, Lieutenant. And yes, it is probable that they are slowing us down."

"Well?"

"Well, what, Lieutenant?"

"Are we going to bounce?"

"Let us allow our pipes to cool and smooth out, Lieutenant. They will not overtake us anytime soon."

"But how are they causing it?"

"The Wayholder said the Korrin vacuum up the interstellar dust." It surprised him that his implant's operating system had let him say so much. Perhaps because he had not mentioned politics or strategies? "One presumes the utilization of . . . call it the inverse of our dustbroom technology. Whereas we use a cigar-shaped shield woven of electromagnetic and antigravity fields to shoulder particles aside as we travel, they seem to be generating a . . . funnel, to draw the particles in."

"And *we're* one of those particles?"

"So it seems, Lieutenant."

They cruised in silence for another four minutes, until McCorcoran said, "I think it's safe now, sir."

"Take us up to threshold speed." As McCorcoran obliged, Daitaku gave the onboards their orders.

"Threshold, sir."

"Bounce us."

#Bounced.#

"How much deeper this time?" asked McCorcoran.

"No deeper. We have gone parallel to the border. We are . . . three hundred light-years from our previous position."

"Another Sol-type star?"

"Yes. And, once again, one light-year out while the computers scan for—"

Alarm shrieks cut him off.

"Oh, this is absurd. Flip us end over end, and use the aft gravpipe to bounce us back to base."

McCorcoran said, "But won't they follow?"

"They haven't yet. Now flip us—"

#Flipped.#

"And bounce us home."

#Bounced.#

"Decelerate, obtain permission to dock, and do it."

"My God, Over Commander!"

"Yes, they are fascinating, aren't they?"

While Liam McCorcoran stammered something about Korrin technology, Daitaku manipulated the data collected by the *Rhone*'s sensors. He said nothing for the twenty minutes of braking. Analysis, extrapolation, and projection kept him too busy.

But he smiled broadly as the *Rhone* docked with the *New Zealand*.

Chapter 19

"Jesus Buddha, we've been talking about your grand-children for an hour now!" Edgy and impatient, Darcy Lee slapped the wooden conference table. Her palm print smudged its shine. "Don't get me wrong—they're probably swell kids; definitely hologenic as hell—but why have we been waiting an entire hour for your people to transmit one simple message?"

Even as O'Flaherty flushed deep red, she scowled. "And just two hours ago you were telling me how good the EM sensors on a fleetship are!" She scrabbled up the holos and shoved them back into her briefcase. "We only have the one satellite, you know."

Darcy Lee froze. Afternoon sun slanted through the open window; the breeze that flirted with the curtains wore the scent of new-mown grass. One satellite? She knew better than that. O'Flaherty had lied. Abrupt fear surged in Lee. The message had gone out, but to the fleetship, not the fighters. At any moment, Corps MPs would arrive to arrest her. They'd take her back to Earth, try her for treason, convict her, execute her—

No. She would not succumb to paranoia. The Long-fallers had their own police, their own army. They did not need TAAC to take two rebels prisoner.

But why had O'Flaherty lied? "Colonel," she said carefully, "we spotted lots of satellites on our way in. Why did you say you only have one?"

"Because it is all we have. We the armed forces, I mean. It's not that we can't use the others, but that we don't operate them. We don't know who else is tapped

278

into them. And I don't think any of us wants the *Morocco* to intercept this message."

"You're right." She began to relax, but her stomach knotted tight again. "That security detail will be shuttling down any minute, if it isn't down already. As soon as they run the *Cuyahoga*'s registration, they'll start hunting Steve and me."

"We'll stall them somehow." Confidence rang in O'Flaherty's firm voice.

Cavendish cleared his throat. "I still don't understand. Is the message being hand-delivered to the transmitter, or what?"

"No, Steven." O'Flaherty pointed at the ceiling. "The *Morocco* is in synchronous orbit directly above the port. Our commsat's much lower. We're waiting for it to reach the far side of the planet before we transmit, so that Longfall itself shields the broadcast from the *Morocco*'s receivers."

He spread his hands. "Use code."

O'Flaherty opened her mouth, snapped it shut, and glanced at Lee.

Well, playing pedant helped pass the time. "Steve, a fleetship's computers can break unknown codes as easily as you can snap a twig."

A sergeant hurried in and saluted. "Transmission complete, Colonel."

"Thank you." O'Flaherty pushed her chair back and rose to her feet. "As long as the task force doesn't bounce out there—"

"They won't." With action imminent, Darcy Lee began to feel good again. "Not here. The Rock's onboards don't know your Oort cloud well enough. It's not that there's a lot of garbage out there; it's just that they don't know where all of it is. They won't take the chance that something solid will be inside the dustbrooms when they emerge. Remember, at threshold speed, hitting a pebble can wreck a ship."

Cavendish already stood by the door. "Are we ready?"

Darcy Lee paused to review her mental checklist. "Where's Kajiwara?"

"In the terminal," said O'Flaherty. "At the reception. Why?"

"Because he might recognize me. His clone did. Daitaku couldn't remember my name, but he knew we had met. So if Kajiwara spots me in the terminal—"

"I'd planned to drive around it."

They passed through the tree farm on the way back to the spaceport. A black dot high overhead swelled into the unmistakable manta-ray shape of a TAAC shuttle. It angled down, sleek and streamlined. The edges of its wings glowed dull red; its belly blushed. It stopped dead in the air and hung motionless over the port's control tower.

"Show-off," said Darcy Lee.

"Pardon?" said O'Flaherty.

The thunder of a sonic boom rolled past them, startling robins out of the pines. The shuttle, waggling its wings twice, continued to hover.

"He's trying to show what a hot pilot he is, so he brings her in at about Mach 3—"

"How do you know it's a man?" Annoyance tinged Cavendish's tone.

"Because women don't grin when they fart," she said.

O'Flaherty chuckled. Cavendish blinked, glanced out the window, and turned back to Darcy Lee, a puzzled expression on his face.

"If a woman were flying that— There, do you see what he's doing now?"

The shuttle dropped straight down, like an elevator in a shaft, slowing as it neared the ground.

"So what's wrong with that?" said Cavendish.

"Not a thing," she said. "But a hot *female* pilot would have brought her down like that from the instant she touched atmosphere—and a woman would have held her descent just below the speed of sound all the way to about a hundred meters off the ground. Fifteen minutes from kiss-air to touchdown, and nobody would have

heard a thing. That's hot. This—'' she gestured at the
shuttle—''this is amateur hour.''

He raised one eyebrow. ''So why didn't you bring *us*
down that way?''

''Because Lieutenant Chou brought you down, and
she is earnest, plodding, and always inclined to go by
the book.''

''I see.'' The car turned onto the main access road.
Traffic thickened. ''Megan, how many ships are on the
ground?''

''Lots,'' said O'Flaherty. ''All of them with the
TAAC insignia painted over the real owner's logo.
They'll be hours getting to the *Cuyahoga.*''

That reminded Darcy Lee of the next item on her
checklist. ''What about clearance for takeoff?''

O'Flaherty looked confused. ''Just ask for it.''

''What worries me is that the security detail might
decide to delay clearance for ships they haven't checked
out yet.''

''Ah.'' The colonel frowned. ''All right. I'll drop
you off and go directly to the control tower. When you
ask for clearance, I'll grant it myself.'' She leaned back
in the seat. Her right hand dropped to the holstered
automatic at her side. ''If it's not me who responds—if
someone else tells you to hold—lift immediately at max,
and best of luck with the *Morocco.*''

''A very cheery thought.'' Darcy Lee slumped back
herself. Lift into the teeth of a fleetship? She would
rather swim in a shark tank.

Fortunately, when Darcy Lee requested clearance,
O'Flaherty's familiar voice answered. ''Any time, *Cuyahoga.* On behalf of the farmers of Longfall, I'd like to
thank the good doctor for his entomological advice. It's
nice to know we don't have to kill the butterflies after
all. *Bon voyage.*''

''Thank you, tower,'' she said, and lifted off. The
ship ascended at a swift, silent angle to the south. The
city disappeared behind them; each succeeding farm-
house below seemed smaller than the last.

"I thought you hot female pilots preferred the vertical to the horizontal," said Cavendish.

"We do."

"Still playing Lieutenant Chou?"

"Nope."

"Then—?"

"Wait." They passed through a cloud layer. She double-checked that the onboards' collision-avoidance system functioned nominally before saying, "The Rock's holding geosynch directly over Port Longfall. A fleetship's programmed to emission-print and identify any approaching vessel within twenty-five kilokay. That's just SOP."

"So?"

"Steve!"

"What?"

She sighed. Steven Cavendish would never pretend to be ignorant. He truly did not grasp the implications. "If the Rock's OBCs ID us, they'll tell the SO—"

"English, please, Darcy."

"If the *Morocco*'s onboard computers identify us, they'll tell the surveillance officer something to the effect of 'That's the *Cuyahoga*, a Lewisanclark-class survey/reconnaissance vessel attached to the *New Zealand*, the fleetship of the 78th, current status unknown but presumed to have been seized by mutineers who deserted to the Sagittarian Guard.' And we don't want that."

"No, we don't," he said.

They emerged from the clouds into brilliant sunshine. "So what we're doing is flying toward the accel lane but away from the Rock. We are also hoping that Kajiwara hasn't put the Rock on Red Alert, because if he has, then his onboards will automatically emission-print and ID any vessel within half a million kilometers. If that happens, this cabin will reach a remarkably high temperature for an astoundingly small fraction of a second, after which it will explode. With us in it."

"They'd do that?"

"Unless, by sheer coincidence, they already have an

ops group on an intercept trajectory, yes, they would do that.'' She twisted around in her seat to look into Cavendish's eyes. His skin had gone dusty gray. "Steve, look on the bright side.''

"What's that?''

"You'd never know what hit you.''

The silver limousine slipped silently down the main avenue of the capital city of Longfall, past one- and two-story buildings, each surrounded by a vast expanse of parking lot. Holoboards promised DANCING and SEED and GUNS. Widely spaced saplings promised shade for parked cars in a decade or two.

Kajiwara Hiroshi sat in the back of the limousine between Michael O'Reilly and Sergeant Redstar, who kept his finger pressed to his implant to relay messages between Kajiwara and the *Morocco*.

"You have honored me with a most impressive demonstration, Michael.'' Kajiwara wanted to reach over and tousle the boy's hair, but seventy-five-year-old men do not appreciate being treated like twelve-year-olds, even by their great-grandfathers. A shame the boy's parents had decided against growth enhancement. Were Michael ten or twenty centimeters taller, Kajiwara would have an easier time viewing him as an adult. "And I agree that for a world like this, an armed reserve is more appropriate than a standing army. As long as you can mobilize quickly enough—''

"We can. As the general said, full mobilization in twelve hours.''

An adequate response time, perhaps, but it did not erase Kajiwara's concerns. An entire branch of his family lived here; he wanted them doubly and triply protected. "Do you need additional instructors? Quite a few of the *Morocco*'s rangers fought the Wayholder on New Napa.'' As ferociously as he would have to fight TAAC HQ if O'Reilly accepted the offer, but Kajiwara would meet the entire bureaucracy in single combat to safeguard his family. 'Something could be arranged, and you might find them useful''

"Well, I'll look into it, but we do have the OBI data that someone on Howland Island—" he winked—"made available to us, and that's been very helpful. Ranger trainers might be a little more sophisticated than we need, or can support, given our limited resources."

He could not restrain himself. How very odd that his self-control, nearly infinite in discussion with his superiors, failed utterly in the presence of his descendants. Then again, he did not truly care whether Pierre LeFebvre and Han Tachun lived or died. "Longfall's resources would stretch further if they were not being diverted into forbidden ventures."

"Forbidden ventures? What do you mean by that?"

"Two hundred seventy-three illegal Zulu-class fighters, Michael." Kajiwara could not keep testiness from his voice. "Nearly one-third the complement of a fleetship. Your people have been very busy."

"Don't blame me for that." O'Reilly folded his arms. Stubborn defiance slid over his face. "I persuaded them to commit to an army, and I argued against building spacecraft. I told them what you told me. Nobody bought it."

"Why was that?"

"Because it doesn't make sense, that's why. Do you personally believe that the Wayholder won't reinforce their combat infantry?"

#Classified.#

Kajiwara closed his eyes and took three deep breaths. Then he looked at his descendant. "No."

"Well, then—"

"But it is your only hope. I do know that all the forces of the Association cannot defeat the Wayholder in space. And I do know that they have said—"

#Classified!#

"What?"

A knitting needle penetrated his skull. "Never mind."

"Yeah, yeah." O'Reilly waved a hand.

Kajiwara could not find the strength to outwit the implant and be persuasive at the same time. He was old,

and tired, and his knees and ankles burned with familiar
fire. Minor things, to be sure, but emotionally abrasive,
erosive. They ground away at the spirit, wore it down.

He gazed forward, through the limousine's smoked
windshield. The port lay dead ahead. A cargo ship
shaped like a sewer pipe was clawing its way into the
sky. As he watched it, a frown began to furrow his
forehead. He touched Redstar's knee. "Is the port under control yet?"

O'Reilly said, "What?" but Kajiwara hushed him.

Redstar cocked his head for a moment. "The detail
landed an hour ago, sir."

"Tell Sergeant Iovini to obtain a verifiable list of all
craft that departed between my arrival and the security
detail's." Kajiwara could have told Iovini that himself,
but he did not like to use the implant as a switchboard.
When he spoke to a human, he preferred to see a human, or at least a holographic representation of one.

"Yes, sir." A moment later, Redstar said, "Sir? The
sergeant would like to double-check his orders, sir. You
instructed him to obtain a full squad and inspect the
documentation of all ships and crew at the spaceport.
Did you also intend him to take over port operations?"

"No, of course not," said Kajiwara. "No one, however, has the authority to interfere with the inspection;
if someone should attempt to, Sergeant Iovini should
place him under arrest and hold him for questioning."

"Very good, sir."

He waited till the sergeant's eyes came back into focus. "Is there any word from the Oort cloud?"

Redstar's lips moved minutely; he nodded once, then
said, "Not yet, sir."

He had not really expected the ops groups to have
reported in, but with time weighing as heavily as his
great-grandson's sullen silence. . . .

At the port, the limousine bypassed the terminal and
drove directly to Kajiwara's shuttle. After helping him
out of the car, O'Reilly bowed. "Sayonara, Kajiwara
Hiroshi. Sayonara."

Squinting against the brightness of the sun, Kajiwara

returned the bow. Heat shimmered off the concrete around them, drawing sweat and drying it immediately. An arid wind pushed between them. He extended his hand.

Obviously startled, O'Reilly stared at it for a moment before he took it. "A handshake?"

"When in Rome." He squeezed hard. At that moment, he wished he himself had had different parents—Italian perhaps, or Russian, or from any culture that taught its children how to embrace each other. He feared he would never see Michael O'Reilly alive again, and he wanted to part in a way that would console him in the years and decades to come. "Goodbye, Michael. Give my—my best regards to your family. Tell them I will be thinking of them." Then he clapped his great-grandson on the shoulder, performed an abrupt about-face, and walked up the ramp to the shuttle.

He spoke to no one on the return flight to the fleetship. He sat alone, his eyes closed, a great and terrible weariness bearing down on him as if to replace the G-forces the gravity generators canceled out.

The pilot docked first at Kajiwara's command module. He thanked the woman and passed through the lock. The pale glow of the star coral filled the module. He ordered his bed to manifest itself. He wanted—no, he needed—many hours of sleep before he would be ready to resume command. He did not look forward to that sleep. Monsters would haunt it, giant green fiends rattling prayer beads strung with babies' skulls.

The holo chimed; he glanced over his shoulder. The *Morocco*'s communications officer peered out of the cube. Kajiwara drew himself up straight and stepped into camera range. "Yes?"

"A hard-copy eyes-only message for you from the chairman came in on the last SitUp, Over Commander. Shall I have it hand-delivered to your module?"

"Yes."

"Two minutes, sir." The cube blanked.

Not time enough really to do anything, but too much time merely to stand and wait. He went to the bathroom, splashed water on his face, and studied the veins in his fatigue-reddened eyes.

The lock buzzed; he emerged to find a young sergeant standing at attention, helmet popped open, an envelope in his hand. Kajiwara took the envelope. "That will be all."

"Yes, sir." The sergeant saluted, locked down his helmet, and left.

The envelope held a card for his holo player. He inserted it into the player's slot, went through the rigmarole of identifying himself properly, then stood, feet apart and hands behind his back, as the interior of the chairman's office took form in the cube.

A fully suited Wayholder paced the office on legs absurdly short and thick. Nearly three meters tall, it had the shoulders of a bull and the arms of a gorilla. It wore a pressure helmet the size of a beachball. Gurkha eyes followed its every move; Gurkha muscles tensed in anticipation of attack.

The alien was speaking through its suit mike. ". . . the Terran Association fleetship that destroyed three Wayholder war zone control craft and all their in-nested ships."

"But I assure you, it is not the TAAC fleetship." Though LeFebvre spoke firmly, sweat beaded his forehead and his cheeks had gone sallow.

"The evidence is indisputable."

"Allow me to explain." LeFebvre picked up a fat silver pen, stared at it as if wondering why he held it, then set it down again. "The ship, it had been one of our fleetships, but most unhappily, its crew mutinied. They act as the pirates—the privateers—entirely without the endorsement or support of the Association."

"So you say."

"Yes!" LeFebvre stopped, gripped the invisible edges of his desktop, and took a deep breath. He continued in a milder, more even tone. "It is as I say. I have explained to you the policy of the Terran Association toward the rebels. If you can destroy them, we will be grateful."

"We can certainly destroy them, human. The question is, what else must we destroy?" It wheeled about and lumbered toward the door of the office.

LeFebvre glared at its back until it had gone, then looked up into the cameras recording the scene. "Kajiwara! You see that which is going on here. The green dogs are losing patience. You have said you could solve the problem. Well, do it! Quickly. And thoroughly." His jaw muscles bulged as he ground his teeth together. "It is my express desire that not a single rebel be left alive when you have done. You are to consider that a direct order from your commander in chief."

The cube blanked.

Kajiwara sat on the nearest chair. Not a single rebel . . . LeFebvre had surely gone too far. No court would rule that a lawful order. But would a civilian court ever have the chance to make that ruling? He thought not. A court-martial might, but it would convene at the chairman's demand, and would find it expedient to ignore the law. . . .

Three war zone control craft! Rebels and mutineers, perhaps; first-class warriors, definitely. And superbly led, of course. Desperation might have forced Daitaku to improvise wildly, both on attack and in retreat, but it had not dulled the edge of his blade.

Kajiwara Hiroshi began to smile, then remembered that he would, sooner or later, have to face the alien-slayer in battle.

His smile faded. He did not know if he could best himself.

The golden cloud in the holo cube coalesced into Mitchell McCorcoran's face. "Over Commander, are you going back into Korrin territory today?"

"I have had quite enough of them." Daitaku placed his calligraphy brush back in its holder. "Their ubiquity and their . . . hunger rather unnerve me." He moved the sheaf of rice paper to a corner of his desk. "However, if you'll grant me the *Rhone* again, and the company of your nephew, I would like to make a similar reconnaissance run through parts of the Wayholder Empire.''

McCorcoran rubbed his lantern jaw. "Same arrangement as before?"

Daitaku placed his hands on his desktop palms-down, and stared directly into the camera. "Absolutely, Mr. McCorcoran."

"That's good enough for me, sir."

Thirty minutes later, Daitaku and Liam McCorcoran bounced into Wayholder Empire territory, to a point a light-year out from a star ringed by two dozen planets.

"Now what?" said McCorcoran.

Daitaku patted the arm of his chair. "We sit, we chat, we wait."

"For what?" McCorcoran began to unbutton his tunic collar.

"For the onboards to scrutinize the system. For . . . whatever."

"That sounds real exciting. Sir." He put his feet up on the edge of his control panel.

Daitaku raised one eyebrow, but did not speak until McCorcoran blushed and dropped his feet back to the deck. "Would you prefer to return to the Korrin, Lieutenant?"

"Uh . . . no, sir."

"Very well, then." Yellow lights flickered as the onboards ran a post-bounce status check; all subsystems confirmed 100 percent functionality. "You really must learn patience, Lieutenant."

McCorcoran's face went stiff. "Yes, sir. I've been told that before."

"Oh, come, Lieutenant, I did not mean to insult you." He rose, and stepped over to the galley for a cup of tea. "I am curious, though, why you entered a profession which someone or other described as 'long stretches of boredom punctuated by moments of sheer terror.' ''

A faint smile touched McCorcoran's lips. "Because life on New Dublin lacked the punctuation, sir."

"Ah." Returning to his place, he set the teacup on

the console. "And I because I thought it the path to honor." He swiveled his chair to the right and studied McCorcoran head-on. "Do you play chess or go, Lieutenant?"

"Not against you, sir." He grinned. "I don't fancy the odds."

"I see." The answer pleased Daitaku. It was good to know that the boy's impulsiveness had limits. "Once upon a time, before I became over commander of Octant Sagittarius, I assisted Raul Santiago in the redesign of the defenses of the Terran System."

"You, sir?"

"Kajiwara Hiroshi, then. I do know that I am not he—that we are different people—but the memories are real, and they come from a time when we were one person. If that makes sense to you, Lieutenant."

"Not really, sir, but gravpipes don't, either."

"Ah." He nodded, more to himself than to McCorcoran. "We investigated the feasibility of installing automatic early-warning stations around the systems. Unfortunately, the realities of the inverse square law, light speed, and TAAC's annual budget defeated us."

McCorcoran cocked his head; his eyes appeared to lose focus. After a moment the said, "Oh! The farther out you go, the more stations you need, and the more it costs."

"Precisely." He queried the onboards. They had located the largest six hundred objects in the system ahead, and had plotted all their orbits. They had also discerned a streak of gravity waves that suggested a deceleration lane. "We were not at war at the time, and did not expect to be invaded, so we could shrug and move on to other matters. The Wayholder Empire, though, is at war. From our observations of the Korrin, I would suspect that the Empire faces continual invasion. That leads one to wonder, what type of early-warning system do the Wayholder have?"

"I don't know, sir."

"Neither do I, Lieutenant. Perhaps we can find out together." He told the onboards to bounce them to the

far end of the apparent deceleration lane, but to hold
the *Rhone* at threshold speed after the bounce.

#Bounced.#

"So." Daitaku leaned back in his chair. Adrenaline
made his muscles restless, twitchy; willpower kept them
still. He had, after all, to set a good example for his
young companion. "Tell me, Lieutenant, how do pilots
of the Sagittarian Guard amuse themselves when off-
duty?"

Ten minutes later, McCorcoran was still answering.
The onboards interrupted to report radio interrogation
from a satellite around the planet at the far end of the
deceleration lane—the planet they had almost reached
by then.

Daitaku scanned the console to reassure himself that
all systems maintained Red Alert. "Interesting."

"Sir?"

"They did not—probably could not—intercept us."

The alarms went off.

Daitaku smiled. *"Now* they pick us up—but a warship
could have devastated that world already. And a Korrin
could have sowed a billion seeds that would fall eventually into its atmosphere."

"Sir, that's a skirmish control craft on our tail—and
my boards say it's at threshold, too."

"Then let us proceed with our tour." He bounced to
the next star in.

The Wayholder ship followed.

"Annoying," he said.

McCorcoran brought up a visual image on the overhead monitor. Three fighters were shooting out of the
forward edge of the pancake-shaped skirk. "It's a lot
closer now, sir."

"Of course it is." He took a sip of tea, and replaced
the cup on the console. "It will get closer still before
we lose it."

"Sir?"

He bounced again. And again. And again.

The alien's lasers found the *Rhone*'s stern. Yellow
warning lights rippled across the boards as sensors on

the stern began to warn of impending structural damage.

Daitaku nodded in satisfaction. "Close enough, I think."

McCorcoran had gone white. "For *what*? A collision?"

"Lieutenant—" he feigned sadness, though he felt glee—"please keep the panic out of your voice. While I would never condemn an officer for knowing fear, I would condemn him for yielding to it. And now—"

They bounced to a spot Daitaku had selected days ago, a spot near the event horizon of a very small black hole. Monstrous gravitational forces seized the *Rhone* immediately, and swung her into a sharp parabola about the object.

The skirk and its fighters, on the other hand, emerged just inside the event horizon.

Or so they assumed.

They certainly never saw it again.

Chapter 20

After slotting the *Cuyahoga* into Longfall's acceleration lane, Darcy Lee stood up to stretch the tension out of her shoulders. She was beginning to appreciate the elbow room a survey/reconnaissance vessel offered. Though the pilot's cabin would fit into a corner of Daitaku's command module, two people could not only share the cabin, but move about without accidental intimacy. She liked that.

Her muscles stayed stiff through twisting and toe-touching. She dropped into her chair and reclined its back one more notch, then checked the readouts. "What the hell are they doing?" she said in a mutter.

Steven Cavendish swiveled the right-hand seat around to face her. "What's the problem?"

"Wait." She double-checked that the onboards still monitored the carriers on every wavelength from infra-red to ultraviolet. "The ops groups off the Rock haven't bounced yet." Her throat was so dry it hurt to talk.

"I thought you said they wouldn't."

"They're not going to bounce straight out, that's guaranteed, but it's about a forty-hour trip at threshold. Not only are they not trying to save time, they're not even heading in the right direction."

"Are they going fast enough to bounce?"

"They've been at threshold for the last forty minutes." She rose, slipped behind Cavendish's chair, and reached into the galley for a tube of cranberry juice. "Steve, do you want anything to drink?"

"Liquid tranquilizer, maybe?"

"Check the med kit in the cupboard by the head."

"I was kidding," he said. "I'm not thirsty. Or hungry. Just nervous. So are we trying to catch them?"

As she edged back to her seat, she tried to be patient. "Steve, this is a surv/recon ship." She set the juice tube on the console. "The only armaments on board are the destruct charges."

"The what?" His voice fluttered slightly.

"Destruct charges." She dimmed the overheads; the control panel threw off enough illumination, although the bottom-lighting made Cavendish's face look ghastly. "In case of capture by the enemy."

"You mean you're supposed to blow yourself up?"

"You're supposed to blow the *ship* up. If you have to go up with it to get the job done, well—" She opened the juice and took a long swallow. Cold tartness soothed her throat. "The point, though, is we really do not want to 'catch' twenty ops groups at full strength and battle readiness. Like a kid chasing a parade—what's he going to do with it if he gets it? We don't want to be anywhere near them."

"Then why are we following them?"

She bit back mounting irritation. "So that—"

#Subjects have bounced,# said the onboards.

"Finally!"

"What's the matter?"

"Wait." As she touched her implant, she checked the time. Then she told the onboards, "Bounce eighty-two light-minutes out from Longfall, toward the Oort, but stay above the plane of the ecliptic. Listen for a transmission from Longfall Astro Command HQ to trainee fighter pilots. Record the message, copy into a SitUp, and bounce the SitUp to the center of the trainee formation in the Oort."

#Bounced. Listening.#

"Darcy," said Cavendish plaintively, "what's going on?"

A few minutes ago she had been admiring the cabin's roominess. Now it seemed unbearably cramped. And hot, too. "They bounced." She reached for the environmental controls and turned the thermostat down.

"Did we?"

She took a deep breath. It did not calm her. "Sure."

"Are you trying to get there before they do?"

"No way. We're trying to copy the message O'Flaherty sent out."

"Why didn't we just get a copy before we left?"

"Because I didn't think of it, okay? Because I didn't anticipate the ops groups right, so I didn't plan this thing right, and now I'm scrambling to recover. All right? Does that satisfy you?" Abruptly she realized that she was screaming. Shame burned her cheeks; nothing is supposed to rattle a fighter pilot. She wished she could loop back in time and clamp a hand over her own mouth.

But Cavendish said, "Hey. Darcy. It's all right. I'm not attacking you. I'm just . . . inquisitive cargo, if you like. Okay?"

"If you'll forgive me for—"

"It's all right. Um . . . would you mind explaining how we can copy that message, though?"

She set the juice tube down and raised her hands to gesture. "Radio waves expand in a sphere that swells outward from the source at light speed. If we bounce to a point outside that sphere, the message will pass by us, and we can record it for replay to the fighters."

"All right. But why? Will it be too faint for them to hear?"

"No. It's just going to take ten or eleven hours to get out to—"

#Recording.#

"—where they are. And if the Rock's ops groups bounce most of the way there, they might beat the message in. So—"

#SitUp away.#

"—the onboards have copied the message into a SitUp capsule and sent that out to the Oort. It just left. It will get there— It's already there. The fighters will hear it, and bounce out of the system." *I hope.*

"To where?"

"Who knows? The rendezvous point's already in their

software. Whoever's in charge will tell them, 'Bounce to Point Gamma,' or whatever.''

"But how do you plan— Oh. The Wayholder tracker."

"Exactly."

"And that way the TAAC forces can't follow."

"You're learning, Steve." Her throat still hurt. After switching the ventilators to high, she set the humidistat to max.

"Because you're teaching. So now what?"

She reached for the juice. "First we bounce to where the ops groups went." She gave the onboards their instructions. "Then—"

"Why? I thought we wanted to avoid them."

"They won't be there. They bounced *to* that point a minute or two ago, and they were traveling at threshold. They've got to be at least five megakay away."

#Bounced.#

"So why are we going there?"

"We came here—" she scanned her boards—"because this is the one place we can be pretty sure they're not."

"We're here already?"

"Steve—" *Patience!* "Yes, we're here already."

"Where are they?"

"Which they?"

"The Longfall fighters. And the carriers, too, for that matter."

She pointed to the bulkhead monitor. "Right there."

"Pardon?"

"It's an overhead simulation. We're in the middle— that point of white light?—headed toward the top. Our light won't move. The background will. The red lights are the TAAC ops groups, they're, ah, six million kilometers ahead of us. About halfway to the edge, and a little off to the right, those green lights?"

"Yes."

"Longfall's Zulus. Call it half a billion kilometers, give or take."

"So are we going to them, or—?"

"No. If they're any good, they've already bounced.

On our current course, we'd intercept their wavefronts in about twenty-five minutes, give or take. The problem, of course, is that the ops groups will notice us any second now, if they haven't already, and they will probably get curious. So what we're going to do is stutter-bounce toward the green lights.''

"Huh?"

She cued the onboards. "Steve, the computers are looking forward for a rock-free lane at least four hundred thousand kilometers long that begins roughly ten megakay ahead of us."

"Why ten megakay?"

"Because beyond that distance the sensors can't pick up anything much smaller than twenty centimeters in diameter—and something that size, even plain old ice, will punch right through the dustbrooms. We need the distance to give the pipes at least five seconds to smooth out before we bounce again. That's still pretty risky. But a surv/recon ship is sleek, so if we've time to spot a rock, we ought to be able to dodge it."

"Uh-huh." His two syllables conveyed a thesaurus worth of doubt. "So then what?"

She sighed. And promised herself she would never again serve as Cavendish's pilot. "The computers bounce us in, we cruise while they look ahead again, they bounce us forward again. And so on and so forth, until the wavefront washes over us and we can follow the Longfallers."

#Bounced.#

The board's lights turned hot red as alarms rang wildly.

She glanced at the display. "Jesus Buddha! Flip us—"

#Flipped.#

"Bounce us back!"

#Bounced.#

The alarms shut off; red lights winked white.

"What the hell was that all about?" said Cavendish.

"Apparently—" she scrutinized the display very carefully—"our TAAC friends also decided to stutter-bounce in.'' That surprised her. The book specifically prohibited stutter-bouncing on that little rest. Had Kajiwara Hiroshi managed to rewrite part of the book? Or had he simply told his pilots to ignore it? "We wound up ten kay behind a carrier."

'Could we have crashed?''

"If they were decelerating at max, yes; otherwise, not a chance. But at that range a carrier could take out the Sly Hog with a can opener, never mind heavy weaponry." She shuddered once. "Okay. Let's do it again."

"What?''

"Check the display."

"So?''

"The ops groups aren't in front of us anymore. They're all stutter-bouncing in. So now we go, knowing they're well ahead of us, and also knowing that we're not going as far as they are." She readied the onboards one more time. "Hold on to your hat, Steve.''

#Bounced.#

Th displays stayed clear that time, and the next time, and the next, until finally the Wayholder device recorded the wavefronts emitted by Zulu-class fighters bouncing out of the system. Darcy Lee let out her breath with a huge sigh, and lifted the juice tube. "Let's go get 'em," she said.

Cavendish said, "Yes. Please. Let's.''

Moonlight fell as cold and merciless as snow. Seven ninja thrust him into the courtyard, pushed him to the moss-ringed stones, and closed a circle around him so he could not escape.

On a timeworn granite boulder sat a black-lacquered katana kake bearing two swords, one long, one short.

One ninja took his name and stood by the boulder.

Another took his honor and stood behind him, there to shift from side to side so that no matter how he twisted or turned, he could not glimpse his honor.

A third took his face and sat cross-legged, a meter away, on the far side of a flat, moonwashed stone.

The go board appeared. He was to play black.

When he slapped a pebble down, it turned white.

He lost, of course. Ignominiously.

The ninja disappeared with his name and his face and his honor, leaving him only the two swords.

He reached.

Moonlight pulsed through metal, and he could not close his fingers around the frost.

Molten steel dripped and ran and puddled like his tears.

A giant hand seized his shoulder. Kajiwara Hiroshi awoke with a shout.

"Sorry, sir," said Sergeant Redstar. "Admiral Wiegand's orders, sir."

He rubbed his eyes as he swung his legs over the edge of his bed. His knees ached abominably. His swollen knuckles throbbed. "How long have I been asleep?"

"Twelve hours, sir." The massive bodyguard stood at attention, his brown eyes focused on the opposite bulkhead.

Kajiwara pushed himself to his feet. The deck chilled his soles. The air smelled sour. Twelve hours? He felt as though he had just closed his eyes. "Get me the admiral."

"Yes, sir." Redstar took a step, then stopped. "Robe, sir?"

He glanced down the front of his nude 167-year-old body and nodded dully. "Please."

Redstar brought him a herringbone-patterned yukata from the closet, then switched on the holo.

Wiegand's image appeared at once. She looked as tired as he felt. "My apologies, Over Commander, but—" She passed a hand over her face. "There's news. All of it bad, but I thought you'd want to know."

"Of course." He walked to his desk. Standing, he touched his fingertips to its slick plastic for the illusion of support.

"The ops groups can't find the Longfall fighters. They did intercept a message originating near Longfall. The message ordered the fighters to bounce to 'Point Theta,' remain there until joined by a Guard vessel, and con-

sider themselves assigned to the Guard until further notice. Finally, Luna has relayed another protest from the
Wayholder Empire. The aliens claim one of our survey/
reconnaissance craft has been running through the Empire to acquire the intelligence necessary to support an
invasion. They demand that we stop this at once.''

'Of course they do.'' He massaged his temples while
he thought. "Send an urgent SitUp to Over Commander
Munez in the *Cheyenne*. Ask him if he knows anything
about this. If it's not one of his ships, he should—'' He
sat down because he could no longer stand.

"Sir?''

Kajiwara Hiroshi had no choice, none at all, and he
hated it. He hated himself for winding up in this position. "He should so inform the Wayholder Empire, and
request that they destroy the intruder on sight.'' His
stomach churned. Asking aliens to murder humans put
him in company with LeFebvre, and he could not think
of more despicable company.

"Yes, sir,'' said Wiegang. "I've brought the ops
groups back.''

"Yes, very good.'' The module seemed darker. Had
the star coral dimmed? Or had his vision? "Do we have
a copy of the message the ops groups intercepted?''

"Yes, sir.''

"Is it signed?''

"No, sir.''

"No, of course not.'' He stroked his jaw. Its silver
stubble offered no real aid to contemplation. "Send an
order over my name to Longfall. The planet is to sever
all ties with the Guard. It is to cease production of war
matériel. And it is to investigate this message we intercepted, arrest the person or persons responsible for its
transmission, and deliver all parties involved to the *Morocco* for court-martial.''

Wiegand blinked. "Sir? TAAC does need all the
gravpipes it can lay its hands on, and KaoHsiung—''

"Once we find a site for them, we shall move their
factories.'' The words soiled his mouth. "Send the
message now.''

"Sir!"

Kajiwara Hiroshi went to a bath that did not cleanse, to a breakfast that left him empty, and to the desk, where he affixed his meaningless but essential thumbprint to one official form after another. His arthritis flared hotly; his print grew more and more smudged. He was glad when the holo chimed, then lit up with Wiegand's worried face. "Yes, Admiral?"

"The reply from Longfall has arrived, sir. In summary, they deny having any ties with the Guard, they refuse to suspend operations at Kaohsiung Gravpipes Limited, and they accuse us of forging the message."

"Then transmit an ultimatum." Kajiwara Hiroshi closed his eyes. He had not expected it to come to this. He had believed himself clever enough to prevent it. He had deluded himself, and now he must pay with his soul. "If they do not accede to my demands, the 79th Fleet will blockade the planet. Nothing will go up—or down. Transmit that now, Admiral."

"Yes, sir."

Daitaku gaped at Mitchell McCorcoran's holo image. "I could not have heard you correctly. Kajiwara is going to blockade Longfall?"

"That's what their SitUp said, Over Commander." Guard members moved behind him on tasks he did not explain. "Unless of course they knuckle under like good little boys and girls, and wait for the Wayholder Empire to come acalling. . . ."

Daitaku eyed his deactivated control console longingly. "Insanity, pure and simple."

"Sir?"

He reached across his desk to tap the button that controlled the fluorescents. Twilight crept over the module. "I have been analyzing and extrapolating—with a great deal of computer assistance—the recordings I made during my forays into Korrin and Wayholder territory." He snapped his fingers at the holo projector.

An overhead view of the Milky Way dispelled the

darkness. The viewpoint zoomed in; the galaxy expanded. Great sheets of stars passed out of the projection area and disappeared, as though they had floated to the edge of the universe and fallen off. The zooming ceased. Two spiral arms burned with cold glory that deepened the black of the rifts that defined them. Beyond the last rift lay a nearly solid bank of light that marked the way to the galactic core. "Are you receiving a copy of this map, Mr. McCorcoran?"

"Yes, sir. What's the scale?"

"One centimeter equals ten parsecs." He told the computer, "Display all stars in white regardless of spectral type. Show TAAC and Guard forces in blue."

Even as the stars shifted to uniform brilliance, blue dots sprinkled the spiral arm closer to Daitaku.

"Wayholder forces in red."

The edge of the Empire facing the Association turned pink, a pink whose hue deepened as it crossed the Empire, until it became a clear, hard ruby along the rift that lay between Wayholder territory and the main disk of the Milky Way.

"Korrin forces in green."

Solid emerald banked the other side of the rift, a gem ledge reaching half a meter back into the realm of the Korrin. Green dust drifted across the rift itself.

"As you can see, Mr. McCorcoran, the Wayholder are badly outnumbered. By at least four to one, if my observations and available stored data extrapolate accurately. The ratio is acceptable for well-led defenders. Not pleasant, or desirable, but acceptable, especially in light of the speed and manner in which the Empire reinforces during battle."

"I'm not entirely sure what you're leading up to, sir."

"The Korrin are invading the Wayholder Empire all along the rift." His sandals whispered on the metal deck as he began to pace. "From what I have seen, they pour in like buffalo on stampede, or a plague of locusts, devouring all in their path. When their enemy flees, they do not pursue, *per se;* rather, they broadcast their seeds and continue at threshold toward the next resource-rich system.''

''Which means that if the Empire pulls out of a star system, it doesn't have the strength to take it back?''

''If there remains anything to take back. . . . Mr. McCorcoran,'' he said with sudden anger, ''the Empire is bluffing!''

''What?''

''Their total forces outnumber ours a hundred to one—but they cannot afford to pull those forces off the Korrin front. A good many, yes, perhaps ten or even fifteen times as many as the combined strengths of TAAC and the Guard, but no more than that. And even that edge can be diminished.''

''Sir, are you saying we could actually attack them?''

Daitaku hooked his thumbs through the belt of his yukata and released a small smile. ''Actually, we *have* to attack them. When their target flees, they pursue—blindly and suicidally. One suspects that a damaged Korrin bounces forward—'' That suspicion, once voiced, evoked a myriad hypotheses. Were the Korrin themselves so long-lived that they remained vital after the interminable sub-c trek across the rift?

Mitchell McCorcoran coughed gently. ''Over Commander?''

''Forgive me. It seems that Wayholder tactical software must mandate instantaneous pursuit lest the Korrin escape in Wayholder territory and infest it. In fact, the Empire might have warned the Association not to attack its ships simply because they cannot afford to lose any.''

''Sir, what if we communicate this information to TAAC—''

''Pierre LeFebvre will not permit the Corps to incur Wayholder wrath.'' He sighed. McCorcoran, the rebel, had suggested giving Daitaku's lord the truth that would set the Association free. Daitaku, the loyal if disposable over commander, recognized how futile that would prove. At times like this he found irony intolerable. ''The Sagittarian Guard will.''

''And?''

"I need to think, Mr. McCorcoran." He gestured to the holo controls. "If it would not displease you—?"

"I understand." Mitchell McCorcoran cut the connection, leaving Daitaku to the agony of his thoughts. Because he knew now how to defeat one foe of the Association, but he could do that only by defecting to the other.

Chapter 21

The cargo ship *Sierra* hit the pop-in point for the Shinkanto System and began to brake. Half the overhead lights in the pilot's cabin went out.

"Don't worry, it's a s-s-software glitch." Anatole Corzini reached over to pat Darcy Lee's hand.

"Stop it." But she said it distractedly, as though she did not really mean it, and that irritated her. She wished she were a cat. Upset cats give marvelous snarls—and are expected to draw blood if touched.

"Sorry. They'll come back on in a minute. Of course, I sort of like it this way, at least when you're my passenger, but—"

"Jesus Buddha." First Cavendish with his inquisitions, then Corzini with his invitations, and only thirty minutes to herself between them. She never should have agreed to go on another mission so soon after returning from Longfall. "This is crazy."

"ETA at Octant Auriga HQ, twenty-one minutes and change. Darcy, this is the very first Sherpa-class transport to be commissioned; we took delivery on it the day before you hijacked us. Once they debug the op sys, it'll be so much better than a Conestoga-class transp—"

"I was talking about the mission." She waited a moment, tapping an impatient rhythm on the arm of her chair. "Did you hear me?"

He turned his thin face toward her. "Of course I did." He spread his hands. "But what do you expect me to s-s-say? You know we need more ships. And TAAC isn't going to give them to us—somebody has to go get them.''

"Sure. But remember who just brought 273 Zulus back from Longfall. At the time, *that* seemed crazy. Now it looks like sanity itself.''

A red light blinked. Corzini cocked his head and listened to his implant. "Okay, the onboards have asked the *Guatemala* for permission to dock.''

She pushed against her chairback, but the damn thing would not recline. "Now we've got a hardware failure. You ingrate. I bring you all those fighters, and what do you do?''

Corzini shifted sideways in his seat and settled back. "Lee, we sent you out for gravpipes, you brought back whole Zulus. Nice gift wrapping, but what did you expect us to do? The *Empire Bane*'s got to be able to bounce, right?''

"I am talking about being handed another fake TAAC uniform, and more fake TAAC ID, and pushed into a freighter with—'' she pointed a finger at him—"you. I've been running on adrenaline and OverTime™ for eighteen hours, and I have to go right back out and do it again. With *you*!''

He smiled, but not convincingly. "That's why I'm piloting this time.''

"It's not going to work.'' The operating system turned the overheads back on. A dull thumping arose in the galley. "Another glitch?''

"Let me check.'' He rose, slipped behind her, and patted her on the head as he passed.

"Jesus Buddha, Zi!'' She clenched her jaws so hard that dull red pain throbbed in her temples. That did not lessen her exasperation, either. "You can't just sneak into an octant headquarters and sabotage a fleetship! It won't work.''

From the galley came the clatter of ice cubes cascading into a bucket. "It's working fine s-s-so far. A lot better than this ice maker, that's for sure.''

"It's too early to tell.''

"Oh, hell, Lee. I know you weren't there, but we

tested Ramesh's emission-distortion gadget real carefully, and it ran just fine.''

"But he wasn't testing it against the sensors of an
octant HQ, was he?''

"No, but— Look, if you're willing to die to s-s-strike
back at the Wayholder Empire, then you ought to be
willing to risk a few years' imprisonment, all right?''

"The punishment for treason *is* death.''

He emerged from the galley wiping his hands on the
front of his tunic. "Fine, then what's the difference?''

"Fighter pilots are not supposed to die by firing
squad.''

"Right. Oh, yeah, that almost makes s-s-sense. Look,
why don't you shut your eyes, take a few deep breaths,
and try to calm down? We'll be there in about eighteen
minutes. Just follow my lead, and look knowledgeable.''

"About *accounting*?''

"No, that's me. You're my mech-handler, remember?'' He winked.

"*The* mech-handler, Corzini. Not yours. *The.*''

"Huh.'' He tapped his implant. "Permission to lock
on at Dock 817. The quartermaster of the *Guatemala*
will meet us at the dock.''

Lee ignored him. She folded her arms, closed her eyes,
and slumped in her seat. If this scheme worked . . .

Twenty minutes later, they floated down the tunnel
linking the *Sierra* to Dock 817 of the *Guatemala*, fleetship of the 58th. Behind them purred an autopallet piled
high with flat plastic boxes and one large crate.

The sentry on duty behind the force field barrier came
to attention. Behind him stood a red-haired lieutenant
wearing Quartermaster Corps insignia and a very worried look.

Corzini snagged the edge of the ID scanner with his
left hand and brought his feet down to the deck. He slid
his ID into the scanner.

A green light flashed. The sentry saluted Corzini and
turned to Lee.

Corzini held out his right hand, but at her scowl he pulled it back. A leg kick touched her down so hard she almost ricocheted. Her nervous fingers trembled; she slotted her card into the scanner. A moment later the light flashed green again. The barrier disappeared with a *pop*. Her stomach twisted as she stepped into gravity. The air smelled of bleach.

The lieutenant drew himself up and saluted. "Yorkson, sir." He looked fresh out of the Academy. "Er . . ." Confusion struggled with poise for control of his smooth cheeks; confusion won. "May I ask what brings an audit team from Howland Island to the *Guatemala*, sir?"

Corzini's eyebrows rose. "You weren't notified of my arrival?"

"Er . . . no, sir, we weren't, sir." Yorkson licked his full lips. Lee figured him for twenty-five, tops. "I mean, not in advance, sir."

Corzini let out a groan. "Lieutenant Lee?"

She was not sure what he wanted from her. "Captain, techies go where they're sent. It's not the lab's job to transmit notification of beta site selection, anyway. For sure it's not *this* techie's job."

"Well, all right. Probably someone in my office, then." Corzini fished in his pocket and pulled out a ROM card. "Here's a duplicate of the orders. Lieutenant, do we have a paper copy of these?"

She put incredulity into her voice. "A paper copy, sir? Us?" She forced a laugh. It did not come easily, but it came.

Corzini clapped the quartermaster on the shoulder. "You can print that out later, then, because we are on one unbelievably tight schedule. Let's talk as we walk."

The boy surrendered to bewilderment. "Yes, sir. Where to, sir?"

"The nearest storeroom."

"Of what type, sir?"

"Anything—linens, food, s-s-spare pallets—just the quickest to get to, that's all."

Yorkson shrugged. "This way, please." He pivoted,

waved aside a jani-mech swabbing the deck, and led them down the central passageway.

"Let me put your mind at ease, Lieutenant York-son," said Corzini. "We're here because you have an excellent record."

"Sir?" They reached the first intersection; he turned right.

Lee lagged behind to make sure the autopallet nego-tiated the turn.

"You've been selected as the beta site for testing—" Corzini sighed—"Mobile Inventory Control Equip-ment. MICE, for short. *Not* a term I would have s-s-selected, but then, the lab gets to name its inventions."

"Yes, sir." Yorkson stopped and pointed to a hatch. "We keep spare spacesuits here. Is that all right?"

Corzini looked over his shoulder at Darcy Lee. "Lieutenant?"

How the hell should I know, Zi? "That should do just fine, Captain."

A bench ran down the middle of the long, narrow chamber. Metal lockers lined two of its bulkheads; di-agnostic equipment covered a third. Corzini opened the large crate without lifting it off the autopallet. "This is the controller, isn't it, Lieutenant?"

You're asking me? "Yes, sir."

He lifted a display screen out of the crate, set it on the bench, and attached the keyboard. Then he plugged the system in. "Now," he told Yorkson, "while my mech-handler's unloading the MICE, let me explain this to you." He stopped and cocked his head. "It just oc-curred to me. If you didn't receive your notification, then you probably haven't received the manuals and other documentation either, have you?"

"I haven't received anything to do with any of this, Captain."

I'm in the dark, too, Zi. Darcy Lee zipped the front off the nearest flat. At least they had taught her this part. Extracting a power cord, she found a wall socket and plugged it in. In a moment, a pink, mouse-sized plastic box appeared at the flat's open end; she set it on the floor. Wheels spinning, it headed for the repair-mech tube entry in the corner, and disappeared. "All of them, Captain?"

"All of them."

While she worked, Corzini spoke to the quartermaster. "These do two things. Obviously, they track consumption of inventory items, but that's child's play. The reader in the doorframe does a very good job of that. The improvement here, though, is that the MICE scatter through the ship and continuously sample all replaceable items, estimating a remaining useful life span, and adjusting your ordering appropriately."

"Sir?" The lieutenant looked baffled.

Corzini waved at the ceiling. "Take those light fixtures. You replace them every—what, nine years?"

"Yes, sir."

Darcy Lee wondered how Corzini had known that, but did not look up.

"Yet these fixtures," Corzini said, "have a rated life of eleven years. You replace early to ensure that none will burn out. The MICE, however, do continuous testing, and are able to list those fixtures likely to expire in any time period you specify. Say you want ten percent more life out of them. Ask it to list those with a useful life of four months or less."

"Can we do that now?"

"Now? We don't even have all the MICE released yet. It will be . . . ten to twelve days before you can begin to extract useful information, useful in the sense of being complete, that is."

"Wait, sir, wait." He held up a hand. " 'Release,' sir?"

"Yes, release." Corzini pointed to Darcy Lee. "What my tech-handler's doing. She activates them, they disperse through the repair-mech ductwork, and start their sampling once they've reached the configuration the controller has determined is optimal for this particular vessel. As their battery packs begin to weaken, they seek out a power source and plug themselves in. While they're plugged in, they use the power line's standing wave to transmit data to the controller. What could be simpler?''

"Sir, I just don't know." His smooth cheeks reddened. "I mean, releasing unknown mechs into the system without authorization is—''

"You have the authorization in your pocket," said Corzini. "Look, I know your real concern, and—''

"Sir?''

He put a hand on the quartermaster's shoulder and dropped his voice so low that Darcy Lee had to strain to hear him. "Look, son, I understand that you're worried that if the MICE don't work, it'll be a black mark on an otherwise spotless record. But I promise you, you don't have to worry about that. As long as Howland Island is using the *Guatemala* as a beta site, you'll be evaluated only on your interfaces with the beta test equipment and teams. If these gizmos botch the job because of inadequate programming or whatever, that's our fault, not yours. All right? You just learn the MICE, son. Learn how to use the controller. You'll come out smelling like roses.''

She had finished the last box. Standing, she said, "All done, sir.''

"Very good, Lieutenant." He glanced at his watch. "Oh, Lord, we're due at the *Morocco*. We'd better—''

Yorkson, his blue eyes wide, said, "The *Morocco* is a beta site?''

Corzini nodded impatiently. "Kajiwara Hiroshi specifically requested it. He ordered the development of the MICE system when he was on Howland Island." He waved to the autopallet and empty flats. "I hate to ask this, but can you have your sergeants dispose of all this?''

"Oh, yes sir, no problem.''

"Fine." He extended his hand. "It's been a pleasure, Lieutenant. Best of luck with the system. We'll be back in about two weeks for the first full-scale test. In the meantime, please record any problems you notice." He turned to Darcy Lee. "Let's go.''

"Yes, sir!" She let him precede her through the door,

and gave Yorkson a pat on the butt. He blushed; she winked. "See you in two weeks." She sauntered after Corzini.

Ten minutes later, as they accelerated up the lane to threshold, she wiped sweat off her forehead. "Jesus Buddha, Zi!"

He laughed out loud, a high, triumphant whoop. "Still think it won't work?"

"The first part worked all right. How's the rest of it supposed to go, though?"

He gave her an odd look. "The way we said."

Her cheeks warmed; she wondered just how pink they had turned. "Uh . . . well, you see, when Mitch explained it back at HQ, I sort of tuned out. Getting in seemed so suicidal that what was supposed to happen afterward didn't really mean anything."

"Uh-huh." He nodded thoughtfully. "Then why'd you go?"

"Because—" She shook her head. "What happens next?"

"All right. The MICE are dispersing through the ductwork, and they are plugging into the power lines, but—" he grinned—"they're searching for the navigational and power systems, not the inventory control systems. The first time the *Guatemala* bounces, it will arrive at the Guard HQ decel lane. The instant the bounce is complete, all power to everything but life-support systems and gravpipes will fail. The pipes will brake at max until the ship has stopped. Then power to the pipes will fail. It will lie there, blacked out—dead in the water, so to speak—just waiting for us to come by and pick it up." He punched the air exuberantly. "Pretty nifty, huh?"

She smiled. "Sure." The smile broadened; a chuckle broke loose. "Sure. Sure, it is, Zi. It really is."

"You know what's even better?"

"How could anything be better than hijacking a fleet-ship?"

"Hijacking two fleetships."

"You've got to be kidding! How—"

"Uh-uh. No joke. Liam and Steven are MICEing the *Burma*. As soon as those ships deliver themselves to us, we're ready to take on the Wayholder."

The holo display in the corner of the command module glimmered softly white as it began to sculpt Admiral Wiegand's frazzled features.

Kajiwara Hiroshi spoke even before the image came into complete focus. "More bad news?"

"Yes, sir." She rubbed her bloodshot eyes, then figured a lock of gray hair off her forehead. With a deep breath, she squared her shoulders. "The over commander may wish to relieve me of my command. While—"

"Why?"

Her jaw muscles tensed visibly. "The gravpipe factory is gone, sir. Someone towed it out of orbit, ran it up to threshold, and bounced out of the system. For whatever reason, my surveillance officer assumed that I had authorized the maneuver, and did not see fit to mention it to me. I take full responsibility, sir."

Kajiwara sank into a chair. He inhaled the warm, humid air of the module till his lungs hurt. He laid his hands on his thighs, palms down. He exhaled very, very slowly. "So." Fury made his teeth chatter. He repeated the breath exercise. It did not calm him. He tried it a third time. "So, Admiral."

"Yes, sir."

He studied the tips of his fingers. Could he do it gracefully, he would dim the lights to hide his lost face. "The fault is mine, Admiral."

Clearly, she had not anticipated that response. Swallowing, she nearly choked. "Sir?"

"It did not occur to me that they might take such a step. Had it, I would have told you to watch for it. It *should* have occurred to me. Speak harshly to your surveillance officer—once!—and consider that adequate reprimand, for both of you. As for myself—" He made a face. "The board of directors will judge me when the rebellion has been put down."

"Sir—"

He waved her to silence. "Earlier you said 'First,' Admiral. That implies 'Second.' Perhaps even 'Third.' Please. Point two?"

"A message from Longfall, sir. In its entirety: 'Come on then. If we can't defend our lands against the minions of tyranny, we don't deserve to hold them.' End of message, sir."

The star coral shone too bright for Kajiwara's ancient eyes. He closed them. Moisture prickled beneath the lids but he would not let it escape. He was samurai, and samurai wept not in the fulfillment of duty.

Those poor, damned fools. What made them think they could stand against the Association? "Admiral."

"Sir?"

"Is there a 'Third'?"

"Yes, sir." She lifted a hand as if in assistance, or sympathy, then let it drop. "The chairman wishes to see you in Geneva at once, sir."

He felt so terribly tired. "Assign me a surv/recon vessel, Admiral, and a pilot who will not fill the journey with mindless chatter."

"Yes, sir."

Ten minutes later the *Han* slipped into the acceleration lane. Twenty minutes after that it bounced, and in another twenty minutes braked to a halt at an L5 shuttleport. An hour later, Kajiwara Hiroshi passed through LeFebvre's ornate door and came to attention.

The chairman raised his bald head. His cold brown eyes focused on Kajiwara's throat. "I have called you here, Over Commander, in order that there be no possibility of the mistake. The planet Longfall has defied the authority of the Terran Association. You are to make such an example of them that no other member of the Association will ever consider defiance again. Dissolve the planetary government. Impose the martial law. Arrest all Guard sympathizers. Convict them of treason. And execute them."

LeFebvre's matter-of-fact tone chilled Kajiwara more than the instructions themselves. Bushido said he must

serve his lord, but could honor possibly require him to
obey one who cared so little for his own people? "Sir,
the cost—"

"Never mind the cost."

"This one referred to lives, ours as well as theirs.
An embargo—"

"You have your orders, Over Commander." A holo
of Earth spun in the plane of his desk. His hands closed
in on it as though it were a basketball and they were
trying to pick it up. His hands met each other at the
planet's core. His fingers interlaced; his wrists quivered.

"Sir, invasion will *not* deter the other colonies. More
likely, it will provoke them to open rebellion also."

"Then we will impose the martial law on them." He
locked gaze with Kajiwara. "It is necessary that you
understand this. The Wayholder believe that we control
our colonies. They hold the entire Association responsible for the activities of the Guard. Until there comes
the time that we can with the hope of success defend
ourselves against the fleets of the Empire, we will suppress any activity that might trigger Wayholder retaliation."

"Sir—" His voice must have trembled with furious
threat, for the Gurkha guards drew their weapons. He
stopped himself. Very slowly, he moved his hands into
plain sight. He spread his fingers. "Sir. One carrier in
synchronous orbit above Port Longfall will effectively
quarantine the entire planet. Thus isolated, the colonists cannot possibly cause any harm to the Wayholder
Empire. The savings in equipment and lives—"

"Damn you!" LeFebvre heaved his bulk out of his
chair and leveled a shaking finger at Kajiwara. "You
continue speaking of the lives, a few here, and a few
there, as though they meant anything whatsoever. I tell
you this, Kajiwara Hiroshi, they are dead already.
Everyone on Longfall is already a corpse. Everyone in
the entire Octant Sagittarius has been already condemned because we will not have the strength to defend
them until long after they have rotted into the dust!"

"Sir, we—"

"Silence!" He slashed the air with his hand. "You worry about a few lives in one octant, on one planet. Me, I worry about all human life in all eight octants, on all twelve hundred planets! You, I entrust to you a mission, and if you fail, what is the cost, ten thousand lives? Ten million? I have my own mission, Kajiwara Hiroshi, and if I fail, the cost is the entire human race! You will do as I have ordered."

He came to full attention and set his jaw. "No, sir."

"You refuse?"

"Yes."

"Then I will tell you this. If you refuse me again, you will be tortured to death."

"So desu." He bowed to the man he had to call his lord.

"But you have not let me finish. We will record your weeks of agony, from beginning to end, and implant them in one of your clones. Who will be given your name, your rank, your options—and your fate, if he also denies me. And so to the second clone, and the third, and all those approaching maturity as well. Kajiwara Hiroshi will take Longfall if I must have him killed a thousand times! Do you understand me, O honorable Over Commander?"

He did. He would gladly die to escape the shame that history would append to his name, but he did not know how many deaths he could endure before his will crumbled. It seemed to him, as he stood in that cavernous office with the mad chairman and the hard-eyed guards, that the disgrace of final submission must increase in direct proportion to his previous resistance. Whichever one of his continuations finally obeyed would know himself inferior to all his predecessors—and to be less than oneself was perhaps the greatest shame of all.

"Have you decided, Kajiwara Hiroshi?"

He nodded.

"And—?"

His throat hurt. "The invasion will commence when this one returns to the *Morocco.*"

LeFebvre sat, gestured brusquely to the door, and turned his attention to documents that materialized on his desk.

Two hours later, Kajiwara Hiroshi entered his command module again. It smelled more like a mausoleum than his home. He flicked on the holo. "Admiral Wiegand."

"Yes, sir?"

He could not meet her honest blue gaze. He could not look at the star coral. He splayed his right hand on his desktop and stared at the webbing between his fingers. "Take Longfall."

The rangers dropped within the hour. Half an hour after that, Wiegand holoed him. "Sir, we need reinforcements from Luna."

His eyebrows went up as his heart sank. Hoarseness roughened his voice. "Reinforcements, Admiral?"

"Yes, sir. Casualties are running five times forecast. The locals turn out to be camouflage experts—our rangers are tripping over positions we never knew existed. More to the point, the Longfallers are very well armed, and astonishingly well trained. Do we have your permission, sir?"

"How many reinforcements?"

"Two more divisions, sir. The ranger CO assures me he'll have the city under control by the end of the week; the planet, within a month or two."

Two more divisions. Had he not persuaded Michael O'Reilly to campaign for the establishment of an infantry, a single ranger company could have taken the whole planet in a weekend. Now it would require two more divisions to seize the city. Probably six more to conquer the world. And guerrilla warfare would smolder for decades.

"Permission granted, Admiral." His shoulders sagged. "I am tired. I must sleep." Without waiting for her response, he switched off the holo.

He went to the wall, and lifted the case of star coral off its hanger. He held it like a book; for a full minute he pondered the silver glow. Then he put the case in the closet and closed the door.

The bed appeared at his command. Not bothering to undress, he stretched out on it.

He slept.

Sleeping, he dreamed a dream from which he could not awake:

Kajiwara Hiroshi bore on his ancient shoulders the responsibility of defending the Terran Association against the Wayholder Empire. The entire Association, not one or more of its parts. He could not allow the few to jeopardize the many. Yet he could not squander his troops on rebels; he would need every ounce of strength later, for the true battle.

He came to a decision. "Withdraw the rangers." Calling for tea, he belted on an old cotton yukata, frayed at the cuffs. He sat at his desk, calligraphy brush in hand. His hand moved—dipping, swirling, slashing across the smooth white field.

The midnight koi snaps;
Resting mayfly disappears.
Ripples shatter stars.

He cleaned his brush and stored it. Returning the yukata to the wardrobe, he donned his dress uniform. He regarded his mirror self. Yes. Clean-shaven, clear-eyed, white hair straight as armies on parade. Yes.

He activated the weapons board and assumed control of the fleetship's armaments. Yes.

He focused the reconnaissance cameras on the moonlit port, and magnified the view till he seemed to be gazing down from the control tower. He set the filters to automatic. Selecting his weapon, he locked the guidance system onto the same patch of shadow-streaked concrete.

He pressed the button.

A missile plunged down through the atmosphere, trailing fire as its ablative shield burned away. Long minutes later, it struck.

Impact smashed the internal circuitry. The magnetic

flask maintained by the circuitry blinked out of existence. One kilogram of antimatter, released and lunging forward at terminal velocity, splashed against the wreckage of the warhead. Matter transmuted to energy.

The filters went black. By the time they returned to normal, the port had disappeared under a sheet of flame that stretched nearly to the city limits. The sheet kept growing, reaching a kilometer more in every direction every two or three seconds, covering trees and buildings and cars and children with its incandescent rage.

Moon-drenched smoke soared up, blocking the scene from his view.

It did not matter. He had locked the guidance system to a particular set of coordinates, above which the *Morocco* itself hung motionless. He did not need to see the broken ground in order to deliver another missile to precisely the same point.

And he had already seen his great-great-grandchildren burn in the night.

He touched the button. Waited two minutes, and touched it again. Waited . . . and touched. Again, and again, and again.

The *Morocco*'s missiles dug a giant crater in the crust of the planet, a crater with walls of fire-fused rock, a crater that bit deeper and deeper until it tore through the bottom of the continental plate. The world screamed, then, screamed as hot magma spurted like blood from a severed artery.

Gray smoke shrouded the globe. Kajiwara Hiroshi studied the instruments that peered through the smoke and told him of conditions on and below the ground.

He nodded once.

He removed his hand from the board.

He went to his bed, lay on his back, and stared at the ceiling of the module.

Wet with sweat, he awoke.

Flames danced before his eyes; the stink of charred flesh filled his nostrils; babies shrieked in his ears.

He knew it for a dream.

And, perhaps, his destiny.

* * *

Yellow light poured through the open hatch. Silhouetted in it, the Lee woman beckoned to him. "They've asked you to come back in, sir."

Daitaku suppressed a smile lest she think it came at her expense. He did not want to offend an officer of such obvious skill. Or a woman of such great beauty, for that matter. "Thank you."

The leadership council of the Sagittarian Guard came to its feet as he entered the conference room. Mitchell McCorcoran coughed into his hand; Steven Cavendish leaned on the long metal table. "I seem to have been chosen as our spokesman, Over Commander, so I'll make it brief." He glanced once around the room, as if for final confirmation. "We accept your offer of assistance with immense gratitude. We have voted, unanimously, to appoint you high commander of the Sagittarian Guard. Will you accept our commission?"

Daitaku bowed. "I am honored."

"So are we, High Commander." He held up two spiral nebulae wrought in gold. "Please wear these in good health and better fortune." He pinned them to Daitaku's epaulets, and shook his hand. "That was the official part. Unofficially, the sense of this meeting is that we have to convince TAAC to withdraw from Longfall. Our recon drones have picked up the colonists' broadcasts and it's pretty grim down there. Retaliation is called for." Again he looked around. No one spoke up. He nodded, and went on. "We recommend an antimatter-missile strike on the city of Geneva, with threats of more to come unless TAAC leaves Longfall alone."

Daitaku blinked once, twice. Though he had expected the council to ask for action against Earth, he did not know how they would react to his response. But that, he supposed, was their problem. They had given him the gold nebulae not as adornment for his broad shoulders, but as a symbol that they expected him to bear the burden of deciding on a strategy to save them from alien and human alike. "I cannot destroy a Terran city."

Mitchell McCorcoran touched his arm. "Do you need more ships? More troops? We can probably find them, somehow."

"No. I have three fleetships, with veteran TAAC crews. Moreover, I myself—in the persona of my original, Kajiwara Hiroshi—designed Earth's defenses. Yet I cannot do it."

Cavendish scowled. "Why? After this slaughter on Longfall—"

"Kajiwara Hiroshi is capable of many things, for he lost his honor at the battle of New Napa. I have not yet lost mine. I will not lose mine. The birthplace of humanity is safe from me."

"But—"

"I do have a plan."

Relief flitted across Cavendish's face. "What?"

Now Daitaku permitted himself to smile. "I will provoke the Wayholder Empire into declaring war upon the Terran Association."

Chapter 22

On the 1st of August, 2351, Darcy Lee wriggled into the *Sydney 10* and strapped herself to the control couch. The flight sergeant closed the canopy for her. She bumped her helmet on it while adjusting the height and angle of the couch. Her right shoulder brushed the Zulu's curved fuselage; her legs fit snugly beneath the forward instrument panel. She made a small, contented sound.

She brought all the monitors alive with the stab of a single button. Impatiently, she ran the preflight check. The Guard was about to launch its campaign against the Wayholder Empire, and she wanted to start *now*. She ached to make the aliens reap some of the pain and sorrow they had sown on the worlds of Octant Sagittarius during the last three years.

The checklist completed, she dipped into the *Empire Bane*'s memory for a holo of Hsing P'ing, her home planet. She windowed the holo into a corner of the main monitor, where she would see it throughout the mission. A wave of the palette changed the color of Hshig P'ing's rivers, lakes, and oceans to red. Blood red. As a reminder. And as a promise.

Daitaku's deep, confident voice filled the cockpit. "Pilots of the Sagittarian Guard, I salute you. You have been briefed about your role in this, the fastest, largest-scale reconnaissance in the history of Terran warfare. We have downloaded unit-specific instructions and mission objectives to your onboards, of course, but I ask you to remember several points. Please approach any target of potential military significance as closely as possible, yet do not forget that Wayholder gravity weapons become effective at approximately fifty thousand kilometers. If a Wayholder ship pursues you, remember to direct your onboards to bounce you past a black hole, and confirm destruction of the enemy before returning home. Finally, the instant you dock at your carrier, dump data into its main banks, and prepare to go again. We must make two or three complete runs today. Again, I salute you. And I thank you.''

The speakers fell silent. Darcy Lee pulled on her gloves and sealed them. Tension clamped her jaws together. She waited.

Five hundred million kilometers above the ecliptic plane of the star called New Napa, the *Guatemala,* the *Burma,* and the *Empire Bane* began to launch their carriers.

Darcy Lee could have commanded a carrier. Daitaku had offered her one. But had she accepted, she would have been stuck in the New Napa. On this mission, wine racks served only as refueling stations and data centers. Their commanders would hurl fighters into the dark, then twiddle their thumbs till the Zulus came home. It would be the fighter pilots who found the soft underbelly of the Wayholder Empire, while the carrier commanders could only fret and pray for their safe return.

Darcy Lee wanted a piece of the action. The Wayholder owed her a home, a family, friends . . . she could not stay behind while others extracted payment on her behalf.

When the fleetship catapulted the *Sydney* into the void, a barely perceptible tremor ran through the *Sydney 10.* Darcy Lee tapped her gauntleted fingers on the padded armrest. The holo of Hsing P'ing glared at her like an angry eye.

A brief pulse of gravpipes thrust the *Sydney* to a spot high above the *Empire Bane.* Falling into line with the other carriers from its fleetship, it came to rest. Spaced one thousand kilometers apart, carriers off all three fleetships would eventually form a line stretching eighty-nine thousand kilometers.

An unfamiliar voice said, "Go in five."

The computer said, #Four. Three. Two. One. Zero.#

Sydney 10 shuddered as the carrier's racks pitched her away. Darcy Lee said, "Accelerate at maximum to threshold."

#Accelerating.#

Behind the *Sydney 10* raced the other nine members of Wing One. Darcy Lee wore a wing leader's scarlet insignia, but led *Sydney*'s Eleven through Nineteen only in the sense that her fighter had come off the rack first, and had accelerated fast enough to stay in front for the twenty minutes it would take the wing to achieve threshold speed.

An odd thing, this business of using fighters as individuals rather than as wings. Definitely against TAAC regulations. She smiled. Thank Buddha Steve and Mitch had not foisted TAAC's rules on the Guard. Although if they had, Daitaku would probably have ignored them, because he needed data on Wayholder star systems, and he needed them quickly.

Considering the way Daitaku's mind worked, it was a wonder that Kajiwara Hiroshi had ever risen to over commander. She had met many ranking officers; occasionally it had occurred to her that TAAC's promotion process screened out anyone capable of independent thought.

If any other over commander or admiral, always excepting Kajiwara Hiroshi, found himself in a situation similar to Daitaku's, he would, almost instinctively, have sent out survey/reconnaissance vessels, because the book said to use them for reconnoitering unknown territory.

If genuinely pressed for time, that same over commander might—just might—dispatch an entire wing to investigate one small volume of space, but with reluctance, because the book advised against it. It would probably never occur to him to assign each fighter pilot a different target for a recon run. If a junior officer suggested it, the CO would point out, with asperity, that the sensors on a Zulu-class fighter would spot less than half what those on a Lewisanclark-class surv/recon vessel would detect. Never mind that a fleetship carried nine hundred fighters, and only thirty SRVs.

Daitaku, though, needed information, and wanted it *now*.

So Wing Leader Darcy Lee drove her Zulu-class fighter to threshold in full awareness of the fact that the nine sleek ships behind her would not back her up if she ran into trouble, nor could she cover for them. On this mission, each flew alone.

On the next mission, though . . .

Her gaze caught the bloody holo. Next time out, she would actually lead the wing into battle. She could hardly wait. She *liked* flying for Daitaku.

#Threshold.#

She came out of her reverie. "Bounce."

#Bounced.#

The star patterns on the screen shifted abruptly. Her destination lay a parsec ahead—a star in the Empire, visually identical to all the rest, that the *Empire Bane*'s main computers judged likely to have inhabited planets.

They ran at threshold for five minutes, while the *Sydney 10*'s antennae combed the electromagnetic spectrum and the onboards listened for artificial emissions. Finding some, they recorded them, and bounced the ship half a light-year closer to the star.

The air dried her nostrils. The screens showed starscapes, unwavering points of light on a black field, so she stared at the numbers on the console. They, at least, changed once in a while. She touched her implant. "Show me a map of the system."

A yellow star appeared at the center of her forward monitor. Faint blue circles haloed it; a blinking blue dot hung on each circle. Across the bottom of the screen appeared the words "Not to scale. Blue indicates a planetary body/orbit suspected but not yet confirmed."

"Then let's get closer." She knew it for a useless suggestion. The software controlled the *Sydney 10*'s approach, and the software would move them in its own good time. Her fingers itched within her gloves.

She bounced toward the alien star half a light-year at a time, coasting after each jump, all sensors eavesdropping on all frequencies, all systems gathering and storing ever-fresher data for later analysis. The map on the monitor grew more detailed, with the blue fading into white as the onboards confirmed the planets' locations and extrapolated their probable orbits. New objects popped up—moons and comets and asteroids.

One quarter of a light-year from the primary, three objects on the map turned red. A thick scarlet line, perpendicular to the ecliptic plane, bisected each. The legend at the bottom changed: "Not to scale. Red indicates apparent spaceports/traffic hubs and accel/decel lanes."

The onboards said, #Decision?#

Ah, now the software wanted the human touch. "Calculate synchronous orbit for each apparent traffic hub," she said crisply.

#Calculated.#

"Bounce to a point . . . one minute's travel at threshold local north of the innermost traffic hub, and twice synchronous orbit width sunward of it. Head due south for two minutes, then repeat for the middle traffic port, then for the outermost. Observe carefully as we pass. Go!"

#Bounced.#

The monitor swapped the map for a real-time image of the "spaceport," and printed "4.8 mkm" at the bottom. That number changed continuously.

Even at maximum magnification, the alleged port had no features beyond a high albedo. The Zulu's dry air made Darcy Lee want to blink, but she watched the bright ball intently. The *Sydney 10* moved so fast that she would have only a few seconds at closest approach to make sense of what she saw. It relieved her that the onboards operated much more efficiently.

The image swelled into a beige ball surrounded by glittering motes that in turn enlarged into metal spheres.

Ships? Factories? Resort hotels? Not her job to decide, thank God. They passed it, then ran for a minute longer. As it dwindled behind them, the onboards leeched every possible datum out of the flyby.

#Bounced.#

The second hub popped up on the monitor. This world had a reddish cast to it, a Martian balefulness that glared out at her and challenged her to come very, very close.

#Bounced.#

One last flashpast and they could go home to the *Sydney,* dump their data, and do it again somewhere else. She stared into the monitor, reluctant to admit, even to herself, that this mission bored her.

The third hub sparkled like silver. An icy hand squeezed her heart. She jabbed her implant. "Kill the gravity generators."

#Gravity generators off line.#

Around a planet-sized assemblage of girders and pipes and modules as big as mountains clustered four—six—*nine* war zone control craft. "0.8 mkm," said the legend at the bottom of the screen.

The *Sydney 10* would approach the Wayholder base for ten more seconds. She had bounced in 50 seconds ago, five million kilometers high. Their detectors would have noticed her 33 seconds ago. Thirty-three seconds! In that much time, a battle computer on red alert could determine her fighter's factory of origin, swivel giant banks of laser mirrors into position with eight decimal places of accuracy, and burn its programmer's surname into her hull.

She gulped. It came down to one question: Were those computers on red alert?

The last few seconds passed like days.

Then the numbers on the bottom of the screen zeroed out and began to increment. She expelled pent-up breath with a gasp. "Watch for pursuit."

#Watching.#

At a megakay she said, "Gravity generators on, accelerate to threshold, but do not bounce."

#Acknowledged.#

To her astonishment, the aliens did not give chase. The *Sydney 10* held the same course for a good thirty minutes—more than long enough for EM emissions from any pursuer to cycle through her sensors—but the onboards said, over and over, #No pursuit.#

It made no sense. It annoyed her. They had not reacted to her intrusion. Were they, by implication, dismissing her as harmless?

Or were they not quite as professional as they had seemed to be, once upon a time in the New Napa?

She stared at the bloody oceans of Hsing P'ing for a minute and a half, then finally said, "Bounce home."

#Bounced.#

Maybe the Guard had a better chance than she had thought.

Kajiwara Hiroshi sat alone in his darkened command module. The atonal music of invasion sang in his skull softly, almost inaudibly, as the deck passed to his tired bones the metallic vibrations of warships docking and departing. The ventilators brought the sound of fans and pumps, and a faint whiff of the algae in the recycling tanks. It smelled like death.

Ghostly light began to suffuse the corner. Kajiwara squinted while the unwelcome illumination reshaped itself into Admiral Wiegand's face. "Sir. A Wayholder war zone control craft is in the decel lane. One of the aliens demands to holo you."

Wearily, he raised his eyebrows. "Did it explain why?"

"No, sir."

He did not know if he had the strength to deal with a Wayholder. In the week since dropping the rangers onto Longfall, he had slept poorly, awakening every day with cries of burnt children in his ears, and visions of moonlit smoke in his eyes. But he had his hateful duty, which no one could do for him. He forced fatigue to the back of his mind. "Patch it through."

The holo blanked, then filled with the image of an alien jungle, all filtered light and tangled green. A Wayholder stepped in front of the mural, clicked its teeth, and patted its belly.

Kajiwara wished he knew whether its pear-shaped waist signified wealth, pregnancy, flab, or something else, something too foreign for a Terran mind to comprehend. When he fought these beings, he would need every fact about them that he could gather and comprehend.

"Over Commander Kajiwara Hiroshi?" Its lips moved, but not in the way that would shape those sounds. A translation program must reside on-line.

Kajiwara hoped it was a good program. "Yes."

"I am First Admiral Screnswinslagerlaimer. I must speak to you."

Kajiwara nodded. "How did you find me?"

"Your chairman gave us your location."

He kept the shock off his face. What was wrong with LeFebvre? Didn't the man—? Never mind. "So."

"I come to warn you. If the intrusions into the Empire are not stopped immediately, the Empire will declare war on the Association."

Once again, experience froze his facial muscles before they could reveal his thoughts—though in this case, he suspected it might not matter. "Intrusions?" he said quietly.

The wrinkles on the alien's torso deepened, smoothed out, then deepened again. "At latest report, over eight thousand separate incursions into our domain have occurred within the last twelve hours. They must cease. Or else the Association will cease."

"We are not responsi—"

"I do not believe you."

"And I have no cause to believe you." He stared into the cameras, completely unable to correlate the other's expression with its emotions. Briefly, it angered him that he had prepared inadequately for this moment, but he set self-reproach aside. Time enough for that later. And for further exploration of the Association's xeno-anthropological databases. Surely there must be more on file than he had found. "Can you present evidence to support your claims?"

"Of course." Looking away, it made a gesture with its left hand. Then it paused, apparently to listen. "I am told that the proof is not in a format which you would recognize. I am also told that the bandwidth of this communications device is insufficient for the transmission of the raw data. My engineers will consult with your engineers to devise an interface to enable data flow from our storage devices to yours. A shuttle will bring my engineers to you. I am told that in a short period of time the interface will be complete and the proof will be in your hands."

The alien lurched forward; the holo turned silver, then black.

Kajiwara switched off his own unit. He paced the unlit perimeter of his module once, then dropped into his desk chair, exhausted. He did not doubt the Wayholder's claim—but thousands of intrusions in half a day?

Daitaku was a clone imprinted with the memories and the mental patterns of his original, was he not? He had to think like Kajiwara Hiroshi. Some divergence had already occurred, as proved by his desertion, but he would have to possess the same basic military instincts as his predecessor.

Because he thought like the man from whom he had been copied, the clone would investigate his enemy before taking any other overt action. He certainly had the means. The *Guatemala*, the *Burma*, and the *New Zealand* gave him ninety survey/reconnaissance vessels, which could make . . . *thousands* of recon runs?

Impossible. The clone had not commanded the other two fleetships long enough to send the SRVs out that many times.

But unless Daitaku had gone thoroughly, completely mad, he would never, ever, wage war without superb intelligence, which verified the alien's complaint. But how could he make so many recon runs with so few ships?

Kajiwara Hiroshi mulled that over, then sat up

straight. Of course. Fighters. Daitaku had twenty-seven hundred of them. Allowing, at minimum, one hour for each mission, the Guard could trespass on the Empire twenty thousand times a *watch*.

So. Since the clone was collecting facts, he was preparing for war. Therefore, Kajiwara Hiroshi knew how to find Daitaku, and by extension the entire Sagittarian Guard.

Daitaku was samurai. Symbolism held him in thrall, as it had every warrior who had walked bushido.

The continuation of a samurai who had lost his honor by losing a world would choose only one world as a base to establish his own honor.

Daitaku had returned to the New Napa.

So. The over commander permitted himself a small smile. He could throw a hundred fleets into the New Napa within four hours. The Guard would cease to exist within five.

He reached for the holo controls, then drew his hand back. Immediate action would cost him the raw data promised by the Wayholder emissary. Those data would almost necessarily reveal far more about the Empire than the Association had in its databases, because for the aliens to prove trespass, they would have to demonstrate location of the alleged offense. And if the data were, indeed, raw—if the emissary submitted unaltered detector readings of incoming electromagnetic emissions—then those readings would contain a wealth of information about background activity at the time of the intrusion.

Kajiwara's analysts would spot traffic patterns and factories and population centers and . . .

And he must also consider Daitaku's nature. No clone of Kajiwara Hiroshi would gather information at considerable risk, and not store a copy in a safe place—a meaningful place. The New Napa shuttleport, for example.

The old man studied the white hairs on the back of his hand. If he were Daitaku, he would strike soon, before the Wayholder realigned their forces and ren-

dered the recon data obsolete. He would strike hard and
fast, and then . . .

A chill ran through Kajiwara Hiroshi. If he were Daitaku, he would step aside, so that the fury of the coun-
terstrike would spend itself elsewhere.

And yet. And yet . . . if he were Daitaku, would he
provoke the annihilation of the human race?

No. In honor or in shame, he would never take that
risk. Thus Daitaku knew something that his original did
not.

"To know and to act are one and the same."

In a short while, Kajiwara would know more than he
did now. Then, perhaps, he could act.

At the moment, he could only prepare to react. He
lit up the holo, and waited till Wiegand's gray hair
showed plainly. "SitUps to all octant HQs and Howland
Island. All Unified Security Forces to full Red Alert.
That is all units in all services. Be ready to defend
against a surprise attack by the Wayholder Empire.
That's all."

Wiegand blinked. "Yes, sir."

He shut off the holo. Suddenly the next few days
promised to be very interesting.

Daitaku paced his command module, barren now that
he had ordered all its furnishing retracted. Though he
would have been more comfortable in yukata and sandals, he wore his dress uniform because the occasion
demanded it. The heels of his shoes rang on the deck.
He thought again about taking them off.

In the module's humid air hung two banks of stars
separated by an empty dark lane, like a Hokkaido street
after the snowplows have passed. He walked down the
rift between the spiral arms. Once in range of the holo
cameras, he said, "I am sending them."

"You can't!" Mitchell McCorcoran spoke with far
more vehemence than usual. His holographic image extended its arms. "They've been flying for twelve hours
now. Some of them have already completed a dozen
missions. You can't ask them to go again!"

Though he empathized with the old man's concern for his nephew and all his nephew's comrades, Daitaku kept his voice level and cold. "A warrior obeys his commander." He touched the gold nebula on his left shoulder. "They will go out before they rest."

"But this is crazy, the—"

"We have revealed our intentions. We must strike now, before the Wayholder Empire can complete its defensive preparations."

McCorcoran scrubbed his face with his hands. "You're trying to trigger the counterattack now, aren't you?"

"Yes."

The former astrophysicist began to speak, stopped, and closed his eyes. He looked far older than his 124 years. "Is it absolutely necessary?"

"Yes." Daitaku gestured to the battle command holo. "The bright yellow dots indicate nearly five thousand targets we have identified within the borders of the Empire. We suspect them to be military factories; their size and traffic suggest great importance. We will strike all of them today."

"But why *now*? Why can't the pilots rest?"

"You know that the Korrin are migrating into the Wayholder Empire."

"Yes, of course, you told us that a long time ago."

"Let me tell you, then, two more things. They are deductions, based on my personal observations, on the shreds of data gathered by TAAC Intelligence some time ago, on computer analysis of the data collected today and on our interpretation of various propaganda holocasts which our reconnaissance runs recorded." Hands behind his back, he faced the holo of McCorcoran. "The defense against the Korrin consumes resources so quickly that the fighting ships on the Association side of the Empire are either under construction or under repair."

McCorcoran said, "How can you be sure?"

"Because we were not challenged once. We plan to

attack here—'' he swept his left hand through a mist of
stars— ''where there are no functioning warships.''

McCorcoran stroked his jaw, but said nothing.

''Moreover, our strike will cut production of essential
war matériel, which will in turn cause all finished output to go to the Korrin front.''

''But they'll shift—''

''Hear me out!'' He glared till the old man nodded
in resignation. ''You recall that the Korrin literally con-
sume that which they conquer.''

''Yes, of course. Like maggots in an apple.''

''Just as maggots swiftly render an apple inedible, the
Korrin can turn a world uninhabitable in less than a
month. Or so claim the Wayholder.''

From the sudden light in McCorcoran's faded blue
eyes, he anticipated Daitaku's point. ''A month?''

''Yes. This is the Wayholder dilemma.'' Daitaku
sensed that the other was ready to withdraw his objections, but needed to save a bit of face. ''This is what
we will take advantage of.''

''If you could just explain that—''

''By striking hard and fast against the productive capabilities of the Empire, we force them to decide which
front has higher priority. If they concentrate on us, their
forces facing the Korrin will weaken steadily, until the
Korrin break through and devour entire star systems. If
they focus on the Korrin, however, they can come to
terms with us.''

McCorcoran rubbed his jaw. ''Yes, but you said they'd
counterattack.''

''They will. And on a scale the Association has never
imagined. But it will be a desperate attempt to shock
us into submission. If we resist their initial onslaught,
they will not have adequate resources to reinforce. On
Earth, during the twentieth century, the losing side in a
major war tried a similar tactic in the Battle of the Bulge.
The counterattack caught the winning side by surprise.
Its ferocity drove them back, but ultimately failed. The
losers did not have enough men and matériel to hold

their advantage. The Wayholder will attack. Kajiwara Hiroshi will defend. The Wayholder Empire will lose.''

Mitchell McCorcoran stood, turned his back on Daitaku, and walked to the wall. He tilted his head to—what? Daitaku did not know if the other stared at the ceiling or prayed to heaven.

After two minutes had passed, McCorcoran said, "Do it."

So he did. Ninety carriers launched twenty-seven hundred fighters. Each Zulu bounced into Wayholder space, to a point less than ten seconds' threshold travel from a major alien factory, and hurled its entire payload at the unsuspecting installation.

Daitaku, sitting in his chair, palms flat against the surface of his desk, could not visualize twenty-seven hundred individual threshold attacks. He imagined, instead, one pilot . . .

Darcy Lee. Almond eyes wide with the effort to see *everything*, she bored in, pinwheels and torpedoes and antimatter missiles spewing out of her fighter, lasers stabbing, while the factory swelled in the monitor to the size of an entire world.

When a bare ten thousand kilometers separated them—when the awakening defenses had just begun to lash back at the black-haired beauty—her onboards cut in. They bounced the Zulu out. They took it to a place of nothingness, a point on a line between stars, simply to see if she was being pursued. She was. They bounced her again. They ran her ship down an intricate route where a microsecond of bad timing would suck it into the whirlpool of a black hole. The Wayholder fell in. The onboards took Darcy Lee back to the carrier above the golden sun of New Napa.

There she would stumble from the cockpit, look around in exhaustion, and wonder numbly if the madman in the command module would issue orders to go again right away.

More than anything else, Daitaku wished he knew the answer to that. The next move, though, was up to the Wayholder Empire—and to Kajiwara Hiroshi.

Chapter 23

Screeching alarms jolted Darcy Lee awake. Reflexes made her throw back the covers, swing her legs off the mattress, lever herself upright. She took a step, shook her head, forced her eyes open. Where—? A low-wattage bulb threw dim red light on a row of metal cots. Ah. Female pilots' quarters, the *Sydney*.

Clumsy from lack of sleep, she pulled on yesterday's tunic and trousers. They reeked, but her Zulu wouldn't mind. She had to sit to get the boots on. She rubbed her eyes, and blinked repeatedly until the clock over the hatch came into focus.

Oh nine hundred hours shiptime. Four and a half hours since she had hit the sheets. Wonderful. She stumbled to the med-kit and drew a shot of fatigue blocker. Pushing aside limp strands of hair, she touched her implant. "Orders?"

#Captain Darcy Lee report to battle station *Sydney 10;* assignment, wing leader Wing One.#

She thrust open the hatch and began to trot down the low-ceilinged gangway. Other pilots fell in with her, red-eyed and yawning and decidedly unsociable. None of them had showered, either. She pressed her neck. "Subject, alarms; query, cause."

#The Wayholder Empire,# said Daitaku, or more likely a recording of him stored in the fleetship's memory, #has attacked fifty colony worlds on or near the rift in retaliation for Guard attacks on its factories. Combat infantry troops are believed to be landing. We must leave the infantry to the colonists; the Guard will destroy the enemy's supporting spacecraft.#

Images from the battle of New Napa swirled unbidden to the top of her memory. Her knees almost failed her. She stopped, leaned against the bulkhead, and breathed deeply, rapidly. The other pilots jogged on.

Sure. The Guard would destroy the Wayholder spacecraft. Fifty worlds, ninety ops groups. Daitaku would probably send one carrier to each planet, and hold the rest in ready reserve.

Ready for the Wayholders' infinite waves of reinforcement.

#Captain Darcy Lee report to battle station *Sydney 10;* assignment, wing leader Wing One.#

"Coming, coming." She pushed away from the bulkhead. The OverTime™ had begun to take effect. She sprinted around the corner, down the ramp, and along the tunnel. The flight sergeant zipped her into a flight suit and dogged down its helmet; he slapped the Zulu's canopy shut as soon as she had squirmed into the fighter.

Strapping herself in, she began the preflight check.

A voice interrupted. "This is Commander Nicholson. The *Sydney* is accelerating to threshold; launch in sixteen minutes fifteen seconds . . . mark. All pertinent data and instructions have been downloaded."

She waited. No carrier commander in her experience had ever been content with such brevity.

Nicholson was no exception. "Your destinations, ladies and gentlemen. Wing One, Journeau. Wing Two, Clarke. Wing Three, Hsinjinshan."

A chill ran through her. Her grandfather's brother had settled on Hsinjinshan and raised an enormous family— very nearly the only family she had left.

She wanted desperately to volunteer her wing for that system. She kept her mouth shut, though. Nicholson and the other wing leaders might have deserted the Corps, but they would hardly engage in a frantic software shuffle just so she could defend a system where some of her family lived. Besides, some of them probably had relatives on Journeau.

Then her eyes widened as the full import of the commander's words hit her. Wing One to Journeau, Wing

Two to Clarke? Daitaku was splitting his ops groups and using the *wing* as the basic tactical unit! Did the man seriously expect ten fighters to drive off a Wayholder invasion party?

Nicholson's voice cut into her thoughts. "A surv/recon vessel has been posted in each system to monitor the situation and to collect Order of Battle Intelligence. The *Hudson* is at Journeau. The *Rhone* is in the Clarke. The *Niger* is at Hsinjinshan. Each is on the scene now; the latest SitUp from each reported one Wayholder skirmish control craft in orbit around each of the worlds. According to High Commander Daitaku, twenty minutes after you attack that skirk, reinforcements will show up. Expect either two skirks or one battle zone control craft."

Oh, yes, she thought, *then either two battleboxes, or one war zone control craft, then. . . . Jesus Buddha. Ten Zulus against sixteen fighters and a skirk. Just for openers. Did he expect miracles?*

"This is in your software, but for God's sake, when you're near a skirk, watch your gravpipes. Outside of fifty kilokay they're safe; inside ten, they're slag. Your systems will bounce you to the SRV monitoring your target. As you flash past, it will feed you new coordinates, which will take you to about forty kilokay from your target. That's just far enough for you to dump pinwheels and torps before shutting down your pipes. Hit their generators with your lasers as you run past. Get out of range before piping up again. Bounce back here to rearm. Again, your onboards know where the *Sydney* will be at all times. Questions?"

The thirty fighter pilots under Nicholson's command stayed silent.

"All right, you have nine minutes forty-five seconds . . . mark! . . . to get ready. Do good, guys."

Forty thousand kilometers away. That bothered her. The onboards could identify the enemy a nanosecond after the fighter's sensors had collected the foe's emissions, but for a successful attack, the wing would have to pop in perfectly aligned to the target. A Zulu's weapons, after all, depended on semimechanical aiming and launch devices—mirrors for the lasers, catapults for the pinwheels, and rockets for the torps.

Half a second of travel at threshold. The pinwheels took longer than that to unfurl. And though the torpedoes would have begun to spread their shrapnel, it would overkill where it struck, and not cover as broad an area as it should.

Well, she had been named wing leader. . . .

She ordered the onboards to display the attack plan. What showed on her monitor appalled her with its simplicity. The fighters would approach in single file, dump weaponry, zap with lasers, zip past, bounce to a regroup point, and do it again.

She did not like that scheme.

"Subject, plan of attack; query, identity of tactician responsible." Because if Daitaku had designed it, she would trust it; if Nicholson had done it, she would revise it with extreme discretion; if—

#Program Crazy Horse, TAAC AI.#

Ah. Computer-generated. That explained. It also meant she could substitute something better without wounding a superior officer's feelings.

One eye on the countdown clock, the other on her monitor, she sketched her own tactics, made sure the onboards understood what she meant, and had them reprogram the other computers in her wing. She was still double-checking that all her fighters had received the instructions correctly when Nicholson said, "The *Sydney* is at threshold speed. Wing One, *go!*"

A microtremor shivered the Zulu as the carrier's catapults hurled them off the rack. She switched over to her wing's frequency. "This is Wing Leader Darcy Lee. Count off with status."

"*Sydney 11,* off-rack and at threshold.'

"Ditto for *Sydney 12.*"

"Kidney 13 in the same flow."

"*Sydney 14* with you all the way."

"Fifteen's systems all go."

"Silly 16, ready when you are."

"*Sydney 17,* off-rack and at threshold."

"Eighteen here, hot to hit."

"Last but not least, *Sydney 19* on track and up to speed."

She nodded. "Thank you. Be aware that plans have changed. The first phase of the attack will run entirely on automatic. Either I or your onboards will tell you when that phase has ended. Good luck."

One last look around her cockpit. She touched her implant. "Bounce."

#Bounced.#

The SRV *Hudson* flashed past five thousand kilometers to port. Finger pressing the switch below her left ear, she asked, "Subject, coordinates of Wayholder skirk; query, did you get them?"

#Coordinates received.#

Wedging herself into her seat, she waited ten seconds for her wing's gravpipes to smooth out. The chance of blowup still remained, but she could not delay much longer. She took a deep breath. She shivered once. "Commence attack."

#Attacking.#

Adrenaline surged through her system. It synergized with her onboard link to warp her perception of time. Time ran slow, now. Her mind ran quick. Minutes seemed to pass between two beats of her heart.

The fighters shifted into a mandala formation ten second's travel time above the face of the Wayholder. Immediately they flipped end over end. Their stern lasers blazed to life, hurling javelins of coherent light at the skirk, burning spears that would not strike for two and two-thirds seconds.

Darcy Lee bit her lip hard enough to draw blood. The skirk would return the wing's fire. The question was, how long would it take the enemy to aim?

If the Wayholder took longer than half a second, their riposte would pierce the void—their targets would be gone.

Four and three-quarters seconds after popping in, each Zulu tossed five torpedoes toward the spot where inertia would place the aliens in five and a quarter seconds.

Now Wayholder lasers stabbed, but too late. The Sajjers were bouncing, in predetermined order, into the plane of the ecliptic, five seconds at threshold from the skirk, and running straight toward its edge.

The metallic taste of blood singed Darcy Lee's tongue. She held her breath. If her fields had re-formed around a pebble that lay in her path—

The onboards targeted the center of the ship, and launched five pinwheels in the pattern of a cross. #Flipped. TAAC forces on scene.#

"What?"

#Bounced.#

"Identify TAAC forces!" If everything ran as planned, 11 and 12 had just popped in, right at four hundred kilokay, 160 meters apart. Each would spin off five pinwheels in the same pattern, and bounce.

Then 13, 14, and 15 would form a triangle at the four-hundred-kilokay mark, pitch five pinwheels apiece, and bounce.

The last four would arrive in a square 160 meters along each side, spit their pinwheels, and leave in a hurry.

But with TAAC ships in the neighborhood—

#Identification: Wing One of the *Sydney,* a carrier—#

"Cancel." She laughed. Just enough distance separated the wing's attack points for EM radiation from the first spot to pass through the second while they were there. They had seen themselves. And now that they had reached their third attack point, presumably—

#TAAC—#

"Disregard."

The wing flew in a vertical column half a megakay out, coming in from the "northwest." She led the way.

She could have sworn they had begun the attack an hour earlier, but only six and a quarter seconds had passed. Their initial laser fire had scorched the Wayholder less than four seconds ago. The alien defenses were probably still facing north, though soon their sensors would spot the wing at the second attack point in the east.

Sajjer lasers blasted out their full fury. In one and two-thirds seconds, the hammer blow of tight light on generator housing would alert the skirk's sensors to the Zulus racing in from the third attack point.

Half a second after that, the aliens would fire back. The wing would have to fly into flame for a full second and a half, because if she gave the order to bounce when the beams struck, their pipes would not have cooled enough, and a bounce could do more harm than that much laser fire.

The onboards displayed a magnified image of the skirk on the monitor. It looked like the innards of a mechanical pancake. She watched closely, not needing to give commands because she had given them all before leaving the *Sydney*.

Yes, there and there and there, ten places in all, metal heated from black to dull red to—

Her alarms flared bright red as Wayholder laser beams washed over the *Sydney 10*'s bow.

She gripped the arms of her chair and clenched her jaws tight. If the skirk had tuned its lasers perfectly, she would die. She had bet her life—and the lives of all her pilots—that she had not given the Wayholder time enough for fine-tuning.

The warning lights blinked green.

She screamed in relief.

Shrapnel from fifty torpedoes had just swept through the coin-shaped skirk, from the obverse to the reverse, vaporizing anything it touched, explosively decompressing one life-support module after another.

At exactly the same instant, fifty pinwheels ripped through the heart of the ship from the east edge to the west, blasting girders and cables and enclosed gangways with impartial fury.

Sajjer lasers drew brilliant lines through outrushing air. The debris cloud thickened. The laser lines sparkled.

"Oh Jesus Buddha!" She had not anticipated the mix of air and vaporized metals and volatilized fluids—but she should have, and she prayed her mistake would not doom her wing.

When the ravaged hulk loomed ten thousand kilometers ahead, the wing's gravpipes shut down for the flyby. The lasers stabbed the murk of noxious gases in the enemy's gut, but she could not tell to what effect.

They passed it in an eighth of a second.

#Target destroyed,# said the onboards.

She drew a breath—her second since the rendezvous with the *Hudson*. She wiped the blood off her lower lip, and touched the radio controls. "Wing One, this is Wing Leader. The skirk is dead. Its fighters aren't. There ought to be sixteen of them around here somewhere. Let's find them, and take them out. Over."

Then she swallowed hard. In nineteen minutes and forty-five seconds, if Daitaku had his timing down to that degree of accuracy, she and her wing might be flying against a battlebox, and she did not have the vaguest idea of how to defeat a force twenty-six times the size of hers. . . .

The Wayholder engineers had left the *Morocco* without completing the interface device they had come to build. Their ship had departed the system without explaining why. Kajiwara Hiroshi did not understand what was happening until a SitUp capsule arrived from Luna.

He read the message in sorrow. Surprise attacks on fifty colony worlds. All TAAC forces except monitoring SRVs withdrawn from Octant Sagittarius systems and concentrated in the Cheyenne. Savage Sajjer-Wayholder space battles near the assaulted worlds.

Kajiwara Hiroshi could not abide the thought of the Association dying fifty worlds at a time. He sent the chairman an urgent request for permission to support the Guard.

Two hours later he received a reply.

To: Kajiwara Hiroshi, Over Commander

From: LeFebvre, Chairman of the Board, Terran Association

Re: Request for permission to support the Guard

The Wayholder Empire has stated that this is a punitive raid, not an attack on the entire Association.

To antagonize the Empire would be to risk the survival of the entire Association.

I was not elected chairman in order to preside over the dissolution of the human race.

Request denied.

Daitaku stroked the gold nebula on his right shoulder as he stared at the console. According to reports from the surv/recon vessels monitoring the various fronts, Wayholder battle control craft had begun to arrive. War zone control craft would come next. Though each fleetship could destroy a few of those, the Empire had as many war nuts as Daitaku had Sajjers.

He had to lessen the pressure on the Guard.

In a moment that approximated satori, the sudden enlightenment of Zen, Daitaku knew the solution, and the knowledge impelled the action. He swiveled his chair about to confront the hologram of Steven Cavendish's worried face. "Mr. Cavendish."

"Sir?"

"Please transfer to base immediately. I am taking the *New Zealand* to the rift between the Wayholder Empire and the territory of the Korrin. I wish you to remain in charge here."

Cavendish looked skeptical. "What are you planning?"

"To attack their border guards from behind, and thus weaken their defenses against the Korrin." He paused to regard his steepled fingers. "Of course, if you would like to accompany us—"

Cavendish swapped ships.

The *New Zealand* bounced across the rift, across the

next spiral arm of the Milky Way, and emerged just within the rift beyond that arm. Daitaku asked his monitors for a wide-angle view. They gave it to him.

A glittering chain-link fence stretched into infinity up, down, and to either side, like a chicken-wire cage around an abyss. On the far side of the fence, brilliant yellow flashes lit up the sky every fifteen or twenty seconds. Dying Korrin composed that random fireworks display.

Daitaku congratulated himself. Here, at the most heavily defended sector of the Wayholder Empire, he would show the aliens their weakness.

He faced the holo of Admiral Duschevski. "Bounce us to a point directly behind that plane," he said, "with a course parallel to it."

At the bounce, the fence disappeared. In the holo, Duschevski's eyes widened. "God, I am never seeing so many ships before!"

"Not ships. Gun emplacements, with conical overlapping fields of fire. They're spaced ten thousand kilometers apart. Our mission is to destroy as many of them as possible. Stay directly above one row, keeping just outside the range of their gravity weapons. Maintain threshold speed. Have Lieutenant Corzini pick off three rows as we pass."

They caught the first Wayholder warriors off-guard. Those, as they died, spread the word, but the word traveled at the speed of light. The *New Zealand* moved at over a fourth that speed. Its lasers, pinwheels, and torpedoes gutted 123 emplacements before the gap between light speed and threshold speed widened enough for the Wayholder to receive the warning, pivot their platforms, and open fire on the fleetship.

"Flip us end over end, and use the stern pipes to bounce ten light-seconds forward," he said.

Duschevski gave the commands. The giant ship responded. They resumed their methodical tearing and rending of the barrier between the realms. Again the platforms swiveled. Again the Wayholder guns lashed out. Again Daitaku said, "Flip and bounce ten light-seconds forward."

"Bounced, High Commander." A moment later, Duschevski cursed. "High Commander, we are needing more time for pipes to cool. Last bounce is blowing nine pipes."

Just when he had found the pattern. After they received the alarm, the aliens took five seconds to swivel their guns about. As long as he struck within that time, he could strike with impunity. But if he had to let the pipes smooth out . . . a thousand on either end. He could spare some, but could not push his luck. Just how long a cool down period did they need to reduce their chances of blowing to less than one in a thousand?

#Ninety-five seconds.#

It seemed he had no choice.

"Admiral, bounce ninety-five light-seconds away from the line. Coast for ninety-five seconds. Return to a spot ninety-five light-seconds from our last point of attack. Flip and run for five seconds, firing on every emplacement we pass. Then repeat the maneuver."

"Yes, sir." The admiral looked over his shoulder and issued the orders.

Ninety-five seconds of cooling, and five seconds of action. The *New Zealand* vaporized three rows of gunposts during each onslaught. Each pass left a rent nearly four times the surface area of Terra—the tiniest imaginable rip in that awesome fence.

But he could tear many such holes in the Wayholder screen, and occasionally return to the perimeter of the first to enlarge it. . . .

They ran for ten hours, clawing at the fence for five seconds out of every hundred, coasting for the rest. In 360 separate strikes, they tore down so much of the Empire's defense against the Korrin that if the holes were joined together, Sol itself could have rolled through the opening with room to spare all around.

"Are beginning run low on munitions, sir," said Duschevski. "Antimatter plants just not keeping up with usage."

"We fly until we are dry," said Daitaku.

Chapter 24

Darcy Lee and her seven surviving pilots circled at threshold a gigakay above Journeau's star. They flew in tight formation because it felt better that way. Nearness promised security, at least psychologically, and her Sajjers needed that. They knew what was coming as well as she did.

A radio voice said, "17 back. Nothing."

"Thank you, 17," she said. "19, go."

She had the next run, so she took another swallow of cranberry juice and shut the tube. Despite her thirst, she had trouble swallowing. The Wayholder reinforcements were due. She prayed that two skirks would appear, because otherwise the wing would face a battle control craft. The thought terrified her. How could mosquitoes bring down an elephant?

"19 back. Nothing."

'Thank you, 19. Wing Leader is going now." She touched her implant. "Triple-jump."

#Bouncing. Flipping.#

Her ship turned end over end so the cooler aft pipe could power the next bounce. She flew alone, up the empty decel lane toward the pop-in point, one of the two places where she thought the enemy likely to enter the system. Her sensors found no sign of the aliens.

#Bouncing. Flipping.#

Again the maneuver put the less recently used pipe in front. The Zulu raced toward the pop-out point at the end of the accel lane. The instruments picked up background EM and broadcasts from the planet.

#Bouncing.#

She rejoined her pilots high above the system. "Wing Leader back. Nothing. 12, go."

She hoped she had picked the right spots to patrol. It seemed probable. Other entry points would either lengthen flight time or increase the battlebox's chances of collision with debris.

Her plan depended on having decided correctly. It would succeed only if she could strike the Wayholder just after they arrived, before they could assess the situation properly.

"12 back. Nothing."

"Thank you, 12. 13, go."

The holo of Hsing P'ing still glowered out of the monitor. So much blood. But not on Journeau, not if she could help it. No human should ever feel a loss like hers, and if that meant taking on a battlebox single-handedly, or even a war zone control craft, well, so be it.

"13 back. They're here." His onboards pumped the invader's trajectory and attitude data to the other fighters' computers. "A battlebox. God, it's the size of Chicago."

"All right." Darcy Lee ran a gloved finger down the image of Hsing P'ing's longest river. "Time to do it. Your onboards have the software. The odds say one pipe's going to blow. If it's yours, hang tight and call for help. If your onboards crash, switch to manual and try to knock out the skirks this sucker's carrying before they can clear the rack. Let's go."

Her computers synchronized timing cycles with all the other onboards. They paused until precisely the right moment. She held her breath. She had programmed the next series of bounces, and it frightened her.

The broken wing bounced to ten light-seconds away from where the enemy would be in ten seconds, and flipped on the way. She and three others popped in to form the corners of a square, twelve kilometers wide and high, that charged the battlebox head-on. Two Sajjers came at it from the side, the last two from above.

They all emerged from the bounce with their lasers aimed and firing.

Her forward monitor flashed a visual of the battlebox. The skirks berthed on its faces looked like silver dollars glued to a black brick. Each of her pilots was attacking a different skirk and would, with luck, destroy it.

After two and a half seconds, the Sajjers bounced 750 kilokay closer to their target, and flipped. Each appeared at the head of the beam it had fired earlier, but just to the side of it. The lasers flared again.

Two and a half seconds later, they jumped another 750 kilokay forward and flipped. They fired. And they bounced.

If the wing's onboards focused, phased, and fired the way she had told them to, the battlebox would notice the wing at exactly the moment that the laser beams slammed home. They would bite with extraordinary intensity, for each would be composed of four individual shots. Granted, each pulse would have spread as it crossed the enormous distance. At the center, though, at the bull's-eye, where all blended together as one, a bit of hell would chew its way through the alien's heart.

Around that burning circle, like a corona around an artificial star, amplified light would fall hard and heavy enough to shock even the best-shielded electronics into incoherence and amnesia.

And as an added bonus, the Wayholder should have the devil's own time trying to identify their attackers, because no TAAC ship created those EM patterns in the sky, or bore lasers that packed quite that kind of punch. If nothing else, the aliens should hesitate before striking back.

Four bounces in seven and a half seconds. Darcy Lee's fighter had matched its own light stride for stride. Now the Zulu shivered as its onboards launched all its torpedoes and popped all its pinwheels.

When only twenty thousand kilometers separated the wing from the immense enemy ship, they would all bounce to the *Sydney* to rearm and return and deliver the *coup de grâce* to—

#Gravpipes out.#

"Out?" She screamed the word because the battle-box lay dead ahead and she traveled at threshold and in—

#Collision in 1.8965 seconds.#

"Mayday!" Her lips moved of their own accord. "Oh my God, I am heartily sorry for having offended thee—"

#Collision in one second.#

The pinwheels raced before her, the torpedoes led them by an increasing margin, and a battering ram of coherent light 750,000 kilometers long had already begun to hammer the foe. Staring at the monitor, she wondered dully if she would have time to glimpse the effect of her attack before she died.

Blazing circles scarred the giant vessel. Each circle encompassed one of the skirmish control craft moored on that face of the battlebox. *Well, four skirks for one fighter is a damn good trade, lady. You should be proud of yourself.*

She laughed, then just as shrapnel from her torpedoes tore into the enemy. Ghastly light flared across the face, and deep into the framework.

One-sixteenth of a second before collision, her pinwheels augered in. She started to frown. The damn pinwheels had not dispersed enough. Then—

Head down, hands behind his back, Kajiwara Hiroshi slowly paced the confines of the command module. He paced in darkness. He did not need the light. He did not need to see his image in the full-length mirror every time he approached that end of the module. He could not stand to see his image, for the Wayholder Empire was destroying the Association fifty worlds at a time. Worlds that he had sworn to defend.

And the chairman still refused to fight back.

Where did honor lie? Did one who had lost his honor have any right to ask that question? Kajiwara did not know.

He paced some more, rephrasing the question in his

mind as his ancient legs turned through one corner after another. Given that he had no honor, which would be the greater shame—to rebel against his lord, or to allow his people to die?

Fifty worlds at a time. . . .

Daitaku had triggered this, deliberately, purposefully. Kajiwara knew that he himself would never—could never—take any action that might endanger humanity unless he had absolute confidence that humankind would not only survive, but prosper.

Could Daitaku have diverged so far from his original that he would act without such confidence?

No. And therefore, Kajiwara Hiroshi must support his clone.

The decision had been forming in his soul since that day off New Napa. Now the last argument clicked into place with such simple finality that he was astonished at how long it had taken him to arrive at such an obvious course of action.

Opening the closet, he retrieved the case of star coral. He hung it on the wall, and basked in its soft silver glow until he was sure.

Then he touched his desk. "General Pensellaer please."

A holo glimmered to life. A ruddy-faced officer with cropped blond hair and square white teeth blinked at the image in his own display. A faint expression of distaste settled on his lips. "Sir?"

"General." Kajiwara sat, leaned back in the chair, and steepled his fingers. "Instruct your forces on Longfall to cease fire, and to withdraw to the port immediately. Retrieve them as soon as possible. The fleets of Octant Sagittarius will no longer wage war on colonists. We are going to relieve the Guard."

Pensellaer smiled slowly, but said nothing.

Kajiwara suppressed a frown. "I take it you offer no objections?"

"None at all, sir. I think it's a damn good idea. If I have any objections, it's that you didn't do it sooner. So can the rangers do anything else for you? Landing parties?''

He shook his head slowly. "No, General. Or, yes, but not in quite the way you think." He cocked his head, stared at the image of the broad-shouldered soldier, and then rolled the dice. "How many rangers are still aboard the *Morocco*?"

"Six thousand, sir—double complement."

"Excellent. Drop on Geneva. Seize the chairman. Hold him incommunicado until further notice."

Pensellaer's smile twisted into a savage grin. "Are you overly particular about the shape the chairman's in when you get back?"

Kajiwara said, "I plan to put him on trial. I would prefer that he be capable of taking the stand."

The general thought a moment. "Long as it works out, Over Commander, that would be a helluva lot more fun than just putting the bastard up against a wall."

"Oh, I plan to do that, General—but after the trial, not before."

Pensellaer rose to his feet and saluted. "Sir. We'll be en route in ten minutes. We'll signal you when we're away."

"Thank you, General." He returned the salute. "Good luck."

Pensellaer winked, and cut the connection.

Kajiwara holoed Admiral Wiegand. "Bring us to threshold speed as soon as the rangers have disembarked."

She raised one eyebrow. She smiled. "Yes, sir."

After sending a SitUp capsule to the other admirals under his command, ordering them to scramble and join the *Morocco* in the Longfall System, he recorded a tape for SitUp capsule distribution to the seven other octant over commanders. "My fellow over commanders. I have resolved to drive the forces of the Wayholder Empire out of Terran Association space. I am dispatching all my fleetships to the worlds currently under siege, effectively stripping the Cheyenne System of its defenses. I request that each of you bring your defenses to full readiness, and prepare yourselves for a Wayholder strike deep within Association territory.''

Wiegand's face appeared in the holo. "The rangers are off, sir.''

"Bring us to threshold. When the other fleetships arrive, form up with them.''

"Yes, sir.''

Nineteen giant ships began to arrive in the Longfall System almost immediately. As they fell into a massive mandala formation centered on the *Morocco,* Kajiwara gave his admirals their assignments. Seventeen were to split their ops groups into three strike forces, each of which would rid one star system of the Wayholders invading it. The fleetship would stay in constant motion, shuttling from one of its assigned star systems to another, re-arming, repairing, and reinforcing as needed.

The *Morocco,* the *Chad,* the *Fiji,* and the 51st Strike Force would not bounce, but would continue on their current course at threshold speed, ready to receive SitUp capsules and respond to any requests for help almost instantaneously.

"Now go,'' he said.

They went, leaving Kajiwara Hiroshi to monitor events from a distance so great as to numb the mind. To run the war by remote control. To pace his silver-lit module and dwell on the irony that if he had fewer arms, he could be *doing,* rather than waiting.

A short time after the last fleetship bounced out, a SitUp report arrived from Over Commander Bjorgeson of Octant Auriga, who had moved all her forces into the vicinity of the Home System.

The news bemused him. Then it alarmed him. Was Terra itself under attack? He pressed he page-scroll button and skimmed the report.

Then he smiled, for Bjorgeson informed him that the other six over commanders and their 120 fleetships would be joining him shortly. When they arrived, they would place themselves under his command.

He began to compose another message.

* * *

As the *New Zealand* coasted to a halt at the Guard base high above the yellow sun of New Napa, a holo glowed in the command module. Daitaku stared at it in dismay. "What?"

"We ran out," said Steven Cavendish. "No more torpedoes, no more pinwheels, and almost no antimatter."

"We can produce that ourselves," he said, "but—"

"We're out of hydrogen, too."

He had never anticipated this. His decades of TAAC service had conditioned him to expect supply lines whose capacity never fell short of the demands placed upon them. He had actually forgotten that he could no longer draw upon the awesome wealth and productive power of the entire Association. "We need—"

His desk lit up with an urgent message—from Kajiwara Hiroshi.

Panic blanked his mind. How had Kajiwara found him? Did this presage an all-out TAAC assault on the Guard? What—

He closed his eyes and inhaled sharply, deeply. That helped. At least it calmed him enough that he understood how Kajiwara had known where to look for him.

The two did, after all, share significant memories. Perhaps he should have eschewed the symbolic gesture. . . .

He sat up straight and read the message carefully.

To: Daitaku
From: Kajiwara Hiroshi, Over Commander, Octant Sagittarius
Re: Defense against the Wayholder Empire
    The fleets of the Terran Association are at our command.
    I will command the 20th through the 79th.
    You will command the 1st through the 19th and the 80th through the 119th.
    Let us destroy the invaders now.

He replied with a short message of his own:

To: Kajiwara Hiroshi, Over Commander,
         Octant Sagittarius
From: Daitaku, High Commander, Sagittarian
         Guard
Re: Defense against the Wayholder Empire
     Thank you.
     You take the invaders.
     I'll take the Empire.
     Best wishes.

He appended a brief summary of tactics the Guard
had found useful, detailed the current disposition of his
forces, and dispatched it in a Situp capsule to the coordinates Kajiwara had provided.

When the fleetships arrived in the New Napa, the *New
Zealand*'s computers presented them with the software
they would need even as Steven Cavendish requisitioned
munitions for the *New Zealand*, the *Burma* and the
Guatemala. Within forty-five minutes, all of them were
ready to go.

The armada climbed away from the New Napa System in a rectangular formation that flew on prearranged
timing, because light itself took two seconds to travel
from the rightmost column to the leftmost, and nearly
three from the bottom row to the top. The armada accelerated toward threshold. It bounced.

It hit the "fence" between the Wayholder and the
Korrin near a densely populated Wayholder planet. Until the alien guns began to return fire, it tore down that
fence. Then it bounced away to let its pipes cool.

Visualize the planet Earth opened up and flattened
out like an orange peel. Put fourteen hundred such areas
together. They will approximate the size of the hole
Daitaku's demons had just snipped in the Wayholder
fence.

For ninety-five seconds the armada ran in the emptiness within the Empire, cooling gravpipes and restock-
ing munitions.

On the computers' commands, the fleets bounced to
the outskirts of a second inhabited system. They ripped

an awesome hole in that system's shield before they rested.

And struck.

And rested.

By the end of one hour, thirty-six Wayholder worlds lay naked and vulnerable to the planet-eaters.

After two hours, the Empire requested peace talks.

Chapter 25

In the worst of her nightmares, Darcy Lee had dreamed that she might die like this, tumbling through darkness in a crippled fighter.

She should have died two days ago, when the *Sydney 10* and the battle control craft met at better than half the speed of light. She should have died in a quick, clean flash of the photons that metal emits as it vaporizes.

But the Wayholder build their ships big—a module here, a module there, and a strut to link them across the intervening vacuum.

Her concentrated laser blast, blue-shifted into a coherent X- and perhaps even gamma-ray beam, pulverized nearly everything ahead of her. Her light drill bored a tunnel though the entire battlebox; her torpedoes and pinwheels sanded its sides smooth.

She plunged into the tunnel she had carved to find it thick with escaping air, ice crystals, and motes of metal coalescing from clouds of incandescent vapor.

Passage through that molecular glow had skinned the *Sydney 10* alive, and driven countless microneedles through its bones. Its heart still beat, but its mind was gone, lost in the general collapse of its nervous system. Deaf, mute, blinded, it rode its own inertia into the unknown, while its passenger tried to remember the prayers she had learned a lifetime ago, on a planet much too far away.

At least the power supply still drove the life-support systems. And the lights. She thought she might go crazy if interstellar darkness invaded the cockpit. She might lose it anyway. The close confines of a Zulu used to reassure her, but now they squeezed her like an undersized coffin. If she bumped her head on the canopy one more time, she would scream.

She ran her gloved hands over the transceiver controls. "Mayday, Mayday—" She paused. She listened. A pointless exercise. The receiver received exactly nothing; not even static. It simply did not work.

Something had lanced through the guts of the Zulu and penetrated that tiny slice of gallium arsenide. A speck of dust, perhaps; or an echo of her own laser beam, its frequency blue-shifted even more by the speed of her approach; or maybe just a massive electromagnetic pulse from her plunge through the Wayholder's framework.

Who knew? And who cared about the *exact* cause—what mattered was that the receiver did not work. Since the transmitter shared the same sliver of gallium arsenide, she could bet that her desperate cries for help spread no farther than the hull of the *Sydney 10*.

She wondered if the emergency beacon had ever gone off. It occupied a separate circuit, so well shielded and padded that in demonstrations the manufacturer dropped it onto concrete from a height of ten thousand meters to prove it would shout "Mayday!" no matter what.

She wondered, too, if anyone still lived who could understand what "Mayday" meant. Did the Wayholder know that word? Did she *want* them to know that word?

Forty-eight hours. Assuming the gas in the tunnel had not robbed her of too much speed, she had traveled, oh . . .

Out of habit, she touched her implant, waited, and then remembered that the onboards had failed.

She dipped her finger in a spot of grease and worked it out on the dead main screen. The equation yielded fourteen gigakay, give or take a couple hundred million.

In what direction?

She slumped in her seat. A sphere with a radius of fourteen gigakay had a volume of— No. Much too depressing, to calculate that one. Just say an awfully large volume for a search party to inspect.

She did not have a single hope that she might have gone into orbit around Journeau or even its star. She could work the equations if she wanted to, since she had nothing else to do but *not* sip the water and *not* eat the food and *not* crack open the canopy and then her helmet and *not*—

But why bother? When you travel so fast that you can skim the event horizon of a small black hole and slip away unscathed, no ordinary star can hold you unless you run into it. Since Darcy Lee was reasonably certain that her heart still beat and her lungs still breathed, she could not have fallen captive to Journeau's primary.

She was heading for nowhere, and making real good time. Time . . .

Forty-eight hours. What had happened out there since the battle?

In a few hours, Kajiwara Hiroshi, commanding just one fleetship, had lost hundreds of ships but cost the Wayholder Empire twice that many.

In this fight, Kajiwara's awesome clone had three fleetships, more experience with the Wayholder, and a bag of tricks that Kajiwara the Original had never imagined.

So was the war over? And if so, who had won? Did it matter to her?

Well, yes, she decided. If the Guard drove off the Wayholder, and if her beacon still shrieked, and if a listener in the Journeau System happened to hear it, she stood an outside chance of being rescued. An awful lot of ifs. Jesus Buddha.

She squeezed shut her eyelids, and wished she could be more optimistic. . . .

The *Morocco*'s rangers held Geneva. Backed by the survivors of the sixty fleets, Kajiwara Hiroshi appointed himself temporary chairman. With Over Commander Frank Munez at his side, he shuttled down to the capital.

Night had fallen. Moonlight bathed the shuttleport in its soft silver glow. As Kajiwara and Munez disembarked the shuttle, General Pensellaer emerged from his car. "Congratulations, Over Commander." He saluted.

Kajiwara hesitated before returning the salute. "I accept your congratulations on behalf of the one who deserves them, General. And I thank you for a job well done. Shall we go?"

Pensellaer escorted Kajiwara and Munez to Corporate Chambers. There he led them to a spacious sitting room half filled with holocasters and cameras. A red velvet rope and a squad of rangers penned the reporters into one side of the room. Pensellaer turned his broad back to the cameras. "I'm sorry about the chairman's office, Over Commander. The plasterers and the carpet cleaners say it'll be ready next week."

Kajiwara sat in an oversized armchair carved of splendid mahogany. Lenses focused on him. He wished he could have the journalists removed. Though a warrior without honor, he could still feel shame, and did not relish witnesses. "The carpet cleaners?"

Pensellaer shrugged. "We disabled the automatic defense system before we went in, but LeFebvre had two Gurkha guards."

"See that their survivors are cared for."

"Of course, sir. Do you want LeFebvre brought in now?"

"Please." He needed to conclude this quickly. Other, more meaningful tasks awaited him.

Pensellaer nodded to a ranger commander, who spoke to a captain, who disappeared into the hallway. He rubbed his palms on the sides of his trousers. He seemed not to know how to fill the time, either. "Tea, sir?"

"Tea?" Kajiwara plucked a spectacular purple chrysanthemum from the vase on the table and held it to his nose. It smelled of a gene lab. "Please."

The general pointed a finger. A sergeant spoke to a tea cart. It floated over to them. As he poured, Pensellaer began describing the attack on the capital in a voice pitched too low for the reporters' ears, though not for their audio pickups. Before he had finished his report, two huge ranger lieutenants dragged a trembling Pierre LeFebvre into the sitting room.

The reporters, hurling questions, pressed against the ropes. The rangers pushed back. The reporters quieted, but scowled.

Kajiwara Hiroshi steepled his fingers. "Mr. LeFebvre. You and your board of directors nearly permitted the destruction of the human race. I had thought of putting the lot of you on trial, but no truly impartial jury could find you anything but guilty. Why should the Association bear the expense of a rubber-stamp trial? Far simpler for me to sentence you to death myself." He gestured to the rangers holding the holocasters at bay. "They could serve as your firing squad."

LeFebvre blanched. His brown eyes widened. His full lips moved, but no sound came out.

Kajiwara wondered if the man would disgrace himself on worldwide holovision. He rather hoped not. He found these proceedings distasteful enough. "And yet," he said slowly, "bushido stills my tongue. It is not honorable for a warrior to slay the vanquished."

LeFebvre staggered as if struck. He made a visible effort to regain his self-control and succeeded, at least, in standing straight.

Kajiwara approved. "I have decided, therefore, to send you and your board of directors into exile." He beckoned to the two lieutenants; they stepped forward and seized the former chairman's arms. "You will be taken to the planet called New Napa. You will be given shovels. When you have buried the dead of New Napa, you will do the same honor to the dead of New Dublin, the dead of Gandhi, the dead of Hsing P'ing, and the dead of Pasteur. Then, and only then, may you return to Earth." He rose from his chair and bowed. "Take him away."

LeFebvre shook off the ranger lieutenants' hands. For a long moment he stared hard at Kajiwara Hiroshi, then turned abruptly and marched out of the room under his own power.

Kajiwara had to admire LeFebvre's poise. He toyed

with the chrysanthemum till the door closed. "Now we will negotiate with the Wayholder." A thought occurred to him. "Frank."

"Sir?"

"Have any of the colonies requested emergency re-provisioning?"

"No, sir."

"I suspect that some will, before too long. The debris from the battles will jeopardize the supply ships."

"I'll have it cleaned up immediately." He touched his implant, but frowned. "I'll have to get the general to patch me in."

"Of course." Munez at his heels, Kajiwara left the sitting room and went down the marble-floored hall to the formal reception chamber.

Within, seven pressure-suited emissaries of the Way-holder Empire awaited his pleasure. The room could have held a thousand such emissaries, and their shuttle as well. Its ceiling disappeared into shadows. The immensity made him feel queasy.

He sat at the head of the table. Moonlight streamed through a tall arched window and shimmered on the glossy wood. "Good evening. I wish this to be simple for each side. I will state the terms of the treaty. You will agree to them. If you do not agree to them, we will send our fleets back to your border with the Korrin and tear down all that you have rebuilt."

The alien in the least ornamented suit spoke. "What are the terms?"

"First, the Wayholder Empire agrees never again to attack a world of the Terran Association."

"Agreed, with the stipulation of self-defense."

"I said *never.*" His voice rang hard and steely, surprising him. He had feared that agoraphobia, even electronically muted, would diminish him.

The Wayholder conferred among themselves for a moment. "Accepted," said their speaker.

"Second. Each shall open its borders to the other for purposes of commerce, scholarship, tourism, et cetera, et cetera."

"Wait." The seven wagged their hands at each other for several minutes. Finally their speaker turned back to Kajiwara. "We will not buy from you, nor talk to you, nor show you anything but the backs of our heads, but we agree."

"Excellent." He stood. "That is the treaty."

"But—"

He walked out.

In the hall, under a blessedly low ceiling, he turned to Munez. "Who follows the most junior member of the board in the line of succession?"

"The Vice-President for Stakeholder Relations, I believe."

Kajiwara nodded. "Bring him to me."

They brought him. He was a little man, with wattled jowls and the signs of many hair transplants. He looked frightened.

"Mr. Vice-President, fate has entrusted to you the responsibility of overseeing the Association's return to constitutional, civilian rule." He beckoned to his left. Lieutenant MacNulty and Sergeants Iovini, Redstar, and Wilson stepped forward. "These men will serve as your guardians. One of them will be with you every moment of the day and of the night until the Association has elected a new board of directors, and it has selected a new chairman. Should you, at any time, diverge from constitutional procedures, your guards will execute you." He handed the vice-president a real letter, on authentic paper. "Here is my resignation. Go and begin."

Two hours later, he walked alone up a garden path in Tokyo. Birds twittered in the bamboo. The breeze blew clean, blew him the scent of the small woman in the plain gray yukata who came around the bend.

"Hiroshi!"

"Mother." He bowed. "I see they have finished rebuilding your city."

"Two weeks ago." She made a face. "They say it's very efficient now."

"That was their goal."

"That, or sterility." She leaned to one side, looked behind him. "Where are your bodyguards?"

"I no longer require them, Mother. I've assigned them to one who does."

"Ah." She nodded thoughtfully. "So you come for your grandfather's swords once more."

"Yes, Mother."

"My eyes are new—" She touched the medals on his chest, rubbed the fabric of his tunic between thumb and forefinger. "But even now they do not see a stain."

"You see with the eyes of a mother."

"And you with the eyes of a samurai, I suppose."

"Yes, Mother."

She pursed her lips. "Will . . . my other son be joining you?"

He raised his eyebrows, grasped her meaning, and sighed. "No."

"Good. I hate parades. You know the way, I believe?"

"Yes, Mother." He bowed again, low and respectful. "Thank you, Mother."

"You are welcome, Hiroshi." She blinked three times rapidly, then turned her head. "Goodbye, my son."

"Goodbye, Mother." He strode down the path to the teahouse.

The sunlight that filled Room B87Q gave the dust in the air a dry, pent-up odor. Daitaku squinted as he looked from Raul Santiago to Steven Cavendish to the pile of documents on the desk before him. "So." He lifted a letter, and let it fall again. "I have inherited everything he owned."

Cavendish said, "That makes you a wealthy man."

Daitaku shrugged. A fortune meant nothing but expanded opportunities for his next sabbatical. "I will assume his name."

Cavendish frowned. "Unchanged?"

"Yes. Was I not meant to be his continuation? He cleansed the name by the manner of his dying. It is an honorable name, now. A name which will demand my

highest to live up to. I will adopt it as is.'' He turned
to his—his original's?—*their* old friend, Raul Santiago.
''I will also accept the title over commander of Octant
Sagittarius.''

Cavendish began to smile. Santiago said, ''No.''

Though stung, Kajiwara lifted one eyebrow in polite
inquiry.

The high commander of the Astro Corps leaned back
in his chair. ''We have forced Han Tachun to resign,
my friend. Someone must take his place as first commander.''

''Have all three high commanders also resigned,
then?''

'Oh, my, no, Hiroshi, not at all. And I assure you
that you will find us quite difficult to work with. But
answer one simple question, my friend—would you
rather take orders from us, or give orders to us?''

He pondered that for a few seconds, then rose to his
feet, and bowed. ''Thank you. I accept.''

He did not move to the first commander's office, because he felt comfortable where he was. He did trade
his desk for one with better communications capabilities. He also reclaimed the tray of star coral from the
command module of the *Morocco*.

In the weeks immediately following the war, traders
fearful of bouncing cargo ships into debris-strewn acceleration lanes suspended shipments to most worlds of
Octant Sagittarius. One colony after another declared a
state of emergency and instituted rationing. The acting
chairman screamed at Kajiwara Hiroshi. Kajiwara called
Raul Santiago, who forwarded Frank Munez's interim
report on the clean-up efforts.

Munez's stilted prose made it harder, rather than easier, to visualize the enormity of the task that confronted
the TAAC teams told to vacuum the vacuum, but the
acting chairman needed data, so Kajiwara brought the
report up on his desk and began paging through it.

The name ''Darcy Lee'' leaped out at him.

''. . . found adrift but alive. Suffering from starvation

and radiation poisoning. Med-evacked to TAAC Main Hospital, Howland Island."

He and an aide paid a visit that afternoon.

She looked up as they entered her room. She looked terrible—hair gone, cheeks hollow, and almond eyes still reflecting the awful darkness between the stars—but the doctors had assured him her prognosis was excellent and her mental state good, all things considered.

She pulled the sheets up to her neck. "Daitaku."

"I am known now as Kajiwara Hiroshi."

"Sure." She blinked, peered at his uniform, then touched her right hand to her forehead. "I'd come to attention if I could, but—" She shrugged. The effort clearly pained her.

With all the gravity he could muster, he drew himself up to his full height and returned her salute. Then he winked. "I have come to present you with the honors you were awarded posthumously." He held out his right hand; the aide placed several kilograms of medals and documents on it. He handed them to her. "I have also come to pay my deepest respects."

"Thank you." Sliding an emaciated arm out from under the sheets, she took the stack of paper and metal and set it on her lap. "For both."

"My pleasure." Staring down at her, he was mildly annoyed with himself for not knowing what to say next.

She gave him a look filled with exhaustion, and terror, and . . . stubbornness. "We'll have to fight again. Either the Wayholder Empire or the Korrin."

He relaxed. Familiar ground, strategy. "Not the Wayholder, but definitely the Korrin.'

Her gaze bored into him, as though she saw nothing in the universe except him. "You've made plans?"

"I am making them." The way she concentrated on him—the way she seemed to be judging his every word, his every motion—challenged him. As he stood by her hospital bed, he realized that he would despise himself if he made this woman disappointed in him. "I'll need the help of a superb tactician. Would you object to a new assignment?"

That put color in her sallow cheeks. "What do you want me to do?"

"Later," he said. "When you have recovered." He gestured to the sheets, to the white walls and the medical machines lining them. "This is not the place to speak of intentional death."

She tilted her head to one side and stared at him for so long that he wanted to fidget. "I see you've been promoted."

"Yes." Despite himself, a smile percolated up to his lips.

"Is something funny?"

"Truthfully, yes. You see, every high administrator has prepared a continuation, but I am the first clone ever to succeed his original. The bureaucrats of the Association won't yield power even to themselves."

She chuckled at that. "Is it hard, being a—a—"

"Clone. Hard?" He lifted his shoulders, and let them fall again. "Strange, perhaps. Even unnerving, to find so many old memories stored in such a young body. There are things which my original did not understand how to accomplish until after he had lost the physical ability to attempt them. Now it is as though I have been given a second chance at them."

"Such as?"

He could not look at her, but neither could he look away. "Friendship. Love. Lasting marriage."

"Ah," she said.

An awkward silence fell, a silence not broken until a large, older nurse approached and tapped him on the shoulder. "Sir, are you really Kajiwara Hiroshi, first commander of the USF, formerly known as Daitaku, high commander of the Sagittarian Guard?"

"Yes," he said. "Why?"

" 'Cause we got a contest going here, sir. The higher the rank of the person you kick out, the more points you get. You're going to be trouble, though, sir. Nobody ever threw out a first commander before, so we're gonna argue about how many points you're worth for the next couple weeks, probably."

He glared at her. "You are asking me to leave?"

"Sir. You got it, sir. Visiting hours are over and I'm gonna collect however many points you're worth."

"But—"

Darcy Lee took his hand and squeezed it. Smiling, she said to the nurse, "What's the most anybody's ever been worth?"

"Fourteen points," said the nurse

"Oh, he's worth a *lot* more than that." She winked at him, and that set glowing an inner warmth that he could not remember ever having felt. "Do what she says, Daitaku. There'll be other times."

"Yes," he said, bending over, kissing her on the forehead. "Yes. Many of them."